P9-APN-115

The Replacement Wife

The Replacement Wife

EILEEN GOUDGE

OPEN ROAD

INTEGRATED MEDIA

NEW YORK

"But love is blind and lovers cannot see
The pretty follies that themselves commit."

—WILLIAM SHAKESPEARE,

THE MERCHANT OF VENICE, ACT II, SCENE 6

To Susan Ginsburg,
who's always had my back,
and whose own love story is an inspiration
to so many.

CONTENTS

CONTENTS

The Replacement Wife

CHAPTER ONE

"We had a nice time," Kat said.

Camille Harte felt her heart sink and the fizz go out of the celebratory bottle of champagne she'd mentally uncorked. In her line of work, she'd learned to read nuances and inflections the way a fortune-teller did tea leaves. *It did not go well*, she thought. Damn. She'd been so *sure*.

"But?" she prompted in a mild tone.

A lengthy pause at the other end of the phone, then Kat said slowly, "Well. He's a great guy and all. But . . . Let's just say I know more about his ex-wife than I do about him."

Camille suppressed a sigh. Clearly, the message figuratively chiseled in stone over the doorway to the Harte to Heart Agency had failed to sink in with Mr. Once-Burned: *Abandon all talk of exes, ye who enter here.* Maybe she should require a minimum wait of one year following a divorce.

"What did you talk about besides his, ah, ex?" she asked.

"Oh, you know, his job, my job . . . the fact that we're both into rock climbing and love jazz." Kat ticked the boxes in a bored voice. "Did you know he has the 'lost' recording of Clifford Brown?" She grew slightly more animated. Camille did know, in fact; Stephen Resler had shown off his vast CD collection and state-of-the art sound system during her home visit. Less impressive to her was his Rat Pack–worthy bachelor pad, which had been in desperate need of a do-over. She'd called in her "commando" decorator, Jeffrey Rabin, and three weeks later, after a fresh paint job, updated window treatments, some new furnishings and throw pillows from West Elm, the place was transformed. Now any woman Stephen brought home wouldn't feel as if she were entering the Playboy mansion circa 1967. Not that Kat would ever venture there; she'd seen enough, apparently. "Like I said, he's a great guy," she repeated without enthusiasm.

"So, no kiss?"

"What?" She gave a nervous laugh. "Oh, that. No. Definitely not."

"If you had to rate the date on a scale of one to ten . . . ?"

"I don't know. A five?"

She was being generous, Camille knew. Excessive talk of one's ex did more than put a damper on the evening: It was the equivalent of a cold shower. She suppressed another sigh and absently pushed a hand through her hair, momentarily taken aback, as always, by its springiness. Hair that for the first thirty-nine years of her life had been bone-straight and in high school the bane of her existence (as well as the victim of several awful home perms and one truly tragic salon job that had left her looking like a cross between Orphan Annie and Lucille Ball), and which, after she'd lost it all to chemo, had grown back curly: her consolation prize, courtesy of the Man Upstairs.

She smiled into the phone. "Not to worry. It wasn't a good fit, that's all. We'll keep trying."

"You still think he's out there?" Kat asked in a small voice. A reporter for a local TV news station, she was known for her fearlessness and hard-charging investigative style, but here she was just another single woman pushing forty who'd caught the brass ring but not the gold.

The "he" in question was someone tall, handsome, kind, family-minded, with a good sense of humor who earned a high six-figure income. "He" drove a luxury car, owned not leased, and lived on a high floor in an upscale neighborhood, preferably in the 212 area code. "He" led an active life and had the body to show for it, and was equally super-charged in his profession (with, ideally, a corner office to show for it). "He" was able to secure prime tables at the best restaurants, knew the difference between gnocchi and *gnudi* and could knowledgeably discuss wines with sommeliers. "He" was a skilled lover who knew how to pleasure a woman. And, last but not least, "he" would never, under any circumstances, cheat on "her."

Camille's high-powered female clients wanted in their personal lives what they strove for in the workplace: the position to which they felt entitled, with all the attendant perks and benefits.

So much for simple kindness and a great smile.

Camille hadn't had a wish list when she met Edward. While these days she might liken herself to a fairy godmother who waved her magic wand to spin white satin out of Calvin Klein executive threads, back then she'd been too inexperienced to know what she did now, at forty-two. As a teenager, she'd devoured paperback novels that featured corseted bosoms and bronzed, bulging pecs on the cover. Other than that, she hadn't had a clue what to look for in a man. She'd merely gotten lucky with Edward. She hoped the same for Kat that she did all her clients: that they wouldn't be so blinded by their expectations they'd fail to see what was in front of them.

"Absolutely," she replied.

"You don't think I'm being too picky?"

"You're entitled."

Camille didn't believe in settling. The right man was out there. And Kat had a lot to offer. Looks-wise, she was an eleven on a scale of ten, with a glamorous and highly visible career. The trouble with her was she had so much on the ball, the ball had just kept rolling. She'd come of age having men fall at her feet and had happily partaken of all that fallen fruit. But as she'd grown older, the pickings had grown thinner. By the time she was in her mid-thirties, most men her age were either taken or had more baggage than the cargo hold of a 747. "I'm not looking to play Florence Nightingale to the walking wounded," she'd stated bluntly in their first interview.

"Aye, aye, Captain," Kat said now. "But if he's still a no-show by the time I turn forty, I'm officially declaring him MIA." She had a sense of humor about it, at least, which put her in good stead.

Camille hung up feeling more spurred on than discouraged. She was reminded of why she'd chosen this profession. It was the Rubik's cube of romance: challenging, yes, but also deeply satisfying when you got all the little colored boxes to line up. Mostly, it was a matter of applying her expertise—a matchmaker was combination headhunter, den mother, makeover artist, and shrink—in finding someone who either fit a client's requirements or fulfilled some subconscious need. But she also had to know when to go with her gut. And judging by the number of successful matches she had made—more than three hundred to date—she figured she must be doing something right.

She thought back to her most recent triumph. At first glance, Alice Veehoffer and Andy Stein appeared to have nothing in common other than that their first names both started with an *A*. Alice was a chemist who spent her days cozying up to test tubes, Andy a customer relations expert whose job relied on the personal touch. The ideal Sunday for Alice was wandering on her own through a museum or curling up with a good book at home, and for Andy hanging out with his pals or bicycling in Central Park. Their first date had been an unmitigated disaster, with Andy doing most of the talking, and Alice, as she put it, relegated to the role of "crash-test dummy." But Camille had had a gut feeling, and she'd prevailed on them to give it another go.

The second time was the charm. Andy took Alice to a showing of *The African Queen* at the Lincoln Center Theater, and afterward they chuckled over the unlikely pairing of Rose and Charlie and how it mirrored their own. Which, in turn, led to a discussion of things they *did* have in common. They'd both minored in Russian in college, were passionate foodies, and loved to travel. Alice described a recent trip to Saint Petersburg; Andy regaled her with tales of his junior year abroad in Florence. They talked for hours—about everything from Russian literature to their careers and what more they wanted out of life—while nibbling on *salumi* and sipping prosecco at Bar Boulud.

Five months later, they were standing under the chuppah, saying their vows. At the reception afterward, Andy raised his glass in a toast to Camille, saying with heartfelt gratitude, "Cupid may be a lousy shot, but you scored a bull's-eye."

She was nothing if not persistent. It was the same persistence that had kept her going when she'd been at death's door the previous year. A year that, to quote the good Queen Elizabeth, had been her own personal annus horribilis. First there was the shock of diagnosis. Radiation and chemo followed, then with the cancer continuing its relentless Sherman's March, a stem cell transplant, which left her battling everything from mouth sores to a blood infection. Even after she was released from the hospital, she was dog-tired most days and prone to nausea and fevers. Nevertheless, she dragged herself to work whenever humanly possible. And when all her hair fell out, she bought a high-priced wig from a shop in Borough Park, Brooklyn, that specialized in *sheytls*—the first goy ever to cross the threshold, from the astonished look on the Hassidic shopkeeper's face. Most importantly, she adhered to her cardinal rule: Never let on. Her clients didn't need to feel sorry for her while fretting about their own uncertain futures.

"Dara, get Stephen Resler on the line," she called to her assistant.

Dara Murray sat at the only other desk in the agency's tiny office on the twenty-ninth floor of the Hearst Tower, at West Fifty-Seventh Street and Eighth Avenue. All client meetings took place outside the office, mainly in restaurants or coffee shops, or if the client was from out of town, Camille traveled to meet with them (at their expense), so the small space suited them. Over time, it had taken on the look of a college dorm room. On Dara's desk sat a framed photo of the all-girl rock band for which she'd been bass guitarist back in the day; next to it, an outsize martini glass from some promotional event. On the table against the wall an iPad dock shared space with an espresso maker, and the loveseat where they took their proverbial coffee breaks held a plush parrot, a souvenir from a recent trip to Key West, and a needlepoint pillow with the slogan *Kiss a frog... you might get lucky.*

"He's in a meeting," Dara informed her after she'd placed the call. "His secretary wants to know if it's urgent."

Urgent? Of course it was urgent, Camille thought. If she'd learned anything from the past year, it was that life was short. And Mr. Once-Burned wasn't getting any younger. He was paying her good money to find him a wife, but so far he'd sabotaged three dates with three separate women. Reports from the front had a disturbingly similar ring: The evening would start out promisingly enough; then a couple of drinks in, as it was getting cozy, talk would turn to the subject of his ex-wife. He wasn't even aware of it half the time and was always remorseful afterward. On the plus side, he didn't get defensive when she pointed out the error of his ways, and unlike many of his Wall Street brethren, Masters of the Universe for whom image was everything, he wasn't out to land the "perfect ten." He was more interested in whether a woman was smart and her heart was in the right place than in her bra size.

"I'm not looking for perfection," he'd informed Camille over lunch at Patsy's, at their first meeting. "I'm not the guy who wants Angelina Jolie but who isn't willing to take a good look in the mirror. I don't delude myself into thinking I'm Brad Pitt. That said, I think I have a lot to offer."

"That you do," she agreed wholeheartedly.

Stephen Resler was an inch or two shorter than most women wanted in a prospective husband, with close-cropped hair that was thinning on top, but he made up for it with an abundance of charm, smarts, and sheer physicality. He'd grown up on the mean streets of the South Bronx having to defend himself with his fists, and despite his Ivy League education and years as a Wall Street mover and shaker, he still looked the part: sturdy as a truncheon, with a gaze that could cut through steel and a muscularity that didn't come from power lifting at the gym.

He had some rough edges—evident in his expansive hand gestures and tendency to drop his r's; also his references to family members who were cops and firefighters—but what might be a turnoff for some would be a refreshing change of pace for others: There was nothing metrosexual about Stephen Resler.

"I just have one question," she said. It was the same thing she asked all prospective clients who were licking their wounds after a divorce. "Are you sure you're ready for this? Because I get the feeling you're still not over your ex."

Stephen gave a rueful smile. "What can I say? Yeah, I still think about Charlene. Probably more than I should. But that's gotta count for something, right? Shows I'm a caring guy."

"For this to work, you first have to get someone to care about *you*," she said in a firm voice. "And that, I can assure you, isn't going to happen if she feels she's in competition with your ex."

He put his hand to his heart. "I'll be on my best behavior. I promise," he vowed.

Famous last words, she thought now, a bead of exasperation rising despite her attempt to squelch it. "No. Have him call me back," she told Dara. The come-to-Jesus with Stephen Resler could wait.

Dara hung up, returning her attention to her computer screen, where the contact info for Stephen Resler was highlighted. "Should I file him under Lost Cause or Hope Springs Eternal?"

Camille sighed. "He just needs some fine-tuning, is all," she said.

"More like a kick in the ass," joked Dara.

"Now, now." Camille cast her a mildly reproachful look. If the situation were reversed—Stephen managing her stock portfolio—she would expect to see results. He should expect nothing less from her.

Dara shook her head in wonderment. "You never quit, do you?"

Dara was the living embodiment of Rule Number One: You didn't have to be beautiful. She had the kind of looks that could be described as either homely or interesting, and yet because she had the confidence of a head turner and dressed the part—today's outfit a slim skirt that hugged her bony hips, vintage rayon top, and death-defying heels—she never lacked for male attention. With her non-surgically-altered nose, blunt-cut hair the color of the Sumatran coffee she consumed by the gallon, wide-set green eyes accentuated by eyeliner, and the gap between her front teeth that had defied orthodontics, she reminded Camille of the young Barbra Streisand.

Camille flashed her a grin. "Nope. Don't know the meaning of the word."

She picked up the phone and punched in another number. She still hadn't heard back from Lauren Shapiro about last night's date with David Cohen. Not a good sign. Could something have happened to nip their romance in the bud? If so, Camille couldn't think what it might be. The museum curator and bookish Columbia professor had hit it off on their first date, he as smitten with her as she with him. Not only that, they were perfect for each other in every way, both in their mid-thirties with similar interests and backgrounds, and both eager to start a family.

Though not necessarily with each other, it now appeared.

"We had sex!" Lauren moaned.

"That bad, huh?"

"No! It was fantastic!"

Camille smiled. "Okaaaaay. So, what seems to be the problem?"

"It's too soon! He probably thinks I jump into bed with every guy I go out with."

"I doubt that. But what if he does? That's not necessarily a bad thing." Camille reminded her that most men wanted a woman who was uninhibited in bed. In her eleven years as a matchmaker, she had yet to have a female client rejected for being too sexual. Usually, it was the opposite.

Lauren was too busy fretting to see reason, however. She sounded on the verge of tears. "The thing is, I really like him. I think he might be the One."

"How do you know he doesn't feel the same way?"

"He hasn't called!"

Camille glanced at her watch. It had been less than twenty-four hours, too soon to panic. "I'll see what I can find out." She spoke in low, soothing tones. "In the meantime, try not to worry. I'm sure there's a perfectly good explan—" She was interrupted by a call-waiting beep at the other end.

"Omigod. That's him!" Lauren exclaimed breathlessly. She sounded more like a girl in junior high than a grown woman who was currently curating a major Rothko exhibition. "Gotta go."

Click.

Camille was smiling as she hung up.

Minutes later, she was in the ladies' room freshening up for her next appointment, with a writer who was interviewing her for an article for *More* magazine. She applied a fresh coat of gloss over her lipstick, then paused in front of the mirror, staring at her reflection as if at an old acquaintance whom she'd randomly bumped into. These days, it was always a bit of a shock whenever she saw herself in the mirror. In place of her bald head was thick hair that fell in loose, coppery curls to her shoulders. Skin once stretched over too-prominent bones now showed a fine tracing of lines around the eyes and mouth. No one would recognize her as one of the gaunt-faced, pink-ribbon-wearing ladies from her survivors' group. Her blue eyes had regained their sparkle, as had her ring finger, where the gold band Edward had placed on it nearly twenty years ago, more recently relegated to her jewelry drawer after it kept slipping off, had resumed its rightful place.

Thank God for Edward. The wives in her group had fallen into two categories: those who'd been emotionally, and in some cases literally, abandoned by their spouses, and those like her whose husbands had been a rock throughout. Although the marriage had had its bumpy spots before she became ill, she had never felt so grateful for Edward as when she'd been bald as an egg, showing more bones than flesh. Nestled in his arms, she was a featherless baby bird that might otherwise be trampled. "You're strong," he'd whispered in her ear. "You'll get through this."

And so she had. Though even with her cancer in remission and her strength regained, she still felt fragile in some respects. There were nights she lay in bed unable to sleep, the old fear stirring like some restless ghost; waking hours when she felt its cold breath on the back of her neck. She didn't tell her husband about those fears. Hadn't she put him through enough already?

She returned to find Dara perusing the menu faxed over by the caterer, for next month's meet-and-greet. The agency hosted one the first Friday of every month, open to all those on their mailing list, which typically meant anywhere from seventy-five to a hundred guests. The buffet supper was an added expense but worth every penny. In Camille's line of work, presentation was everything. Good food and decent wine, low lighting and music conducive to romance kept it from being just another crackers-and-cheese event. Guests were inspired to dress up rather than wear what they'd worn to work that day. Everyone looked their best and shone their brightest.

"Your two o'clock called to confirm," Dara reported without glancing up. Camille consulted her watch. Just enough time to get to the Mandarin Oriental, three blocks away, where she was to meet the writer who was interviewing her. "Oh, and don't forget your three-thirty doctor's appointment." Dara had a mind like a motherboard when it came to keeping track of appointments.

Camille gave a short, mirthless laugh. "As if." Today was the day she was to learn the results of her most recent PET scan, a moment

THE REPLACEMENT WIFE · 11

of truth that loomed over her each time like the sword of Damocles. She put on her Burberry raincoat and grabbed her umbrella; it had been drizzling on and off all week, April showers that showed no sign of giving way to May flowers anytime soon, and if she couldn't arm herself against potential bad news, at least she could stay dry.

IF CAMILLE HADN'T known better, she'd have taken Yvonne Vickers for a prospective client. The writer looked to be in her late thirties, with the body fat percentage of an Olympic athlete and blond hair boasting natural-looking highlights affordable only to someone with a six-figure income. The kind of woman who understood it was more about looking good in a T-shirt and jeans than in designer labels. Who, if she was looking for a husband (she wasn't wearing a ring, Camille had noticed), would see it as an enhancement, not the antidote to lonely spinsterhood.

"What do you say to those who call your profession antiquated?" Yvonne smiled as she lobbed the question at Camille, tape recorder whirring on the table between them.

"We're not all like Yentl in *Fiddler on the Roof*." Camille gave a dry chuckle. It was a common misconception. She, for one, was the furthest thing from the stereotypical Jewish *shadchen*. She wasn't even Jewish and if old-world matchmakers put a premium on modesty and virtue, she was all about style, flair, and the loosening of inhibitions. "Besides, my clients are the ones calling the shots, not their parents. *They* decide when and who they'll marry. And believe me, the majority of them don't have any trouble finding dates on their own."

Yvonne eyed her quizzically. "Why do they need you in that case?"

"They're busy with their careers and don't have the time to keep testing new waters," Camille explained. "Or in some cases, they've struck out a few times and don't trust their own instincts."

Yvonne arched an eyebrow. "But isn't that just a highbrow form of pimping?"

Another misconception, this one not so benign. Camille struggled to hide her impatience. "My clients are looking for a life partner, not someone to have sex with," she replied evenly. "It's a simple matter of expediency. What might take them years, I can accomplish in weeks or months."

The writer looked vaguely disappointed at not being able to get a rise out of her, but quickly moved to the next question. "So, Ms. Harte, what makes for a good match, in your experience?"

"Similar backgrounds and values mostly. That, and common interests." Camille paused before going on. How to put it delicately? "I also have to keep in mind certain, um, physical preferences."

Yvonne rolled her eyes, momentarily dropping her professional stance. "You're telling me. The guys I've gone out with? Most were overage frat boys obsessed with big tits," she confided.

Camille, aware of the whirring tape recorder, didn't comment except to say, "I can't deny looks are at the top of the wish list for most of my clients," she replied with a small shrug. "Though women are more willing than men to overlook . . . certain flaws if the rest of the package is to their liking."

"You mean if the guy's filthy rich?" The blonde gave a cynical laugh.

"Well, yes, there's that. But money isn't everything." *I certainly didn't marry for money.* Edward was a struggling med student at the time. Rail-thin and badly in need of a haircut, with the pallor of someone who spent his days in a library carrel when he wasn't in class. No, what had drawn her to him initially, in addition to the handsome face peering from under all that hair, was his inherent kindness and intelligence. "Mainly what women want is someone who's smart and nice and can make her laugh."

"And who's good in bed," Yvonne supplied. Camille smiled and sipped her Perrier. The blonde's eyes dropped to Camille's left hand. "You're married, I take it."

"Coming up on twenty years." Camille's face relaxed in her first heartfelt smile of the interview.

"How did you and your husband meet?"

"A suicide hotline, if you can believe it." She laughed at the look of astonishment on Yvonne's face—the story never lost its shock value. "Don't worry, neither of us is suicidal," she hastened to add. "I was concerned about a friend of mine, and Edward was the one who took the call."

"How romantic," observed Yvonne, her tone wry.

"It goes to show, you never know where you might find your soul mate."

Yvonne dropped her gaze, leaning forward to adjust the volume control on the tape recorder. She consulted her notes before moving on to another topic. "I understand you were a marriage counselor before you became a matchmaker. Why the career switch, if you don't mind my asking?"

"It's a long story," Camille said. "The short version is, I got tired of being around unhappy couples all day long." There had been days when she used to drag home from work bruised from the verbal battles she refereed. "Now, instead, I get to play Cupid. It's way more satisfying."

Camille thought she saw a wistful look flit across the blonde's face as she commented, "You must go to a lot of weddings."

Camille smiled. "You'd think so, wouldn't you? But I don't get invited to them all."

Yvonne looked surprised by that. "Really? Why not?"

"Not everyone wants it known they required the services of a matchmaker." Camille gave a sanguine shrug. "I don't take it personally. As long as the story has a happy ending, that's all that matters."

"So you believe in happy endings?"

Camille thought of her husband and children, fourteen-year-old Kyra and eight-year-old Zach. Despite the past year's ordeal, she was luckier than most. Not many forty-two-year-old women could say they had it all and mean it: a loving family, a fulfilling career. Her health, too, though it seemed she couldn't entirely count on that. "Yes," she answered unhesitatingly. "I truly believe there's someone for everyone. Some people just need a little help finding that special someone."

Yvonne smiled and sat back, crossing her slender legs and settling her notebook on one knee. "Which is where you come in."

"Exactly."

"How do they find *you?*"

"By referral mostly. But a lot of it is just chatting people up." Camille was naturally friendly—when she was a child, her mother was constantly scolding her for talking to strangers—whether it was fellow guests at a social function, other ladies in department store dressing rooms or public restrooms, or seatmates on planes. Once, on the shuttle from La Guardia to Boston, she struck up a conversation with an attractive older man. By the time the plane touched down, she'd learned his wife of forty years had died four years prior and he was finally ready to start dating again. She gave him her business card, and six months later she was dancing at his wedding.

After she'd told the story, Camille glanced at her watch. A quarter to three. She'd have to leave now if she was to get to the doctor's in time. Her stomach twisted. Never mind the results of the last two PET scans had showed no recurrence of her cancer, she was never able to face that moment of truth without a sense of dread. She rose, signaling the interview was at an end.

"Call if you have any more questions," she said, shaking the blonde's hand.

"Thanks for your time. I'll let you know when the article comes out. Oh, one more thing," she said as Camille was turning to go. Camille heard the note of hesitation in her voice and thought, *Here it comes.* She'd been expecting it since the moment she'd laid eyes on Yvonne Vickers.

"Yes?" she said, maintaining a pleasant, neutral expression so as not to betray her thoughts.

Yvonne confirmed her suspicion by blushing to the roots of her highlighted hair and asking. "Just out of curiosity. Do you, um, have anyone you think might be right for me?"

CAMILLE'S HEMATOLOGIST-ONCOLOGIST GREETED her with the usual dose of cheer. "Camille, you're the only woman I know who manages to look fresh as a daisy even when it's pouring rain outside."

The same could be said of Regina Hawkins, MD. However frazzled or harried, she always looked as if she'd stepped out of an ad for Oil of Olay. Her tawny skin glowed like burnished sandalwood. Her black hair, pulled back in a bun, was as smooth as if naturally straight. Only her alert brown eyes hinted at what lay beneath the smooth exterior. They seemed to impart a challenge of some kind, as if she were mentally laying down the gauntlet. *Cancer, you may think you've got this patient beat, but I'm one badass doctor you're not going to want to mess with.*

"It comes from being on intimate terms with my car service," replied Camille with a laugh.

"How's the shoulder?"

"Still a little sore. I'm sure it's nothing. You know us Type A's, we tend to overdo it at the gym. It's probably just a pulled muscle." Camille massaged her right shoulder, wincing slightly.

Her doctor nodded slowly, offering no comment. "Why don't we step into my office?"

Camille tensed up again. Her fate awaited her. What would it be, the lady or the tiger? The discomfort of the test itself, lying perfectly still for an hour inside the scanner while the radionuclide that had been injected into bloodstream did its work, seemed a minor inconvenience compared to the gut-churning anxiety of waiting for the results. Then, she'd imagined her body a traveler en route to an undisclosed destination. Now she'd arrived.

Regina's office was more homey than officelike, with its handsome furnishings and beautiful old Berber rug over polished floorboards, its walls covered in cream wallpaper flecked with pale blue, which made her think of vanilla ice cream topped with sprinkles, and hung with watercolors painted by Regina's husband, a well-known artist. She headed for the cozy seating arrangement where she and her doctor had sat on numerous prior occasions, discussing test results and treatment options while sipping tea. Even on a rainy day, the room was filled with light, and though the view out the mullioned windows was of the hospital across the street where she'd spent so many bleak hours, she was heartened by signs of spring: new grass and rows of tulips and daffodils, which fluttered in the breeze like bright-colored pennants heralding a grand opening.

Regina sat down across from her and pulled a set of computer-generated prints from a manila envelope that bore the return address of the radiology lab. Wordlessly, she spread them out on the table in front of Camille, like a fortune-teller laying out Tarot cards. Camille stared at them. Over the past year, she'd become as adept as a medical professional at reading test results, so she knew instantly what she was looking at. Time slowed to a standstill. She felt a vein at the base of her neck start to throb. At last, she lifted her head and looked her hematologist-oncologist in the eye.

"Does this mean what I think it means?"

CHAPTER TWO

"Beach, or are you more interested in sightseeing?" asked the travel agent, a trim blonde in a blue suit and gold earrings, whose colors mirrored those in the poster on the wall behind her, of some tropical vacation destination: blue sky, sunny beach. A beach, strangely, without tourists.

Edward smiled and shook his head, contemplating the poster. "I'm not really sure, to be honest." His and Camille's last vacation was . . . what? Anguilla, the Cap Juluca resort, four anniversaries ago. Between their busy schedules and the children, it seemed there was never a good time to get away. Then, this past year, it became impossible. The weeks and months were consumed with tests and procedures and hospital stays, not just the usual demands. There had been no talk of the future, then; it had been enough just to get by day to day. He felt the old burning in his ribcage at the memory, and fought the urge to press a hand to his chest—he didn't want the travel agent to think he was having a heart attack—straightening his tie instead. *No sense dwelling on the past.* Camille was fine now. No reason they couldn't plan a getaway. "I'd ask my wife, but I want it to be a surprise. We're celebrating our anniversary next month."

"Oh?" The woman brightened. "Is it a big one?"

He nodded his head. "Our twentieth."

"Well, that makes it even more special. Let's see . . ." Her hand skimmed over the stacks of glossy brochures on her desk before she selected one and handed it to Edward. "What about a cruise?"

He glanced at the brochure, suppressing a shudder. "I'm not much of one for cruises." He'd never been on one, but as he eyed the photo on the brochure all he could see was a floating hotel from which there was no escape, peopled with card-carrying AARP members and featuring endless games of shuffleboard and all-you-can-eat buffets. Besides, the entire time Camille would be schmoozing up the other passengers—not exactly the second honeymoon he had in mind. He set the brochure aside. "I'm thinking maybe the beach."

"Well, that leaves us plenty of options," she said. *Us?* He envisioned the trim blonde in the blue suit trotting alongside him and Camille as they made their way down the ramp at the airport. "I could get you a honeymoon package. It's near the end of the season, so there are lots of deals. What about Bermuda? The weather's nice, and it shouldn't be too crowded this time of year."

"Bermuda?" He considered it while absently rubbing his chin, which was scratchy with beard stubble—no matter how closely he shaved in the mornings, he always came home from work looking like an extra in a gangster movie. "Isn't that where they have the pink sand?"

"Why, yes." She beamed at him. "In fact, there's a lovely hotel on the South Shore that might interest you . . ." With a few keystrokes on her computer, she summoned up the hotel website, which showed a sandy beach the color of the laundry after he'd thrown the whites in with the colors (he was as bad at housekeeping, he'd discovered when Camille was ill, as he was at cooking), lapped by turquoise water, a cluster of cottages perched on the hillside above. "I could see if one of the ocean-view cottages is available, if you like." He eyed her fingers on the keyboard, poised to strike, and shook his head.

"Let me think about it." Already, he was regretting his impulse. He'd spotted the travel agency on his way home from work, and . . . well, it had seemed like a good idea at the time. God knew he and

Camille could use a romantic getaway. He couldn't recall the last time they'd so much as made love. But maybe surprising her with a trip to some exotic locale wasn't the way to go about it. His mother, with her old-country superstitions, would call it tempting fate. "I'll get back to you," he said, rising to his feet.

Minutes later, he was striding along Amsterdam Avenue, headed back to his offices, at New York–Presbyterian. As he was leaving the travel agency he'd remembered the new batch of interns. They'd have that old crank Wendell Marsh, who covered up for his failing faculties by barking at everyone around him, for evening rounds if he didn't offer to fill in (Marsh welcomed any excuse to shovel his workload onto others). It would keep the spark he'd seen in those eager, shiny-eyed faces from being trampled on, but Edward felt a ripple of guilt nonetheless. He ought to go home. Camille never complained about his long hours, but he knew it irked her. Another thing they didn't talk about. What excuse could he give, anyway? The plain fact was he didn't look forward to going home the way he used to before his wife became ill and almost died. It wasn't her fault; none of it was anyone's fault. But there it was. He loved his wife—that hadn't changed and never would—but he felt as if he were continually holding his breath around her, looking up at the sky, knowing it could fall at any moment. It had once. It could do so again. Today, for instance, he'd been waiting to hear the results of the latest PET scan. He'd phoned Camille several times, but each time he'd gotten her voicemail. That, plus the fact that she hadn't returned his calls, had him on edge, the ever-present fear, like a caged animal in the back of his mind, batting at its confines.

She'd have called if it was bad news, he consoled himself. Still, he wouldn't be able to relax until he knew for sure. He slowed his step, pulling his cell phone from his coat pocket. It had stopped raining, so thankfully he had no umbrella to juggle while he dialed. He frowned when, once more, the recorded message with his wife's voice clicked on. Damn. Why wasn't she picking up?

She was always available to her clients. He couldn't recall the last time they'd gotten through an entire meal in a restaurant without her having to attend to her buzzing BlackBerry or cell phone. Sometimes they called late at night, usually in a panic over some minor incident. It was as if these grown men and women had been transported back in time to their high school years, with Camille as combination best friend and guidance counselor. Why did she have to hold their hands every step of the way? *It's my job,* she'd always say. *It's what I get paid to do.* But what about *him?* Why couldn't she pick up the damn phone for own husband?

Don't be a prick. He blew out a breath, then when he could trust himself to speak in a normal voice, left another message. They both had demanding jobs; it wasn't just Camille's. All the more reason for a getaway. A week, ten days, would do them a world of good. He fingered the brochures the travel agent had given him as he was slipping the phone back into his pocket. He pictured himself strolling along that pink-sand beach in Bermuda with Camille. Afterward, they'd go back to their cottage and make love like they used to, back when the sight of her naked body stirred passion in him, not pity. When he didn't have to shut his eyes to get aroused or keep from tearing up.

We'll get there, my love, he thought, quickening his step. It started to rain again, heavy drops splatting against his scalp as he ducked his head, making him wish now for his umbrella. Up ahead loomed the Harkness Pavilion, where his offices were. Its lit windows glowed in the gathering twilight, a beacon of hope for some, and for others the last they would see of this earth. For him, it was the refuge home had once been . . . and would be again, God willing. He missed the old days. Eating dinner with his family, then cuddling with his wife on the sofa, watching old movies on TV after the children had gone to bed. Someday soon, he vowed, he'd find his way back to that.

In the meantime, what better way to begin again than with a

romantic getaway? The question was where? He smiled to himself
as he contemplated it. That should be their biggest problem.

CAMILLE ARRIVED HOME shortly before seven p.m. to find her children on the sofa in front of the TV and her husband nowhere in
evidence. She hung her dripping Burberry on the antique coat rack
in the vestibule. "Hey, what's this? Don't you have homework?" she
called to Kyra and Zach. She was careful to inject a stern note into
her voice. She didn't want them to suspect anything was wrong.

Zach acknowledged her with a grunt, not taking his eyes off the
TV, while Kyra, who like most teenagers was used to multitask-
ing—at the moment, she was text-messaging one friend while talking on the phone with another—looked up at her with an innocent
expression. "I *am* studying, Mom. Alexia's helping me with my
homework." She gestured toward the textbook that lay open on her
lap. It was unclear whether Alexia was the friend she was talking to
on the phone or the one she was texting. "Oh, and FYI, Dad called.
He said to tell you he had to work late."

Camille already knew this from the last message he'd left on her
voicemail. Normally, it would have annoyed her, but right now she
was too numb to care. Earlier, she'd thought about calling him, but
then she'd have had to explain why she was in a bar on Lexington
Avenue, drinking a gin and tonic at an hour when she was usually
home with the kids, and she didn't want to have to break the news
to him over the phone. Funny, though, even after two gin and ton-
ics she didn't feel the least bit drunk. Stranger still, she noticed as
she stooped to retrieve a stray sock—one of Zach's—from under the
coffee table, she had no feeling in her fingers; they were as numb as
the rest of her.

Leaving the children to their devices, Camille walked through
the adjoining sitting room and dining room beyond on her way to
the kitchen. The apartment, a classic nine in one of the gracious

prewar buildings that lined West End Avenue, was almost sinfully large by Manhattan standards. She and Edward had bought it as a fixer-upper when she was pregnant with Kyra, and she recalled thinking she'd never have enough stuff to fill all its rooms. Now, fifteen years later, the spacious apartment, chockablock with furnishings and knickknacks and strewn with evidence of growing children as it'd once been with their toys—backpacks and Rollerblades, shoes and items of clothing, a hand-held Gameboy (Zach's) here, a shiny pink iPod (Kyra's) caught in a tangle of wires there—felt, like Baby Bear's chair, just right somehow.

Not like the Upper West Side apartment she'd grown up in, which had been smaller but which had seemed enormous after her mother died. Memories flitted at the back of her mind. She'd been fourteen at the time, the same age as Kyra, and her sister, Holly, was eleven. The proverbial poor little rich girls, with their dad on the road three weeks out of every month, and their only living relative, Grandma Agnes, on the other side of the continent. There had been just the live-in housekeeper, Rosa, who was kind but spoke only broken English and who pined for her own children back in Puerto Rico. The burden fell to Camille to look after herself and her sister. It was she who took Holly shopping at Bloomingdale's, where their father had a charge account, when she needed new clothes, and who helped Holly with her homework and made sure she bundled up before going outside in cold weather. She reminded their dad whenever there was a parent-teacher conference or school play. She even had to remind him about their birthdays, so he wouldn't forget to buy a gift . . . or show up, period.

One time, Grandma Agnes became suspicious of the fact that their father was almost never around when she phoned. She demanded to know who, besides Rosa, was looking after them.

"Well, um, there's Maureen." Camille experienced a moment of panic before she plucked the name from midair. She didn't want for her and Holly to be sent to live with their grandmother.

"Maureen? Maureen who? Is your father seeing someone?" Her grandmother was instantly on high alert, no doubt imagining that her former son-in-law had taken up with some floozy.

"No! Nothing like that." Camille made no mention of her father's secretary, with whom he'd been spending far more time than when their mother was alive—Louise, who'd become suddenly indispensable, even going with him on his business trips. Louise was no floozy. "She was, um, Mom's friend. Her *good* friend," she threw in for extra measure. It amazed her how easily she could lie.

"Funny. I don't recall your mother ever mentioning anyone by the name of Maureen." Camille pictured her grandmother standing in her kitchen, in Del Mar, with its view of the orange trees in the backyard, wearing one of her grandma outfits—no-iron slacks and a color-coordinated blouse, of which she seemed to have an endless variety—her hair teased into its signature apricot poof. She'd be on her way to a bridge game or to meet one of her friends at the country club.

"You probably just forgot, is all," Camille said helpfully.

"I'm not *senile*," her grandmother snapped, then her voice softened. "So does she come around often, this Maureen?"

"Oh, yes. She's here practically all the time. She's helping Holly with her homework right now." The lie gathered momentum, like a kite caught in an updraft, tugging Camille along with it.

"Is she? That's nice." Grandma Agnes seemed satisfied. But before Camille could breathe a sigh of relief, she said, "Why don't you put her on? I'd like to have a word with her."

Camille broke out in a sweat, thinking she would never get away with this. But somehow the lies just kept tumbling out of her mouth, like the toads in the fairy tale about the two princesses. "Um, she can't come to the phone right now. She . . . she just went into the bathroom."

"In that case, I'll wait." Grandma Agnes was clearly in no hurry. Either that, or she still had her suspicions.

Camille was panicking now, imagining all sorts of things. Being put in foster care would be worse than having to live with Grandma Agnes. Would her grandmother sic the authorities on her dad if she knew the truth? She scrambled to extricate herself from the tight spot she was in. "It might be a while," she told her grandmother. "She said she had an upset stomach."

"Maybe she shouldn't be around you and Holly if she's sick."

"Oh, it's not that. She ate some bad sushi or something."

Lie upon lie, springing from nowhere, but somehow she'd stumbled upon the magic words. If Grandma Agnes was suspicious of her dad's activities, she was even more suspicious of raw fish: To her, sushi was downright barbaric. Naturally, if you were foolish enough to eat it, you'd get sick.

That was the end of her interrogation. Maybe because to pursue it would have meant getting on a plane, and Grandma Agnes was even more afraid of flying than of raw fish; their mom had always taken them to visit her instead. After that, whenever her grandmother phoned, Camille would sneak in casual references to Maureen, as if they were so used to having her around it was hardly worth mentioning.

Years later, at Grandma Agnes's funeral, they were approached by a dear friend of hers, a woman by the name of Ivy Klausen. "What a comfort it was for Agnes knowing you girls always had someone to look after you when your father was away," declared Ivy, sniffling into her lace-trimmed handkerchief. "If I heard it once, I heard it a thousand times—'Thank God for Maureen!'"

Their father gave them a baffled look, as if say, *Who the hell is Maureen?*

The memory was a painful reminder, and now she moved about the kitchen as if on autopilot. The numbness was wearing off. Her fingertips prickled with sensation as she took out the chicken breasts their housekeeper, Graciela, had left to marinate in the fridge. She sliced French bread and assembled the fixings for a salad. She was sliding the chicken into the oven when her daughter walked in. "Need any help?" Kyra asked.

Camille was touched by the offer. Kyra used to love hanging out with her in the kitchen, helping with supper, but these days it seemed every spare moment when she wasn't with her friends was spent either texting them or gabbing with them on the phone. When Camille had bemoaned this fact to Edward, he'd reminded her, in that oh-so-reasonable tone of his that had a way of setting her teeth on edge, "She's a teenager. What do you expect?" He was right, of course. And there was little to be done about it. So she tried to be more patient with their teenage daughter's growing pains— which, truth to tell, pained her more than they did Kyra—and to delight in moments such as these.

She put on a smile. "Don't you have homework?"

"All done, except for my English essay." Kyra got out a knife and began slicing tomatoes, dropping them into the salad bowl. "Mr. Costello's always giving us these bogus assignments. Like, whoever heard of doing a book report all in dialogue?"

"I don't know. Sounds like fun."

Kyra rolled her eyes. "With the *Gossip Girls* maybe. Not *Pride and Prejudice*."

When Kyra was done with the tomatoes, Camille gave her a cucumber to peel. "When I was your age, I had a mad crush on Mr. Darcy," she said. "I planned to marry a man just like him when I grew up."

"Yeah, Dad kind of reminds me of Mr. Darcy." Kyra smiled at her own joke. She was the spitting image of Edward: lean and lanky, with his olive skin and amber eyes and wavy dark hair, which when she was an infant had stuck straight up like down on a baby chick. Kyra was also the first to pick up on anything amiss—unlike her brother, who wouldn't notice if bombs were falling—as evidenced when she looked up a minute later from chopping green onions to peer at Camille with a creased brow. "Mom, is everything okay?" she asked.

"Sure. Why?" Camille paused as she opening a bottle of salad dressing.

"You're crying."

Camille brought a hand to her cheek, surprised, and at the same time not surprised, to find it wet with tears. "Must be the onions," she said, gesturing toward the green bits strewn over the chopping block.

"They're scallions," Kyra corrected.

"Can I help it if my nose is more sensitive than most people's?" Camille attempted to make light of it, which was an effort in her current state. She felt as if she might crumple like a piece of aluminum foil with the slightest pressure.

Kyra let it go, but the worried look on her face remained. Life in their household was back to normal in most respects, but the after-effects of the past year's ordeal lingered still. Zach couldn't sleep at night unless the night-light in his room was on. And Kyra remained watchful, quick to pick up on any change in mood.

Mindful of this, Camille was quick to change the subject. "How's the new boy?" she inquired. Kyra looked up at her with what seemed a purposely blank expression. "I'm talking about Jan. Unless there's another new kid I don't know about." Camille knew next to nothing about the mysterious exchange student from Norway, except that Kyra had a crush on him (which she would die rather than admit). "Is he getting along all right?"

"I guess." Kyra's expression turned glum. "Chloe Corbett volunteered to be his study partner."

"And that's a problem?"

Kyra frowned, bits of scallion flying from the end of her knife. "She's such a bitch!"

"Language," Camille chided.

Kyra stood with her knife poised in midair as if she'd like to bring it down on Chloe Corbett's pinkie. "Sorry, but she *is*. She's so pushy. She put her hand up before anyone else could."

"Maybe you should've been a little quicker."

"Mom! You act like it's my fault." Kyra's brown eyes flashed with indignation.

"It's not a case of being at fault, sweetie. You know the saying *All things come to he who waits*? Well, it's a crock. If you want something, you have to grab it before someone else does."

"How do I know if he even likes me?"

"You won't know if you don't go to the trouble to find out."

Kyra's shoulders slumped. "Chloe is prettier than I am."

"Not true. You're way prettier." *You just don't know it yet.*

"You're only saying that because you're my mom."

"I also know what boys want. It's what I do for a living, remember."

Kyra said with mock gravity, "Mom, I'm only in ninth grade. I'm too young to get married." Camille chuckled, but she was thinking that in some ways her daughter was more mature than other girls her age. She'd been through so much, more than any child should have to. No one knew better than Camille what it was to face the threat of losing a parent. A threat that had been realized, in her case. Would the same be true for her children? Her heart clenched at the thought.

Zach wandered in as she was taking the chicken out of the oven. Camille gave him the job of setting the table. "Should I set a place for Dad?" he asked hopefully as he was putting out plates and cutlery.

"Sure, but I don't know if he'll be back in time," Camille told him.

Zach looked a little downcast but rallied as soon as they sat down to eat. At eight going on nine, he was like a half-grown Labrador puppy, all over the place when he wasn't glued to the TV screen or some electronic device, with feet that were growing at twice the rate of his lanky frame. "Mom, guess what Ronnie got for his birthday?" he said excitedly as he was reaching into the breadbasket. Ronnie Chu was his best friend at school. "An iPhone!" he announced before she could take a guess. He took a bite out of his bread. "It's so awesome. You should see all the cool apps it has."

"Lovely," Camille muttered.

Zach went on, "Isn't that the coolest present ever?" Bits of chewed bread flew from his mouth as he spoke.

Camille ignored the not-so-subtle hint. "Why? Do you know someone who has a birthday coming up?"

"Mooooom." He gave an exaggerated roll of his eyes.

My son, heart of my hearts. Camille recalled when Zach had entered the world nearly nine years ago, the joy she'd felt when the doctor announced, "It's a boy!" Not that she wouldn't have been as happy with another girl, but she'd always pictured herself with one of each. The complete family.

"Oh, it's *your* birthday." She smacked her forehead with the heel of her hand. "Geez, I almost forgot."

"You didn't *really* forget, did you?" Zach eyed her uncertainly.

If Kyra was the image of her dad, Zach was unmistakably the child of Camille's womb. Auburn-haired, with Irish eyes that danced with mischief even when he wasn't misbehaving and a mouth that frequently got him in trouble with his teachers at school. She took in the spray of freckles over his snub nose, the pouty lower lip and long eyelashes that would break hearts some-day, the cowlick that made him look like a pint-size sixties doo-wop singer. A sense of impending doom slammed through her with the force of a freight train. *How can I bear it? How will they bear it?*

"Of course she didn't forget, you moron," said Kyra, giving her brother a playful swat.

"Can I have an iPhone? Please, Mom?" Zach begged openly,

gyrating in his chair like when he had to go to the bathroom. "I swear I'll never ask for anything again the whole rest of my life."

"That's, like, seventy more years going by the average life expectancy," Kyra pointed out in a dry, pedantic tone. She sounded so much like her father, it brought a thin smile to Camille's lips.

Zach, ignoring her, continued to plead, "Can I? Please?"

"It's 'may' not 'can,' and no, you may not," said Camille.

Zach's lower lip edged out. "Give me one good reason."

"I'll give you two: One, it's not a toy, and two, you're too young. In a year or two, maybe we'll consider it."

You may not be here in a year, whispered a voice in her head. She almost relented then. Why deny him? But she knew she had to stand firm. Experience had taught her that consistency was key.

"That is so unfair!" cried Zach, throwing his fork down with a clatter.

Life is unfair. Get used to it.

But she only said mildly, "I know someone who won't be getting dessert if he doesn't stop acting up."

Zach gave her a mutinous look. But it didn't stop him from asking, "What's for dessert?"

"You won't know if you don't behave. But I'll give you a hint: It's chocolate." Camille had stopped at Sarabeth's on her way home. "I'll even throw in a kiss on the house if you're *really* good."

This time, when Zach protested "Moooom," he was grinning as he said it.

After supper, the kids helped clean up, then they all changed into their pj's and piled onto the sofa to watch *Harry Potter and the Deathly Hallows: Part 1* on DVD for the umpteenth time. Normally, Camille spent the hours before bedtime helping her children with their homework. Sometimes they played games—Scrabble or Pictionary or Chinese checkers—the kind that would keep their brains from going digital and remind them they were a family, not just a group of people who happened to live together under one roof. But tonight, a movie was all she was up for. Bookended by Zach and Kyra, she gladly gave herself over to the action on-screen.

It was well past Zach's bedtime before she tucked him in and kissed him good night. "Who's my favorite boy in the whole wide world?" she asked, as she had every night since he was a toddler. He grinned up at her from his pillow. "I dunno. Who?"

"I'll give you a hint: His name starts with a Z."

Zach considered himself too mature for such "baby" games, but he played along nonetheless. He wrinkled his brow in mock concentration before delivering his line: "Me!"

"That's right. And don't you forget it." She felt her throat tighten as she planted another kiss on his forehead. In his Spiderman pajamas, his cheeks ruddy from the washcloth she'd used to scrub his face, he looked more like five going on six than eight about to be nine. "Night, buddy. Sleep tight."

Kyra was out cold by the time Camille looked in on her. Camille tiptoed over to the bed, smoothing the hair from her daughter's brow. Asleep, Kyra didn't look much older than Zach, the same angelic expression, smoothed of all fears and worries. Camille used to wish her children would stay little forever. Now she only wished she would be around to watch them grow up.

CAMILLE WAS SITTING up in bed, reading, when Edward walked in an hour later. "Sorry I'm so late." He bent to kiss her cheek, bringing the cool breath of the outdoors. She closed the book on the page she'd been staring at, unseeingly, for the past forty minutes. "Rounds took longer than I expected. This new bunch of interns, you never saw such eager beavers—so many questions." He grinned, and she felt a stab of irritation. Were those kids more important than his own?

But she only asked mildly, "Have you eaten?"

"I had a slice of pizza. Does that count?" he said.

She let out a small, involuntary sigh. Couldn't he have made it home in time for dinner? She nearly said something, but bit her tongue instead. What did it matter in light of the news she was about to impart? News that would shatter whatever normalcy they'd regained.

"You didn't get my messages?" He paused to give her a quizzical look as he was loosening his tie.

"I got them," she said in a flat voice.

He eyed her anxiously. "You're not mad, are you?"

"No, I'm not mad."

He sat down beside her on the bed. "Did it go okay at the doctor's? I figured when I didn't hear from you . . ." He trailed off at the look on her face, his eyes searching hers as he sat there with his tie hanging askew. She said nothing, and his anxiety turned to worry. "Cam?"

She shook her head, the enormity of the news she had to impart expanding inside her and forcing the air from her lungs. She took in her husband's dear face. His brown eyes, the color of whiskey straight-up; the close-cropped dark curls that in his student days used to brush his collar; his angular jaw shadowed with stubble. He'd always been handsome but had grown even more so with age. The only signs of wear and tear were the lines bracketing his mouth and the crease between his eyebrows. She reached up now to smooth the crease away, but it only deepened.

She drew in a deep breath and told him.

CHAPTER THREE

When the time came, Edward wanted it inscribed on his tombstone, not that he'd been the best doctor, but that he'd been a good husband and father. Or had tried to be—at this point it was more a goal than a statement. During Camille's last bout with cancer, he had realized just how inadequate he was at running a household and caring for two children on his own. He wasn't sure how it had happened, but what had once been a shared obligation had become primarily Camille's. He was like the passenger in that old movie *The High and the Mighty* who was forced to fly the jet after the pilot fell ill. Somehow—more by the grace of God than his own efforts— he'd managed to keep the plane aloft. Now he was being told it was going to crash.

He sat on the bed, blinking rapidly to stave off tears, a fist-size lump in his throat. "We'll get a second opinion," he said, amazed at how steady his voice was. "I'll call Gene first thing in the morning." Gene Ketchum, chief of oncology at Sloan-Kettering, was an old friend from medical school. He took Camille by the shoulders, forcing her to meet his gaze. She looked like death. Jesus. "And even if it's what we think it is, there are options. It's not hopeless."

"No, it's not," she agreed. "But the odds aren't exactly in my favor."

"You can still beat this. You did once before."

"It was different then." He shook his head in denial, and she went on, her voice rising, "Edward, the cancer isn't just back—it's *spread.*" The picture formed in his mind then: the bright spots dotting the radiologic image like emergency flares on a darkened roadway after a car wreck.

Still, he went on shaking his head. "It's not hopeless," he repeated. "Regina didn't say it was hopeless, did she?"

"No, but you doctors never do." She smiled grimly. "She was honest, at least—she told me I have a three percent chance at best. And that's only if I undergo another stem cell transplant." Camille shuddered visibly at the prospect. "Otherwise, I have maybe six, nine months."

A jolt of alarm went through him, like the aftershock of an earthquake, more at the defeat in her voice than the bleak prognosis. "Refusing treatment isn't an option," he said firmly. She took his hand and squeezed it, her eyes mournful.

"Edward, I'm not sure I can go through that again." The defeated look she wore matched her voice. But she was a fighter, he knew. He clung to the belief that she would regain that spirit once she'd gotten over the shock. "I'd like to spend what time I have left at home, not in a hospital bed hooked up to machines. That's not how I want our children to remember me."

"Better that than have them thinking you gave up," he said more harshly than he'd intended.

She winced, and what little color remained in her face drained away. He knew she was thinking of her own mother, and he felt a stab of remorse. Here she was facing the worst, and he was making it even more difficult for her. He gathered her in his arms. She'd regained some of the weight she'd lost last year, but she was still too thin. Back then, she'd jokingly threatened to have "Handle with Care" tattooed on her rear end. He, in turn, had insisted she was indestructible. Now he was conscious of her breathing, and it was an effort not to count each breath.

He murmured into her hair, "We'll get through this. Just like we did before."

"Before, I had a fighting chance." She drew back to look at him, her haunted expression piercing him.

Edward wanted to rail against God, shake his fist at the sky. But instead, he replied evenly, "The odds aren't as good, no. But new treatments and protocols are being developed all the time."

She gave a wan smile. "That's just what Regina said."

"She's right. We could get lucky. You never know." But even as he spoke, he knew it was only a remote possibililty. Years of testing and blind trials went into developing each new drug. Even if there were one shown to be effective for her type of cancer in the trial phase now, approval from the FDA could still be many months or years away.

"Good thing you're not a gambling man, or we'd be bankrupt by now." She shook her head, wearing a wobbly smile. Then the smile broke and the tears in her eyes spilled down her cheeks. "Oh, God. I don't think I could bear it—holding on to hope. Maybe I just need to work on acceptance."

Nowhere in Edward's vocabulary were the words *I can't.* And until now he'd never expected to hear those words out of his wife's mouth. For Camille, the proverbial glass had always been seven-eighths full. It was one of the reasons he'd fallen in love with her. A memory surfaced, from when they were first engaged. They'd been on their way to grab a bite to eat one evening and he'd apologized for not being able to afford to take her someplace nicer than the neighborhood kebab joint, at which, she'd smiled and said, "I get to be a part of your future. Believe me, that's way better than beef Wellington and a bottle of a fancy wine." She tucked her arm through his as they strolled along the sidewalk near the Morningside Heights walkup he was sharing with a classmate until he and Camille could afford a place of their own. "As for that other stuff, we've got all kinds of time."

"I won't let you die," he said now through gritted teeth.

She caressed his cheek, saying in a choked voice, "My darling. I know you'd move heaven and Earth if you could. That's why I love you so much. Who else would've thought to take snapshots of the tulips along Park Avenue so I wouldn't totally miss out on spring?" A smile touched her lips at the reminder of the last time she'd been confined to a hospital bed fighting for her life. "But even you can't perform miracles."

Desperation set in. "You can't just give up," he insisted.

"Oh, Edward." She wiped away a tear. "I may not have a choice."

A dozen arguments howled through his head, like the storm gathering force outside, but he didn't voice them. She looked so spent. *She'll come to her senses after a good night's sleep,* he told himself. "We'll talk in the morning," he said. "Everything always looks brighter in the morning."

"Come lie next to me." She scooted over to make room for him.

Edward stretched out beside her, still in his suit and tie. How many evenings had they lain together like this, discussing the events of the day or venting some work-related frustration? It was generally run-of-the-mill stuff—a cranky patient or a demanding client, or one of the children acting up—complaints he'd have welcomed now. Instead, he could only stare up at the ceiling, taking shallow breaths to keep from reminding himself, and her, of his own disgustingly robust health. Neither of them spoke. It was several minutes before he felt Camille stir beside him.

"Kyra has a crush on a boy in her class," she informed him. Her voice had a soft, dreamy quality. "His name is Jan." She pronounced it "*Yah*n." "He's an exchange student from Norway."

"Tall, blond, and strapping, no doubt." He wondered why he was just now learning of this. Since when did his little girl have crushes on boys? Wasn't it only yesterday she'd been playing with dolls?

"I have no idea what he looks like. I haven't met him yet."

"Will anything come of it, do you think?"

"Hard to say. According to her, he doesn't even know she exists."

"Good. Let's keep it that way." Edward used to think he'd be open-minded, even liberal to a point, when his daughter was old enough to date. But that was before his baby girl blossomed into a fetching fourteen-year-old who could easily get her heart broken.

"Oh, I don't know," Camille said. "I was thinking she should invite him over."

Edward frowned in confusion. "Am I missing something? You just said the guy doesn't know she exists."

"All the more reason. The only thing standing in the way is shyness."

"His or hers?"

"Both, if my guess is correct."

"Our daughter," he said, "is anything but shy." Kyra was very vocal in expressing her opinions.

"Not at home, no, but in school? With boys? Don't you remember what it was like at that age?"

"Sure, and I'd have died of embarrassment if my parents had invited over some girl I liked."

"I didn't say *we* should invite him."

"Doesn't it amount to the same thing?"

"I was only going to suggest it."

"You want my advice? Stay out of it."

Camille rolled onto her side so they were face-to-face. "So we should just let her flounder?"

"She's not floundering. As far as I can tell, she's doing just fine." He added on a lighter note, "Besides, I have it on good authority that meddling in a teenager's love life can bite you in the ass."

"Whose authority would that be?"

"Yours. Those were your exact words when I suggested she ask Seth Conway to the Sadie Hawkins dance."

"This is different," she said. "Seth's a junior. Jan is her age, at least."

He smiled. "Spoken like a true matchmaker."

"Yes, and a damned good one at that." She was quiet for a minute, studying his face. When she spoke again, her voice was low and tremulous. "Edward, I need to ask something of you."

"Of course. Anything," he replied without hesitation, but for some reason he felt a chill tiptoe up his spine.

"Promise me you'll marry again after I'm gone."

It was the last thing he wished to think about now or ever. He'd never looked at another woman, not even during the months Camille had been so ill, with their sex life on hold. He couldn't imagine lying next to another woman like this. Holding her in his arms. Making love to her.

"We are not having this conversation." He spoke in a tone that invited no dissent. "You're my wife. The only one I want. And you're not going anywhere. That's all there is to say on the subject."

"But if—"

He pressed a finger to her lips. "Don't. This is hard enough as it is."

Camille's gaze remained fixed on him. Her eyes were a shade of blue so vivid it seemed color-enhanced, like that of the sky in the glossy brochures still tucked in his coat pocket. He recalled thinking, when they had first met, *I could spend the rest of my life gazing into those eyes*. It hadn't occurred to him that he might outlive her; it was as unthinkable then as it was now.

THEY MET ON a rainy night in September of 1989. George Bush senior was in office and the Gulf War was heating up in the Middle East. That, and reports of the massacre in Tiananmen Square, had campus activists in a foment, waving placards and chanting protests, though Edward was too intent on his studies to pay much attention, steeped in subjects whose names he'd have had difficulty pronouncing when he was a boy merely dreaming of becoming a doctor: neurobiology, microbial pathogenesis, general virology, molecular diagnostics. Sometimes he'd nod off in the middle of a late-night cram session and wake hours later to find his head resting on an open book, its pages pressing a ridge into his cheek. One of his roommates, Darryl Hornquist, after finding him in that pitiful state once too often, urged him to get out more, find some other interests before he caved under the pressure. "I've already lost one roommate to the psych ward," Darryl had said. He was referring to Lewis Karlinsky, who'd had to drop out the previous semester after he became obsessed with light switches and doorknobs and keeping all his pens and colored markers precisely lined up. Edward, after giving it some thought, decided Darryl was right, so he began volunteering at a crisis center in the East Village, where his job was to man the suicide hotline Tuesday and Thursday nights between the hours of eight and midnight.

The night Camille phoned in, it was pouring rain. He recalled thinking, as he slogged across campus on his way to the subway station, that if anyone were contemplating suicide they'd be twice as likely to go through with it on a night like this. The rain had been coming down so long and hard, the campus walkways were flooded and the lawn in front of Low Memorial Library a bog. Armed with only a flimsy folding umbrella, he was soaked to the skin by the time he reached the crisis center. He'd only just settled in at his desk, with a large container of coffee and the textbooks he'd brought in case it turned out to be a slow night, when one of the phone lines lit up. He picked up and a breathless voice, that of a girl so agitated he couldn't make much sense of what she was saying, began to babble—something about a bad breakup and an asshole of a boyfriend.

"Take a breath," he said calmly. "Tell me what the problem is."

"Pills, I think. I'm not sure."

"You're not sure if you took pills?" *This is a new one,* he thought.

"No. I mean, yes, I'm sure."

"But you might have. Is that what you're saying?" He spoke slowly and carefully, in case she turned out to be even crazier than she sounded. You never knew, with some of these people.

"No! I didn't take any pills!" she cried.

He frowned in confusion. "Then who did?"

"No one. Yet. As far as I know."

"So, no pills . . . okay." He exhaled. "Let's start at the beginning. Have you been depressed lately?"

"Not me! My roommate. I'm afraid she might try to hurt herself." She went on in a rush, "She's been a mess ever since that dickhead broke up with her. Excuse me, but he is, and that's putting it mildly. Then today I find this vial of prescription pills in her dresser drawer, and I can't think of why someone who has absolutely nothing wrong with her, except bad taste in boyfriends, needs Codeine." Finally, she took a breath, saying a bit more calmly, "I didn't know who else to call."

"You did the right thing." He was momentarily at a loss, then after he'd collected his thoughts, he suggested, "Why don't you put your roommate on? Maybe it would help if I talked to her."

"No! She'd kill me if she knew I called this number." She made a sound halfway between a groan and a giggle. "Oh, God. I can't believe I just said that. Now you're going to think she's homicidal on top of suicidal. She's really not that bad, I swear. Just a little mixed up."

"Well, you did the right thing. She's lucky to have you as a friend. What's your name, by the way?"

"Camille."

"Like in the movie?"

"You know it?" She sounded surprised. She was probably thinking he wasn't the average medical student, and she'd be right. Thanks to his nana Clara. Growing up, every day after school that he didn't have homework he and Nana Clara would watch the black-and-white movies from her girlhood on TV while she did her ironing—films like *Red Dust* and *The Lady Eve* and *The Public Enemy*. By the time he was twelve, he'd seen the entire *Thin Man* series and could quote lines from movies his friends had never even heard of.

"Of course," he said. "Garbo's finest hour."

"My parents were huge fans," she explained. "Apparently, they didn't see it as a bad omen that her character dies in the end." She gave another helpless giggle. "Sorry, I seem to have death on the brain."

"Join the club. I spent the morning dissecting a cadaver."

"Which means you're either a serial killer or a med student. I'm assuming the latter."

"Third year," he said.

"So this isn't your real job? You don't get paid to talk people off ledges?"

"No. I'm just a lowly volunteer."

"Well, I'm glad I got you." There was a brief pause, as if she were considering what to do with him now that she had him, before she went on, "So, Mr. Dissects-Cadavers-by-Day-Talks-People-Off-Ledges-by-Night, are you allowed to give your name? Or is that against the rules?"

"Edward," he told her, smiling as he leaned back in his swivel chair, his textbooks forgotten for the moment and his unopened container of coffee growing cold. "Edward Constantin."

"Edward, huh? Not Ed or Eddie?"

"No, just Edward." Even as a child, he'd only ever been called by his full name. He'd been named after his great-grandfather, whom he was said to resemble. When he was younger, Nana Clara would often remark on it, but it wasn't until he was older that he saw the resemblance, in the framed studio portrait that hung on the wall of his parent's cramped row house in Milwaukee, between himself and the young naval officer with the wavy dark hair and solemn brown eyes posing stiffly in his WWI uniform, fresh from the battlefields of Verdun and Ypres.

"Ah, the traditional type. I like that," she said. "I suppose you also open doors and pull out chairs for us poor, helpless females." He heard the lilt in her voice and realized she was flirting. She must have realized it, too, because her tone at once became more subdued. "So, um, Edward, what do you think I should do? About Melissa—my roommate. Should I confront her?"

Following the crisis center's guidelines, he instructed, "Yes. But if she denies it or refuses to get help, you need to speak to someone about it. A guidance counselor or her parents."

"What if I'm overreacting?"

"Do you want to take that chance?"

"She could end up hating me."

"You'd hate yourself even more if she ended up harming herself."

Camille sighed. "You're right."

Edward, quite outside the center's guidelines, found himself offering, "Look, this isn't strictly protocol, but I'm going to give you my home number. Just in case. That is, if you, um, need . . ."

"Thank you. That's very nice of you," she said, not letting him finish. He braced himself for a polite brush-off. Maybe she thought he was some creepy guy who was hard up for dates. "But you don't know me. I could be some crazy person who's making this up just to get attention."

"Somehow I doubt that," he said, feeling the tension go out him.

"We should probably meet in person, though, so you can be sure. In a public place, of course. You never know with crazy people, even the ones who seem harmless. You can't be too careful these days."

"How do you know *I'm* not some lunatic?" He played along.

"Easy. If you were, we wouldn't be having this conversation." He chuckled, and she went on, "So, Edward, do you ever get time off from dissecting cadavers and talking to depressed people?"

"Not too often," he admitted.

"Tell me about it." She gave a sigh of solidarity. In the next five minutes, he learned Camille was in her junior year at NYU and that she worked part-time cataloguing data at a research lab. "How about breakfast then? You can spare an hour on Sunday, can't you? I'll see if I can get Melissa to join us. She needs to be reminded that not all men are assholes."

He laughed. "Thanks for the vote of confidence."

"Not at all. I have a good feeling about you, Edward Constantin."

They arranged to meet at Barney Greengrass, at nine a.m. on Sunday. She promised to call and give him an update on Melissa before then. He wished her luck. "I hope it turns out okay."

"Yeah, me, too," she said. "But either way, no backing out on me."

"I wouldn't dream of it." Edward was grinning as he hung up. He felt strangely buoyant the rest of the evening for someone taking calls at a suicide hotline on a dark and stormy night. He wasn't even able to concentrate on his studies between calls—a first for him. He kept thinking about the girl. What did she look like? Was she pretty? All he knew was, he couldn't wait to meet her.

She phoned the following evening to let him know she'd spoken with her roommate. The crisis was a false alarm, as it turned out— the vial of prescription pills was for an old injury; Melissa had no intention of killing herself. After that, talk turned to other things. When he finally hung up, he was surprised to note that more than an hour had passed, during which time he hadn't given a single thought to his studies or the paper that was due tomorrow.

Sunday morning, at nine a.m. on the dot, Edward arrived at Barney Greengrass, on the Upper West Side. As he walked into the deli, his gaze was drawn to a girl seated at a table by the window who fit Camille's description. Slender and fair-skinned with blue eyes and auburn hair, wearing a red sweater and faded blue jeans, a pink scarf looped around her neck. She was pretty; prettier even than he'd imagined. He stood rooted to the spot for a moment, dazed by her beauty and all those blazing, sunset colors converging on him at once. Then she spotted him and waved, breaking into a smile so dazzling it was all he could do to keep from tripping over his own feet as he wound his way toward her through the maze of Formica tables.

As he drew near, he could see she was even more beautiful up close. Fine-boned, with delicate features, and, sweet Jesus, those *eyes*—they were the bluest of blues. He saw, too, that her hair wasn't just one color; it was a dozen shades ranging from russet to pale gold. As she rose to greet him, it glimmered like firelight. "You're taller than I expected," she said as they shook hands.

Edward was speechless for a moment. When he finally recovered his wits, he blurted unthinkingly, "Am I?" As if it weren't perfectly obvious that he towered over her, at six feet four inches.

"You're also better looking," she went on with a frankness that made his face warm. "You should've warned me."

"I don't think of myself that way," he replied self-consciously.

"Really." She cocked her head, smiling at him. "You don't have girls telling you that all the time?"

"The only girls I come into contact with these days wouldn't know a live body from a cadaver," he replied with a laugh. "Med students are notorious for being bad romantic prospects."

"I see. Well, that explains it." Her smile turned coquettish, and she announced as they sat down, "Oh, by the way, my roommate won't be joining us. Melissa's not speaking to me at the moment."

"She's not?" Edward adopted an appropriately sober expression so she wouldn't guess how relieved he was to learn he'd have her all to himself. "I thought you'd sorted things out with her."

"Yeah, well, that was before Dickhead begged her to take him back and I told her she'd be crazy if she did." Their waitress, who had to be at least a hundred years old and looked as if she'd been working there since the Nixon administration, handed them laminated menus and went to fetch the coffeepot. Camille waited until she was gone to confide, "In case you haven't noticed, I'm fairly outspoken."

"I've noticed," he said, pressing his lips together to keep from smiling.

Over an enormous breakfast of scrambled eggs and lox washed down with endless cups of coffee, Edward told her about the courses he was taking at Columbia and some of the challenges he faced as a third-year med student. When Camille asked what had made him go into medicine, he answered, "It was my grandmother, actually. Though she didn't have much faith in doctors." Camille eyed him curiously, and he explained, "She was from the old country; she relied on folk remedies." He saw clearly in his mind the jars of mysterious herbs and roots that had lined the kitchen cupboards when he was growing up, each one bearing a handwritten label. "Though in the end, she didn't have a cure for what killed her," he said, his voice turning hard.

Camille was quiet for a moment. "I'm sorry. Were you and she close?"

"Very." He saw she was waiting for him to go on, but he hesitated to divulge more. He'd never told anyone the story of how he'd carried his beloved *bunicuța* in his arms to the hospital, when he was just thirteen and she was little more than a bundle of sticks covered in skin. The memory was too painful, even after all these years. "It was hard seeing her suffer at the end, but I'll spare you the gruesome details. Anyway, you'd have to know my family for any of it to make sense."

She regarded him with a thoughtful expression, as if sensing it was a painful topic. But she only remarked, "Well, I don't see how your family could be any more screwed up than mine."

"Was it as bad as all that?" he asked as he sipped his coffee.

She shrugged. "I wasn't starved or beaten, if that's what you mean."

"You don't have to be, to have a miserable childhood."

"My mom died when I was fourteen." Her tone was matter of fact, but he could see the flicker of some deep emotion in her eyes. "And my dad . . . let's just say he wasn't around much after that."

"Who looked after you when he was away?"

"No one, really. We had a live-in housekeeper, but it wasn't really her job to take care of us. Mostly it was just me and my sister." He caught an undercurrent of bitterness in her voice. "Holly was only eleven at the time. She doesn't remember it as being all that bad, but that's probably because she had her big sister looking out for her." She pushed her plate aside as if she'd suddenly lost interest in her food. He felt a pang of sympathy for the young girl she'd been. "There weren't any relatives who could help out?"

"Just my grandmother in California, but we only saw her when we went for visits in the summertime."

To Edward, it was unfathomable: two young girls left to more or less fend for themselves. He was an only child, but the community he'd grown up in was a close-knit one. Growing up, he'd been surrounded by adults. Everyone he knew was related to him in some way, whether by marriage or blood, or simply by virtue of having come from the same region in Romania as his parents. "What sort of work does your dad do?" he asked, sensing the need to tread carefully.

"He's vice president of operations for Pan Am. Before that, he was a pilot." She began tearing off pieces of bagel, leaving them scattered over her plate. "We never know what time zone he's in, much less when we'll see him. When I was a kid, I used to count the days until he came home from trips, but I don't bother to keep track anymore. What would be the point? I wouldn't go home at all if it weren't for Holly. Though she's not around much, either."

"Holly," he mused aloud. "Don't tell me. She was named after—"

"Holly Golightly." Camille broke into a grin. "Good guess."

Edward scooted his chair in to keep from getting poked by the very large purse of the woman seated behind him, bringing himself into even closer contact with Camille. He was hyperaware of her presence across from him; the narrow space between them seemed charged with ions. "Is she anything like the fictional Holly?" he asked in what he hoped was a normal voice.

Camille rolled her eyes, but he didn't miss the way her expression softened. "Believe me, she gives new meaning to the term *free spirit.*"

"In other words, she's nothing like you," he teased.

Camille swatted him with her napkin. "Bite your tongue. Just because I happen to care about my allegedly suicidal roommate, it doesn't make me the super-responsible type." A tiny smile surfaced. "Well, maybe a little. But I come by it honestly. Holly was a handful, let me tell you. She still is."

"How so?" he asked, inching his chair in a little closer.

"Well, for one thing, she practically lives with her boyfriend. Which might not seem so unusual, except that she's only seventeen and he's ten years older." At the expression he must have worn, she went on, "I know. Jailbait. But that's Holly for you. Or maybe it says more about my dad. You'd think he'd check up on her once in a while—officially, she stays with her best friend when he's out of town—but with him, it's out of sight, out of mind."

"Wow." Edward didn't know what to say to that.

"You know what she used to do when she was younger? Crash bar mitzvahs. Seriously." Tavern on the Green, back when it was a happening enterprise, was only a few blocks from where they lived, she explained, and there was always at least one bar or bat mitzvah on any given Saturday. "She figured no one would notice one more kid. I thought it was strange that she got so many invitations, but I figured there must be a lot of Jewish kids in her class. She got away with it, too. For a whole year. Until one of the moms smoked her out. When I confronted her, she just shrugged and said, 'It was something to do.' That's my sister for you, in a nutshell."

He chuckled. "A career criminal in the making."

Camille laughed and pushed her hands through her hair, which caught the light and his breath along with it, spilling through her fingers to fan across her back. "You joke," she said. "But it's a fact. Truancy, underage drinking, sneaking out at night, you name it, Holly's done it."

"I'm sure she'll straighten out in time. She's still young."

"I suppose." Camille sighed, slumped over her plate with her elbows propped on the table as she stared into the distance, lost in thought. Then she straightened suddenly, bringing her gaze back to him and saying in an exasperated voice, "Listen to me. I'm twenty and I sound like a worried mom. Between Holly and my stupid roommate, it's a wonder I have a life."

"You can't help it if you're the super-responsible type," he teased.

They both laughed. The woman behind him, with the purse, turned around to stare at them, which only made Camille laugh harder, covering her mouth with her hands to stifle her giggles.

Edward wanted to lean in and kiss her, then and there. Lick the dab of cream cheese from the corner of her mouth and run the tip of his tongue over her sweetly parted lips. It shocked him, how close he came to doing just that. He had never felt so strongly about a girl.

The following Saturday, he used his meager savings to take her to dinner at an Italian restaurant in the Village. Afterward, they went back to her dorm room at NYU. Her roommate was out with her boyfriend, so they had it to themselves. Before she'd even switched on the lights, they were in each other's arms. They kissed, and then she took his hand and led him to her bed.

They lay together on the mattress, kissing and touching each other for the longest time without taking their clothes off. But if she was going slow, it wasn't out of shyness. She wanted to make each moment last, she told him. They weren't just making love, they were making memories.

Edward was in no hurry, either. All week, he'd been at a fever pitch imagining this: Camille naked in his arms. He wanted to savor each moment. He'd been with other girls—three, to be exact—but Camille, unlike his previous girlfriends, needed no guidance when it came to what to do with her hands and mouth. It quickly became obvious, somewhat to his consternation, that despite his being several years older, she was the more experienced.

"You've never done this before? Seriously?" she asked when he hesitated to go down on her.

"Once," he confessed. "She didn't like it."

"I promise I'll like it," Camille purred, urging him lower. Listening to her moans of pleasure as he brought her to climax, he thought no sound could be sweeter. Afterward, he fumbled in the pocket of his jeans for the condom he kept in his wallet. He always found this part awkward, and to make matters worse his fingers weren't cooperating for some reason. He felt like a bumbling teenager. Once again, it was Camille who took charge, pulling the foil packet from his hand and tearing it open in a single, deft move. When he finally entered her, he could barely contain himself. If she hadn't been equally impatient, he wouldn't have been able to hold back long enough to bring her to climax a second time.

"That," she murmured, "was amazing." She eased out from under him and rolled onto her side, propping her head on her elbow. She grinned at him in the darkness, her face inches from his.

"Better than with your other lovers?" He couldn't resist.

"Yes. But to be a hundred percent sure, I think we should review the material one more time," she replied in a mock studious voice. She wriggled in closer, and they began kissing again. He wouldn't have thought it humanly possible, but within seconds he felt himself stir in response.

She climbed on top, and they rocked together. She gave herself over to him with abandon, her head thrown back, exposing the smooth, white column of her throat, her bright hair spilling over her shoulders and back. The exquisite pleasure mounted with each thrust, and he felt the last vestiges of control slip away. When they finally collapsed, trembling, their bodies slick with sweat, he felt as if he'd arrived at a destination to which he hadn't known he was headed.

·   ·   ·

NOW, ALL THESE years later, he looked at his wife, lying still and pale beside him. Panic rose in him. *What if I were to lose her?* It was like trying to imagine a world without the sun or moon. Had he been a man of faith he'd have railed at God. Why *her*? What had she done to deserve this? Hadn't she—they—suffered enough? To make matters worse, she was already thinking ahead to a future that didn't include her. Christ. As if they didn't have enough to deal with.

"I don't want anyone but you," he told her.

She eyed him mournfully. "I know. But I might not always be here."

He felt his chest constrict. "Don't say that."

"I hate this as much as you do," she went on, her voice shaky. "But we have to face the fact that in all likelihood you'll outlive me. I'd feel better knowing you wouldn't be facing the future alone."

"I wouldn't be alone. I'd have the kids."

"I'm thinking of them, too. I know what it's like to lose a mother."

"They'd still have me," he choked out.

"Yes, but you'll need someone to help look after them." She was putting it delicately, he knew. The implication hung heavy in the air: He had already proven woefully inadequate in that area.

"No one could replace you," he insisted. Jesus. Why were they even discussing this?

"I know," she said, wiping away the tear rolling down her cheek. "I felt the same way when my mom died. But you know what? It would've been better for Holly and me if our dad had remarried."

"I'm not your dad," he said, though deep down he suspected he and his father-in-law had more in common than he cared to admit. "I wouldn't just leave my children to fend for themselves."

"*Our* children." She placed a hand against his cheek. "Don't I get a say in it, too?"

He shook his head. "I can't make any promises."

"Even if it was my dying wish?" It was what she always said in jest whenever they disagreed on anything, but hearing it now was like a shot through the heart. He winced.

"You're not dying," he said. *I won't let you.*

The tears were flowing faster now, rolling down her cheeks to drip off her chin; she no longer bothered to wipe them away. "Oh, Edward. Don't you see? I only want you to be happy."

"How could I be happy without you?" His mouth contorted, and he felt the hot sting of tears. He breathed in and out, slowly and deliberately, until he'd regained a measure of composure.

"You feel that way now, but you won't always. I know. I see it every day. Remember Manny Horowitz?" She named a former client whose wedding they'd attended several years ago. Manny's first wife had died shortly before their fiftieth anniversary and, after an extended period of mourning, Camille had introduced him to the woman who became his second wife. "He didn't think he could ever love again. He only wanted companionship. Then he met Corinne."

"I don't need some random woman to keep me company in my old age," he growled.

"It wasn't like that with Manny," she told him. "He fell in love again. So, you see, it's possible."

If anything was possible, didn't that also hold true for her chances of recovery? he thought. "I'm not giving up on you just yet," he said, using a corner of the sheet to wipe away her tears.

"Oh, Edward." She looked so woebegone, his heart broke a little more.

He gathered her in his arms. "I love you," he whispered hoarsely.

"I know," she whispered in return. "That's what makes this so hard."

"I can't make any promises."

"Okay, no promises. Just keep an open mind, okay?"

Edward thought of all the times they'd clung to each other like this, giving each other solace when the going got rough. Often it had led to their making love. But cancer had robbed them of that, too. What the past year's ordeal had taught him was that love and desire weren't inextricably bound; one didn't necessarily ebb with the other. His love for Camille was different than before—he felt more protective of her than anything—but no less strong. If that meant humoring her until she regained her natural sense of optimism, he supposed there was no harm in it.

"I'll try," he said with a sigh.

CHAPTER FOUR

Growing up, Camille and her sister had amused themselves during their father's long absences by playing word games like Twenty Questions and I Spy. Their all-time favorite was Would You Rather. Would you rather be beautiful but brainless, or the smartest person in the world with an ugly face? Swallow a live cockroach, or kiss a boy with food stuck in his braces? Be stranded on a desert island, or swim through shark-infested waters? If you had only six months to live, would you spend it in the arms of Robert Redford, or doing good works like Mother Teresa?

The last one, posed by Holly, had been a real head-scratcher. Camille was sure she'd win more points toward heaven doing good works. On the other hand, if the hottest guy on the planet were crazy enough to take on a dying girl . . .

This was how it went in reality: In the morning, you got up and fixed breakfast, then got your kids off to school. At work, you put on a smiling face. And maybe at some point in the midst of your hectic day, if you weren't too swamped, you had a few minutes to yourself in which to wallow in self-pity before it was time to go home and get supper ready. In short, life went on.

She met with clients. She balanced her checkbook. She went grocery shopping (though now it was with a sense of irony that she checked expiration dates). She planned her son's birthday party. She got her hair cut (only giving a cryptic smile in response when her

stylist asked if she'd consider coloring it, after finding a gray hair).
The difference was, she was keenly aware of the passage of time.
Before, the days and weeks would slide one into the next; she'd
never given much thought to their being in ever-dwindling supply,
which she now saw as a shocking waste. These days, whenever Zach
said something that made her laugh or Kyra doled out one of her
rare hugs, she savored it like hard candy dissolving slowly on her
tongue. She'd recall what her own mother used to say to her, when
giving out her weekly allowance: *This is all you're getting, so spend
it wisely.* Back then, it was dimes and quarters; now it was minutes
and hours.

The morning of Zach's birthday, she phoned her husband at
work to remind him to pick up the cake at the bakery on his way to
the all-boy party at Chelsea Piers. When Edward showed up several
hours later, after the six boys had worn themselves out in the batting cages and were digging in to the pizza she'd had delivered, her
heart sank when she saw he was empty-handed.

"You forgot." She stared at him in disbelief.

He paused, giving her a blank look, then grimaced. "The cake.
Damn." His expression turned contrite as he continued toward her.
"I'm sorry, Cam. There was so much going on at work . . ."

Like I don't have a lot going on, too? But she didn't voice her frustration; she only sighed.

"I'll run back and get it," he said.

"Never mind," she told him, her voice weary. "By the time you
made it back, it'd be too late." The bakery was all the way up on
West Seventy-Ninth Street, easily a forty-minute round trip.

Edward flashed a guilty look at their son, who at the moment
was too busy chowing down with his friends to notice either his
father's presence or the absence of the cake. The boys all had red
clown mouths and cheese dripping from their chins. Then Zach
spotted his dad and came charging over.

"Hey, Dad! Guess what? I hit more balls than anyone!"

Edward grinned and ruffled Zach's hair. "Way to go, slugger. Sorry I wasn't here to see it." He grabbed a wad of napkins and handed it to Zach, who gave his stained mouth a cursory swipe.

"I only struck out *twice*." Zach beamed at his dad.

"Looks like we have a future MVP on our hands." Edward turned to smile at Camille, who didn't smile back. She wasn't in a forgiving mood at the moment. "I would've gotten here sooner if I could have," he told Zack, bending down so they were eye level. "You know that, don't you?"

"Yeah, I know." Zach's tone was matter of fact. *He shouldn't be so used to it,* Camille thought.

"But, listen," Edward went on, "I have a surprise for you."

Zach's eyes widened. "Bigger than the bike?" His main present was the razor bike he'd been begging for since he was six.

"No, but it's one I think you'll like," Edward answered with a wink. "Instead of boring old cake, how would you feel about us all going to Serendipity for frozen hot chocolate sundaes?"

"Awwwwwesome." Zach jumped up and down in his excitement. "Can we go now?"

"Sure, as soon as you finish your pizza."

"Great," Camille muttered to her husband after Zach had run off to give the good news to his friends. "Now all we have to do is figure out a way to fit six kids and two adults into one cab."

"So we'll take two cabs," Edward said with a shrug. Problem solved.

If only it were as simple as that. Now she had to phone the other moms and inform them of the change in plans, then pray it wouldn't be too long a wait once they got there. The popular eatery was always packed this time of day; it could be an hour or more before they got a table. Which meant six rowdy boys jammed into the waiting area, or worse, racing up and down the sidewalk in front.

Why did mothers always get stuck with the boring details while fathers got to play the hero? she thought with frustration. It wasn't intentional, she knew; they *meant* well. Still. The upshot was, while

Zach would remember this day as one filled with fun and surprises, her memory of the last birthday of his she was likely to celebrate would be of her husband neglecting to do the one thing she'd asked of him and then compounding it by making even more work for her. She sighed again. Maybe it wasn't so unintentional. Maybe, deep down, he wanted to punish her.

"You're angry with me, aren't you?" She confronted him while the boys were in the restroom washing up.

Edward looked at her, a play of emotions flitting over his handsome face like wind-chased clouds across a winter sky. "Angry? Why would I be angry at *you*? I'm the one who screwed up."

"You know perfectly well what I mean," she said through gritted teeth. "You blame me, don't you?"

His eyes flashed, and in that instant, she caught a glimpse of what he'd kept under wraps in the days since she'd come to a decision about whether or not to seek treatment. After a second opinion, from Edward's oncologist friend at Sloan-Kettering, confirmed the original prognosis, she hadn't seen the point. For what? Another three to six months shackled to a hospital bed, so shot full of painkillers she wouldn't know what planet she was on? She and Edward had discussed it, of course, until they were both blue in the face, but he refused to accept her decision. As if she hadn't agonized over it herself! As if she were doing this for her own selfish reasons! She couldn't make him understand. So much was being taken from her—the opportunity to grow old with her husband and watch her children grow up, see them graduate and get married and have children of their own—why squander a single, precious moment of the time she had left?

"Camille, I don't think this is the time . . ." He lowered his voice, glancing over at the restroom as if he expected the boys to come tumbling out that very moment. "Can we talk about this later on?"

"Talk about *what*? Why don't you just say it?" she hissed. "You're mad because I'm not doing what you want. I'm not choosing to subject myself to torture on the practically nonexistent chance I'll live to see our son's next birthday."

She'd been witness to her own mother's slow, agonizing death. She knew what it was like. The hospital bed in the dining room. The nurses coming and going at all hours. Each night, she'd lay awake in bed listening to the creak of footfalls in the hallway and voices speaking in low tones, wishing she still believed in Santa Claus so she could believe, too, that her mom would get better.

"I have patients who'd be grateful for any chance at all," he said in a tight voice. "How do you know what's possible unless you try? Miracles do happen. We doctors think we know everything, but we don't. We—" He broke off abruptly as the boys trooped noisily out of the restroom.

They didn't speak of it again.

THE FOLLOWING SATURDAY, they sat the children down and told them a modified version of the truth. At the stricken looks they wore, she reassured them, "I don't want you worrying. I'm in good hands." Her doctor had started her on a mild dose of chemo, just enough to slow the cancer's spread. It would buy her more time and meant she could go about her business as usual for the next few months, barring any side effects. Her children wouldn't have to know how serious it was until it was absolutely necessary.

Zach's eyes filled with tears. "Are you going to die, Mommy?" he asked, his voice quavering.

Camille darted a helpless glance at Edward, who was quick to step in. "We all die sometime. You know that," he reminded their son, his voice gentle. "It's part of the circle of life." They'd explained it to Zach when he'd come to them with questions after watching *The Lion King* for the first time. Then he'd been too young to know the meaning of death. It had helped having a vehicle to make him understand. *Thank God for Disney*, she thought now with irony.

"But I'm not going anywhere so fast," she put in, "so I don't want to see any moping. I'll still be there to cheer you on at soccer games. And to embarrass your sister at her piano recitals," she added with a wry glance at her daughter, who always complained that she clapped too hard. Kyra only gave a wan smile in response. Zach wriggled onto Camille's lap, which he hadn't done since he was small. Never mind, at nine, he weighed almost as much as she did—he would be tall like his father. "Will you have to go to the hospital like the last time?" he asked with his scruffy head buried against her chest.

"I hope not," she told him, wondering if he could hear the sound of her heart breaking. "We'll see."

She glanced again at Edward, who she could see was struggling with his own emotions. She watched him swallow before saying in a hoarse voice, "Your mom is getting the best care possible. That much I can promise."

"Plus, I'm counting on you guys," Camille said. "Hugs and kisses are the best medicine, as we all know." She looked pointedly at her teenaged daughter, who sat with her arms crossed over her chest scowling at no one in particular.

"It's so *unfair!*" Kyra burst out.

Camille put an arm around her. "I know, honey. But life isn't always fair."

"We'll just have to pull together like the last time," Edward said.

"You mean like when you were in charge and we had pizza every night for a week?" Kyra gently reproached. "Dad, I'm sorry, but you're hopeless."

They all laughed, and Camille breathed a sigh of relief. The children were taking it in stride. They seemed fine. Mostly. That night, when she tucked Zach into bed, he wanted his teddy bear in addition to the night-light on. And Kyra ignored the usual flood of phone calls and text messages from her friends, choosing instead to cuddle with Camille on the sofa while they watched TV.

Dara and Holly were the only ones to whom she'd confided the whole truth. Dara, after the initial shock wore off, had the right attitude. Instead of projecting an air of gloom, she used gallows humor to lighten the atmosphere around the office. Like when she quipped, after Camille had gotten off the phone with a client who'd whined that there were no "truly hot" guys left, "Maybe you could have a word with Heath Ledger when you get to the other side, and see if you can get him to come back." Trust Dara to keep the elephant in the room in plain sight. Holly was trying her best, too, though it was more difficult for her. If Dara made bearable what would otherwise be awkward and oppressive, it was Camille's sister who provided a sounding board.

"Edward's pissed at me," Camille told her. It was the last week in April, and they were at the obstetrician's, Holly seated on the examining table dressed in a paper gown while they waited for her doctor. Holly had asked Camille along because today was the day of her first ultrasound: She wanted her sister to share the experience when she got her first look at her unborn child.

"If he is, it's at the situation, not you," Holly replied.

"No, it's more than that," Camille insisted. "He acts like I have a *choice*."

Holly sighed and reached for Camille's hand. "It's hard for us all, Cam. Here I am feeling guilty for bringing a new life into the world while you're—" She broke off, her eyes welling with tears. "Damn. Now look what you made me do." Camille snatched up a box of what at a quick glance looked to be tissues, and they both laughed when Holly withdrew a latex examining glove instead. She held it up, limp and wrinkled, observing, "Reminds me of a condom. Though it's a little late for that, in my case."

"I won't have you feeling guilty," Camille said after they had both dried their eyes. She gave her sister an admonishing look. "This is supposed to be the happiest time of your life. I, for one, am thrilled about the baby." *I just hope I live to see it born.* "It certainly took you long enough."

"God, remember that pregnancy scare I had in high school? I was scared I was going to end up pushing a stroller while all my friends were graduating. I was never so happy to get my period. Now I'll probably be the only one in Mommy and Me who got knocked up from a one-night stand."

Camille smiled and shook her head. Her sister had always gone her own way. Why should this be any different? Camille recalled how scandalized she'd been when Holly lost her virginity, at fourteen, to a popular senior at their school whom she'd known all of three weeks. "He won't respect you now," Camille had cried angrily. "He'll tell all his friends." To which Holly had replied nonchalantly, "Who cares? I don't have anything to hide. Anyway, I liked it as much as he did."

By the time Holly was in her twenties, she'd been living on her own for years, traveling the country with the nineties grunge band Wrath, as personal assistant and sometime girlfriend to its lead singer, Ronan Quist. Camille had despaired of her ever getting a real job or settling down. But Holly had surprised everyone by enrolling in college at the age of thirty, taking a job managing a small radio station to make ends meet while she worked toward her degree. After that, she started her own online business selling rock-and-roll memorabilia. Fittingly enough, the Web site's address was rockon.com.

Camille smiled now at the sight of her thirty-nine-year-old sister, who at twelve weeks pregnant was now convex in all the places she'd been concave. Her speed bumps, as she used to jokingly call her breasts, were fuller and her face rounder. Her porcelain skin, once the envy of the Goth crowd she'd hung out with in high school, was peaches and cream. With her curly light-brown hair, wide blue eyes, and dimples, she looked positively angelic. If not for the tattoo on her left butt cheek—a pear with a bite taken out of it—no one would guess Holly was a former bad girl.

"Well, at least you got something out of it," Camille observed wryly, her gaze dropping to her sister's barely discernible baby bump.

"Besides the sex, you mean. God, the sex . . ." Holly's expression turned dreamy. "Did I mention it was the best I ever had?" And that was saying a lot, given the multitude of lovers through the years.

"Only about five zillion times."

Holly had been smitten with Curtis McBride after just one date, despite the fact that they had little in common—he was a banker and she'd made it a rule never to date a man who wore a suit and tie to work—but when he told her he was being transferred overseas to his bank's London branch, she preemptively broke it off. Transatlantic relationships, she claimed, were strictly for the Very Rich or Very Deluded. The phone bills alone would be enough to bankrupt her. It wasn't until after Curtis left for London that she discovered she was pregnant. She briefly considered terminating it, but after the shock wore off, she came to the realization that this might be her only shot at motherhood. She had since grown excited about having a baby.

"Can I help it if my baby's father is an amazing lover?" Holly placed a hand over her belly.

"Speaking of which, have you told him the big news yet?" Camille eyed her sternly, strongly suspecting she hadn't. Holly, among other things, was a procrastinator.

Holly became suddenly absorbed in the display of baby photos stuck with colored pushpins to the bulletin board on the wall. "I will. I just haven't gotten around to it," she replied with an airy wave of her hand, as if they were talking about a friend of a friend, not the father of her child.

"And just when *do* you plan on telling him? When it's time for him to kick in for college tuition?"

"There's no rush. I still have five more months to go. Besides, he's not all that easy to get hold of."

"You could leave a message on his voicemail."

"I would, but apparently he switched carriers. I don't have his new cell number."

Camille just looked at her. "Why do I get the feeling you're just making excuses?"

Holly shrugged, unrepentant. "Wouldn't you, if you had to tell some guy you barely knew you were having his kid? I mean, what's the protocol here? You're the expert, you tell me."

"You're hopeless, you know that?" At the same time, Camille didn't doubt Holly's child would turn out fine despite what was sure to be an unorthodox upbringing. At least, he'd always know his mother's love. Would the same be true of her own children? She felt a pang at the thought.

"Maybe, but I always manage somehow," Holly replied, adding in a gentler voice, "It's *you* I'm worried about. You need to stop fretting about your pregnant sister and whether or not your husband's pissed at you, and start taking it easier. Because I am *not* having this baby without you. Is that understood?" She paused to dab again at her eyes, saying, "I don't want Dad to be the one holding my hand in the delivery room."

"Not much chance of that," Camille replied bitterly.

"Well, he would if I asked." Holly had always been more forgiving toward their dad. Maybe because she hadn't borne the brunt of his absenteeism. "Still . . . he'd probably pass out, and then where would I be?"

"Better off, no doubt."

"Come on, Cam. Cut him a break. I'm sure he felt horrible about it when you told him your news."

Camille said nothing.

Holly stared at her, head cocked to one side. "Oh, my God. He doesn't know, does he?"

Camille sighed. "No."

Holly stared at her with slack-jawed incredulity. "Let me get this straight: I get a load of crap for not telling Curtis about the baby, and you haven't told Dad your cancer is back. Don't you think that's a tad hypocritical?"

"It's not the same thing," Camille replied defensively. "You don't know how Curtis will react—he might be thrilled, for all you know—but Dad is Dad. He's totally predictable. Which is why there's no reason for him to know until it's absolutely necessary. What difference would it make?"

"For one thing, I'm sure he'd want to spend more time with you."

Camille snorted in derision. "Right. Like the one time he came to see me in the hospital and then spent the whole time talking about his golf game? No, thanks. I don't need that right now."

"What about what *he* needs?"

Camille shrugged. "He'll survive just fine without me. He's already demonstrated that."

"But . . . but you're his daughter!"

Camille's gaze drifted once more to the photos of new moms cradling their infants. Snapshots taken by the proud papas, no doubt. Where had her own father been when she and Holly had needed him most? She flashed back to the day she and her sister had been helping him clear out his apartment in preparation for the move to Fort Lauderdale, following his retirement ten years ago. They were emptying a cabinet in his study when they came across a leather-bound scrapbook, one they'd never seen before. They were excited at first, imagining it filled with mementos of their childhood—old report cards, diplomas, and certificates, the award Camille had gotten for the best English essay her senior year of high school. It wasn't until they opened it that the stark truth of their lives was revealed, in page after page of scorecards from their dad's golf games.

Yes, if nothing else, Larry Harte was predictable.

Dr. Farber, an otherwise competent-seeming middle-aged woman with graying hair in an untidy bun and eyeglasses slipping down her nose, swept into the examining room just then. After checking Holly's blood pressure and asking the routine questions, she pronounced her in good health and asked, smiling, "Now, are we ready for our first peek?" Holly nodded, wearing a goofy grin as Dr. Farber smeared goo over her belly in preparation for the ultrasound.

When the grainy image appeared on the screen, Holly, propped on her elbows to get a better look, observed, "It looks like the dancing peanut on the Planters jar."

"The most beautiful peanut I've ever seen," said Camille.

"It won't be dancing for a while yet," said Dr. Farber, "but so far everything looks good."

Good. Camille had almost forgotten what that was like.

Afterward, they went to a French café in Holly's neighborhood—near Prospect Park, in Brooklyn—for cappuccinos and croissants. Holly talked of her plans to turn her spare bedroom into a nursery and about her latest "score": a leather jacket worn onstage by Bruce Springsteen during his *Born to Run* tour. A cascade of bright chatter designed to keep at bay the topic neither of them wished to discuss. But there was no escaping it, Camille knew. When it was her turn, she said, "I've been thinking a lot about Mom lately."

Holly's smile drooped. "Yeah, I know. Me, too."

"Imagine what it must have been like for her at the end. Lying in bed day after day, knowing she'd never get well, then having to say good-bye to everyone she loved." Her throat tightened at the memory.

"I remember," Holly murmured, her eyes welling with tears. Tears that weren't just for their mother, Camille suspected. "Poor Mom."

"She never complained. Not once. She was always thinking of us, never herself. Remember that video she made?" They'd found it among their mother's things after she died, in an envelope marked *For my girls.* She'd filmed herself while she was still well enough to do so. In it, she told them how much she loved them and gave advice for when they were older. *Always send a thank-you note.*

Never spend more than you make. Don't be afraid to try new things. Kiss your children every single day. Take a trip to Africa. Camille had sobbed so hard the first viewing she could barely make out her mother's words. But in the years since, she had tried her best to live by those words. The only thing she hadn't done was take the trip to Africa, and now it looked as if she never would, any more than her mom had been able to realize that lifelong dream.

"She had on that ugly scarf I gave her for her birthday," Holly recalled.

"She loved that scarf." Camille could see it in her mind's eye, a pink-and-blue Gucci knockoff only a fifth grader would find beautiful, but her mom wore it every day after all her hair fell out.

"Yeah, I know. That was the problem." Holly gave a choked laugh.

They were both quiet for a minute. There was only the sound of the spoon clinking against the cup as Holly stirred another packet of sugar into her decaf cappuccino (she'd always had a sweet tooth, but now it was times two), and the ambient noises of the café in the background.

"Remember Louise?" Camille ventured at last.

Louise had been their dad's secretary when he was vice president of operations at Pan Am. Pretty in a fresh-faced, captain-of-the-girls'-soccer-team kind of way, she was from a small town in Kansas and had once told Camille that everyone back home thought her a "glamorous" big-city girl. "Actually, I live on Long Island," she said, "but it's all the same to them." Louise wasn't glamorous. She commuted to work by train. She shopped for clothes at Bolton's. And she was nice in the way that people from the Midwest were: She smiled even at people she didn't know, and when she told them "have a nice day," she truly meant it. Camille and Holly had always liked her in the distant way one likes one's father's secretary; she was part of his other life, his work life, which to them was as remote as the far-flung locales he traveled to on business trips. Then their mother got sick, and Louise became more of a fixture in their lives. On

Saturdays, she would take Camille and Holly to a movie or museum and chatter away as if nothing were wrong, as if their mom weren't lying in a hospital bed at home. That was when Camille began to hate Louise. She hated everything about her: her big teeth and blue eye shadow; the way she dotted her *i*'s with big round *o*'s like smiley faces; her annoying habit of folding her napkins neatly before tossing them in the trash; even her stupid banana-yellow Walkman. But mainly what she hated about Louise was the adoring way she looked at their dad.

Finally, she couldn't take it any longer. "I hate her!" she cried to her mom after Louise had taken her and Holly to the Children's Museum to look at antique dollhouses. Dollhouses, for God's sake! She was fourteen!

"Oh, sweetie." Mom sighed. She looked tiny and frail, her bald head wrapped in the scarf Holly had given her and her legs barely making a dent in the bedcovers: a stick figure in a child's drawing. "You mustn't hate her—she's trying her best. She really cares about you and Holly."

Camille shook her head. "No, she doesn't. She only cares about Dad."

"I remember when I first met your dad, how handsome he looked in his captain's uniform." Her mother's eyes glazed over. With the meds she was on, she had a habit of drifting off in the middle of a conversation or switching to another subject. Now, in her wan, hollow-eyed face, Camille caught a glimpse of the red-lipstick-wearing mom who used to dance in the living room in her bare feet to the tune of Sam Cooke's 'Twistin' the Night Away.' Oh, he was something. All us stews were mad for him."

"Mom. We were talking about Louise?" Camille prompted gently.

"Louise . . . yes." Her mother's eyes cleared in that moment, like fog shifting to reveal the contours of the surrounding landscape. "Well, of course she has a crush on him. How could she not?"

Ugh. It was a disgusting thought. Camille felt her stomach turn, imagining her dad and Louise doing what she herself had done with Tim Watkins, a boy in her ninth-grade class with whom she'd made out at Serena Hughes's Christmas party the year before. She had a feeling it wouldn't stop at Seven Minutes in Heaven for her dad. "You need to talk to Dad about it," she said primly as she lowered herself onto the bed. "You have to warn him. He probably thinks she's just being nice."

Her mother sighed again. "I've already spoken to Dad about it."

"You did? What did he say?"

"If it makes you feel better, he wasn't any happier about it than you were when I first suggested he ask Louise to get more . . . involved."

"You mean . . . you mean this was *your* idea?" Camille eyed her in confusion.

"Sweetie pie." Her mother shook her head sadly. "Trust me, it's for the best."

Camille, too shocked and upset to understand what her mother was trying to tell her, blurted "How can you say that? Can't you see she's trying to take your place?"

"I won't always be here," her mother said.

Hearing the sad resignation in her voice, Camille could no longer deny what she'd known for some time: Her mother was dying. The days of hospital stays were over; now there were just the nurses who worked in shifts and twice-a-week visits from the hospice lady. Camille felt faint with the knowledge.

"No one could ever take your place," she choked out.

Mom brought a hand as thin and light as an origami bird to Camille's cheek. "I'll always be your mom no matter what. But your dad will need someone to help look after you and your sister when I'm gone."

"We can look after ourselves," Camille declared staunchly.

Mom eyed her sorrowfully, maybe because she knew her

husband wasn't up to the task. Even with her doing all the work, he wasn't the most attentive of fathers.

Wrapped in that ridiculous scarf of Holly's, her head looked too big for her neck to support, as if it might snap with the weight were it not resting on the pillows at her back. Her eyes burned amid bruised-looking hollows. "I know you can, sweetie. But that doesn't mean you should have to." She closed her eyes, taking shallow breaths—even with the tube feeding oxygen into her lungs through her nose, it was often hard for her to breathe. "Louise is a good person, Cammie. All I ask is that you give her a chance. For my sake. Will you do that?"

Camille swallowed hard against the lump in her throat. "I . . . I'll try."

Her mother summoned a faint smile. "Good. Now come kiss me good night." She held out her stick-figure arms, and Camille carefully navigated her way around the plastic tubing to lay her head against her mom's bony chest. She smelled of the medicine bottles on the tray beside the bed, and her heart fluttered like a baby bird in its nest. She stroked Camille's hair, murmuring, "My big girl. I know I can always count on you." When Camille finally drew back, she saw that her mom's eyes had drifted shut. She got up and tiptoed out of the room. Then she went to her own room and lay down on the bed, where she cried herself to sleep.

All these years later, the tears surfaced once more at the memory. She'd never told Holly the story—her sister had been too young at the time—and as she related it to her now, Holly nodded in understanding.

"Yeah, it makes sense," she commented when Camille was done. "What I don't get is what Dad ever saw in Louise—she wasn't exactly his type." Though they both agreed he never would have cheated on their mother while she was alive—for all his faults, he'd been loyal to her—but it was understood that he and Louise had become lovers afterward. "I guess she was . . . convenient."

"I wonder what ever happened to her," Camille mused aloud.

"Who knows?" Holly shrugged and took a bite of her croissant. "Probably she went back to Kansas and married some nice dentist and had a passel of kids. I'm sure she's a grandmother by now."

"I wonder why she and Dad didn't get married."

"Probably because he didn't ask. Let's face it: He wasn't in love with her. Also, we were pretty mean to her. I think that might have had something to do with it."

"If I was I mean, it wasn't because I hated her. I just hated the fact that she wasn't Mom." Camille watched her sister take another bite of her croissant, scattering crumbs over the tabletop, before adding thoughtfully, "Actually, we'd have been better off if he had married Louise."

Holly paused in mid-chew, staring at Camille in disbelief. "You've got to be kidding."

"She wasn't a bad person," Camille went on. "And Mom was right about one thing: We needed someone to look out for us, with Dad gone all the time."

Holly dropped what was left of her croissant onto her plate and wiped her buttery fingers on her napkin. "Why do I get the feeling this isn't just about Louise?" She spoke slowly, her gaze remaining fixed on Camille.

"It's not," Camille replied, sighing. "I was thinking about my own children. I worry about what it'll be like for them after—" She broke off at the pained look her sister wore. "You know how Edward is. He adores them, but . . ." She gave a helpless shrug. After her extended hospital stay the previous year, she had returned home to find the refrigerator bare except for take-out cartons and the children out of sorts from having stayed up past their bedtimes. Not only that, Edward had been late several times picking up Zach from soccer practice and had neglected to sign the permission slip required for a field trip Kyra's class had gone on, leaving their daughter in tears when the bus was ready to leave and he couldn't be reached. Though the worst was when Ellie Keenan, the mother of Kyra's best friend, Alexia, offered to have Kyra stay with them until Camille was "back on her feet." Camille learned later that it had been at Kyra's request.

"He'll get it together." Holly defended her brother-in-law. "He's just used to having you do everything."

"Kids can't be put on hold," Camille reminded her. "It'd be better for everyone if he didn't have to go it alone."

"What, exactly, did you have in mind?" Holly asked warily.

"Maybe Mom had the right idea." *Even if she picked the wrong person.*

"Oh, my God." Holly's blue eyes widened. "Please tell me you're not thinking what I think you're thinking."

Camille nodded slowly, taking a deep breath before going on. "I want to be the one to find him his next wife." The idea had gradually taken shape in her mind over this past week, and like the cancer eating away at her insides it was inescapable—she couldn't dismiss it.

Holly's eyes widened and her mouth fell open. With crumbs of croissant stuck to her lips, she looked childlike in that moment. Then she whispered furiously, "Christ Almighty. Have you lost your fucking mind?"

Camille didn't back down. "Is it so terrible to want to make sure my family will be okay after I'm gone?"

Holly shook her head, still gaping at her in disbelief. "No, but this is going too far."

"Is it? Holly, it's what I *do*. What I'm good at. How can I just leave it up to the whims of fate? You know how clueless Edward is. If he ever gets around to it, he'll marry whoever's the most persistent." Half the female personnel in his department at New York–Presbyterian had crushes on him—anyone with eyes in their head could see that—but he always gave her a blank look whenever she teased him about it. And it wasn't just that he was clueless; he'd be drowning in grief after she was gone. Any woman who managed to snag his attention would have to be a pit bull. *Is that what I want for my family?*

Holly went on shaking her head. "I can't believe you'd even consider such a thing."

Camille's mouth twisted in a smile that held no humor. "That's the funny thing about dying: You find yourself considering all sorts of things you couldn't have imagined before."

Her sister's expression softened. "And what does Edward have to say about all this?"

"He doesn't know. I haven't gotten that far yet." She was waiting for the right moment to broach it with him. Though she had a feeling there would never be a right moment. Her resolve wavered momentarily as she recalled the stricken look on his face when she'd told him she was dying. Her voice cracked. "It's just . . . oh, God, Holly, I'm so scared. I don't know what else to do."

Holly reached for her hand, blinking against the tears that welled in her own eyes. "I know you're scared . . . you have every right to be. I also know what a control freak you are." She managed a wobbly smile. "But, Cam, there are some things even *you* can't control. First off, Edward would never go for it. I've never seen a man so devoted to his wife."

"I know." Camille felt as if an invisible band were tightening around her chest. "That's what makes it so hard." The selfish part of her wanted her husband to mourn forever after she was gone. She pictured him in his bereavement, a lonely figure in black wandering the windswept moors like Heathcliff in *Wuthering Heights.* But this was real life. And real life was messy, full of pieces needing to be picked up. "But we're not talking about romance. It would be strictly platonic."

"Like a stock with growth potential?" Holly supplied, her tone grim.

"Something like that." Camille looked down at her hands.

"What if," Holly ventured cautiously, "this hypothetical woman, assuming she *is* hypothetical—" She shot Camille a sharp look.

"—should develop feelings for him. You can't always predict how someone will react."

The band around Camille's chest tightened further. "I guess that's the chance I'll have to take. But whomever I ended up choosing, she wouldn't be the type to act on those feelings. Give me some credit."

"It's not you I'm worried about," Holly said darkly, but at the look Camille gave her, she immediately backed off. "Okay, let say it *is* strictly platonic. In that case, why bother? Isn't that what friends are for?"

"Yes, and he has friends, but not someone he could call at two in the morning if he needed to talk. Or who'd drop everything, without being asked, to help out in a pinch," Camille pointed out. Even Hugh, kind and caring though he was, couldn't be expected to fill in all the gaps. "He needs someone who'll be there for him and the kids like another parent would."

"What am I, chopped liver?" Holly replied indignantly.

"No, of course not. But you'll have your hands full."

"I'm having a baby, not dropping off the planet."

"I know. And believe me, I'm counting on you to be there. And to spoil my kids rotten."

Holly gave a tremulous laugh and reached for a napkin, using it to dab at her eyes. "You mean you won't roll over in your grave if I let them eat Froot Loops and watch R-rated movies?"

"I might. But don't let that stop you."

Holly blew her nose into the napkin. "While we're on the subject, I have a confession of my own: I'm with Edward—I think you're jumping the gun. There's still a chance you can beat this."

Camille shook her head mournfully. "You can afford to believe in divine intervention, but I have to be realistic." There was more she could have said—about how much this was hurting her and how the last thing she wanted was to drive a wedge between her and her husband by introducing another woman into the mix—but she held her tongue. There were no words to express how she was feeling, or to convince Holly. All she knew was she couldn't allow her family to fall apart when she had the means to spare them at her fingertips, no further away than her client list. They spoke no more on the subject. They finished their croissants—Holly polishing off hers as well as Camille's—and Camille paid the bill. She glanced at her watch as they were leaving, surprised to see it was nearly lunchtime. As they walked to the subway station, Camille told her sister about the Texas oil magnate, newly divorced, who'd flown in from Houston to discuss the possibility of her finding his next wife for him. She was on her way to meet him now; he was taking her to lunch at Jean Georges. "If you're interested, he's filthy rich." She hadn't yet given up on Holly, who so far had resisted all her matchmaking efforts.

"No, thanks. I don't do filthy rich, just filthy," Holly said, grinning as she placed a hand on her belly. "Speaking of which, you, um, wouldn't happen to know what time it is in London?"

THEIR FIRST ANNIVERSARY, Edward had taken her to dinner at the Four Seasons. Camille would long remember that night. How handsome he looked in his best suit and tie, and how elegant she felt in the new dress he'd insisted she buy for herself. She'd questioned the wisdom of splurging on such a pricey meal—at the time, they were subsisting on student loans and the meager salary from her part-time job as a research assistant—but he'd assured her they could afford it. He didn't bat an eye at the menu prices, nor did he select the least expensive bottle on the wine list. After they'd eaten, he whisked her off to Central Park, where they'd gone for a carriage ride—the final treat of the evening. Only then did he confess he'd sold his collection of jazz CDs to finance the occasion. Camille, deeply moved by the knowledge that he would make such a sacrifice for her, could have wept. She had never loved her husband more than she did that night.

This week, they would celebrate their twentieth anniversary. Edward had warned her ahead of time not to make any plans, saying with a wink he wanted to surprise her. Camille could only hope it wouldn't involve her getting on a plane. There had been a time she'd have loved nothing more than to be spirited off to Paris or Rome for a romantic weekend, but these days she simply wasn't up for it. The course of chemo she was on was mild, aimed only at slowing the progression of her disease, but she was feeling the effects. Her appetite was off, and she tired easily.

Camille was relieved, the evening of their anniversary, when their hired car made the turn onto Fifty-Second Street instead heading for the airport. Minutes later, they were pulling up in front of the Four Seasons restaurant. "You remembered," she said, leaning in to kiss Edward on the lips.

He smiled, looking pleased with himself. "I even booked us the same table."

"By the pool? What, did you pull the sympathy card?"

His smile faded, and he shot her a reproachful look.

It set the tone for the evening. Conversation was strained after that. Camille could only pick at her food, and even the bottle of champagne they sipped throughout the meal did nothing to lift the leaden mood. She knew she was lucky to have a husband who was sentimental enough to want to recapture the happiness they'd known as newlyweds, but it only served to remind her of what she'd lost . . . and what she stood to lose still. Even if they could somehow turn the clock back, time was running out. And there was nothing either of them could do about that.

Her mood improved a bit when they went for the commemorative carriage ride in Central Park afterward. Snuggled next to her husband under the lap robe provided by the driver, she allowed her mind to drift. It was early spring, and blossoms fluttered down around them like pink snowflakes, from the cherry trees lining the roadway down which they rattled. A full moon could be glimpsed through the treetops, floating like a ghostly galleon above the tall buildings along Central Park West. The only sounds were the *clip-clop* of hooves and distant blare of traffic.

"A perfect end to the perfect evening." She sighed contentedly.

"Better yet, I still have my CD collection," he replied with a chuckle. *And you.* The unspoken words hovered in the air.

"I still find it hard to believe you let a woman come between you and Charlie Parker," she teased.

"Not just any woman." He gazed at her tenderly, shadows from the street lamps that illuminated the roadway flickering over his face. "Which reminds me, I have something for you." He withdrew a jeweler's box from his coat pocket and handed it to her. "Happy anniversary, darling."

Inside the box was a diamond teardrop pendant on a delicate gold chain. Beautiful but also a bittersweet reminder. The band around her chest squeezed tighter until she could scarcely breathe. As Edward fastened the chain around her neck, she envisioned him doing the same for their daughter someday. Kyra getting ready for her first prom or her wedding, wearing this same necklace.

"It's lovely," she said in a small, cracked voice.

"Sorry my fingers are so cold," he apologized when she began to shiver. "Perfect," he pronounced when she turned around so he could see how the necklace looked on her. "I just wish I'd been able to afford something this nice our first anniversary." Back then, his gift to her had been a silver bracelet purchased from a sidewalk vendor, which she secretly treasured more than all the expensive jewelry he'd given her since. "But then I would have had to sell one my kidneys."

She laughed. "Only a hopeless romantic would go to such extremes."

"Are you saying I'm not romantic?"

"No, just that you're not hopeless."

They lapsed into companionable silence, each wrapped in his and her own memories. "I'm glad we could do this one last time," she murmured as they were heading back the way they'd come.

Her husband remained silent, but now it was a brooding silence. She felt the coiled tension in his muscles as he sat beside her, gazing into the darkness. When he finally spoke, his voice was low and tight. "It doesn't have to be the last time. We could have years more."

"Oh, Edward." She exhaled deeply, and it seemed all the air she'd ever breathed went out of her lungs. "I'm not doing this to hurt you. I'm simply choosing not to live in a dream world."

"You think I don't know what you're up against? Why do you think I went to all this trouble? I wanted tonight to be special, because I didn't know if—" He broke off with a choked sound.

She fingered the necklace, feeling her own throat tighten. "I didn't get you anything. I'm sorry."

In a sudden movement that startled her, he seized hold of her and crushed her to him, whispering hoarsely in her ear, "*You're* all I want. Don't you see? Without you, nothing else matters."

She clung to him, fighting back tears, before reluctantly drawing back. "I love you, Edward. More than you'll ever know. But the fact remains I have stage-four cancer. You know what that means. You know that whatever I do or don't do, the chances of survival are next to nil." She paused, looking him in the eye. "So I have one more favor to ask of you, my darling. And it's a big one."

He regarded her warily. *Probably he thinks I'm going to ask him to put me out of my misery when the time comes.* But what she'd be asking of him was much more: to imagine a life without her. Nonetheless, his voice was gentle as he replied, "You know I'd do anything for you."

She felt a stab of guilt nonetheless. She was doing this for his own good, but he wouldn't see it that way. "Remember what we talked about before?" she ventured.

He nodded his head, his expression growing warier. He attempted to make light of it, though. "Sorry to disappoint you, but I don't have any candidates lined up yet to be the next Mrs. Constantin."

She took his hand in hers, lacing her fingers through his and squeezing tightly. Oh, God. This was so hard. "That's what I wanted to talk to you about. I don't want you to be alone when the time comes."

"I told you I'd keep an open mind. What more do you want?" he replied testily.

"I want to be the one to find her for you."

He stared at her, wearing the same look of horrified disbelief Holly had worn when Camille had shared the idea with her, only with an overlay of anger. Finally, he exploded, "What is this, some kind of joke?"

Camille pressed on, "Please, just hear me out. I know how it sounds, but it's not what you think. I'm not suggesting you . . . you take a lover. Nothing like that. I'm talking about someone who'd be a friend to you. Someone who'd help with the children. I don't expect you to fall in love again right away. If at all," she hastened to add at his thunderous expression. "It's just . . . if you do end up marrying again, I want her to be special. As special as you deserve."

"So I'm not to be trusted to make my own decisions, is that it?"

"I didn't say that. It's just . . ." Her voice trailed off.

"This is what comes of being married to a matchmaker, I guess," he muttered angrily. "No one's safe from your meddling."

"If the situation were reversed and I came to you for some life-saving operation, wouldn't you do everything in your power to save me?" she reasoned.

"I don't see how you can compare the two." She heard the throttled fury in his voice. "You're talking about *playing* with lives, not saving one. And who the hell appointed you God all of a sudden?"

"Would it hurt just to meet with her?"

"*Her?* You mean you have someone lined up already?"

"No, of course not. I'd never do that without your permission."

"Well, when you put it that way, how can I refuse?" he replied sarcastically.

"Is it any crazier than us getting married when we didn't have two nickels to rub together?" she persisted. "Everyone said we were too young, that we should wait until we were both out of school. But we didn't listen. We were determined, even if it meant living in a fifth-floor walkup with cockroaches coming out of the woodwork and a toilet that didn't flush properly."

"Stop."

"My point is—"

"Just . . . stop." His eyes flashed. "I wanted tonight to be about *us.*" He looked down at the jeweler's box caught in a fold of the lap robe, then he picked it up and with a violent jerk his arm sent it sailing into the shrubbery alongside the path. When he brought his gaze back to her, she saw the hurt on his face. "Why are you so eager to palm me off? Should I be worried about that, too?"

Mournfully, Camille shook her head as she regarded her husband of twenty years. "I love you with all my heart," she told him. "But it doesn't change the fact that I'm going to die."

He was silent for so long she didn't think he would respond. At last, he gave a deep sigh and said in a hollow voice that seemed to rise from the depths of a well, "I know. I know."

CHAPTER FIVE

"How are you feeling today, Mr. Szegedy?" Edward inquired.
His elderly patient looked like Yoda from *Star Wars* sitting
scrunched in his chair, his head, covered in spun-white hair so
sparse it hovered like a fine mist over his freckled skull, seemingly
too big for his shrunken body. The old man answered in a barely
audible rasp, "Not so good."

"How long has it been since your surgery?" Mr. Szegedy, his
hand trembling, held up two fingers. "Two weeks?" A slow nod in
response. "And do you remember how long were you on ventila-
tion?"

The old man shrugged. His wife answered for him, "A few hours
maybe? He doesn't remember so good. You've had a rough time of
it, haven't you, Georgie?" she said in a louder voice to her husband,
who in addition to having difficulty with his speech was also hard
of hearing. The old woman reminded Edward of his grandmother,
with her ruddy complexion and high cheekbones, her old-country
articulation. There was something beautiful, too, in the way her
movements blended seamlessly with those of her husband—the pas
de deux of a couple who's lived together so long they've lost track of
where one leaves off and the other begins.

He tried to imagine Camille at that age, with silver hair and
wrinkles, but he couldn't quite picture it. A familiar heaviness
descended on him. "When did you lose your voice, Mr. Szegedy?"

Again, it was the wife who answered. "Right after the surgery. Before that, he could talk just fine. You couldn't shut him up! Isn't that right, Georgie?" She gave her husband's shoulder an affectionate pat. Edward could see the lines of worry on her face, and he smiled to put her at ease.

"Loss of speech isn't uncommon after an aortic valve replacement," he explained. "During the operation, the vocal cord is displaced, which can cause it to become temporarily paralyzed. I can't say how long it'll take, but it usually corrects itself with time. Let me have a look. . ." He nodded to Dev Patel, the male intern who was currently acting as his assistant. Dev administered a topical anesthetic before carefully threading a thin plastic tube through the patient's nasal cavity. A minute later, they were looking at a live camera feed of the vocal cords on the computer screen connected to the rhino-laryngeal stroboscope, which confirmed the diagnosis.

Soon Mr. and Mrs. Szegedy were on their way out the door of his office, the old lady clutching a slip of paper with the name and number of a speech therapist written on it. Edward handed the chart to his assistant, asking if Mr. Szegedy had been the last of his morning's patients.

Dev nodded in response without having to consult the Palm Pilot that Edward jokingly referred to as Dev's third hand. A slightly built young Pakistani with an infectious smile, Dev was known for his efficiency. "Your two o'clock called to cancel, and your next one's not until two-forty," Dev informed him, breaking into a grin. "You're free for a whole two hours. Lucky you."

Lucky? Edward couldn't recall when he'd last felt lucky. But he kept his tone light as he replied, "If my luck holds, maybe I can get the old man to pledge some of his millions." He was having lunch today, at the Knickerbocker Club, with Liam McPhail, a former patient and potential donor for the West Harlem Clinic where Edward donated his services two afternoons a week.

"That might be pushing it. I hear he's a real tightwad."

"In that case, maybe I should send you as my emissary," Edward joked. Dev was also known for his charm.

"No, thanks. He'd eat me for lunch."

"Speaking of which, no more skipping lunch—doctor's orders. Can't have people start thinking you have a slave driver for a boss." Dev reminded Edward of himself when he was that age: ambitious to a fault. Not much had changed in the intervening years. He wasn't as ambitious—his only goal these days was to help other people, though the irony didn't escape him that it was often at his family's expense—but he was just as absorbed in his work. It wasn't unusual for Edward to look up from his desk and see that it had grown dark outside and realize he hadn't eaten a thing all day.

Dev just laughed. "They already think that."

Minutes later, Edward was striding out the entrance of the Harkness Pavilion on his way to the building that housed the Neuro-Psych Center. He had half-an-hour to kill before lunch and was overdue for a visit with his old friend and mentor, Hugh Lieberman. He hadn't told Hugh the bad news about Camille yet; he'd wanted to get a grip on his emotions first, which so far hadn't happened. He couldn't get past his anger and frustration. As a doctor, he understood Camille's decision not to seek further treatment, but as her husband, it was unfathomable. Yes, the odds were slim. But how could she not want to fight to stay alive? She had once before. Why not now?

As if that weren't bad enough, she was talking about lining up his next wife. It was as if she'd become a stranger to him overnight. The Camille he knew and loved would never have asked this of him. Not that he doubted her motives: She believed it to be in his and their children's best interests. But what did that say about their marriage? Why wouldn't she want to make the most of the time they had left together instead? He understood her fears regarding the children—she'd lost her own mom when she was fourteen, and her dad had pretty much dropped the ball when it came to caring for his kids—but that, too, had left a bitter taste in his mouth. Did she honestly think he was like her dad, that he'd neglect his kids the way Larry had? Jesus. At the same time, Edward felt a niggling disquiet knowing he wasn't entirely above reproach in that regard. A memory surfaced, one that seemed to sum up his inadequacies: Camille in the hospital and the kids hungry for supper while he, Edward, stood in the kitchen dolefully contemplating a block of frozen hamburger. He'd meant to take it out to thaw before leaving for work that day. Just as he'd meant to buy groceries on his way home and pick up the dry cleaning and write a check for his daughter's glee club fund-raiser. None of which had gotten done. As a result, there was only the food that Camille, sick as she was, had stockpiled in the freezer. He wouldn't soon forget the resigned look on his then thirteen-year-old daughter's face when she'd wandered in at that moment, as if she'd expected nothing more from him but loved him anyway. She didn't comment; she just reached for the stack of takeout menus by the phone, asking, "Pizza or Chinese?"

Edward liked to think he would do a better job of raising his kids on his own, if it came to that, than Larry had with Camille and Holly. But was he only deluding himself? The thought made him pull up his coat collar as he hurried along the sidewalk, as if to ward off a sudden blast of chill air.

THE HARKNESS PAVILION was part of a loose sprawl of buildings over several city blocks that comprised the vast medical complex of New York–Presbyterian. Edward was winded by the time he reached the Neuro-Psych Center, where he rode the elevator to the fifth floor. Hugh was on the phone when he walked in.

A massive bear of a man seated at an even more massive desk with a view of the East River, Hugh broke into a grin as he hung up the phone. Edward had been assigned to Dr. Hugh Lieberman as an intern, during his psych rotation, and had formed a lasting bond with the older man. Hugh was the wisest person Edward knew, which was underscored by the fact that he looked like a shrink from Central Casting, with his squirrely Einstein hair and sharp blue eyes caught in nets of wrinkles. "So, my friend, what gives?" he said. "I don't see you for weeks, and now here you are looking like something the cat dragged in. Whatever's eating you, it's got teeth."

Edward shrugged, attempting to make light of it. "What is it with you guys? Does everyone who walks in your door have to have a problem?"

Hugh eyed him closely, as if he suspected there was indeed a problem in Edward's case, a big one, but he refrained from any further comment. He heaved himself out of his chair and shambled around to clear the chair opposite his desk of its pile of books and files. "Sit down, sit down." It was only midday, but already his tie sported a stain and the lapels of his corduroy blazer were dusted with what was either dandruff flakes or powdered sugar from the doughnuts he consumed by the dozen. "How have you been? How's Camille?" he asked as he stood leaning against his desk, looking like another of its untidy stacks. Hugh's organizational system was one of controlled chaos, but he could pluck any given item from the jumble at a moment's notice. "Ruth was saying the other day we're way overdue to have you two over for supper."

"Love to. But can we take a rain check? Some . . . stuff has come up." Edward was purposely vague, but when the older man just stood there, shaggy eyebrows raised, waiting for him to continue, Edward knew it was no use. He gave a sigh. "It's Camille. Her cancer's back."

He saw dismay register on the older man's face. "I see." Hugh pushed a hand through his squirrely gray hair. "And this is why you've been avoiding me?" Every Wednesday, they had a standing date to play racquetball at Hugh's athletic club, but Edward had made excuses the past few weeks.

"It's not just you. I haven't told anyone."

"How bad is it?"

"Bad."

"*Gottenyu,*" Hugh muttered to himself, shaking his head. As a psychiatrist he was trained not to show emotion, but now there was no hiding how he felt. He was fond of Camille and like an uncle to Kyra and Zach. During Camille's last bout with cancer, Hugh and his wife, Ruth, had been a godsend, delivering home-cooked meals and taking the children with them to their country house in Rhinebeck on weekends. "What course of treatment does her doctor recommend?"

"Dr. Hawkins says another stem cell transplant is really the only option, and my friend Mitch at Sloan-Kettering concurs, but it's a moot point, I'm afraid." Frustration welled in him as he explained that Camille had opted not to seek further treatment, even though it was her only hope.

Hugh nodded thoughtfully but gave no indication of whether he approved or disapproved. He only commented, "I'm sure it wasn't an easy decision."

"Yeah, well, I sure as hell didn't get a say in it." Edward recalled how powerless he'd felt watching his grandmother slowly wither away and die. He'd vowed to never again let that happen to a loved one. And here he was, all these years later, once more with his hands tied behind his back.

"I know this isn't easy for you, either," Hugh said gently. "If there's anything I can do . . ."

"Say a prayer. That's about all there is left."

"Never underestimate the power of prayer, my friend." Hugh was an observant Jew, with a mezuzah on the door frame at the entrance to his office to show for it. But he was also a man of medicine, evidenced when he asked, "What about a clinical trial? Is that something worth exploring?"

"Sure," Edward replied dully. "But there's nothing right now." The past few weeks, he'd spent every free moment making phone calls and scouring the Internet, to no avail. "I haven't given up, but if something does turn up, it'd have to be soon." He didn't need to say it: Time was running out.

"I know some people. I can ask around," Hugh offered. "In the meantime, if you ever need to talk, you know where to find me."

"What's the use of talking about it? Her mind is made up." Edward looked down and saw his hands were balled into fists. He flexed his fingers, but they felt stiff, as if they'd been in that position for a while. He shook his head, saying bitterly, "She won't listen to reason. It's like she *wants* to die. She even has my next wife all picked out." The last part was stretching the truth a bit. Camille hadn't acted on her suggestion. He didn't think she would go that far, not without his go-ahead, but then, what the hell did he know? He didn't know his own wife anymore.

Even Hugh, who'd no doubt heard it all as a psychiatrist, couldn't imagine a scenario as bizarre as the one Camille had sketched out—he must have interpreted it as an overstatement brought on by extreme frustration—because he only said, "It's not unusual for people who are terminally ill to find comfort in knowing their spouse will find happiness again after they're gone."

"It's more than that with her. Don't forget, she does this for a living."

"I see," Hugh said, frowning. "And does she intend for you to—"

"No. God, no." Edward was quick to disabuse him of *that* notion. "It'd be strictly platonic. Think of it as a lease with an option to buy," he said bitterly. "The way Camille sees it, unless I have someone waiting in the wings, I'll either die of grief or turn into a crusty old widower."

Hugh scratched his head, wearing a troubled look as he considered this. But like always, he quickly rose to the occasion. "There's no one-size-fits-all in dealing with terminal illness," he said, speaking in measured tones. "I've had patients refuse to accept the inevitable; they cling to the hope that a cure is imminent. Others accept that they're going to die but feel the need to control every aspect."

Camille was like that, Edward thought. When she'd gone back to work after the births of their children, she'd compiled a list of instructions for the nanny so detailed it could have served as a child-rearing manual. Before every business trip or hospital stay, she'd stocked up on enough food to feed a family of ten. And already she'd assembled an entire layette for Holly's baby.

"Camille wouldn't stop at that," he said. "She'll be orchestrating everything from the grave."

Hugh gave a knowing smile. Some years ago, he'd approached her about a nephew of his who, at age forty, showed no sign of wanting to settle down, to the despair of Hugh's sister. Camille had swung into action, and six months later, the once confirmed bachelor was walking down the aisle. "It might help if she had something to distract her," he said after giving it some thought.

"What do you suggest?"

"When was the last time you went on vacation, just the two of you?"

Edward thought of the glossy brochures from the travel agency, which he'd ended up discarding. If he had briefly considered the tantalizing possibility they offered, he now saw it merely as wishful thinking. Besides, a "romantic" getaway would only underscore the fact that the spark had gone out of their marriage. He and his wife hadn't had sex in so long, he couldn't remember the last time they did. Camille was usually too tired, and in all fairness, he hadn't actively pursued it. Only in the shower did he allow his fantasies to run wild. He'd close his eyes as he was soaping himself down and picture himself making slow, sweet love to his wife. Back when they were first married, they couldn't get enough of each other—all it would take was a brush of fingertips or meaningful look to send them ducking out of a theater in the middle of a movie or slipping away early from a party—and now he was reduced to masturbating in the shower. It wasn't that he didn't still find his wife desirable. But mostly what he felt was the desire to protect.

"I don't think a second honeymoon is the answer," he said wearily.

"It doesn't have to be a getaway," Hugh said. "The important thing is for the two of you to find something mutually fulfilling that will make both of you feel her final days were well spent."

"Such as?"

"That's for you to decide, not me. But if you want my advice, I suggest that you listen to what she has to say," Hugh counseled. "Even if it makes no sense. Even it seems downright crazy. There's power in that, my friend. You and your wife may even find something you can agree on."

"You mean like my going along with this crazy scheme of hers?" Edward replied sarcastically.

"If nothing else, you'd be in it together," Hugh said.

EVERY SUNDAY, WITHOUT FAIL, Edward phoned his parents in Milwaukee. He always timed his calls so as to catch them when they were likely to be home from mass, but on this particular Sunday, the third in his season in hell, he found himself hoping he'd get the answering machine instead.

No such luck. His father picked up after two rings. "Heya, kid. What's cooking?"

"Not much," Edward lied. "How've you been, Pop?"

"Not bad, not bad. Back's been acting up, but other than that I got no complaints."

As with many retired brewery employees, Vasile Constantin was suffering the effects of having hoisted heavy barrels for decades in the era before forklifts. "What does the doctor say?" Edward asked.

"He wants me to have an operation. Like I can afford to be laid up for six months," he scoffed. These days, Vasile worked part-time as a security guard to make ends meet. He was too proud to accept his son's offer of assistance, other than the airline tickets Edward sent so his parents could come visit once a year. "Hell with it," he threw in for good measure. *Like mother, like son.* Edward thought once more of Nana Clara. Normally he'd have injected one of his speeches about the importance of listening to one's physician, but right now he didn't have the heart to get into it with his dad. He had bigger problems.

"How's Mom? She taking her medication?" he asked.

"Sure, sure. Doc says it ain't serious, though. You know, just old age."

"Is she resting like he told her to?"

"You know your mom; only time you can get her to sit still is in church." Vasile gave a throaty chuckle. He'd been a two-pack-a-day man for years, until he finally quit smoking at his wife's insistence, but he still sounded like Edward G. Robinson with a bad cold.

"How're the kids? How's Camille?"

"Everyone's fine." Edward squeezed his eyes shut, massaging his forehead with his thumb and forefinger where a headache was setting in above his right eyebrow. They chatted for several minutes more, about the weather in Milwaukee and which of the relatives were ailing or had another grandchild on the way, and why next season was sure to be a winning one for the Brewers.

When Edward finally asked to speak with his mom, Vasile informed him, "She's at Mrs. Dubieski's. She stopped in to check up on her on the way home from mass." He recalled that his parents' elderly neighbor had recently suffered a fall that left her with a broken hip. "I'll have her call you when she gets back."

"No, don't. I'll try her later," Edward said, with a glance at the open door to his and Camille's bedroom across the hall. "Camille's still asleep. I don't want the phone to wake her."

"She not sick, is she?"

A lifetime of getting up to go to work each morning before dawn had made an early riser of Vasile even in semi-retirement, so he assumed anyone who slept in past nine was either sick or lazy, and since Camille was the opposite of lazy, it could only be the former. Edward felt his incipient headache take root like some noxious weed. But he kept his tone even. "It's Sunday, Pop. People sleep in on Sundays."

"Other people, not your old man. The day I'm not up with the sun is the day they carry me outta here in a box."

His dad chuckled, and Edward winced. "Don't talk that way, Pop."

"What? We all gotta go sometime."

Edward was quick to change the subject. "Listen, Pop, I don't know that we'll be able to have you and mom out for a visit this year. There's a lot going on." An understatement. "We'll see how it goes."

Normally, his parents came for a week every summer, and they all went to their beach house, in Southampton.

Thinking of the beach house reminded him of happier days: splashing in the surf with his kids when they were little; he and Camille, each with a child on their lap, sitting around a campfire at night roasting wienies; the four of them strolling along the tide line, Kyra and Zach squealing with delight as they stomped on the tangled strands of kelp to make them pop. Soundlessly, he drew in a breath and eased it out of his lungs.

"Sure, I understand. You'll let us know, okay?" His dad was nothing if not easygoing.

"You bet. Listen, Pop, I've got to go. I'd put the kids on but they're eating breakfast." In actual fact, Kyra and Zach had already eaten and at the moment were battling it out, playing a heated game of Nintendo "NASCAR Unleashed," but right now, he'd have sawed off his own leg to escape. His head was throbbing, and his gut burned from the two cups of coffee he'd drunk on an empty stomach.

"Okay, sure. Give 'em a kiss from Pop-Pop. And tell the little slugger, next time he visits he'll be rootin' for the Brewers whether he likes it or not." His dad gave another throaty chuckle.

Edward hung up feeling more depressed than ever. Why hadn't

he told his father the truth? He would have to eventually. *Because you're still holding out for a miracle,* answered a voice in his head. Also, because his devoutly Catholic parents, who placed more stock in religion than in medicine, might support Camille in her decision. He didn't need to give her ammunition.

He could see Camille stirring in her sleep in their bedroom across the hall. Fearful of disturbing her, he got up and went to close the door to the study. But his hand lingered on the doorknob, and some impulse made him step into the hallway instead. He crossed over into the bedroom, his footfalls muffled by the carpet. Moments later, as he stood gazing at his slumbering wife, her brow creased even in sleep, the past and present collided and he was caught in the crush.

EDWARD HAD BEEN thirteen when Nana Clara fell ill. She refused to see a doctor, and when she finally went, it was only to confirm her deeply held belief that the medical profession was of little use outside stitching cuts and setting broken limbs. *What do I need with doctors?* she'd say. All they ever did was poke and prod, then charge a fortune for it. She relied on folk medicine, and had gained somewhat of a reputation in their community, as had her mother before her in their village in Romania, as a healer.

"This will make the swelling go down," she informed Edward when he was nine, after a cut on his arm had become infected and she applied a poultice of finely shredded cabbage to the inflamed area. Another time, after a neighbor had suffered a heart attack, she brought him a jar of dried, ground hot peppers and instructed him to put a pinch on his tongue if he should have any more chest pains. (Mr. Janovich later reported that it had worked like a charm.)

Edward could see Nana Clara clearly in his mind's eye: a leathery strip of a woman with hair like spun glass and dark eyes in a round face quilted with lines. If she was missing a few teeth, her smile was no less quick because of it, and if her step had slowed with age, it never wavered in coming to the aid of anyone who was in need. When she wasn't brewing some potion that stank up the house, she was filling it with delicious smells, that of *caltaboşi* or the garlicky *stufat de miel,* or the mouthwatering stew *tochitură moldovenească* from her native Moldavia.

He recalled sitting on her lap as a very young child while she sang to him—Romanian lullabies and the few pop tunes she knew, for which she always garbled the lyrics. She smelled of starch from the laundry she took in and more strongly of the unfiltered cigarettes she smoked. When she was a young girl growing up in Romania, the films shown at the village cinema, starring the likes of Mae West and James Cagney, were all she'd known of American culture before she came to this country, and as a result, her English was peppered with slang from that era. "Hiya, doll," she would greet the neighbor ladies who brought her their laundry. And to Mr. Sokolowski, the owner of the Polish grocery on the corner where she did her marketing, she'd carp, when returning some perishable item she'd deemed inedible, "Mister, I got a beef with you."

One time, Mr. Sokolowski saw her coming and ducked into the storeroom in back. He learned the hard way there was no avoiding the force of nature known as Nana Clara. When he poked his head out a short while later, it was only to find her instructing a gaggle of female customers in the proper way to select produce by demonstrating the flaws in his. "See that? All wax, no taste," she sniffed, holding up a shiny red apple. "You want wax, you come eat off my kitchen floor. You want fruit, go to Mr. Santangelo down the street." To suggest patronizing an Italian's place of business over a fellow Eastern European's was tantamount to heresy, but to her, fair was fair.

Nana Clara, all four feet and eleven inches of her, took nothing lying down. But even she was powerless against the kidney disease that ultimately claimed her life. Neither her potions nor the pills the doctor had prescribed did any good. She grew weaker by the day while Edward watched with growing despair.

His parents were of little help. Vasile had been informed his mother wasn't eligible for benefits under his company's insurance plan and instead of contesting it, he'd accepted it, as he did all edicts from his superiors, with shoulders bowed. When Edward urged him to appeal to his boss, Vasile only shook his head while Edward's mother, Anca, wept and wrung her hands, saying, "Your father could lose his job. These are important people. What are we to them?"

Meanwhile, Nana Clara grew ever more frail. Then one morning, when he was getting up to go to school, Edward found her passed out on the bathroom floor. He shouted for his mother—his father had already left for work—and when she came running, he cried, "We have to get her to the hospital!"

"No! Look, she's coming around." His grandmother had begun to stir by then. He knew what his mother was thinking: Hospitals were for rich people, people with insurance, not the likes of them. It wasn't that she didn't care about Nana Clara, but her fear that they would be ruined financially by an extended hospital stay eclipsed all else in the moment. "I'll send for Dr. Costa. He'll know what to do."

Edward knew with a sinking heart there would be no relying on his parents. After his mother had dashed off to phone the doctor, he did what any normal thirteen-year-old would do, in his view. He donned his sturdiest pair of shoes and then picked his grandmother up in his arms, carrying her downstairs, where he paused only long enough to bundle her in a blanket and throw a coat over himself before stepping out the door into the frozen grip of winter in Milwaukee. He was tall and strong for his age—six feet one and still growing, and on the junior varsity track team at his school—and his grandmother so tiny and frail, he was able to carry her without too much difficulty as he navigated the icy sidewalk. Even so, every muscle in his body was on fire by the time he reached the bus stop, four blocks away. The other passengers gaped at him—the tall boy with the shock of black hair, still in his pajamas and with his coat flapping open, carrying an old woman in his arms as if she weighed no more than a sack of laundry—as he boarded the bus. Ignoring the curious stares, he appealed to the driver in a breathless voice, "Sir, I need to get my grandmother to the hospital. Can you help me?"

In the emergency room at Saint Mary's, he bypassed the admissions desk, instead approaching a burly black man wearing a white lab coat who was seeing to one of the patients in the waiting area, a small girl with what looked to be a broken arm. "Please," he croaked. It was all he could manage.

The next thing he knew, his grandmother was on a gurney. She had regained consciousness by then, and she smiled weakly up at him, rasping, "Ya big lug, you coulda got us both killed."

She died the next day.

Now, as Edward gazed at his sleeping wife, the thought of her dying was almost more than he could bear.

Normally, Camille was the first to rise in the mornings; she usually had breakfast on the table before anyone else was up. But she hadn't slept well last night. He'd been woken several times in the night by her tossing and turning and once by her crying out in her sleep. Even now, as she lay sound asleep, he could see, from the tight curl of her body, that whatever she was dreaming it wasn't of happier days. A knot formed in his throat. *If only there was something I could do.*

AS IF HE'D expressed the thought aloud, she stirred and her eyelids fluttered open. At the sight of her husband standing over her, Camille was instantly awake. He looked so woebegone, her first thought was, *Someone died.* Then it hit her: *She* was that someone . . . or would be soon enough. Remembering, she felt the familiar despair descend on her like some crushing weight. But this time, the pain she felt was entirely for Edward. It tore at her seeing him this way. If only she could ease his burden! She longed to comfort the slump-shouldered man with the red-rimmed eyes. *I won't let you face the future alone, my darling. Not if I can help it.*

She sat up, squinting against the sunlight that slanted through the blinds. "What time is it?"

"Quarter to eleven." He sat down next to her on the bed, smoothing her hair from her forehead. From the living room at the other end of the hall drifted the sounds of some video game being played—the roaring of engines and gnashing of gears, the *kaboom* of virtual car crashes.

She groaned. "Why didn't you wake me?"

"I thought you could use the sleep. You were pretty restless last night."

"Sorry. Did I keep you up?"

"Not at all," he said, but she knew it was a lie. He looked tired. She laid a hand on his cheek. "You're a good husband."

"I try." He smiled at her. "While we're on the subject, what would you say to breakfast in bed?"

She felt a pang, seeing how hard he was trying. "It's a nice idea. But I'm more in need of a shower right now," she told him.

"What do you say we go out for brunch, then?" he suggested. "The kids have eaten, but I'm sure they wouldn't say no to pancakes."

"You know what would make me even happier?"

"What?"

"If you'd come with me on Friday."

"Why, what's happening on Friday?"

"This month's meet-and-greet." She took note of his darkening expression and hurried to clear up any misunderstanding. "I just thought it'd be nice. We don't spend enough time together." Also, she thought, it would give him more of a feel for what she did for a living. He'd never been to one of the meet-and-greets and had attended only a handful of the weddings. Not that he was dismissive of what she did for a living, he just had no frame of reference. In the tight-knit community in which he'd grown up, there was always someone who knew of a nice girl or boy who'd be perfect for someone else's son or daughter, so there was little need for professional matchmakers. He'd never said as much, but she knew it bothered him when clients phoned after hours needing moral support or reassurance and that he considered them more than a tad neurotic. Maybe if he saw how nice and normal most of them were, he'd be more open to the idea of—

"Thanks, but I'll pass," he said brusquely before she could complete the thought.

"Oh, Edward," she beseeched. "Would it hurt, just this once?"

IF THE ROAD to hell was paved with good intentions, Edward thought, its paving stones surely had those very words carved into them: *Just this once.* He knew if he agreed to this he would be signing on for more than an evening of socializing. Knowing Camille, she probably had someone in mind for him already. And if she couldn't bring Mohammed to the mountain . . .

He opened his mouth to say no effing way, then he recalled Hugh's advice. Was this what he wanted, to spend what might be his wife's last days on Earth locked in combat? Perhaps it would be better, as Hugh had suggested, for them to join in a common purpose instead. He didn't want to look back someday and wish he'd done it differently, nor did he want to add to his wife's misery. Maybe if she had something to hold on to, if only the hope that her family wouldn't be left rudderless after she was gone, it would make this more bearable for her. Or—a new thought occurred to him—what if her plan, once put into action, made her realize how wrongheaded it was?

Still, he resisted. In the past, whenever he and Camille had disagreed about something, they'd usually managed to strike a compromise. But this time, there could be no compromise. His goal was to get her to hang on and hers to get him to let go. Where was the middle ground in that?

CHAPTER SIX

Angie D'Amato had grown up believing herself to be unique in only one respect: She possessed none of the talents of her older sisters. She wasn't musically gifted like Rosemary, nor was she athletic like Susanne. She didn't have Julia's beauty (which, given how Julia cultivated hers as if it were a rare hothouse flower, could be considered a talent), and she wasn't a brain like Francine, whose SAT scores had earned her a full scholarship to Northwestern. The only thing Angie could do was cook.

"Angie, do me a favor and start supper," her mom would say whenever she had errands to run or laundry to fold or one of Angie's sisters needed to be picked up from some afterschool activity. So Angie would peel potatoes or boil macaroni or chop vegetables, and because her mother was forever running behind schedule, she'd usually end up preparing the entire meal. Over time, her family grew to expect it. "Angie! When's supper going to be ready? My date'll be here practically any minute!" Julia would yell over the droning of the blow-dryer. "Angie, would you make extra tonight? I'm having some of my teammates over," Susanne would request as she breezed through the kitchen on her way to soccer practice. "God, Angie, not fish again! You'll stink up the whole house," Rosemary would bitch as she plied the piano keys. "If only you'd put as much effort into your home-work," Francine would say, shaking her head. If Angie's father didn't grouse or put in requests, it was only because he barely noticed what was on his plate as long as it was hot and there was plenty of it. The only real gratitude she ever got was from her mom. "My little chef. What would I do without you?" she'd say, pausing in the midst of her rushing around to drop a kiss on Angie's cheek or dip a spoon into whatever was bubbling on the stove. Angie didn't mind; she enjoyed cooking. As the years passed, she progressed beyond the recipes scribbled on stained cards in her mother's hand to the more complicated ones in cookbooks: snowcapped lamb chops, Oriental-style chicken, crab-stuffed sole. She learned to make rice perfectly each time, polenta that didn't stick to the pot, biscuits as fluffy as the ones depicted in the photos. She used fresh herbs instead of the dried ones from the spice rack. Desserts were made from scratch: cookies, pies and cobblers, layer cakes frosted with buttercream. Her senior year of high school, while her friends were applying to colleges, Angie had her heart set on culinary school.

Before long, she was mastering preparations such as a *mirepoix* and a *brunoise* and learning the proper methods for braising, sautéing, and saucing. After graduating from the Culinary Institute, she went to work, moving up the ladder from *saucier* to line chef to *garde manger* and eventually *chef de cuisine* in restaurant kitchens in and around Manhattan over the next ten years. All the while, she dreamed of one day opening a restaurant of her own. Unfortunately, without a financial backer, it remained just that: a dream. So, at thirty, she started a catering business instead. In the eight years since, she hadn't once regretted the decision. The hours sucked, her overhead gobbled up the lion's share of her profits, and she was often busier than she would've liked, but she was her own boss and had free rein to create her own dishes instead of re-creating those of others.

One of her regular clients was the Harte to Heart agency; she'd been catering their monthly meet-and-greets for the past three years. She'd more or less stumbled onto the gig after a friend of hers had dragged her to one of the meet-and-greets as a guest. Angie had hit it off at once with the attractive, personable matchmaker who was hosting the event. When Camille, after learning what she did for a living, asked what she thought of the uninspired array of food on offer that evening, Angie wasn't shy in giving her opinion along with her business card.

Camille glanced at the card. "'A Catered Affair.' I like it. And may I say," she added with a wry smile, "tailor-made for this crowd."

Angie was pleased by the show of interest and also intrigued by the venue, if only from the standpoint of an observer. "Do they ever find what they're looking for?" she asked, glancing around the rented West Chelsea space at the attractive and obviously well-heeled singles, most around her age or a little older, all happily mingling.

"Most do, yes. If they're in it for the right reasons," Camille told her.

"What if you're just unlucky in love?" At the time, Angie had just been dumped by Thierry, the French-Canadian *sous chef* at Langoustine, the last restaurant she'd worked at. Before him, there had been a string of other disappointments: Ben, the butcher, who could break down a side of beef in no time flat but didn't know the first thing about women; the handsome and highly-sexed Darius whom she'd caught in bed with another man; Danny Osborn, the brilliant, temperamental chef who'd broken her heart when he took a job at a restaurant in L.A., informing her only after the fact, by email. And that wasn't even counting the boys she'd burned her way through in high school.

"I believe we make our own luck. Especially in love." The pretty, auburn-haired matchmaker lifted her wineglass to her lips, and as she did Angie took note of the gold band on her ring finger. Clearly she knew what she was talking about from a personal as well as professional standpoint.

"What's the secret?" Angie adopted a casual tone so the matchmaker wouldn't see her as a potential client.

"There's no secret," Camille said. "Mostly it's about being open to possibilities. I've had people come to me with a list of requirements so long, no one could possibly measure up. I had one woman tell me the guy I'd fixed her up with would be perfect if only he didn't have a mustache."

"What did you say to that?"

"I told her to either get over it or get him to shave it off."

Angie laughed. "You don't mince words, do you?"

"That's what they pay me for. I tell them what their friends won't."

"What if you don't know what you're looking for?"

"Believe me, you know when you find it."

After Camille had drifted off to see to her other guests, Angie was left wondering if she would ever find her soul mate or even recognize him if she did. She'd since concluded that, while Mr. or Ms. Right might be out there for most, if not all, of the singles she encountered at the meet-and-greets (she'd witnessed enough hookups over the past three years to be convinced of it), a husband probably wasn't in the cards for her. She hadn't found anyone she loved enough to make that kind of commitment and, at thirty-eight, what were the chances she ever would? Besides, marriage wasn't all it was cracked up to be, from what she could see. Her sisters were all married, and though they'd never in a million years admit it, Angie knew from the occasional comments they'd let slip that they felt they'd missed out in some ways. Francine, with her three children, the youngest still in diapers, and her job teaching middle school, was perpetually worn to a frazzle; Rosemary and her husband were currently in counseling; Susanne ran around like the Energizer Bunny, staying active in lieu of a once-promising athletic career (the closest she got to playing field these days was coaching her oldest son's soccer team); and Julia's attempts to get pregnant over the course of ten years and two husbands had made her even more looks-obsessed (if she couldn't have a baby, then damn it, she'd be the hottest housewife on the block!), though she'd toned it down a bit since becoming a mother to the two little girls she'd adopted with her second husband.

Angie's parents set an even worse example. They no longer had sex, according to her mother. Worse, her mom didn't seem bothered by the fact. Angie wondered if she herself would feel that way after forty years of sleeping next to the same man every night. In her mom's case, one who rattled the whole house when he snored, farted openly, and had more hair on his back than a mountain gorilla. Did familiarity breed, if not contempt (her parents were devoted to each other if not still madly in love), then an inferior-grade contentment? If so, she'd rather live alone the rest of her life, thank you very much.

No, she had no regrets. She had a career she loved, a family she was close to (if at times those bonds chafed), and good friends. She would have liked to have had children of her own but took joy in spending time with her nieces and nephews and the kids in her cooking class at the Bedford-Stuyvesant Youth Center—Raul, Julio, Jermaine, Tre'Shawn and Daarel, Tamika, D'Enice, and Chandra— where she volunteered one night a week. What more did she need?

At the Harte to Heart meet-and-greets, she was content to be a fly on the wall. As she put out platters or circulated with trays she could watch the mating dance from a safe remove: the women being hit on by guys in whom she could tell they had zero interest, from the bored looks they wore, and the men who surreptitiously scoped out the competition while chatting up a sure bet. She took note of which guests went home alone at the end of the evening and which ones hooked up. She silently cheered when sparks flew and sometimes had to bite her tongue when she overheard a guy deliver some lame pickup line. "Dude, you're never going to get laid that way!" she'd come close to blurting on more than one occasion.

Oddly enough, looks weren't as much a factor as she'd once thought. At every meet-and-greet, there was the usual bevy of beauties, but not everyone was gorgeous or handsome. Camille's assistant was the embodiment of the agency's unwritten motto: You didn't have to be a princess to find a prince. Dara might look like the love child of Sandra Bernhard and Lyle Lovett, but with her combination of style, sexiness, and sass, she had men eating out of her hand. At the opposite end of the scale were the babes who, after sparking some initial interest, fizzled like dud Roman candles and the oh-so-hip and handsome who were bypassed in favor of the sweet, fun-loving guys who were more cuddly than cute. There were no hard-and-fast rules, Angie had learned. You just had to put yourself out there and hope for the best. Camille was good at her job—you could tell just by watching her work the room—but more often than not it was a matter of being in the right place at the right time. Which was where Angie was the first Friday in May when she spotted a tall, strikingly handsome man who momentarily made her forget her aching feet and the heavy platter she was carrying.

He was standing alone by the buffet table, sipping a drink and trying to look inconspicuous. *Fat chance,* she thought. With his soulful dark eyes and thick, wavy black hair flecked with gray at the temples, his swarthy complexion and face that screamed *Take me to the casbah!,* he had as much chance of blending in as a rare tropical tetra in a bowlful of goldfish. She pegged him as a newcomer. She'd never seen him before, and a face like his you didn't forget.

Angie wasn't in the habit of striking up conversations with the guests at these events, but she found herself inquiring of Mr. Tall-Dark-and-Handsome as she set down her platter, "First time?"

He turned to her, smiling sheepishly. "Is it that obvious?"

"I'm a trained observer," she said, doing her best impression of an international spy by lowering her voice to a near whisper and tapping the corner of her eye.

He chuckled. "Clearly, that's not your only talent," he said, gesturing toward the sumptuous spread she and her staff were in the process of laying out. "I'm sure it tastes as good as it looks."

Angie was warmed by the compliment. "I don't think you'll be disappointed," she said, confident in her abilities in that one area even if she was no competition for the glamorous women circulating about. "By the way, I highly recommend the eggplant *involtini.* It's my signature dish."

He gave a full-on smile then that went through her like a warm knife through buttercream. Up close, she could see his eyes were more amber than brown, with thick lashes and emphatic brows, which at the moment were arched in bemusement. With his noble forehead and strong jaw offset by a sensuous mouth, he looked . . . princely. There was no other word to describe it.

"You must be Angie." He put out his hand, and she noted with approval that he had a nice, firm grip. "Edward Constantin. It's nice to meet you. My wife has told me a lot about you."

His wife? Angie felt her heart sink as her eyebrows shot up, despite knowing she wouldn't have stood a chance with this guy even if he were up for grabs. "You're married?" She kept her voice light. Before he could reply, she went on in an arch tone, "At the risk of pointing out the obvious, aren't you in the wrong place?"

His smile widened. "I'm Camille's husband," he explained.

"Oh." It made perfect sense. Naturally, Camille would be married to a walking billboard for her services. Angie put on her brightest smile. "Well, I've heard a lot about you, too." It wasn't strictly true—she and Camille communicated mostly by email and at the meet-and-greets were usually too busy to chat with each other—but she knew enough. "You're a doctor, right?"

He nodded, and she thought, *Ma would have a field day.* Loretta D'Amato's last, great hope was that she'd live to see her youngest daughter walk down the aisle. If Angie were to marry a doctor, her mom would think she'd died and gone to heaven. *Why can't you meet someone nice?* she'd say. *Not the riffraff you go out with.* Meaning a man who wore a suit and tie to work instead of chef's whites and who wasn't covered in tattoos or scars from cuts and burns.

Edward leaned in to confide, "Don't tell anyone, but I'm here under duress." His gaze drifted to his wife, wearing a red halter dress and chatting with one of the other guests, a tall brunette who looked like a fashion model. "Parties aren't really my thing."

That explained why she hadn't seen him at any of the prior meet-and-greets. "They're not really my thing, either," she told him. "Reminds me of when I was in my twenties, and they were just an excuse to get drunk. Now I get to watch other people drink too much and makes asses of themselves," she added with a laugh, eyeing a bosomy blonde standing nearby, whose efforts to make an impression on the man with whom she was chatting were working in all the wrong ways, from the trapped look he wore. "Also, I don't wake up the next morning with a hangover. Sore feet maybe but no regrets. Though," she added in a wry voice, "if I were looking for a husband, I'd be the proverbial kid with her nose pressed against the window of the candy store."

"But you're not looking?" He gave her a questioning look.

"Nope," she replied cheerfully, and she went on to explain, "I have four sisters, all married but not all happily so. They'd sooner die than admit it—they enjoy lording it over me too much—but if they had it to do over again . . ." She shrugged. "So the way I figure it, I'm just avoiding the mistakes they wish they hadn't made."

"Not every marriage is unhappy."

"No, but it's still a crapshoot. You never know what you're going to get."

"It's not like winning the lottery. You have to work at it."

"Some people have to work a little too hard, from what I can see." Angie caught a flicker of some buried emotion in his eyes and was quick to say, "But hey, what do I know? I'm just the armchair quarterback." She turned to gaze out the window. The rented space they were in, the top floor of a converted factory in West Chelsea, had floor-to-ceiling windows that wrapped around two sides of the building. From where she stood, she could see all the way across the Hudson River to New Jersey. Closer to shore, the reflected glow from the buildings along the waterfront showed the remnants of an old pier jutting from the water like rotted teeth. "You know the saying *Always a bridesmaid, never a bride?* That's me. Not because I never caught the bouquet, but because I'd rather be single than stuck in a miserable marriage."

"You never wanted kids?" he asked.

Angie brought her gaze back to him. Edward was smiling in a way that made her weak in the knees. The hard little nugget of cynicism that kept her from making a fool of herself with attractive men—attractive married men in particular—had turned into a quivering *panna cotta.* "Sure. But I have nieces and nephews coming out of my ears. Little beasts, every one of them," she added with a fond chuckle. "The birthday cakes alone keep me plenty busy. In addition to being a caterer by trade, I'm also the family baker," she explained with a laugh at the quizzical look he gave her.

"I can't imagine my life without kids." His expression softened as he told her about his children, a son and daughter. "Kyra's fourteen going on forty, and Zach's your typical nine-year-old, all knees and elbows. They can be a handful at times, but they never cease to amaze me."

"You also have an amazing wife," Angie reminded him.

"That I do." His gaze traveled once more to Camille. In her red dress, with her tumble of auburn curls against skin so fair it was almost translucent, she glowed. Any man would be proud to call such a woman his wife. Yet, strangely, the look on his face was one of melancholy.

"Hey, are you all right?" Angie touched his elbow.

He blinked and returned his gaze to her, his smile slipping back into place. "What? Yes, I'm fine. I was just thinking of something." He didn't volunteer any more than that.

Angie felt a queer urge to comfort him nonetheless, which would have been entirely presumptuous since they'd only just met. He would think she was pushy or possibly coming on to him. So instead she did what any self-respecting Italian girl would do in a situation like this. "Why don't I get you a plate of food?" she offered. "You look as if you could use something to eat."

THE MOMENT EDWARD had walked into the crowded room, he'd known it was a mistake to come. Instead of the soft music drifting from the speakers, he heard the sound of the band playing as the *Titanic* went down. His gut churned at the thought of the evening ahead, which—he suspected—was just the opener before Camille got down to the real business at hand. As she guided him around, introducing him to people, it was an effort to make polite conversation when he longed to head for the nearest exit. But he'd agreed to accompany Camille to the meet-and-greet and he was a man of his word, so he soldiered on.

One woman caught his eye: a striking brunette in a tailored black business suit that was in marked contrast to the cocktail attire worn by the other female guests. She was tall, six feet, at least, and not at all self-conscious about her height, judging by the five-inch heels that had her towering over the balding man with whom she was chatting. The man looked smitten, and it was easy to see why. She was a knockout, with her willowy figure and exotic good looks: high cheekbones and jade-green eyes that stood out against her golden-hued skin. Part Asian, he guessed. She looked familiar. Had he seen her somewhere? Probably in a magazine or on a billboard.

She caught him staring and flashed him a look over the balding head of her admirer, one that said, *Don't go anywhere. I'll be with you as soon as I can get rid of this guy.* Edward realized, to his chagrin, she must have thought he was scoping her. It was a reminder of his real purpose in being here, in Camille's mind, at least—for all he knew the brunette in the black suit was earmarked as his next wife—and he regretted once more having agreed to come. *What the hell was I thinking?*

Not that the women he'd met tonight weren't attractive, but he had no interest in any of them. To him, they were like paintings in a museum, to be admired but not possessed . . . or desired. He had eyes only for his wife. When the brunette in the black suit parted company with her balding admirer and began moving in Edward's direction, he took advantage of the opportunity, as she momentarily passed from his line of sight, to duck away and lose himself in the crowd.

KAT FISHER HAD almost decided not to come. A late-breaking news story had kept her banging out copy until after the end of her shift, leaving her no time to dash home and change for the party. She'd have bagged on it on altogether if she hadn't been so damn pissed. It was that girl, Natalie, from the assignment desk. Flashing her industrial-chip diamond around the newsroom, complete with cutesy story about how her boyfriend—now fiancé—had hidden it inside a fortune cookie prior to popping the question over Chinese takeout. It had been all Kat could do not to gag.

Not that she had anything against the girl; Natalie was nice enough. But why *her*? She wasn't pretty or even especially interesting. How had she managed to get engaged when Kat, who was known to cause men to grow weak in the knees just walking into a room, *just breathing the same air,* was still husbandless? Was it just that she was unwilling to settle? Or was there something wrong with her, some hidden flaw, like in a diamond, that was invisible to the naked eye?

The irony was she'd had no interest in getting married until recently. Marriage meant settling down, and she couldn't afford to do that in the early years of her career. She'd been too busy climbing the ladder, which had meant working the farm teams until she was ready for the big leagues. She'd started out as a junior copy editor at one of the local news stations in Sacramento. After six months, she moved on to Abilene, where for two years she cut her teeth with her first on-air gig, before it was on to Buffalo, followed by stints at WOFR in

Miami and then WSB in Atlanta. It wasn't until Kat had made it to the top, as a reporter for the number-one station in the number-one market, WABC-TV in New York City, that she could pause to take a breath and focus more on her personal life, only to discover that life didn't sit still while you pursued your career. At thirty-nine, she had as much male interest as ever, only now the men in her age group were either married and looking for some action on the side or carrying so much baggage she'd need a forklift.

Three years ago, she'd gotten her wakeup call when her ob-gyn had informed her, during her annual checkup, that her window for childbearing was rapidly closing. "You have less than fifty percent chance of getting pregnant at your age." Dr. Berg gave it to her straight. "By the time you're forty, the odds will be even slimmer. I'm sorry," she said at the look of dismay Kat must have worn, "but those are the facts. Better to know now than to have regrets later on."

"But that doesn't apply to *me*," Kat protested. "Look at me! I work out like crazy. I run marathons, for God's sake. I know women half my age who can't even make it to the five-mile mark."

"It's not a race, Kat," her doctor said gently. "What you see on the outside doesn't always reflect what's on the inside."

"So what you're saying is my expiration date is almost up?" Kat, who almost never cried—she viewed it as a sign of weakness—found herself suddenly, and perilously, on the verge of tears.

Dr. Berg nodded her graying head. "That's one way of way of looking at it. I'm not saying this to worry you, but if you want children, you're going to have to get on it fairly quickly."

"But I don't even have a husband!"

"That can wait. Your biological clock can't."

Dr. Berg gave her a comforting pat on the arm. But there was no comforting Kat. How could she relax knowing her ovaries, to which she'd scarcely given a thought all these years except when she was on her period or getting a Pap smear, were decomposing as rapidly as roadkill.

As luck would have it, that same day she had a lunch date scheduled with a woman whom she'd met while doing a piece for WABC-TV on top female executives of Fortune 500 companies. Over lunch at the Modern, when Susan Longmire let it drop that she'd met her husband through a professional matchmaker, Kat was astounded. Susan was gorgeous and smart, with an MBA from Harvard. Why on earth would she have to *pay* someone to find her a husband?

"You should give her a call." Susan pressed a business card into her hand when Kat remarked jokingly that she ought to give it a try, since she hadn't had much luck on her own. "It couldn't hurt."

It was all Kat could do not to wrinkle her nose in distaste. "How is that different from Match.com and eHarmony?" Online dating services, in her view, were the last stop on Desperation Express.

"I know what you're thinking." Susan smiled. "I thought the same thing when someone first suggested it to me. But really, is it any different from going to a headhunter? Except the goal here is to find the perfect match."

"Not to sound conceited or anything, but I have plenty of men who want to go out with me," Kat replied with a frankness she could only have used with another woman who was equally desirable.

"Of course! Look at you, you're gorgeous! I'm only talking about narrowing the field so you don't waste time looking for love in all the wrong places," Susan told her. "Believe me, I know. I dated my share of losers. Until I met Bradley." With that, she whipped out her iPhone, flashing a photo of her husband, a six-foot-two heart-stopper with blond hair, blue eyes, and the kind of body that blue jeans were made for. And he wasn't just eye candy. The thirty-nine-year-old Bradley was also a top cardiologist who'd been on the US Olympic ski team in his youth. In his free time, when he and Susan weren't off skiing in Gstaad or deep-sea diving at the Great Barrier Reef, he volunteered his services for Doctors Without Borders.

Kat phoned the number for the Harte to Heart agency that very day. She met with Camille Harte the following week, and within minutes of chatting with the stylish, energetic matchmaker, she was ready to sign on. The first man with whom Camille fixed her up was a forty-two-year-old systems analyst by the name of Daniel Sides. Daniel was good looking with a full head of hair and the brains to match, so Kat was hopeful at first, and when he oh-so-casually let it drop over dinner at Bouley that he was a Mensa member, mildly impressed. But by the third mention of his Mensa membership, she'd mentally checked out. Then there was Kenneth, the architect, who had the dream house he'd one day share with his dream wife already sketched out. It wasn't until Kat took him to visit her friend Gretchen, and Gretchen's three-year-old, who wasn't fully potty-trained, peed on Kenneth while they were roughhousing on the rug, that she learned he wasn't as eager to start a family as he was to find a wife. Stephen Resler was the most recent bomb-out. The forty-two-year-old financier seemed promising at first, if a bit rough around the edges. But when he'd started in about his ex-wife, on whom he was obviously still hung up, her interest fizzled. After they left the the restaurant, she thanked him for a lovely evening and hightailed it on home.

Now here she was, once more back in the fray. Earlier in the evening, she'd run into Daniel Sides, sporting a goatee but as pompous as ever, and was relieved when, after a brief exchange of pleasantries, they went their separate ways with apparently no hard feelings on his part. It seemed to set the tone. As she circulated about, no sparks flew with any of the men she met. She wasn't at her liveliest and knew it; it didn't help, either, that she was dressed in her work clothes, attire more appropriate for a televised standup on the courthouse steps than a festive occasion. The only interest she got was from a balding stockbroker who stuck to her like a sock fresh from the dryer. It wasn't until she was attempting to give Mr. Static Cling the polite brush-off that she spotted a man who made her take a second look. And she didn't just look; she gasped in recognition.

It was *him*. The guy she'd always pictured in her mind's eye standing at her side on her wedding day. Tall and so handsome he literally took her breath away, with close-cropped dark curls and George Clooney eyes, which at the moment were fixed on her, she realized with a delicious chill of anticipation. She wondered what his story was. Divorced? Widowed? Or was he, like her, a formerly devout single turned romantic hopeful? Whatever, she was dying to meet him.

Unfortunately, by the time she'd peeled away from Mr. Static Cling, George Clooney Eyes was nowhere to be seen. Damn. She could only hope some other woman hadn't snagged him already. She scanned the crowd, finally spotting him over by the buffet table. She was headed in that direction when she ran into Camille. Kat wasted no time in pointing him out. "Who," she demanded, "is *that*?"

"You mean Edward?" Camille peered in the direction Kat was pointing. "He's—"

"Don't tell me," Kat groaned, not letting her finish. "He's taken. I knew it. Damn, just my luck."

Camille smiled. "I was going to say he's my husband."

Kat gasped again, this time in dismay. "Oh." She struggled to hide her disappointment, making a joke of it. "Well, looks like you got the pick of the litter."

Camille gave Kat's arm a consoling pat. "He's not the only one. Just be patient a little while longer."

"Oh, I've got all kinds of time," Kat replied sarcastically, thinking of her rapidly shriveling eggs. "Though at the rate I'm going, I'll be able to pay for the wedding out of my retirement fund."

Camille's smile fell away briefly, and Kat noticed how tired she looked. She seemed sad, too, which surprised her. It had never occurred to Kat that the perennially upbeat matchmaker might have problems of her own. Before she could ponder it further, Camille was once more her cheerful self. "Trust me, I've been doing this a long time, and I have yet to have anyone ask for a refund."

But when Camille excused herself to attend to her other guests, Kat caught the flash of tears in her eyes as she was turning to go. There was no doubt about it: Camille was hurting. Kat could only wonder why. Did it have anything to do with that gorgeous husband of hers?

ANGIE PILED A PLATE with food and then led the way down a corridor that opened onto a kitchen crammed with stacks of cardboard cartons, large plastic containers of food, and platters ready to go out. She had to move some boxes to make room for Edward to sit down. Then, while she bustled about putting the finishing touches on the platters and servers darted in and out, he ate. He hadn't had much of an appetite lately, but everything tasted so good he suddenly couldn't get enough: airy little pillows of gnocchi in herb cream sauce, seafood salad with shaved fennel, braised duck breast in ginger-soy sauce, focaccia fragrant with rosemary and garlic, eggplant *involtini* every bit as delicious as promised.

When he'd finally had his fill, he exclaimed, "My God. Where did you learn to cook like that?"

Angie beamed as if he'd paid her the world's greatest compliment. "The usual way," she told him. "Culinary school. That, and being screamed at by chefs in the restaurant kitchens I've worked in. It makes a real impression, believe me, when you have some big, tattooed dude waving a butcher knife this close to your face." She held up a thumb and forefinger spread a scant inch apart.

He watched as she sprinkled Parmesan cheese over another platter of eggplant *involtini*. She wasn't beautiful or glamorous like many of the women he'd met tonight. Her face was free of makeup except for a touch of sheer lip gloss, and the only jewelry she wore was the gold studs in her ears; her hair, the shiny brown of molasses, was pulled back in a ponytail and her attire equally toned down: a plain white cotton blouse and sensible black slacks with a pair of lime-green Crocs peeking from under the cuffs. But maybe it was because she wasn't going out of her way to impress that he found her so refreshing. He took in the spray of freckles over her nose and cheeks, which made her appear more youthful than was suggested by the fine lines at the corners of her eyes. Eyes that were easily her best feature, huge and dark and thickly lashed: those of an Italian film star. Though it was her smile that got to him the most: a smile that made him feel hopeful when he had no reason to, like a shaft of light penetrating a collapsed mine shaft.

"Did you ever stand up to them?" he asked.

"Hell no. I've been known to be reckless, but I'm not suicidal."

"My first year of internship was like that," he recalled. "You either got tough or got chewed up."

"Makes for good knife skills," she said. "Are you a surgeon?"

"No, why?"

"Your hands. They look like those of a surgeon."

Edward looked down at his hands, loosely curled on the table. He'd only ever thought of them as tools of his trade. But looking at them now, he saw his grandfather's hands. His father's father had made his living as a cabinetmaker. As a boy, Edward had loved watching the old man work, the way his supple brown hands caressed the wood as he plied it with his tools. "I thought about going into surgery," he told her, "but it would've meant another four years of residency. You have to draw the line somewhere or you never see your family." *Not that I see enough of them as it is.*

One of the servers, a slim dark-skinned woman with green eyes and hair in tiny braids looped in a bun, popped in just then, pausing long enough for Angie to introduce her. "Edward, this is Cleo. If you want to know the secret to my success, you're looking at her." Cleo flashed him a smile and said a quick hello before dashing off with the platter Angie had finished assembling.

"So, what kind of doctor are you?" Angie brought her attention back to Edward.

"I'm an ear, nose, and throat man." His specialty was otolaryngology, but most people didn't know what that entailed or even how to pronounce it, so he seldom bothered to elaborate.

She scooped ground coffee beans into a commercial-size coffeemaker. "Well, now I know who to call next time I have an earache. Though I can't remember the last time I had to go to the doctor's. I don't know if it's because I'm naturally healthy or because I can't afford to be sick."

Edward felt a pang, thinking of Camille. "Be thankful," he said.

She must have heard something in his voice because she paused to study him, those big, dark eyes of hers fixing on him with an intensity he found a bit unsettling. "Look," she said finally, "you don't know me so it's none of my business, but I couldn't help noticing you seem kind of . . . tense. Is there anything more I can get you? I think there's some brandy around here somewhere."

Was it that obvious, he wondered, or was she just more perceptive than most? Either way, he was disarmed by her candor and sincere-seeming concern. "I wouldn't say no to a shot of brandy," he said.

She flashed him her infectious smile, then spent the next couple of minutes rummaging around in the boxes until she found what she was looking for. From another carton, she pulled a couple of glasses and poured a finger of brandy into each. She handed him one, and they clinked glasses.

"*Salut!*" she toasted.

He took a few sips, the brandy, along with the food he'd just eaten, warming his insides and prying at the coiled tension in his muscles. "Thanks," he said. "I feel better already."

"It's known as the Italian school of medicine," she replied as she stood leaning against the counter. "My nonna always said food and wine were the best cure for what ails. So, Edward," she asked after a bit, "do you feel like talking about it? Again, not that it's any of my business, so please feel free to tell me to butt out. You wouldn't be the first."

"It's Camille," he found himself confiding, somewhat to his surprise. The brandy had loosened his tongue. Or maybe it had more to do with Angie herself: She was like a hot toddy on a winter's day. "I don't know if she's told you, but she's been having some . . . health problems." Angie's smile faded, replaced by a look of concern. "I'm sorry to hear it. She hasn't said anything to me, but then she wouldn't. In the three years I've known her, I've never heard one complaint out of her, not even when she had cancer." She paused, letting out a gasp. "Oh, my God. Is that it? Is the cancer back?" He nodded gravely, and her face crumpled in dismay. "When I asked what was wrong, I thought maybe you'd had a bad day at the office. I never imagined . . ." Her voice trailed off, her face reddening. "I didn't mean to bring up a sore subject."

"Actually, it's a relief to have it out in the open," he said. "We haven't told many people."

Hesitantly, she asked, "What's the prognosis?"

"Not good."

"God, I'm so sorry." Tears glittered in Angie's eyes.

"It's not a death sentence," he hastened to add, though more to reassure himself than her. "We haven't run out of options yet." He hadn't given up hope that his wife would come to her senses, though every day lost made the already slim chance of recovery that much slimmer.

"Still . . . it's got to be tough."

"It is," he said quietly. "More for her than for me."

"How's she taking it?"

"Surprisingly well, considering."

"She's amazing," Angie said. "Honestly, I don't know how she does it. If it were me, I'd be a total mess. I'd never leave the kitchen. That's what I do when I'm stressed, I cook. I once cooked so much stuff I had to invite over everyone in my building so the food wouldn't go to waste. All because my stupid sister decided to have a face-lift and almost died on the operating table."

"Is she all right now?"

"She's fine," Angie said with a dismissive wave of her hand. "Julia says it cured her of ever having any more plastic surgery, but I'll believe it when she's still saying that at sixty. Though I hope to God she means it, because I don't ever want to go through that again. A word of advice: Never make marinara sauce when you're freaking out. It's not a pretty sight, believe me."

"At least you had something to show for it." What did he have except a heap of bitterness?

She leaned in to place a hand on his arm, saying gently. "You have each other, that's something."

At the reminder, he rose to his feet. "Speaking of which, I should get back to the party. Camille will be wondering where I disappeared to." He found himself lingering even so. Being with Angie soothed him in a way he couldn't explain. They'd only just met but he felt as if he'd known her all his life. "Thanks. You've been very kind," he said as he shook her hand, which was small but strong, like Angie herself.

"My pleasure." She pulled a business card from her pocket and handed it to him. "Look, if you ever need anything, don't hesitate to call. I work weird hours, so I'm usually available when no one else is." She smiled crookedly. "Sometimes it helps to talk to the bartender."

Edward was used to women slipping him their phone numbers. Camille didn't think he noticed when other women came on to him, but he only pretended not to because it embarrassed him. Yet he sensed this wasn't that; Angie was merely reaching out. Nevertheless, he knew, even as he tucked the card in his wallet, he wouldn't contact her. His wife might get the wrong idea.

He smiled grimly at the irony as he made his way back to the party.

CHAPTER SEVEN

"I have someone who'd be right for you."

The woman seated across from Camille at the Blue Ribbon Sushi Bar & Grill, where they were having lunch, eyed her apprehensively. "Who said I was looking?" she replied, but Camille could see a glimmer of curiosity, and perhaps a spark of hope, in Elise Osgood's gray-green eyes.

Camille smiled to put her at ease. "You must have known when I asked you to lunch, it wasn't strictly social."

Elise nodded slowly. "Okay. I'm listening."

"It's, um, a bit delicate." Camille paused to take a sip of her Perrier. Why was it so hot in here? Maybe it was just her. She was nervous, a first for her—usually she was the one doing the soothing with prospective clients. "Just hear me out before you make up your mind, that's all I ask."

"Fair enough." Elise sat back, smoothing her napkin over her lap.

So far so good. Camille had had a good feeling about Elise from the start. They'd met several months ago, at a Literacy Partners fund-raiser, and after learning the attractive thirty-eight-year-old schoolteacher was divorced, Camille had slipped Elise her business card. Elise wasn't quite ready to start dating again, but they'd stayed in touch. Every time they'd talked, Camille had felt more and more drawn to the other woman. She had thought she and Elise could actually become friends, though she hadn't given up on finding her a new husband when the time came. Never was there a woman more cut out to be a wife and mother. Which was why Camille had asked her to lunch today.

Elise Osgood had all the right qualifications. She was smart, sweet-natured, and wholesome, and pretty enough without being a temptress, with an open, guileless face and shiny light-brown hair worn in an attractive feathered cut. She loved children—her face had lit up when she'd spoken of her students at Saint Luke's School, where she taught fourth grade—and was a regular churchgoer as well as active in several charities. She came from a solid background; she'd grown up in a small town in Wisconsin, the youngest of three children, where her father was a family practitioner and her mother a nurse. Above all else, she wasn't in a hurry to get married again.

None of which made this any easier.

Camille had woken that morning feeling as if she had a dry-swallowed aspirin stuck in her throat. The thought of her husband with another woman, however benign the relationship, made her want to throw up. She'd almost chickened out and canceled her lunch date. Only after a good cry, a long hot shower, and a cup of strong coffee, did she find the courage to stay the course. *You can't afford to be selfish,* she'd lectured herself. This wasn't about what *she* needed but about what was best for her family. Now, as she sat facing the woman who might be her husband's future wife, she drew in a deep breath before continuing, "He's married . . ." At the look of shock on Elise's face, she put her hand up, palm out, to still the words of protest forming on her lips. ". . . but his wife knows all about it. It was her idea actually. She's terminally ill, you see."

Elise's shocked look gave way to one of sympathy. "The poor woman. My God, how awful!"

"Yes. Which is why it's important she find the right person." Camille sought to keep her voice steady. She wasn't here to get sympathy but to secure her family's future.

"And you think *I* could be that person?" Elise shook her head. "No, I'm sorry, it's out of the question."

Camille had known it would be a tough sell. Elise was a deeply moral person; she'd also been badly burned by her ex-husband, who'd cheated on her, which made the thought of becoming a home-wrecker downright repugnant. Camille had to convince her she would, in fact, be rescuing a home, not wrecking one. "I'm not talking about sex. Just friendship, for the time being."

Elise eyed her in confusion. "I'm sure this man has his own friends. Why would he need me?"

"I'm talking about something a bit more . . . involved than the kind of friend who delivers casseroles and babysits the children now and then."

"There are children? Oh, God." Elise grew even paler.

"Yes, two—a boy and a girl. Both great kids." Camille's voice caught, and she reached again for her water glass.

"That makes it even worse."

"Why? You love kids."

"Exactly. Which is why I could see myself getting sucked in."

"Would that be so terrible?"

"Yes, if you're me. I could end up marrying a man I didn't love because I was crazy about his kids."

"I'm not talking about marriage. Though in time, if you and he should develop feelings for each other . . ." Here Camille faltered, taking a breath to bolster herself and loosen the knot in her throat before going on. "Then marriage would certainly be an option." Elise stared at her, not saying anything. "Look, I realize it's a lot to ask. It's also a huge leap of faith. But you're exactly what this family needs, Elise. And if you're not ready to start dating again, it could be what you need, too."

"I—I don't know," Elise stammered.

"Why don't you meet them before you make up your mind."

Elise looked torn, but after a moment she shook her head. "No, I don't think so."

"How could it hurt? There'd be no obligation."

"Maybe not, but I'd end up feeling even sorrier for the poor woman."

"She doesn't want your pity. She only wants your help."

"Which is exactly why I need to steer clear. You have me pegged. I'll give you that much," she told Camille, her mouth twisting in a rueful smile. "I'm always the first person with my hand in the air whenever a job needs doing. But serving meals to the homeless on Thanksgiving is a far cry from getting involved in something like this. I don't need that kind of commitment right now. If and when I marry again, it'll be for love."

"But didn't you marry for love the first time?" Camille reminded her.

Elise winced and looked down. "Yes," she said in a small voice. "But I didn't know what he was like when I married him."

"All the more reason to go a different route. How do you know you wouldn't grow to love this man in time?" It pained her deeply to say it, but she had to look to the future. She wanted her husband to know happiness again after she was gone and for her children to grow up in a happy home. She swallowed hard, struggling to quell the tears that threatened.

Elise absently fingered the Tiffany heart on a chain around her neck (a gift from her former husband?) as she frowned in thought, the pain of those memories etched on her face. Their entrées had arrived, but neither of them had picked up their forks. "That's partly what worries me," she said. "If that were to happen, how could I be sure it was love and not something else? After I found out Dennis was cheating on me, I stopped trusting my own instincts."

"Just because you chose wrong the first time, it doesn't mean you will the next time."

Camille knew she had a nibble when Elise asked tentatively, "What about the husband, what does he have to say about all this?" "He wasn't too keen on the idea at first, as you might imagine." Camille gave a smile that held no humor as she thought back to the verbal battles of the past few weeks. Never had a victory been as hard-won or as hollow. "He's only doing it for his family. For him, it's an act of love."

"He sounds like quite a guy," Elise observed, her tone wistful.

"He is." Camille spoke softly, her gaze drifting past Elise. She was seeing Edward in her mind's eye holding their daughter in his arms when she was minutes old, tears of joy streaming down his cheeks. If anyone had told her then she would one day be not only willing to give him up but working to persuade another woman to take her place, she'd have thought they were crazy.

"You sound as if you know him fairly well."

Camille brought her gaze back to Elise. "I ought to. He's my husband."

Elise's eyes widened. "Oh, my God. You don't mean to tell me—?"

"I have cancer."

Elise stared at her in disbelief. "But . . . but you don't look sick!"

"I know. Ironic, isn't it?"

"God, I feel so awful. I had no idea. Why didn't you say something?"

"I didn't want you to be biased."

"I'm sorry if I seemed insensitive." Elise's eyes pooled with tears. "Is there anything I can do?"

"Yes. Meet my family."

"You're really serious about this?"

Dead serious, Camille almost said, but this was no time for gallows humor. Elise deserved an explanation. "If you're asking if this is how I pictured my life turning out, the answer is no. But things don't always turn out the way you expect." Elise ought to know that better than anyone. "I'm just playing the hand I've been dealt. I don't like it. In fact, I hate it. But I can't let my own needs get in the way of doing what's best for my family. Which is where you come in."

"Why me?" Elise dabbed at her eyes with her napkin.

"You and Edward would be a good fit. And my children would love you."

Elise gave a wobbly smile. "What are their names?"

"Kyra and Zach. She's fourteen, and he just turned nine." A true smile surfaced as she spoke. She couldn't speak of her children without smiling. "You'd love them. They're wonderful kids."

"This must be hard for them, too."

"It is. But they don't know the extent of it. Not yet."

Elise put a hand over Camille's. "I can only imagine what you must be going through."

Camille felt deeply grateful toward this kind, caring woman. But knowing she'd picked the right person didn't make it hurt any less. "It *is* hard," she said, "which is why it's important my family be in good hands after I'm gone." Elise nodded slowly, and Camille could see she was softening. "Would you like to see a picture of them?" She pulled a snapshot from her purse and handed it to Elise, one taken by her sister at their beach house a few summers ago. In it, Edward was carrying the then five-year-old Zach on his shoulders, bookended by his wife and daughter, the four of them brown as mariners and wearing identical grins. It was her favorite photo of her family.

Elise studied it longer than mere politeness dictated. "You have a beautiful family," she said softly when she finally handed it back. If eyes were windows to the soul, Elise's were the floor-to-ceiling kind: You could see every emotion in their gray-green depths. Right now, the look in them was that of a woman longing for the child she might have had by now if her marriage hadn't ended. "All right," she said. "I'll think about it. But I'm not making any promises."

·　·　·

ELISE USED TO think that if you married for love only good would come of it. Her parents were living proof—they still held hands when they sat on the couch watching TV in the evenings, and after her dad had dragged her mom to a ball game or golf tournament, he always followed it up with something he knew she'd enjoy: an evening out at the Rainbow or a movie he wouldn't in a million years have chosen to see on his own (the kind that had him snoozing by the time it got to the part where Elise's mom was sniffling into her handkerchief). When Elise had fallen in love and gotten married, she had taken it for granted her marriage would be as solid and loving.

Dennis had all the makings for the perfect husband. He had the same small-town values as she did and revered God, country, and the Saint Louis Cardinals, in that order. He was thoughtful and attentive, as sentimental as he was passionate, and he made an effort with her family. The first Christmas she took him home to meet them, Dennis brought a suitcase full of gifts—a handsome coffee-table book for her parents, a box of fancy chocolates for each of her brothers and their wives, toys for her nieces and nephews. Before he popped the question, he made sure to get her father's blessing, though Elise, thirty-one at the time, had lived on her own since college.

Dennis fit in so well he might have been an Osgood himself. He was big, blond, and blue-eyed like her dad and brothers. He loved to tinker with car engines and, like Rob and Brett, had played football in college. And he treated Elise like a queen. The only thing they ever disagreed on was the wedding. Elise had her heart set on a church wedding, and Dennis lobbied for a simple ceremony before a justice of the peace, with just their families and close friends in attendance. "Why go to a lot of fuss?" he'd argued. "Wouldn't you rather be on the beach in Aruba than stressing out about seating arrangements?" In the end, he'd gotten his way. Not that it had mattered; on her wedding day, all she could see was her groom standing before her, his eyes shining with love.

And their passion didn't ebb once the honeymoon was over. A junior associate at his law firm, Dennis put in long hours at the office. But whenever he had to work late, he always arrived home with something he'd picked up for her along the way, to make up for it—flowers, a box of strawberries, the latest edition of *The New Yorker* or *Cosmopolitan* fresh off the press. On the rare occasion when she was the one who had to work late, she'd often as not arrive home to find candles lit and music playing softly on the stereo and Dennis at the ready with a bottle of massage oil.

He was insatiable in the bedroom. Elise would often smile, as they lay curled together after making love, thinking how lucky she was. Once, she'd told him, "I read in *Cosmo* that most married couples have sex only four or five times a month. Which makes us either incredibly horny or totally aberrant." She giggled, feeling a sense of abandon she'd never known with another man, though admittedly her experience was limited—she'd only had two other lovers before Dennis.

He chuckled. "Four or five times a month, huh? You know what I call that? Just getting started."

Five years into their marriage, he was assigned to a team handling an important case that had him flying out to L.A. every other week. The first few trips, he called home every night he was away to say he missed her. He'd list, in a throaty voice, all the ways he planned to make it up to her when he got home, or ask playfully what kind of underwear she had on. But as the months wore on, the calls became less frequent with each trip. There were nights when he didn't call at all, though he always had a perfectly good excuse—a meeting that ran over, a late dinner with a client—so she didn't worry; she simply chalked it up to the price of his being made junior partner.

Then one day, he phoned from L.A. to say he was taking a few days off, for a long weekend of R&R in Palm Desert "God knows I've earned it," he said, sounding so exhausted she didn't question it for an instant. And if she was the tiniest bit hurt he hadn't asked her to join him, she told herself it didn't mean he had fallen out of love with her. Even happily married couples needed time apart now and then. It was normal. It was *healthy*, in fact.

It didn't mean your husband was having an affair.

So Elise picked up the proverbial hammer to unwittingly pound the nails into her own coffin in saying, "Of course, sweetie. I'll miss you like mad, but I'll have Glenn to keep me company." Glenn Stokowski, a close friend and colleague of hers, was so mild-mannered not even a jealous husband would consider him a threat. "I'll see if he wants to go to the movies or something."

Incredibly, she didn't grow suspicious even when repeated calls to Dennis's number over the course of the next few days went straight to voicemail. She merely assumed, as he later confirmed, the resort he was at was in a remote place that was out of cell phone range. What possible reason would he have to cheat on her? They still had sex regularly, and if he wasn't quite as attentive as before it was only natural—they weren't newlyweds anymore—and didn't mean they had grown apart. "We're like a pair of swans," he had once told her. "We're mated for life."

The way she found out about the affair was so prosaic it made her cringe almost as much as the betrayal itself: lipstick. Not lipstick on his collar, a tube of lipstick wedged between the couch cushions, which she came across while vacuuming one day, several months later. At first, she'd merely wondered idly whose it was. They hadn't had company in a while—Dennis was always too busy or tired to have friends over for dinner, and unlike her parents' neighbors in Granstburg, New Yorkers weren't in the habit of dropping in unannounced. Then finally comprehension dawned, all the clues she'd ignored until now coming together, connecting in a hard punch to her solar plexus: *He's cheating on me.* The breath went out of her lungs, and she sank to the floor, where she lay curled in a ball, sobbing. The pain she felt was worse than any she'd ever known.

Elise half expected—half hoped even—Dennis would come up

with a plausible explanation when she confronted him. Instead, he broke down and confessed. There were the usual disclaimers: He hadn't meant for it to happen . . . it was only because he and Amanda, the team leader on the case that had them both flying out to L.A. every other week, were together so much of the time . . . and no, God no, they had never done it in his and Elise's bed, he wouldn't do that to Elise. As if it made the betrayal any less hurtful that he'd had the decency to screw his girlfriend on the couch instead. He begged her forgiveness, promising to break it off with Amanda. "It's *you* I love, not her," he wept. "Whatever you think of me right now, we can fix this."

"*You* might be able to fix this. I can't," she told him as she stood by the bed he claimed not to have desecrated (though how could she be sure?), watching him pack the suitcase she'd dragged from the closet, saving him the trouble. He thought he was only going away for a few days, but she had other ideas.

"I made a mistake," he said, tears rolling down his cheeks as he beseeched her, a pair of rolled-up dress socks in one hand and a canister of shaving cream in the other. He looked like a man packing for a trip from which there was no return (some part of him must have known, even then). "But if you can find a way to forgive me, I'll make it up to you, I swear. I'm still the same guy you married."

What Elise felt then was like the blue northers she recalled from childhood—storms that would roll in over the Great Plains like freight trains—as anger surged through her, ripping away the last, trembling blade of faith. "No, you're not," she told him. "The man I married would never have done this to me." With that, she walked out, leaving him to finish his packing . . . and begin his new life. Six months later, as soon as the ink was dry on their divorce papers, he married Amanda. Recently, Elise had heard they were expecting their first child.

Now, a year later, she pondered the strange request from Camille Harte. The irony was too rich: Elise, whose husband had cheated on her, was expected to play the part of the other woman in this new scenario.

Except it wouldn't be cheating. Camille had been quite clear about its being strictly platonic, at least in the beginning. Not that Elise was looking for love—she hadn't been on a date since her divorce and had no wish to ever again be in a position where a man could wound her the way Dennis had. In that sense, she was indeed the perfect candidate. And from Camille's description of him, her husband sounded like a devoted family man, so there'd be no unwanted overtures on his part. Still, every instinct told her to steer clear. Even if she wasn't going to be tempted to sneak off to a motel with another woman's husband, she didn't want the idea to so much as cross her mind even in rejecting it.

Nevertheless, her heart went out to Camille. How could she refuse the request of a dying woman? Maybe it wouldn't hurt just to meet Camille's family. Probably nothing would come of it, and then she could walk away with nothing to weigh on her conscience. She contemplated this as she rode the subway to work, the day after her lunch with Camille, and was still in a quandary when she reached the gated entrance to the school grounds. Making her way up the path to the main building, she passed mock cherry trees in bloom and flowerbeds ablaze with tulips and daffodils. Unlike the public schools, and most private schools, in Manhattan, Saint Luke's School, on Hudson Street, looked more like the elementary school in Grantsburg that she'd gone to as a child, its landscape dominated by trees and grass rather than concrete and asphalt. Normally, it soothed her, all that greenery, but today she was too lost in thought to take much notice.

Elise didn't realize she wasn't alone, as she entered the faculty lounge and made a beeline for the coffee machine, until she heard a familiar voice observe glumly, "So it's true." She turned to find her friend Glenn seated at the round Formica table, hunched over a steaming mug of tea.

"Oh, hey. I didn't see you. Is what true?" she asked as she poured herself a cup of coffee.

"I really am invisible to the opposite sex."

"Uh-oh. Does this have something to do with last night's date?"

"Yup. Another one bites the dust."

She sat down across from him. "As bad as the woman who turned out to be ten years older and eighty pounds heavier than in her photo and who moaned about her dead dog the whole time?"

"Worse. In fact, I think this was the worst one yet."

Elise found that hard to believe. Who could be worse than the dead-dog lady or the female executive who'd insisted they go Dutch treat—to Gramercy Tavern, no less—then when the check came, had sat back as if she expected Glenn to pay? Or the vegan who told him she couldn't see herself dating anyone who ate meat? Glenn's tales of woe about the women he'd met online were partly why Elise herself didn't date. Each week brought some new horror story.

"What was it this time?" she asked.

"She shot me down before we even got around to ordering drinks."

"That's it?"

"You had to be there. It was the *way* she did it."

"What did she say?"

"That she didn't think I was her type, and there was no point in either of us wasting our time."

"Ouch." Elise winced in sympathy.

"Actually, in a weird way she did me a favor," he went on in the same glum tone. "It forced me to take a good look at myself. Let's face it. I'm no Casanova. You know what I am? I'm Charlie Brown with the football. Which is why"—he straightened his shoulders, wearing a grim look of resolve—"I've decided it's time to throw in the towel. What's the point of putting myself out there if every time I either get shot down or end up being the bad guy?"

"I guess the point is to keep going until you find the right person," she replied cautiously.

"Frankly, I don't think she's out there."

"You won't know unless you keep looking."

"Isn't that a tad hypocritical?" He raised his eyebrows at her over the rim of his mug as he sipped his tea. She frowned, and he went on, "I seem to recall your telling me you'd rather walk over a bed of hot coals than put yourself out there again."

"That was when I was in the middle of a divorce."

"And how many dates have you been on since then? Oh, let's see . . . zero." He held up his hand, making a circle with his thumb and index finger. "Admit it, you're worse than I am. You won't even go out with perfectly reasonable-seeming guys who are into you and who don't obsess about dead dogs or try to get you to eat seitan."

"Okay, you've made your point. But at least I'm not wallowing in misery."

"No, just popcorn and DVDs." He smirked at her, reminding her of their standing Saturday-night date. Usually, they stayed in. They had dinner together at her place or his, then afterward they'd watch a movie on DVD, whatever had come in the mail that week from Netflix, which often made for an eclectic mix, since Glenn was into action pictures and Japanese anime, and her taste ran more toward the likes of *Sleepless in Seattle* and *Julie & Julia*. Elise didn't know how she'd have gotten through the past year without Glenn. He'd been more than just supportive; he'd been her entire support system, with her family and childhood friends so far away.

Elise reached across the table to give his hand a squeeze. "Just because I'm gun-shy, it doesn't mean you should give up. Anyway, don't forget, I found what I was looking for."

"Right. What's-his-name." Glenn refused to speak Dennis's name. It was his lone, small revenge against the man who'd hurt his dearest friend. "The guy who soured you on all other men."

"Except you," she said.

"That doesn't count—we're not dating."

Elise wondered why she and Glenn had never clicked romantically.

She didn't know if it was because they'd met while she was still married or because they were colleagues and she'd long ago made it a rule never to date a coworker, after she was fired from her first job, at the Dairy Queen in Grantsburg when she was in high school, because the assistant manager, who was also her boyfriend, decided to break up with her and thought it would be too awkward to continue to work together. It wasn't that she didn't find Glenn attractive or fun to be with. She smiled, remembering the time they'd gotten into a water pistol fight in the backyard of his parents' house, in Amagansett, that had ended with them tussling on the lawn, soaked to the skin and laughing like a pair of goons, while he attempted to wrest her pistol from her grip. Later that same day, they'd gone bowling, and she recalled thinking at the time how nice it was that she could do stuff like that with Glenn, stuff her more sophisticated friends would find boring or provincial.

Glenn's dismal track record with women was a mystery as well. She suspected it was partly because he wasn't exactly the stuff of fantasies: neither the bad boy with the day-old stubble and washboard abs, nor a slick, Master-of-the-Universe type who wore shirts with monogrammed French cuffs. Glenn was just . . . average. Average height and build, with a face neither handsome nor homely but somewhere in-between and hair the color of the brown corduroy jacket he had on. His eyes were his best feature—eyes the blue of a picture-postcard sky.

Elise didn't doubt he'd find love eventually. As for herself, she wasn't so sure. Maybe it was time she got out of her rut and tried something new. She took a sip of her coffee and made a face. "Ish. How can anyone drink this stuff? It could double as paint thinner." Normally, she stopped at the Starbucks on the way to work, but this morning she'd been running late. She hadn't slept well the night before—she couldn't stop thinking about Camille's proposal—and as a result had fallen back to sleep after shutting off her alarm when it went off at the usual ungodly hour.

"Want me to make you a cup of tea?" he offered.

She shook her head. "Thanks, but I should get to my classroom. I still have some papers to grade." She rose and walked over to the sink, dumping the remains of her coffee down the drain.

"You mean you didn't get to them last night?" She heard the surprise in his voice. Usually, she had her students' papers graded before her favorite TV shows came on in the evenings.

She kept her face averted as she rinsed out her mug. "I was busy."

"Oh, I get it. Hot date?" She turned to find him grinning at her.

"Very funny."

Glenn stood up, gathering his things, and together they exited the faculty lounge. Other faculty members waved to them as they strolled along the corridor on the way to their classrooms. Elise was cheered by the stir of activity and bright display of student paintings on the walls. Even Glenn was smiling. He paused outside her classroom and gave her a light tap on the forearm with the rolled-up papers in his hand. "Hey, you doing anything this weekend?" he asked.

"Why, what did you have in mind?"

"There's a Truffaut festival at Film Forum. We could catch whatever's playing, then go out for Chinese afterward."

"Sounds good, but I'm not sure what my plans are this weekend." It depended on the answer she gave Camille. She felt a fluttering in her belly at the thought. Briefly, she thought about confiding in Glenn, but he'd tell her she was crazy to even consider it. "I'll have to get back to you."

"You're not keeping something from me, are you?" He leaned in, his eyes dancing, and she smelled the peppermint tea on his breath. "Something involving a practicing member of the opposite sex?"

Elise opened her mouth to tell Glenn to stop being obnoxious, then thought better of it. "Of course not," she said, then flashed him a secretive smile before turning to let herself into her classroom.

CHAPTER EIGHT

"If you don't tell him, I will," Holly said as she made the turn onto Park Avenue. She was driving the "Juicemobile," which was what she called the OJ-era white Bronco she'd bought, used, so she could travel to flea markets outside the city in search of rock memorabilia. Camille sat in the passenger seat, hanging on for dear life even though she was strapped in, because her sister was a kamikaze behind the wheel.

They were on the way to the Waldorf Astoria hotel to meet their dad, who was in town for the annual golf tournament at his old club in Bronxville. They always had dinner with Larry, at Peacock Alley, the first night of his stay. Camille and Holly hadn't celebrated holidays with their dad since they were children, so it was what passed for tradition in the Harte family. Usually, Edward and the kids joined them, but this year Camille had thought it best she and Holly go alone. She didn't want her dad to know she was sick (with Larry, everything was on a need-to-know basis as far as she was concerned) and couldn't risk having her nine-year-old blurt it out. What she hadn't taken into consideration was her sister's big mouth.

"Don't you dare," she warned Holly.

"Well, someone has to, since you're obviously not going to."

Camille gave a sigh. She was tired and out of sorts from having spent the better part of the afternoon in the infusion suite at New

York–Presbyterian hooked to an IV, and in no mood to play make-believe, in pretending their dad gave a damn. "Can't you wait until after I'm dead?"

Either way, it wouldn't make a difference. Her father had never been there for her. Not after Brendan Garver broke her heart in eighth grade or when she was devastated after getting rejected by her top two picks when applying to colleges her senior year or even when she was at death's door the previous year. The most she could expect from him was a murmur of sympathy or consoling pat on the head. It wasn't that he didn't care, just that he didn't care enough. And half-baked love, she'd learned the hard way, was worse than no love at all, because it left you wanting more.

Holly shot her an admonishing look. She was dressed all in green—pale green pashmina shawl over an emerald wrap dress, green faux-crocodile sandal heels, and dangly jade earrings. No one else could have pulled off such an ensemble, but somehow Holly did. "Enough with the morbid talk," she chided. "I'm not ready to bury you just yet."

Camille sighed again. "Fine, if you stop making excuses for Dad. He was a shitty dad and you know it. And he's not much better as a grandfather. Kyra and Zach barely know him, for God's sake."

She stiffened and braced herself as her sister swung into the next lane, nearly clipping a black Escalade in doing so. "Okay, so maybe he could make more of an effort," Holly conceded, "but you don't exactly knock yourself out, either. How long has it been since you visited him—four, five years?"

"The last visit, the kids and I spent the whole time at the pool while he and Edward played golf. That, and hanging out with a bunch of people we didn't know. Not exactly my idea of fun."

"He did make a special trip to see you when you were in the hospital," Holly reminded her.

"Only out of a sense of duty, I'm sure." Camille wished her sister could see their father for what he was. Holly saw a whole cake where there were only crumbs and the bare minimum as an act of fatherly devotion.

Holly zipped through the intersection at Park and Fifty-Second as the light changed from yellow to red. "He's not as bad as you make him out to be. He's just not good at showing his emotions."

"There you go again, making excuses."

"Well, it's not like he's some loser dad!"

"No, and we weren't starved or beaten, either."

"Whatever happened to *forgive those who trespass against us?*"

"I'm not Catholic, and unless you converted without me knowing it, neither are you."

"My point is, you may not have many more opportunities," Holly said in a more subdued voice. "Do you want this to be like all the other times, with him making nice and you making him pay for his sins."

"What do you mean? I'm always perfectly polite."

"Yeah, when you're not acting like it's torture just to have to sit through a meal with him."

"That is so not true!" But even as Camille protested, she knew her sister was right: She didn't make it easier for their dad. On the other hand, any attempt to get close to Larry at this late date would seem forced. Maybe she should aim for the middle ground: general forgiveness of those who'd trespassed against her without naming any names.

"Is too," Holly said in a sing-song voice, like when they were eight and eleven.

"Okay, okay." Camille gave in. "I'll be on my best behavior. But in exchange, you have to promise not to say anything about me being sick. Seriously, Holl, I mean it." She gave her sister a stern look. "I don't want this to get maudlin." Not that there was much chance of that with Larry.

"Don't pregnancy hormones entitle me to a Kodak moment, at least?"

"Uh-uh. Nothing doing."

Now it was Holly's turn to sigh. "Fine. Have it your way."

Soon they were pulling into a parking garage a block from the Waldorf Astoria. Holly phoned their dad as they were leaving the garage, and he was there to meet them when they stepped through the revolving glass door of the hotel lobby minutes later. He broke into a wide grin when he saw them. "Ah, and who are these two lovely ladies? Don't tell me they're my daughters!" It was the same tired line with which he greeted them each time, and they chuckled dutifully.

The mingled scents of Old Spice and Mac Baren pipe tobacco reached through the years to grab Camille by the throat as she hugged her father. "Hi, Dad. You're looking good," she said.

It was true. At seventy-nine ("seventy-nine years young!") he was still in good shape, not an ounce of fat on him, and his face, although deeply lined, had retained its rugged contours. He had all his own teeth and a full head of hair—hair once blond and now the ivory of old piano keys. It was easy to see why he was the most sought-after man at Heritage Acres.

"So are you, baby, so are you," he said, as if he hadn't noticed how pale and drawn she was, which he probably hadn't. He turned to Holly. "And how's my newest grandchild? He kicking yet?"

"We're still taking bets on whether it's a he or a she. You in, Grandpa?" Holly said, hooking an arm through his as they strolled through the lobby to Peacock Alley, Camille bringing up the rear.

"How are the kids?" Larry asked Camille when they were seated.

"They're fine," she said, smoothing her napkin over her lap. "They send their love." Mindful of her promise to Holly, she made a conscious effort to strike an upbeat tone. "You should see Kyra—she's become quite the young lady. She's been after us to let her wear makeup to school, but so far we've been able to hold the line. And Zach"—she shook her head in mock despair—"we'll be shopping for his clothes in the men's department before long. He's shot up at least a foot since you last saw him."

"I'm sorry they couldn't make it tonight." Her father sounded genuinely disappointed. He was good at making all the right noises—she'd give him that. "I don't remember you and Holly having so much homework when you were in school, but I guess it's different nowadays."

How would you know, you were never around? Camille wanted to retort. But she held her tongue, not wanting to spoil the evening for her sister. She only replied, "It *is* a school night, Dad."

Larry seemed to accept this and moved on to another topic. "How's Edward? He still racking up those frequent flyer miles?" he inquired as he sipped the wine their waiter had just poured.

Camille felt a prickle of irritation. The only trips her husband made were when he visited his parents, in Milwaukee, or was flown in to speak at medical conferences, but trust Larry to make him sound like . . . well, like Larry. She replied with an edge in her voice, "As a matter of fact, he's home with the kids right now. We don't like leaving them unsupervised. But maybe that's another thing that's different than it was in your day."

"Dad, guess who I ran into the other day?" Holly shot her a warning look before launching into a shaggy-dog story involving some old crony of their dad's whom she'd randomly bumped into on the street. After that, they stuck to neutral topics. Camille spoke of the increasingly stiff competition in her business—there were more ads for matchmakers in *New York* magazine than for gentlemen's escorts these days. Larry recounted a recent moment of triumph on the golf course when he'd shot a hole-in-one. Holly told about the leather jacket once belonging to the Boss that had fetched a high price on eBay, money that would tide her over when the baby came. It seemed almost an afterthought when she casually mentioned that she'd been in touch with the baby's father.

"Curtis and I had a long talk, and he was really cool about it. He wants to be supportive, whatever I'm comfortable with. He even offered to send money, but I told him I have it covered," she said blithely.

This was news to Camille. Why hadn't Holly said something earlier? Trust her to bring it up now, with their dad. "Did he also offer to make an honest woman of you?" she asked in an arch tone.

"God, no!" Holly gave a mock shudder.

"Am I missing something?" Larry looked confused as his gaze traveled from Holly to Camille.

"I barely know the guy," Holly explained. "I don't see any reason to get married just because I happen to be knocked up. So if you were planning on going after him with a shotgun, Dad, there's no need."

He gave a wry chuckle. "Just because I'm old, it doesn't mean I'm old-fashioned. Honestly, you young people act like you invented sex. This may come as a shock, but your mother and I were hardly virgins when we married."

The sisters exchanged a look, and Holly nearly choked as she was swallowing a mouthful of the Pelligrino she was drinking in lieu of wine. She coughed and reached for her napkin, wheezing, "Too much information, Dad."

Larry's blue eyes twinkled beneath silver brows. "So let me get this straight. You can have a child out of wedlock, but I'm supposed to act as if you and your sister were brought by the stork?"

"Wow. And all this time I thought we came out of a cabbage patch," Holly quipped.

"The difference is," he went on, "your mom and I were in love."

"Oh, so now you're saying I'm a tramp?" Holly pretended to take insult.

Larry smiled indulgently, reaching over to pat her hand. "No, but then I stopped worrying about your moral fiber a long time ago, around the time you ran off with that head bumper."

"Head banger," Holly corrected at the mention of her ex-boyfriend Ronan Quist.

"Dad, why didn't you ever get married again?" Camille asked. Conversations with her father seldom got past the polite chitchat stage—discussing anything more personal than news, sports, and weather made him uncomfortable—so she seized the opportunity to delve a little deeper.

"Who would I have married?" he replied lightly.

"You certainly had your share of opportunities," she reminded him. Even before he moved to Fort Lauderdale and became the heartthrob of Heritage Acres, he'd had women flocking around him. "Louise, for one." A slight crease appeared between his brows at the mention of his former secretary-turned-mistress, but other than that no chinks appeared in his Teflon armor.

"No one could ever replace your mom," he said.

"Maybe not, but she wanted you to get married again. She told me so herself." *She was worried about what would become of Holly and me. She knew you too well. And she wasn't wrong.* Holly shot her another warning look, but she ignored it—the emotions she was normally able to keep contained had been bubbling to the surface, like runoff from a toxic waste dump, ever since she'd learned her cancer was back. She spoke with cold deliberateness. "Instead, you chose to honor her memory by abandoning your children."

He eyed her with reproach, but his voice was mild when he spoke. "Abandon? Don't you think that's too strong a word? Anyway, why dredge that up now? It's ancient history."

"Not for me, it isn't."

"Cam—" Holly started to interject, but Camille cut her off.

"And no, I don't think *abandon* is too strong a word. What else would you call leaving two kids to fend for themselves for weeks at a time?" she went on. "Sure, we had Rosa, but you know as well as I do, as far as childcare went she was just for show. God, Dad, I was only fourteen!" Now that she had a fourteen-year-old daughter of her own, her father's transgressions seemed even more egregious. "Holly had her big sister, at least. *I* was the one who calmed her when she had nightmares, who made sure she was dressed warmly before she went out and that she took her vitamins. I forged your signature on permission slips. I even had to lie to Grandma Agnes when she got suspicious because you were never there when she phoned—I was afraid we'd be sent to live with her. Though, in retrospect, we'd have been better off. Even foster care would have been better." She shot a glance at Holly, who sat perfectly still, wearing a stricken look.

Larry sighed, visibly annoyed now and maybe even a bit unsettled. But he replied in a purposefully even voice, what she thought of his cockpit voice, the one he must have used to calm passengers when there was turbulence in the air, "Really, Cam. Do we have to discuss this now? I'd prefer to just enjoy my meal if that's all right with you." As if he were used to such outbursts, though this was the first time she'd confronted him about his past actions.

Camille watched in disbelief as he sawed off a piece of his steak and popped it in his mouth, as though the subject were closed as far as he was concerned. It was the final straw; she felt something inside her snap. Her voice rose, and she was only dimly aware of other diners glancing their way. "It was easier for you, wasn't it, just to walk away? Easier than having to face up to your responsibilities."

He sighed and put his fork down. "I had a job to do," he said. "You know that."

"Wasn't it also your job to look after your children?"

"I couldn't be with you all the time," he said defensively.

"How about *some* of the time? We would have settled for that."

"Cam, I don't think . . ." Holly started to say.

Camille ignored her. The feelings she'd kept tamped down for so long continued to bubble up. "Did you honestly think you could do as you damn well pleased and *not* have us resent you?"

"Speak for yourself," Holly muttered.

"Deny it all you like, but I know the truth," Camille went on, her voice mounting to a tremulous pitch. She realized to her horror she sounded more than a little unhinged, but she couldn't stop herself. Her anger was an express train hurtling down the tracks. "You were a crap dad! There, I said it. And if you're looking for an apology, you're not getting one."

Camille braced herself for a blast of fury or at the very least a show of indignation. But strangely, her dad seemed more concerned than angered. He leaned in, placing a hand on her arm. She saw only worry in his eyes. "What is it, Cam? What's wrong? This isn't like you."

Just like that her anger drained away, tears rising in its place. "My cancer's back," she choked out.

For the longest time, he just sat there staring at her uncomprehendingly. When at last he spoke, he sounded deeply shaken, which surprised her—she hadn't expected him to get emotional, or maybe she'd only hoped he wouldn't, because black-and-white was easier than dealing with shades of gray. "Baby, I'm so sorry. For you to have to go through that again . . ." He shook his head, and then, true to form, forced a game smile and said, "But you beat it the last time. And with all the new drugs that have come along since then, I'm sure you'll—"

"It's too late for that," she cut him off.

The color drained from his face beneath his golfer's tan. "Are you telling me there's no hope?" Camille just sighed while Holly discreetly dabbed at her eyes. "There must be something that can be done," he said, his shoulders slumping. For the first time ever, he looked his age.

"I'm afraid not," she said. "But there is something *you* can do."

"Anything. You name it," he said eagerly. Camille pictured him reaching for his checkbook, his automatic reflex through the years whenever she or Holly had hit a rough patch. She supposed it was his way of showing he cared, but he would have to do better than that from now on.

"Be there for my kids," she told him.

⋄ ⋄ ⋄

AT WORK, CAMILLE referred all new business to Dara. She had neither the time nor energy to do more than tend to her existing clients. No one would blame her if she walked away altogether, but she needed the distraction work provided. It gave her a reason, other than her husband and children, to get out of bed each morning. She was like a farmer nurturing the seeds she'd planted. It gave her hope to see a budding romance blossom and kept her from being crushed under the weight of knowing there was no hope for her. She was bolstered when Laura Shapiro told her that David the professor had popped the question, when Sam Braverman took her advice and ditched his hairpiece, and when Alex Wilcox's date with Ellen Pratt, a smart hospital administrator his age—not the trophy wife the forty-two-year-old hedge fund manager had envisioned for himself—went so well he asked her to go away with him for the weekend.

There were two clients, however, who'd defied all her efforts thus far: Kat Fisher and Stephen Resler. So she was encouraged when she met with Stephen, the day after her ill-fated dinner with her dad, and learned his date with Carole Fellows, the thirty-seven-year-old attorney she'd fixed him up with, had been a success. "You were right about Carole," he told her over coffee at the Starbucks near his firm's Wall Street offices. "She's really something. Not to mention she's an even bigger Yankees fan than I am." He grinned. Stephen lived for the Yankees; he'd have sold his car if need be, he'd once joked, to pay for season tickets. "Not only that, she gets me, you know?"

Camille was pleased to hear it. "So, you weren't put off by her line of work?"

"Not at all," he said. "Jesus. She has stories that make my divorce seem like a walk in the park." Camille gave him a quizzical look and he admitted, "Yeah, we talked about it, but I wasn't the one who brought it up. She asked me, so I told her. And you know what?" His blue eyes sparkled. "It wasn't a turnoff for her. In fact, she told me she wished she'd known me back then. She said if she'd been my divorce lawyer, she'd have made damn sure I didn't get screwed."

Camille smiled. "So I guess this means you'd go out with her again."

"Already on it. I'm taking her to the ball game on Saturday. Then we'll see who's the biggest Yankees fan." He chuckled as he sipped his coffee, and she thought, *He made it to first base, at least.*

"I have a good feeling about this," she told him.

He shrugged, his optimism all at once giving way to caution. "Yeah, well, it's too soon to say."

"Just be careful to—"

"I know, I know," he said. "Keep my mouth shut about my ex."

Camille was smiling as they parted ways. It looked as if the hard-charging, bullheaded Stephen Resler had finally met his match. Which reminded her: She still hadn't heard back from Elise. She automatically reached for her cell phone. But no, she had to wait, let Elise come to her. It was a tough decision, and tough decisions weren't made overnight. Nevertheless, she fretted the whole way back to her office. What would she do if Elise's answer was no? It wasn't as if she had a Plan B. The deeply kind, down-to-earth school-teacher was the only person she knew who ticked all the boxes.

Plenty of women would be interested in a handsome, well-heeled widower, but how many would be willing to take on a ready-made family or have the patience to wait until he was ready to love again? Edward, left to his own devices, might pick the wrong person, which would be worse than if he ended up alone. If she couldn't always be there, she wanted her children to always know a mother's love. Elise would be a loving stepmother—that much she was certain of.

DARA WAS SIFTING through the stack of applications that had arrived in that day's mail when Camille arrived back at the office. Dara held up one of the headshots. "What do you think?"

"She's pretty," Camille said, giving it a cursory glance.

"Um. You don't think she's a tad . . . masculine?"

Camille hung up her coat and sat down at her desk. "Are you going somewhere with this?"

"Yeah." Dara thrust the photo out so she could get a closer look. "It's a man. In drag."

"Oh." Camille could see now what should've been obvious at first glance: the strong jaw and neck, the stubbled cheeks beneath a thick layer of foundation. She shrugged. "Well, it takes all kinds. I'm sure he'll find someone." If not through the Harte to Heart Agency, then perhaps the drag-queen scene.

"It's not him I'm worried about, it's you," said Dara, swinging a stiletto-heeled boot around as she crossed her legs. Her brow was furrowed beneath her straight-cut black bangs. "In the old days, you'd have spotted that right away. You're working too hard. You need to take some time off."

"I'm fine," Camille replied impatiently.

"No one said you had to die with your boots on."

"I'm not dead yet, so back off."

"Whatever you say, Boss," Dara said smartly, swiveling her chair around to face her desk.

"I'm not your boss anymore," Camille reminded her, a smile edging its way onto her face. She'd recently promoted Dara from assistant to partner, with an eye toward her taking the helm one day. "Look, I hear you, and I promise as soon as I—" The phone rang before she could finish the sentence.

It was Kat Fisher.

"Camille? I'm glad I caught you."

Camille said brightly, "Well, you beat me to it. I was going to call you. I just spoke with Gabriel Noonan, and he's eager to meet you." More like smitten the instant he'd laid eyes on Kat's headshot. When Kat didn't react, she prompted, "The guy I was telling you about? The art dealer?"

"Great." Kat sounded distracted. "But that's not what I wanted to talk to you about. I'm having some people over for dinner this Saturday and was hoping you and your husband could come."

Camille was about to decline the invitation but thought better of it. Dara was right; she *had* been working too hard, and an evening out in a relaxed atmosphere among fun, interesting people might be just what the doctor ordered. "Sounds good, but I'll have to check with Edward."

"Tell him I refuse to take no for an answer," Kat said playfully. "I need something to remind me of what I'm playing for, and if that handsome husband of yours can't do it, no one can."

CHAPTER NINE

"What's your hurry? Have another drink," Kat said after she'd ushered out the last of the other guests.

Edward had risen to his feet, and now he glanced at his watch. He wondered how he'd gotten roped into going to this dinner party in the first place. When Camille had bailed at the last minute, saying she wasn't feeling well, and then had urged him to go without her so as not to disappoint their hostess, he should have put his foot down. It wasn't until Kat greeted him at the door and he recognized her as the striking woman who'd caught his eye at the meet-and-greet that he understood what this was: a setup. Kat Fisher, for all intents and purposes, was his "date." Sickened by the realization, it had been all he could do to act normal with Kat and her other guests, an effort that had left him drained.

"I really should go," he said, smiling. "It's late."

"Not that late," she cajoled, putting a hand on his arm. "Just one more drink. I've barely had a chance to talk to you all evening, the way my friend Barbara had you corralled." Already, he'd forgotten which one Barbara was. The attractive blond stylist or the pudgy brunette stock analyst?

Kat, on the other hand, was the kind of woman you wouldn't forget. Especially in the form-fitting, midnight-blue cocktail dress she had on. She was a real stunner, he had to admit, with her willowy build and exotic features—the product of a German father and Vietnamese mother, he'd learned over supper. Intelligent, too, with the kind of smarts they don't teach in college. Camille had chosen well, he thought bitterly. No man in his right mind would reject what Kat had to offer. Though, at present, he could hardly be described as a man in his right mind.

"Well, I suppose I could stay a few more minutes," he relented. He didn't want to be rude. This had to be awkward for Kat, too, and she was trying her best. Nothing would come of it, but he didn't want to hurt her feelings. Still, he thought longingly of his easy chair at home as he sank onto the low-slung sofa in Kat's sleekly appointed living room, which was more stylish than comfortable.

It had been a rough week. One of his favorite patients, sweet old Mrs. Coleman, who was in the early stages of Alzheimer's, had showed up twice thinking she had an appointment when she didn't. Then there had been the run-in with Howard Brody, a petty dictator in administration, who had given him grief about budget overruns. To cap it off, his son had thrown a tantrum as he was getting ready to leave tonight: Zach was bent out of shape because his Nintendo was off-limits for the time being, a consequence of poor grades on his last report card.

And always, like a splinter in his heart, there was the thought of Camille.

Forty-five minutes later he was still ensconced on the sofa in Kat's condo on the Upper East Side. He'd lost track of time with his second nightcap and Kat was such good company, with her stories about her travels and various adventures in the news business, he found he was no longer in a hurry to leave.

It didn't hurt, either, that she seemed to find him equally fascinating. Gone were the days when Camille had hung on his every word. His wife didn't even want him around, apparently. Hurt and resentment rose, hot and thick, in his throat. How could she have blindsided him like this? He had agreed to go along with her preposterous plan, admittedly more to humor her than anything, but still. Why couldn't she, at least, have been honest about Kat?

". . . and poor Daniel. I invited him because I thought it would cheer him up," Kat was saying. Edward realized his mind had wandered and he brought his attention back to her. "He and his boyfriend, Keith, just broke up. Which is awkward, because Keith is also a friend of mine, so I couldn't invite them both." She reached for the wine bottle on the coffee table and offered it to Edward, who shook his head, before refilling her glass. "God. Don't you hate when you have to choose?"

Edward murmured in sympathy.

Kat sighed and went on, "Story of my life: My closest friends are all gay. No wonder I'm still single." She sat next to him on the sofa, her bare feet tucked under her as she sipped her wine.

"I find it hard to believe that's the only reason you haven't found a husband," he replied gallantly. He wasn't just trying to make her feel better, it also happened to be true: Kat was beautiful and accomplished, with much to offer.

"Finding one isn't a problem. It's finding the right one."

"So, what is it you look for in a man?" he asked.

"For starters, someone who isn't threatened by the fact that other men find me attractive," she replied frankly. "I had this one boyfriend, in college, who was so jealous he once threw a punch at this other guy just for talking to me at a party." She grimaced at the memory. "Though I'm not sure which is worse, that or the ones who like showing me off like I'm some prize they won."

"You can't blame a guy for wanting to show off a beautiful woman," he said in defense of his gender.

"Yes, but a woman wants to be appreciated for more than just her looks."

"Well, I don't think you have anything to worry about on that score. Your accomplishments speak for themselves."

She smiled at him, her smoky-green eyes shining in the soft

THE REPLACEMENT WIFE · 147

glow of the candles that provided the room's only light. "Spoken like a true gentleman." She set her wineglass down on the coffee table and angled her body so she was all but leaning against him. "Frankly, if I found someone like you I'd be willing to bend the rules," she said, with a directness he'd come to expect from her. He felt a rippling sensation, low in his belly, that was part unease and part excitement. "When I saw you at the meet-and-greet, naturally I thought you were there for the same reason I was. I couldn't believe it when Camille told me who you were. I finally come across a guy who I could actually see myself with, and he turns out to be my matchmaker's husband. If it weren't so funny, it'd be pathetic."

Edward was getting a clearer picture now. Camille, after discovering Kat Fisher had her eye on him, had decided to run with it. Was the plan hatched then and there or had it taken a few days to formulate? Either way, here they were, alone together, and the implication was clear: Kat was his for the taking. Was that secretly part of the plan, too? Was he supposed to make love to her?

Heat climbed into his face at the thought. He was pondering how to politely extricate himself before the situation grew any stickier when Kat closed the few inches of space between them, winding her arms around his neck, her breasts, spilling from the low neckline of her dress, pressing into him. At first, he was too startled to pull away; then he realized to his dismay he felt no inclination to do so. She was so beautiful, and it had been so long . . .

It wasn't until she tilted her head toward his with the look of someone waiting to be kissed that he was jolted to his senses. He quickly disentangled himself and stood up. "Trust me, this isn't a good idea. I apologize if I gave you the wrong impression," he added, ever the gentleman.

Belatedly, Kat seemed to come to her senses as well. A chastened look came over her face and she sat up straight, tugging at the hem of her dress. "Honestly, I never intended—" She gulped, red stripes outlining the curves of her cheekbones. "You must think I'm a horrible person."

"No, nothing of the sort," Edward hastened to assure her. If anyone was at fault, it was Camille. Maybe she hadn't meant for it to happen, but this was what came of playing with fire.

"I adore your wife. I just thought . . ." Kat bit down on her lower lip, her eyes welling with tears. "I don't know what I was thinking. But that's me: the girl who's got it all but who can't seem to get it together. Shit, I shouldn't have had so much to drink. Red wine always does this to me." She bowed her head and began to weep. Edward fought the impulse to flee and sank back down on the sofa. He couldn't just abandon her when she was so upset. This wasn't her fault.

He patted her on the back in an awkward attempt to comfort her. "We both had too much to drink," he said, speaking in a soothing tone. "Let's pretend it never happened, all right?"

Kat lifted her head to flash him a teary smile. "You're a good man, Edward. Why can't I find someone like you?"

"You will," he said.

She followed him to the door, where she planted a demure kiss on his cheek. "Friends?"

"Friends," he said, though he knew he wouldn't see her again if he could help it. Too dangerous.

Edward felt sick inside as he rode down in the elevator. All those years ago on his wedding day, he couldn't imagined it would come to this: that one day he'd be slipping away from another woman's apartment, late at night, with a guilty conscience. *I did nothing wrong*, he told himself. But he'd been tempted, if only for a moment. And sometimes a moment was all it took.

Outside, he paused as he was heading for the corner to hail a cab. Suddenly, he couldn't bear the prospect of going home and having to face his wife after what had just happened. Better he stay away until he was sure she'd gone to bed, and then they could talk in the morning when he was less likely to say something he'd regret. What he needed right now, he realized, was a friend. Out of the blue, he thought of the caterer from the meet-and-greet. Angie. He remembered how comfortable he'd felt with her, and before he knew it, he was fishing her card from his wallet, which thankfully he'd saved. He punched in her number on his cell phone, and she picked up after three rings.

"Edward. What's up?" she said cheerfully, sounding not at all surprised to hear from him. He might have been an old friend checking in. "Don't tell me. You're at a party and need rescuing."

"Something like that," he said, wincing anew at the thought of Kat. "I hope I'm not calling at a bad time." She'd mentioned that she worked late hours, but it was nearly midnight.

"Not at all. I just got off work. I'm headed out for a bite to eat. Care to join me?"

"Sure, why not?" he said, glad for the invitation.

"I hope you like sushi."

"Just what I'm in the mood for." He realized suddenly he was starving. His stomach had been in knots when he was at Kat's, so he had eaten only enough of the meal she'd served to be polite.

He hailed a cab and ten minutes later he was at the restaurant, at East Sixty-First and First. He spotted Angie at the blond-wood sushi bar as he pushed his way in the door. Seated alongside her were two Hispanic men, one with a scruffy beard and the other covered in tattoos, whom she seemed to know from the way they were inter-acting. "This is where a lot of chefs hang out," she explained after she'd introduced him to her friends, Miguel and Julio. "Best sushi in the city and it's open until three a.m.—the shank of the evening in our line of work. Have a seat. The guys were just leaving." She waved good-bye to Miguel and Julio as they headed off.

"Do you always dine this late?" he asked as he sat down next to her.

"Only when I'm working a gig. Usually, by the time I knock off, I'm starved. One of the ironies of my profession—you're constantly surrounded by food, but there's no time to even nibble. You won't need that," she told him, plucking the menu from his hand as he was picking it up. She explained that ordering from the menu in a sushi restaurant was strictly for amateurs.

"I see. So all these years I've been going about it all wrong?"

"You and everyone else, unless you're a serious foodie. For us chefs, it's basic 101."

"So, how do we do this?"

In response, she signaled to one of the chefs, a rather austere-looking Japanese man wearing spotless chef's whites, who broke into a smile and hurried over. She ordered two pieces of tuna sashimi.

"Is that all we're having?" Edward asked.

"No, but you don't want it to look like you don't know what you're doing. It's like with wine, you taste first before you have them pour you a glass." When the order arrived, he watched her delicately tweeze one of the glistening pink oblongs with her chopsticks and pop it in her mouth. She chewed thoughtfully under the chef's watchful gaze, then nodded to him, indicating it met with her satisfaction. Edward followed suit, though he wasn't as nimble with his chopsticks.

Angie ordered *omakase*—chef's choice—and soon small, impeccably prepared dishes began arriving, one after another. Petite as she was, she matched Edward bite for bite. He found her enjoyment of the food as refreshing as he did Angie herself. Though he squirmed a little when she asked lightly what a family man like him was doing out so late on a Saturday night without his wife.

"Camille and I were invited to a dinner party," he explained. "But at the last minute, she wasn't feeling well, so I went without her. She insisted. She didn't want the hostess to be disappointed by us both being a no-show." *Or ruin any chance of said hostess becoming my future wife,* he thought dismally, struck anew by the bizarreness of the situation he was in.

"Must've been some party," Angie said, eyeing his plate, which was scraped clean of the last of the dozen small courses. "Was the food bad, or was it the company that put you off your feed?"

"Neither. I had a nice time," he said in a flat voice.

Angie's ponytail had wandered onto her shoulder, and now she pushed it back as she cocked her head to study him, those dark Fellini eyes of hers seeming to see right through him. "If you don't want to talk about it, that's cool. We can just hang out. But for the record, I'm a good listener."

"Trust me, you don't want to know," he replied dolefully.

"Try me."

His defenses were down and there was something about Angie that made him want to confide in her. Before he knew it he was telling her about his wife's dying wish and his "date," if that's what it was, with Kat Fisher, leaving out only the part about Kat coming on to him—the quicker he put that out of his mind the better. Angie didn't bat an eye, though it must have seemed as bizarre to her as it did to him. "It's only because she wants what's best for me and the kids," he defended Camille, in case Angie had gotten the wrong impression.

She nodded slowly. "Understandable."

"She grew up without a mom, and she's afraid the same thing will happen to our kids."

"So she's doing this for the kids?"

Edward sighed and shook his head. "No, she worries about me, too. She thinks I'm in danger of becoming a crusty old widower. Loveless and probably friendless. Oh, and a workaholic, though that wouldn't be much of a stretch." He refilled both their sake cups. His head felt fuzzy from all the alcohol he'd consumed tonight and he realized he was ever so slightly drunk.

"You don't sound like you're too keen on the alternative," she observed.

"Having her pick out my next wife? Oh, I'm thrilled. Isn't what every husband wants?"

She regarded him curiously. "Why did you agree to it, if you don't mind my asking?"

"She's dying." Edward grimaced as he spoke; saying the words made it more real. He stared bleakly into the cloudy depths of his sake cup before lifting it to his lips. "It's what she wants."

"And what do *you* want?"

"Does it matter?"

"Of course it matters."

His fingers tightened around the cup. "What I want is to hold on to what I've got."

She nodded, eyeing him with sympathy. "Look, I'm no shrink," she said. "But I know one thing: When you go against your principles, it usually backfires. I bent over backwards with my former boyfriends trying to please them, and all it did was drive them away. Because I wasn't the person they fell in love with; I wasn't being true to myself. So now I live alone and work weird hours and eat sushi at one a.m., and any guy who has a problem with that can take a flying fuck."

"Those former boyfriends of yours are jerks. They don't know what they're missing," he said, feeling a rush of indignation on her behalf. "Any man would be lucky to have you as a wife."

She blushed and looked down. "Oh, I don't know about that. I'm not exactly wife material."

"Maybe you just haven't found the right person."

Angie fiddled with the wrapper from her chopsticks, folding it into neat accordion pleats. He thought how pretty she was; not a knockout like Kat, but there was something so appealing about her. She was tough on the outside but had a kindness that manifested itself even in small ways, like when she'd brushed away the stray grains of rice and bits of dropped food at the end of the meal, folding it into her napkin so their server wouldn't have to clean up after them. "Maybe," she said.

He paid the bill, and they went outside. It was nearly two a.m. but strangely he didn't feel the least bit tired. As they lingered on the sidewalk saying their good-byes, she told him about the cooking class she taught at the Bedford-Stuyvesant Youth Center, where she volunteered one night a week. "You should come by sometime and meet my kids," she said. "Some of them have never met a doctor outside the ER. It'd do them good to see there are other career options besides the fast food industry or a life of crime. Though I shudder to think of any of them wielding a scalpel. They're bad enough with kitchen knives. They can be a bit, um, boisterous at times," she explained, and he chuckled at the image of petite Angie riding herd on a bunch of rowdy teenagers.

"Sounds like fun," he said.

"You doing anything this coming Wednesday?"

"Not that I know of. What time?"

"Six to eight. And you wouldn't have to do anything except show up. That is," she said with a sly grin, "unless you want to go *mano a mano* with me, show off those knife skills."

He grinned in return. "Count me in, in that case." Camille might have plans for that night, but to hell with it. He'd gone along with tonight's plan and look where it had gotten him. At least with Angie, he didn't have to worry about her trying to seduce him—she was like a little sister. Not that Camille needed to know about Angie. She might get the wrong idea. Though, really, she wasn't exactly in a position to hurl accusations after the dirty trick she'd pulled on him tonight, with Kat. He handed Angie his business card. "Email me the details."

Seconds later, Angie was climbing into the back of a cab. She paused to look up at him as she was pulling the door shut, a petite figure in a faded Che Guevara T-shirt and holey jeans, her dark hair trailing in wisps about her freckled face where it had escaped her ponytail. "See you next week," she said, adding with an impish smile, "Oh, and Edward? Try and stay out of trouble until then."

CHAPTER TEN

"Daarel, I said to *debone* the chicken, not massacre it." Angie shook her head in despair at the mangled lump on the boy's cutting board, which bore only a vague resemblance to a chicken breast.

"Yeah, like you be boning Tamika," snickered Raul, in the next station.

Angie cast Raul a stern look. "That's enough out of you, Romeo."

He adopted an air of innocence. "Me? I ain't the one got a group rate at Planned Parenthood."

The others cracked up, and Angie had to struggle to keep a straight face. This was generally how it went the evenings she taught her cooking class: One of her students would make a wisecrack, and pretty soon they were all in on it, tossing good-natured insults back and forth like popcorn at a kiddie matinee. She wouldn't have it any other way, though. She adored these kids, and in their own smart-mouthed and occasionally riotous way, they *were* making an effort. Take Raul, for instance. He was the class clown, but his home life was no laughing matter. His mom was living on the streets and his dad in Nicaragua. The one time Angie had paid him a visit, after he'd failed to show up for class two times in a row, she'd found him caring for his ailing grandmother. Seeing how sweet he was with his *abuelita* and how little they had, it had been all she could do not to cry. But they didn't want her pity, she knew, so she stayed and cooked them dinner instead.

Before they'd been introduced to the pleasures of freshly prepared meals, her kids had known only the kind that came out of a
box or can or from fast-food joints, with the exception of those, like
Julio, who lived in homes where the parents still cooked the foods of
their native lands. They all had one thing in common, though: They
were considered "at risk." The boys of ending up in a gang or prison
and the girls, except for Tamika, a straight-A student who was looking to better herself, of getting knocked up and having to drop out
of school. Even with a strong hand to guide them, some would slip
between the cracks, Angie knew. *Not on my watch, though.*

She inspected the other students' efforts, which ranged from
decent to downright disastrous. They were in the cafeteria at the
youth center, where several tables had been placed end to end and
divided into stations with masking tape, each with its own cutting board, utensils, and hot plate. When she was done making the
rounds, she called the class to attention. "Okay, not a bad start, but
you're going to have to do better than that to impress our guest."
Earlier, she'd told them about tonight's "special guest," due to arrive
any minute, which had caused them to perk up. The only other time
they'd had a guest was when Angie's mom came—she showed them
how to make spaghetti and meatballs. "Also, I want you guys to be
on your best behavior. I don't want him thinking you're a bunch of
hooligans," she added in a sterner voice.

"Is that, like, a real word?" asked D'Enice, a generously proportioned girl who looked far more mature than her sixteen years. She
resembled her mother, who'd been sixteen when she'd had D'Enice.
The first time Angie had encountered the mom, she'd mistaken her
for an older sister.

"Look it up. It's in the dictionary under your name!" yelled
skinny Raul.

"Yo, Miss D. This dude, he yo' *man*?" called a loud voice. She
turned to see Julio smirking at her. A thickset boy with spiky brown
hair and big eyes that were all innocence, he could dismantle a car

faster than she could a rack of lamb, with the police record to show for it. His miscreant days had ended when he'd found Jesus, as evidenced by the gold crucifix around his neck and Jesus tattoo on his arm, but he hadn't lost the knack for stirring up other kinds of trouble.

"Miss D got a boooyfriend," chanted Chandra and D'Enice.

Angie felt her cheeks warm, but she kept her tone light. "If you guys would stop running your mouths and pay attention, you might actually learn something. Now, listen up, because I'm going to show you a really cool trick." She picked up her knife and made a deep cut down the center of her neatly deboned breast, and then folded open the two halves. "See, just like opening a book."

"That's, like, if you actually know how to crack a book," interjected Tamika, casting a pointed look at Daarel. She was determined to be the first in her family to go to college, a goal that wasn't shared by her boyfriend. Lately, Daarel had been talking about dropping out of school. That is, if he didn't flunk out first. Tamika alternated between browbeating him and tutoring him in her spare time. Recently, she'd given him an ultimatum: If he didn't get serious about his schoolwork, she had no further use for him. Angie hadn't given up hope on Daarel, though. He wasn't lazy or stupid; he just needed to find something he was good at. She was encouraged by the interest he'd shown in cooking. At the end of last week's class, when his vegetable stir-fry was deemed the best of the bunch, he'd looked as proud as if he'd gotten into Harvard.

It was hard to believe, looking at him, that he was only seventeen. Daarel, built like a Sub-Zero, with a deep rumble of a voice, could probably get into any nightclub without being carded. He'd met his match in Tamika, though. Tall and regal, with cheekbones that could cut glass and eyes a startling blue against her coffee-with-milk skin, she took no shit from anyone, least of all him. When Daarel flashed her a grin and said, "Shut yo' mouth, bitch," she flipped him the bird.

"Guys, show some respect," Angie scolded. She knew there was no real malice in it, but still . . .

"Yes, Miss D," they chorused in unison.

Smart-asses, she thought affectionately. "Okay, now we sear this puppy to lock in the juices and get a nice brown crust." She drizzled oil into the skillet on her hot plate. "You want to get the oil plenty hot, and remember to stay out of the way when it starts to sizzle. You don't want to get burned." She was interrupted when someone's cell phone erupted, to the tone of Cee Lo Green's "Forget You." Chandra retrieved the offending item from her purse, scowling at the screen.

"It's Ronald," she muttered.

Her friend D'Enice observed indignantly, "Guess he not gettin' enough from that ho Marisol." The week before, Chandra's boyfriend, Ronald, had cheated on her with another girl in their class, and they'd broken up over it. Now it seemed he was trying to get back with Chandra.

Chandra, a skinny girl with crooked teeth and hair cut in an asymmetrical wedge, soaked up the sympathy when Tre'Shawn looped an arm around her shoulders and said, "That fat-ass bitch got nothin' on you."

Big and muscular, Tre'Shawn could match Daarel pound for pound, but he was more teddy bear than testosterone-driven. A few weeks ago, he'd shown up for class with a bunch of slightly wilted flowers. After thrusting them into Angie's hand, he'd muttered in an embarrassed voice that they were from his parents' deli and would've been thrown out otherwise, then had scowled at her as if daring her to make something of it. She'd appreciated the gesture nonetheless.

"Yeah, but us fat-ass bitches know how to strut our stuff," said D'Enice, waggling her own considerable behind.

Everyone cracked up, and once again Angie had to restrain herself to keep from joining in. She constantly toed the line between friend and authority figure. Though with these kids, you always knew where you stood. There might be a concealed weapon or two, but nothing else was hidden. Here, in the neighborhood known as Bed-Stuy, a world away from the safe, civilized one she'd go home to, just over the bridge but on the other side of the rainbow, life was lived out loud.

Just then, the door to the cafeteria swung open. Eight pairs of eyes—nine including Angie's—fixed on the tall, dark-haired man who walked in. Edward, wearing jeans and a navy blazer over an open-collared white shirt as crisp as an envelope containing an invitation to some exclusive event, paused and looked around, his amber eyes crinkling in a smile as he took in the circle of openly staring faces. In a voice that resonated in the hush that had fallen, broken only by the sizzling in Angie's skillet, he said, "Something sure smells good, so I must be in the right place."

"Come on in, the party's just getting started," Angie called to him. Her heart was racing, and she felt short of breath all of a sudden. "Guys, this is Dr. Constantin," she introduced him, gratified to see that the kids were on their best behavior. If anything, they were too polite, shy almost. They hadn't been that way with Angie's mom—no one could be shy with Loretta—but Edward, with his princely bearing, was like a movie star appearing in their midst. He was so friendly and low-key, though, he soon had them clustered around him, peppering him with questions.

"Do you, like, cut people open and stuff?" Raul wanted to know.

"I'm not that kind of doctor," Edward told him. "And I'm happy to report a patient has never been lost on my watch." He looked down at the mangled chicken breast on Raul's cutting board, and shook his head sorrowfully. "Which is more than I can say for that poor fellow."

The remark was met with guffaws and some good-natured jostling of Raul. D'Enice wanted to know if the hospital Edward worked at was like the one on *Grey's Anatomy,* where everyone was always "hooking up." Edward laughed and told her, no, it wasn't as steamy as all that.

Listening to him, Angie noticed that the temperature in the room seemed to have gone up, and a moment later, she caught a whiff of something burning. With a quick downward glance, she saw it wasn't her imagination—her skillet was smoking. She grabbed a dishtowel and wrapped it around the handle, snatching the skillet off the hot plate, while the class looked on in amusement as if they knew what had had her so distracted.

"Miss D, you don't watch out, you gon get *burned*," teased Jermaine. At fifteen, he was the youngest of the bunch and small for his age, but he aped the sass and swagger of the older kids.

All too true, thought Angie, casting a surreptitious glance at Edward out of the corner of her eye. She needed to watch out in more ways than one. When he came over and asked if there was anything he could do to help, she tossed him an apron along with a challenge. "Okay, Big Shot. Time to put your money where your mouth is and show us some of those knife skills."

He grinned and went to work deboning a chicken breast while she supervised the students as they butterflied and then pan-seared their earlier efforts, with varying degrees of success. Finally, when they were ready to go into the oven, she placed all the breasts on a baking sheet, each one speared with a different colored toothpick to mark its ownership. While they finished cooking, she demonstrated the making of the sauce. She stirred white wine and broth into the combined chicken juices, and when the liquids were reduced by half, threw in a few pats of butter along with some salt and pepper and a handful of chopped herbs. She'd chosen easy side dishes—pan-fried potatoes and sautéed snow peas—which the kids would have no difficulty mastering. When everything was ready and the table cleared, they sat down to enjoy the fruits of their labor.

Tonight, though, the kids seemed more interested in their guest than in the food. Tamika quizzed Edward about colleges, which ones he thought had the best premed programs, and the boys wanted to know what it was like to dissect a cadaver. D'Enice and Chandra teased him about his knife skills, which were less impressive when it came to deboning than, one would hope, in making surgical cuts. When the time came, they seemed sorry to see him go. It was the most excitement they'd had since Raul had set a dishtowel on fire, triggering the smoke alarms and thus summoning a crew of firefighters.

Together, Edward and Angie walked to the subway after seeing the kids off. "Thanks for coming. It meant a lot to them," she said as they strolled along the sidewalk. *And to me,* she added silently.

"My pleasure," he said. "I don't remember when I last had so much fun." He wasn't just being polite, she could tell; he sounded as if he meant it. The knowledge warmed her.

"You're a natural. You had them eating out of your hand."

"They're good kids."

"Though not always so well behaved," she said. "Don't get me wrong—I adore them, but there are times I could happily wring their necks. They remind me of the thugs I used to work with when I was a line cook, so they should do okay if they decide to go into my profession." Her tone turned serious. "They don't have it easy, though. Most of them come from broken homes and Tre'Shawn's and Daarel's dads are doing time. It's a wonder none are in gangs or on drugs or have kids of their own. So far," she was careful to add. "I always say a little prayer each time that they'll show up."

They turned the corner onto Bedford Avenue, and Angie took note of the brownstones lining the block on either side, most in various stages of disrepair. The neighborhood was slowly becoming gentrified; everywhere she looked she saw evidence of it—scaffolding erected around a building, a trendy shop or restaurant sprinkled here and there among the tired-looking storefronts—but it still wasn't entirely safe to walk the streets alone after dark. Usually one of the bigger boys, Tre'Shawn or Daarel, escorted her to the subway station.

"You're making a difference, that's what matters," Edward said. Angie hoped so, but she knew there was a fine line between doing good and being a do-gooder. Her kids might be at a disadvantage in some ways, but they had a lot to offer; she got as much from them as she gave. Also, she was no saint, far from it. Her acute awareness of the man walking alongside her—make that *married* man—was testament to that fact; it was an effort to keep her hand from "accidentally" brushing up against his. "I just wish I could do more," she replied. "I only have them a couple of hours each week."

"Have you thought about doing it full-time? Teaching, I mean."

"What, and trade working insane hours just to break even for a steady job with benefits? Besides, what do you think finances this little operation? The center is barely hanging on, and with the economy in the toilet, donations are hard to come by. I pay for supplies out of my own pocket, and it doesn't come cheap." Some of the parents were out of work, she explained, so she always made extra to send home with the kids. "I'll never be rich, but I wouldn't have it any other way."

"Money isn't everything," he agreed.

"No, but according to my mom, you haven't made it, either, until you have a ring on your finger and have produced at least one child, so I guess I come up short on both counts."

"There's still time for that," he said, smiling.

"I'm not as young as you think. I'll be thirty-nine next week," she informed him. "By the Italian-American scale, which is measured in dog years, that makes me practically a senior citizen."

She thought of the birthday party her mom was planning. It was with a heavy sense of obligation that she faced each year's, knowing Loretta would be offended were she to say no to the cake and balloons and cast of thousands. If Angie never again had to hear her family sing "Happy Birthday" while she blew out the candles on the cake, knowing, as she made her wish, that her mom was wishing for something entirely different, it would be fine by her.

Yet her pulse quickened and a small jolt of electricity shot through her when Edward said, with a twinkle in his eye, "Well, you're never too old to celebrate a birthday. What do you say I buy you a drink?" It was all perfectly innocent. She knew every move in the book—from her own experience and from observing others at the Harte to Heart meet-and-greets—and nothing he'd said or done hinted even remotely that he was looking to get into her pants. He merely enjoyed her company, for which she was glad. Still, she knew she had to be careful, because her own motives weren't as pure and her heart didn't always take orders from her head. Even a lapsed Catholic like her knew better than to get involved with a married man, whatever his circumstances. A voice in her head warned, *If you knew what was good for you, you'd put a stop to this now.*

Instead, she found herself saying, "Sure, but I don't know where you'd go for a drink around here." They passed a seedy-looking bodega. Two doors down a shabbily dressed man sat on the front stoop of a derelict brownstone. "I'm not too picky, but I prefer drinking out of a glass to a bottle wrapped in a paper bag."

He chuckled. "I was thinking of someplace in your neighborhood."

"Oh. Well, there's a tavern near where I live that's pretty nice." Belatedly, she asked, "But don't you have to get home?" They'd reached the entrance to the subway station and she paused to look up at him. His gaze drifted past her, his face clouding over. Then he shook his head, as if to clear it of whatever had been troubling him, and smiled at her.

"It's just one drink," he said.

"ANGIE, IS THAT you?" Her mom's voice came bulleting down the line. Loretta always knew which of her daughters was calling before said daughter so much as breathed into the phone.

Angie suppressed a sigh. "It's me."

"You okay? You sound funny." Built-in caller ID wasn't Loretta's only talent.

"I'm fine, Ma. I just called to say hi." If Angie let more than a week go by between phone calls, her mom assumed something was wrong. Her busy schedule was no excuse. Loretta would remind her that her sisters phoned daily and they had jobs, too (not to mention husbands and children). Angie's infrequent visits were another bone of contention. Whenever she reminded her mom that, unlike her sisters, all of whom lived within close driving distance, she had to take the train from the city, Loretta would wave away the excuse. Her attitude was summed up by a comment she'd once made: "That's why they call it the *Long Island* Rail Road, so people like you can come see their families once in a while."

If only it were as easy as taking the train.

More like going back in time. At family get-togethers, at her childhood home in Oyster Bay, the old rivalries and squabbles were alive and well. Angie's sisters still argued with one another about who'd had the messiest room when they were growing up or the most friends or the cutest boyfriends in high school. They discussed ancient history as if it were breaking news, and they were fond of dredging up past incidents—everything from when Angie wet her pants in kindergarten to when she was caught making out with Brendan Soper behind the bleachers in ninth grade—that were guaranteed to make her cringe. Her parents were even worse; they acted as if she'd never left home. Her dad still called her by her childhood nickname, "Jellybean," and her mom was constantly nagging her to stand up straight, watch her mouth, or stop biting her nails. It was comforting in a way, like an old teddy bear with half its fur rubbed off, but mostly it was just irritating.

In the background, Angie could hear the sound of a baby crying. "I was watching Frannie's kids while she was at her PTA meeting." Loretta raised her voice to be heard above the racket.

"Nick couldn't watch them?" Angie said.

Loretta informed her that Francine's husband, Nick, who was the baseball coach at Hofstra University, had a game that night and that Ann Marie, the babysitter who looked after the kids during the day while Francine taught school, was sick. "I don't know why your sister even bothers with a babysitter when she has me," she sniffed. "What, I raised five kids and I can't look after my own grandchildren?" Angie heard Francine make some unintelligible comment in the background, at which Loretta yelled in response, "Oh, yeah? Well, you'll be old, too, one day, Miss Smart Mouth!"

"Tell Frannie I said hi," Angie said, stifling a giggle.

Francine was the sister to whom she was closest, and not just in age. They shared the same sense of humor and unsparing worldview. Francine was the only one who didn't paint a rosy picture of married life. Being a wife and mother had its rewards, Francine had once told her, but usually she was too tired to enjoy them. When she'd turned forty, Angie had treated her to a day of pampering at the Elizabeth Arden spa. Francine fell asleep during the pedicure.

Angie and her mom talked a while longer. Loretta told her about the Alaskan cruise she and Angie's dad had booked for September, and Angie brought her mom up-to-date on her latest venture, a former pizza parlor in the Bowery that she'd leased and planned to renovate, her business having outgrown its current space. Then, as if the conversation had been just the warm-up for the main event, Loretta inquired casually, "So, you met anyone interesting lately?"

Angie, still flush from the evening spent in Edward's company, felt a twinge of guilt. She had nothing to hide except her own lustful thoughts, but if her mom were to find out she was so much as entertaining fantasies about a married man, burning in hell would be the least of her worries.

"Yeah, Ma. I ran into Johnny Depp the other day and he asked me out on a date."

"Ha, ha. You should write jokes for Letterman."

"I wasn't trying to be funny."

"You think your sisters found husbands by sitting home alone every night?"

"You think I sit home every night? I wish." Angie was glad her mom couldn't see her now, sitting on the sofa in her pj's, a pint of chocolate Häagen-Dazs in hand. "The only reason I'm not working tonight is because it's Wednesday. Remember, I have my cooking class on Wednesdays? The kids said to say hello, by the way. They're still talking about your meatballs."

Loretta chuckled at the memory. "Ha! You tell them they can come over to my house anytime."

Angie smiled. Her mom could be a pain in the ass at times, but her heart was in the right place. There was always room for one more her table. "I'll be sure to do that, Ma."

In the next moment, her mother erased any points she'd earned in the goodwill department by seizing the chance to deliver another of her public service announcements. "You'd have kids of your own by now if you weren't so stubborn. Just remember, you're not getting any younger."

Angie, in her exasperation, blurted, "Maybe I should just marry a man with kids. That way you'd have ready-made grandchildren, and I wouldn't have you bugging me all the time."

She might as well have dangled a bloodied limb into a shark pond. Her mother pounced. "So you *are* seeing someone. Why didn't you say so? Is he divorced, is that it? Because if you think your dad and I would have a problem with that, may I remind you we're very broad-minded. Did we try to talk your sister out of getting divorced?" Whenever she told the story she edited out the part where she'd begged Julia to go to the family priest before leaving her first husband. "If he's good to you, that's all that matters. So, when do we get to meet him?"

"I'll let you know as soon as I've met him myself."

"Fine. Be that way," Loretta said in a mock-injured tone. "I'm only looking out for you, you know."

"I know, Ma, and I'm sure I'll thank you someday. Now will you put Frannie on?"

Moments later, the extension was picked up. "Hi, Ange," her sister's voice greeted her. "Sorry. The kids are hopped up on all the sugar Ma's been feeding them. I was just—" She broke off at the sound of a yowl. "Nicky, stop that or I swear! Your brother is *not* a punching bag."

Amid the din, Angie heard the sound of someone breathing into the phone who wasn't Francine, and she said pointedly, "You can hang up now, Ma." She waited until she heard the click at the other end before giving in to a sigh.

Francine chuckled knowingly. "Tell me about it."

"She driving you nuts, too?"

"Oh, yeah. She won't let up about the babysitter. You'd think Ann Marie was totally unreliable the way Ma carries on. I know it's only because she can't stand it that *she's* not the one taking care the kids, but it still gets to me. Though God only knows why she'd want the job. Didn't get enough of dirty diapers and snotty noses when we were growing up? I swear, the woman is a glutton for punishment."

Angie heard the sound of a door closing as Francine went into the next room, followed by the snick of a cigarette lighter. Francine had been trying for years to quit smoking, though she claimed she was more likely to drop dead of exhaustion than die from lung cancer.

"What did you tell her?"

Now it was her sister's turn to sigh. "That I'd think about it." Few could withstand the force of nature that was Loretta D'Amato. "As if I don't have enough problems."

"Why, what's going on?" Angie asked.

Francine took an audible drag off her cigarette. "Let's see. Nicky was sent home from school last week with a case of head lice. Then he and Bobby got into a fight because Bobby said he had 'cooties.' And now Caitlin's coming down with the same thing Ann Marie has. Oh, and did I mention there's talk of another teachers' strike?

But hey, other than that everything's just peachy." Angie pictured her sister, still pretty but tired-looking and working on the twenty pounds she'd gained with her last pregnancy. "So, did I hear Ma say something about you dating some divorced guy?"

Angie groaned. "Will somebody please just shoot me now and put me out of my misery?"

"What, and leave us to deal with Ma on our own? Not a chance. I'd sooner shoot myself." Francine dropped her voice as if their mother might be listening in. "Seriously, Ange, if you're seeing someone, you can tell me. I promise I won't breathe a word to Ma."

"There's nothing to tell." Angie would have left it at that, but she knew it was no use trying to keep anything from Francine. Her sister would ferret out what little there was to know. "First of all, I'm not 'seeing' him—we're just friends. And secondly, he's not divorced."

"Oh, God. Please tell me you're not having an affair with a married man."

"Of course not! I told you, we're just friends."

"That's what I said about Nick before I got knocked up."

Angie recalled what a huge deal it had been at the time. Francine having to drop out of graduate school when she found out she was pregnant and marry Nick, whom she'd only been dating a short while. Thirteen years and three children later they were still together . . . and Francine was still wondering what might have been. Angie dug into the Häagen-Dazs container with her spoon, ladling up a soupy pocket where the ice cream had partially melted. "I'm not going to get knocked up," she told her sister as she slurped down the spoonful of ice cream. "I'm not even sleeping with him."

"Just watch yourself, that's all I'm saying." Francine fell silent a moment before venturing, "So, is he is good looking, this friend of yours who's married and who you're not sleeping with?"

"Yeah, I guess." Angie was careful to downplay it, but Francine must have heard something more in her voice because she muttered under her breath, "Lord help us." Angie insisted, "It's not what you're thinking, I swear."

"You also swore you weren't going to lose your virginity to Kevin Boyle, and who was walking around with condoms in her purse no more than a month later?" Francine reminded her.

"I was sixteen!"

"Yeah, well, some things never change." Francine paused to let that sink in before saying, "Listen, I've gotta go. I have to get the kids home. I'll call you tomorrow, okay? In the meantime . . ."

"I know. Don't do anything you wouldn't do." Angie pictured her sister grinning at the other end as she stubbed out her Parliament Light. You wouldn't know it to look at Francine now, but inside the suburban mom's body was the teenage girl who'd once mooned a carload of boys out the window of her best friend's Camry on the way home from a party after too many wine coolers.

Angie hung up and closed her eyes, leaning back against the sofa cushions. She pictured Edward as he'd looked tonight, when they were lingering on the sidewalk outside the tavern after the "one quick drink" that had stretched to several hours, his face glowing as he spoke, not about taking it back to her place, but about his daughter's starring role in her school play. No, he'd done or said nothing to warrant the feelings he evoked in her, but she'd wanted to feel his fingers in her hair and his lips on hers nonetheless. She'd wanted—

She gave a guilty start at the wayward direction her thoughts had taken. She couldn't help having feelings, she supposed, but God help her if she were ever to act on them. Might as well dig a hole and jump in before her family could dig it for her.

CHAPTER ELEVEN

"Are you sure this is such a good idea?" Holly asked as they loaded the last of the shopping bags into the cargo hold of Camille's Volvo station wagon, parked at the curb in front of her building.

Camille turned to face her sister. "You're always telling me to think outside the box. Well, I'm finally taking your advice."

"This isn't just outside the box. It's in outer space circling the planet."

Holly, in her fifth month of pregnancy, was finally showing. Not like Camille when she was at that stage in her pregnancies, when her feet and ankles had been puffy as the rest of her. Holly's baby bump was of the movie star variety: the only thing protruding on an otherwise sylph-like body. Standing next to her, Camille felt like a dog's dinner in comparison. She knew she looked awful, thin and drawn, and she felt even worse. She was running a low-grade fever, which she hadn't mentioned to anyone because she didn't want to spoil her family's weekend plans. They hadn't been out to the beach house since last Thanksgiving, and they were all looking forward to the start of the season.

There was also the matter of their houseguest.

"I don't have a lot of time to explore other options," she said simply.

Holly was quiet for a moment, wearing the pained look that had become all too familiar of late: the one that said she knew her big sister wouldn't always be there. "Still," she said. "Are you sure you're going about this the right way? Why not just have her over for dinner instead? That way, if Edward and the kids decide they hate her, the entire weekend won't be blown."

"They won't hate her. She's a nice person. You'll see." Camille spoke with more conviction than she felt. Privately, she shared her sister's qualms and wondered if perhaps she'd been hasty in inviting Elise for the weekend in lieu of simply having her over for dinner, as Holly had suggested. But she'd been caught off guard when Elise had phoned—it had been over a week and Camille had all but given up on her—and when Elise let it drop, in the course of their conversation, that she'd be visiting a friend in Amagansett on Sunday, Camille seized the opportunity. Why not make a weekend of it? she had said. Elise could stay with them Friday and Saturday nights before joining her friend. It had seemed like a good idea at the time; she'd thought it would give Edward and the children— Holly, too—a chance to really get to know Elise. Only afterward did she regret the impulse. Edward was still upset with her—for some reason he seemed to think the dinner party at Kat's had been some sort of setup—and she'd been unable to convince him otherwise. She didn't want to make an already tense situation worse. But it was too late now to back out; the arrangements had already been made and she wasn't going to risk having Elise change her mind due to a change of plans.

"I don't doubt she's a nice person," Holly said, "But that's beside the point."

"She's just coming to meet you guys and for you to get to know her. That's all." Camille attempted to make less of it, but her matter-of-fact tone didn't match the leaden feeling in her gut.

"Even so, it's weird."

Camille couldn't disagree with that, so she only shrugged and resumed the task of stowing items in the back of the Volvo.

"What have you told the kids?" Holly wanted to know.

"Just that a friend is coming for the weekend." And maybe a "friend" was all Elise would ever be.

"How does Edward feel about it?"

Camille straightened and sighed. "He's not too happy about it," she admitted.

Holly stood with her arms crossed over her chest, wearing a look of disapproval. "Sometimes I wonder if you know how lucky you are to have a husband who loves you as much as he does."

Camille felt a pang at her sister's words. She knew Edward loved her, but since the argument they'd had after the night at Kat's, he'd been strangely withdrawn. His hours at work had grown increasingly irregular and one evening the previous week he hadn't made it home until after eleven p.m. His excuse was that he'd stopped for a drink with one of his colleagues on the way home from a seminar, and while she had no reason to doubt his story, it had left her feeling unsettled nonetheless. One thing was clear: He'd been in no hurry to get home to his wife.

"I know," she said in a small voice. "But right now, I don't feel very lucky."

Holly's face creased in sympathy, knowing Camille wasn't just talking about Edward, and she reached for her, hugging her tightly until Camille pulled back to fish the tissues she kept on hand at all times these days from the pocket of her hoodie. She helped herself to one before offering the pack to Holly. "Well, don't just stand there, we don't have all day," she said after they'd both dried their eyes. Holly gave a snappy salute, saying, "Aye, aye, Captain."

Camille watched her sister wriggle her way in back among the packed contents of the Volvo and begin rearranging things to make room for more stuff. "Are you sure you want to take all these beach towels?" Holly called over her shoulder. "Don't you have enough at the house?"

"You can never have too many beach towels, not with kids," Camille told her.

She recalled lazy summer afternoons at the beach in South-ampton, building sand castles with her kids when they were little and wading with them in the surf. In her mind's eye, she saw her younger self, a baby on her hip and a toddler in tow, gingerly making her way into the surf, the children squealing in delight as the waves rolled in to splash them. However warm the weather, Kyra and Zach were always shivering by the time they emerged from the water, soaking wet. She'd swaddle them in towels like caterpillars in cocoons, and they'd burrow into her lap to get warm. She ached now knowing those days were behind her. However hard she strove to hold on to each moment, to stay in the present, it was like the sand that slipped from underfoot when she stood at the water's edge with the tide rushing in.

Her sister emerged from the back of the car, her face flushed and hair in disarray, a piece of lint stuck to one cheek. "I think that's everything," she announced. "Should we go round up the kids?"

Camille locked the Volvo, and they headed back inside. She'd been lucky to find a parking space in front of their building. Friday afternoons in the warm-weather months always brought a caravan of cars and SUVs double-parked along this stretch of West End Avenue, the owners of said vehicles shuttling back and forth, loading them with stuff they'd need for the weekend.

Kyra was ready and waiting when they walked in the door of the apartment. "What took you guys so long? It'll be dark by the time we get there!" she cried. She'd recently acquired her first "grown-up" two-piece, and she was dying to show it off at the beach. Camille hoped the spring weather would cooperate. This time of year, it alternated between stretches of warm, sunny days and weekends when they stayed indoors, a fire lit in the hearth while cold ocean winds gusted outside.

"Is your brother ready?" Camille asked calmly.

"I don't know, but I've been ready for *hours*," declared her eldest.

"The beach will still be there in the morning," Holly reminded her niece, adding with a wink, "and so will the boys." Kyra's face went pink and she hurried off to fetch her brother.

Camille headed for the kitchen to fetch the snacks she'd packed for the trip. Holly trailed after her, scooting onto one of the stools at the counter. "So," she said, "I'm seeing Curtis next week."

Camille grew suddenly alert and she paused, looking up at her sister, as she was putting juice boxes and apples from the fridge into the bag with the soy nuts and SunChips. "He's in town?"

"Only for a few days." From the casualness with which she spoke, anyone would've thought it wasn't that big a deal, but Camille knew better. The bigger the event, the more Holly downplayed it—she'd been that way ever since she was a kid. She wondered if Curtis was making a special trip just to see Holly or if she was just a loose end to tie up before he flew back to London.

"Well, I'm sure you two have lots to discuss," she said pointedly.

"I guess." Holly shrugged.

Camille frowned. "What do you mean, you 'guess'? You're not in this alone, remember."

Holly helped herself to a banana from the fruit bowl. "He didn't even know I was preggers until a few weeks ago, and if I hadn't told him, he'd be none the wiser," she reminded Camille. "The point is, he's not a fixture in my life, and no one's holding a gun to his head. So it's his choice whether or not he wants to get involved. Either way, Junior and I will be just fine."

"He should at least pay child support."

"Why, because it's the law?"

"It's the law for a reason, and let's face it, you could use the money." Holly's online business generated a decent enough income, but as often as not it was a case of feast or famine. A major score, like the Springsteen jacket or the guitar played by Jimi Hendrix at Woodstock, could tide her over during lean times, but with a child to raise, she'd need a steadier source of income.

Holly had other concerns, though. "Those support checks come with a whole lot of strings attached from what I've seen. I know women whose exes think it gives them all kinds of rights, even stuff like deciding who they should go out with. I have this one friend whose ex took her to court because it was 'harmful to their kids'"—she made her air quotes, speaking in a derisive tone that was offset by a mouthful of banana—"that her live-in boyfriend was in a rock band. Imagine!" To Holly, who lived and breathed rock and roll, such a statement was just shy of heresy.

Camille let it go for now. Her sister had never listened to reason. Why should the fact that she had a baby on the way make a difference? She'd continue to go her own way just as she always had.

Just then Kyra reappeared, with Zach in tow. Minutes later, they were all buckled into the Volvo, headed for the Throgs Neck Bridge. Edward would join them later; he was taking the jitney. Holly kept the children entertained while Camille drove. Kyra considered herself too mature, at fourteen, for such games as seeing who could spot the most out-of-state license plates and only reluctantly joined in, but she soon got into the spirit of it and was craning her neck, shouting in glee at each new sighting of a vehicle that didn't bear New York plates. It wasn't until they were stuck in bumper-to-bumper traffic on the LIE that the children grew restless.

"What's there to eat?" Zach's voice rose, petulant, from the backseat as he and Kyra rifled through the bag of snacks their mom had packed. "Apples and chips? That's it? Can we stop at McDonald's?"

"It's 'may' not 'can.' And no, we may not," Camille answered mildly, inching forward another car length as the traffic began to move again. "I don't want you to spoil your appetite."

"But I'm hungry *now*." She could see her son in the rearview mirror working himself into a major pout.

She ignored it. If there was a silver lining to living on borrowed time, it was that she had learned not to let the small stuff get to her. When one of her children whined or mouthed off, she saw it as evidence of normalcy. Better that than have them minding their manners because they were fearful of making their sick mother even sicker. "We'll eat dinner when we get to the house," she said in her don't-try-my-patience voice. "I'm fairly certain you won't starve before then."

It was growing dark by the time they pulled into the driveway of the modest 1850s Cape Cod, on a tree-shaded lane in Southampton. Camille and Edward had purchased the house shortly after Zach was born. Juggling their busy careers with the demands of a five-year-old and an infant had made them see the need for a place where they could slow down and enjoy life more. Toward that end, they'd declared the beach house a television-free zone, a rule that applied to computers and video games as well. Anywhere else the kids would have balked at such a rule, but here they accepted it as the natural order of things. She'd noticed they were happier and better behaved as a result. Most evenings after supper, they played card games or Scrabble or worked on a jigsaw puzzle together. When the kids were younger, Camille or Edward would often read aloud to them from books they themselves had loved as children— *The Borrowers* or *The Witch of Blackbird Pond* or *Twenty Thousand Leagues Under the Sea*—while a fire crackled in the hearth and Kyra and Zach listened raptly. Here, more than anywhere else, they were a family.

And now, with Elise, she'd possibly be introducing a new member. A fresh ripple of apprehension went through her at the thought. What if her husband refused to give Elise a chance? What if Elise decided against taking on such a huge commitment once she saw what it entailed? Camille would be back at square one, without a plan and her family without a safety net.

You can't think that way, she told herself as she flipped open the Volvo's hatch and began pulling boxes and bags out of the back. She had to stay positive. Even if the desired outcome was one she never could have imagined wishing for back in the days when she'd had a choice.

She'd arranged for Elise and Edward to arrive on the same jitney. When she pulled into the parking lot of the Omni a short while later, she spotted them standing together in front of the station chatting amiably. *So far so good,* she thought. A small seed of jealousy sprouted nonetheless. She'd been so worried they wouldn't like each other, it hadn't occurred to her they might like each other a little too much. Watching their animated faces and the way Edward nodded his head as if deeply interested in whatever Elise was saying, she suddenly had trouble getting enough air into her lungs. It felt like the time she'd cracked a rib falling off a ladder, when it had hurt just to breathe. This was the hard part. The part where she had to grit her teeth and smile while her husband bonded with—and possibly grew to love—another woman.

She tooted her horn to get their attention. As they approached, she noted with approval the canvas tote Elise carried in lieu of a suitcase. One of Edward's pet peeves was women who packed for a weekend in the country as if they were going abroad for an entire summer. Elise's casual attire, khakis and a cotton-knit sweater with a lightweight quilted jacket thrown over it, also struck the right note. Camille was reminded of when her friend Nicole had come for a visit several summers ago. Nicole had arrived looking as if she'd stepped from a glossy ad in *Town & Country.* All weekend, while the rest of them ran around in shorts and flip-flops, she minced about daintily in pressed slacks and wedge-heeled espadrilles. Even at the beach, she was in full makeup, wearing a matching cover-up over her swimsuit. She hadn't been invited back since.

When they got back to the house, Camille showed their guest around while Edward and Holly saw to the refreshments and the kids set the table out on the deck. She was tired and still not feeling well but determined to play the good hostess. It was important that Elise feel welcome.

Elise took it all in, seeming genuinely interested. "I prefer these old houses to the newer ones," she said, admiring the dining room's built-in china cabinet. "They have character, and I'll take that over modern any day." She darted Camille a worried glance, as if it had only just occurred to her that Camille might think she was eyeing the house with future ownership in mind.

Camille pretended she hadn't noticed, saying smoothly as they continued on upstairs, "You should have seen it when we first bought it, before we fixed it up." It had been the victim of a godawful seventies remodel, complete with faux-brick linoleum and aqua bathroom fixtures, the memory of which made her cringe even all these years later, with no evidence of it anywhere in sight. "We had to tear out all the bathroom fixtures and completely redo the kitchen. And the shag carpeting—you don't even want to know. It was a nightmare."

"Anyone who would cover these beautiful old wood floors in shag carpeting should be taken out back and shot, in my opinion," said the churchgoing schoolteacher, showing a side of herself Camille hadn't previously seen. Elise, she guessed, could handle anything that came her way.

Camille led the way into the guestroom, which was in keeping with the period like the rest of the house. An antique pencil-post bed covered in a white chenille spread and flanked by mismatched nightstands faced a pair of double-hung windows, which provided a peekaboo view of the ocean during daylight hours. Against the opposite wall was a Victorian pine washstand, on it a pitcher in which Camille had placed fresh-cut flowers from the backyard. "It doesn't have its own bathroom, but I think you'll be comfortable," she said.

"I'm sure I will—it's lovely. But where will your sister sleep?" Elise asked, eyeing the lone bed.

"Don't worry about her—she always bunks with Kyra when she visits," Camille assured her. After the one and only night Holly had spent in this room, she commented that she'd felt like Little Red Riding Hood visiting Grandma without the Big Bad Wolf to make it interesting.

"Your sister's nice, but she isn't at all what I expected," Elise observed as she dropped her tote onto the luggage rack by the cherry lowboy. "You two don't seem to have very much in common."

Camille laughed. "You can say that again."

"Are either of you anything like your parents?"

Camille pondered a moment before replying, "I guess I'm more like mom. As for Holly, well, she's Holly—they broke the mold with her. She looks a little like my dad, but other than that, the only thing she got from him was his height." Not for the first time Camille blessed the fact that neither she nor her sister had inherited any of her dad's traits, though now the thought was accompanied by a twinge of guilt. Larry had left several messages on her answering machine over the past couple of weeks, and she had yet to return his calls. She suspected the only reason he was making an effort was because she'd shamed him into it. Still, the fact remained that he *was* making an effort. She owed him a call at least, if only as a courtesy.

"People say I'm like my dad," Elise said. "Which, if you met him, you'd know was a compliment. In fact, your husband reminds me a little of him. I don't mean just because they're both doctors, but I get the sense he . . ." Her voice trailed off, and her cheeks reddened. "Not that you can know someone just from talking to them on the bus. I only meant . . . well, he seems nice."

Camille decided the time had come to confront the elephant in the room. They couldn't go on like this all weekend, with Elise second-guessing her every remark. "I'm glad you two hit it off, but if you're worried I'll read too much into it, you can relax. As far as I'm concerned you're here to enjoy yourself, nothing more. After that . . . well, we'll see how it goes." Elise nodded, and some of the tension went out of her face. Satisfied, Camille left her to unpack and freshen up.

Minutes later, Elise joined the other adults out on the back deck. Holly had made mojitos—virgin for herself—and Camille had set out the crackers and cheeses and prosciutto she'd picked up at

Zabar's. Holly, ensconced in one of the old rattan chairs that had come with the house, remarked contentedly from its cushioned depths as she sipped her drink, "Man, this is the life."

"She's says that each time, and then after a day or two, when she's covered in mosquito bites and sick to death of Parcheesi and Monopoly, she wonders why anyone in their right mind would choose this over city life," Camille told their guest, prompting Holly to cry out in mock indignation.

"I'm not *that* bad! Anyway, I may see it differently when I'm a mom."

"I doubt that." Edward smiled indulgently at his sister-in-law. "If he's anything like you, your kid will have the entire subway system mapped out before he's reciting his ABCs." He turned to their guest. "What about you, Elise? Are you more of a city mouse or a country mouse?"

"A little of both, I think," she replied thoughtfully as she sipped her drink. "I grew up in a small town, so there's a part of me that will always miss that. But I know if I were to move back to Grantsburg, I'd miss my life here even more. The theaters and museums and restaurants, and, oh, just that fact that you can never walk down the same street twice—it's different each time." In the glow of the candles flickering on the low table in front of her, she looked especially pretty in the flowered dress she'd changed into, which showed off her slender figure without flaunting it.

Holly turned to her. "So, my sister tells me you're a teacher."

Elise brightened. "Yes, I teach fourth grade at Saint Luke's."

"You must like kids, in that case."

Camille darted Holly a warning look, but if Elise was aware that she was being subtly grilled, it didn't show. She replied enthusiastically, "Oh, yes! The best part about being a teacher is that it keeps you from becoming just another jaded adult. Where we see the ordinary, kids see a world full of wonders. At the end of the day, I always come away feeling there's hope for mankind."

Edward smiled his approval, his gaze drifting to his own children, who could be seen through the sliding glass door, sprawled on the braided rug in front of the fireplace playing a card game. "I just wish more teachers felt as you do," he commented. "Your students are lucky to have you."

Camille felt a vicious stab as the sprout of jealousy inside her sunk its roots deeper. Edward was clearly enjoying Elise's company. Her sweetness and sunny nature seemed to have melted any initial reservations he might have had. She thought of the saying *Be careful what you wish for.*

She was getting up to freshen everyone's drinks when a wave of dizziness swept over her. She didn't know if it was due to the mojito or the fact that she was running a fever, but she felt decidedly woozy. She was wondering if she could slip away for a quick lie-down without it being too noticeable, but before she could excuse herself, her husband turned to her and asked, "Dinner about ready? I should put the steaks on."

"I just need to boil the water for the corn," she told him.

Elise jumped up. "Anything I can do to help?"

"Thanks, but Holly and I have it covered. Why don't you stay and keep Edward company?" Camille replied, keeping her tone light. She couldn't allow herself to show any sign of weakness, not when she'd made it this far, so she summoned every ounce of will she possessed to keep her smile from becoming a grimace and her knees from buckling as she headed inside.

She somehow managed to get the corn boiled and the potatoes microwaved to the proper consistency while Holly made the salad. But when the food was on the table and everyone else digging in, she could only pick at what was on her plate. She had no appetite whatsoever and barely enough energy to saw at her steak. She didn't feel as woozy anymore, but she was having trouble staying focused—the conversation at the dinner table buzzed in her ears like white noise. Though she didn't miss the keen look of interest Elise wore as she listened to Edward talk about his work.

"It's nice to meet a doctor who's more concerned about his patients than the bottom line," Elise commented. "My dad's like that. If a patient can't afford his fee, he has them pay what they can."

"*My* dad works for free!" piped Zach.

"Not quite." Edward chuckled, explaining to their guest that he hadn't given up his day job, he only volunteered his services at a free clinic in the Bronx a couple of afternoons each week.

"That's admirable," she murmured, looking at him as if he'd hung the moon.

Camille felt the crack in her heart widen.

Just then, Kyra let out a cry of dismay and began dabbing with her napkin at the front of her dress, where a stain now showed. "It's ruined!" she said. "And this is only the first time I've worn it!"

While Camille just sat there, too out of it to respond, Elise came to the rescue. "The trick is to treat the stain before it sets. Come on, I'll show you." As she and Kyra headed inside, Camille heard her remark, "By the way, I tried on that same dress at H&M, and it didn't look nearly as good on me. It really suits you." Kyra beamed at her, while Camille's heart broke a little more.

After dessert, a strawberry pie from Sarabeth's, everyone pitched in on the cleanup. Edward and Zach cleared the table while Camille, moving about as if underwater, loaded the dishwasher and Holly and Elise went to work scrubbing the pots and pans. Camille was bending to stack the last of the plates in the dishwasher when she was overcome by a fresh wave of dizziness. She straightened and swayed on her feet, black specks gathering at the periphery of her vision. Then the floor tipped sideways, and everything went dark.

When she came to, she was lying on the kitchen floor, looking up into her husband's worried face. "How long have you been running a fever?" he asked, holding a hand to her forehead. She muttered something unintelligible and his frown deepened. "We've got to get you to the hospital."

Her disorientation gave way to panic. She'd had enough of hospitals to last three lifetimes. "No! Please, I just need to lie down," she told him. "If you could just help me up to bed . . ."

"Mom! Do what he says!" Kyra shrieked. She looked pale as she stood with her arm around an equally white-faced Zach.

Edward's voice was gentle as he helped her to her feet. "Do you think you can make it to the car, or do you need me to carry you?" He was making it clear the matter wasn't up for debate.

"I . . . I think I can walk," Camille told him.

Holly rushed to take her other arm, and together she and Edward maneuvered her out the door and down the driveway. "Don't worry about the kids. I'll keep an eye on them," Holly promised.

Camille was vaguely aware of Elise climbing into the backseat; then she lost consciousness once more. When she came to again, she was lying on her back on a gurney under a bank of fluorescent lights, Edward standing at her side. As he bent to kiss her on the forehead, she saw he was still wearing the worried look from before. Before she could reassure him, she was wheeled away.

Everything was a blur after that, until a smiling face framed by curly blond hair swam into focus. "Just a quick pinch," said the pretty young nurse as she inserted an IV needle into Camille's arm. There was a sharp prick followed by a burning sensation and then a warm weightlessness as the drug took effect, setting her afloat like a bit of flotsam being swept out to sea. "Are you married?" she asked groggily. She'd noticed the girl wasn't wearing a wedding ring.

The nurse only smiled in reply.

Camille slept. She didn't know how long. Periodically, she was roused by the nurses who came to check her vitals or administer more drugs, but each time it was as though it were happening in a dream. In her semiconscious state, she found herself drifting back in time. At one point, she heard a baby crying down the hall and imagined it was Zach when he was little, needing to be rocked back to sleep. Her one lucid thought in the middle of it all was *I'm not ready yet.* She couldn't die until she'd made sure her family would be safe and secure after she was gone.

When she woke again, it was to a room filled with light. A vacuum cleaner droned in the corridor. There were other noises, too: the sound of voices and rattle of carts. A different nurse from the one last night, a stout older lady with gray hair, took her temperature and declared, "Ninety-eight point nine. Well, that's an improvement! You gave us quite a scare last night, young lady."

Young lady? Camille felt a hundred years old.

"Where's my husband?" she croaked.

The nurse smiled. "He should be along any minute. He's just having a word with the doctor."

Soon after, Camille heard the squeak of rubber soles in the corridor, then the door whooshed open and Edward came striding in, looking tired and disheveled and sporting a day's worth of beard stubble. Coming up behind him was Elise. "Dr. Harding tells me you're doing much better," he said, taking her hand and smiling down at her. "You really had us worried there."

"Thank goodness, we got you to the hospital when we did," Elise said, stepping up alongside him.

Camille glanced from Edward to Elise. When had they become an "us" and a "we"? She noticed that Elise still had on the dress she'd been wearing last night. "You've been here all night?"

Elise nodded, explaining, "I was going to call my friend in Amagensett and have him pick me up. I was afraid I'd be in the way, but your husband said he could use the company, so I stayed." Edward flashed her a grateful smile. "It was the least I could do," she said modestly.

But Camille saw from the veiled look she gave him that it had been more than a kind gesture on her part: She was smitten. An icy hand gripped her heart. Edward talked about her blood readings and white cell count, but it was as if he were speaking a foreign language. She couldn't focus on his words, only on the picture he and Elise made. No one would guess they'd known each other less than twenty-four hours; they might have been a husband and wife come to visit a sick friend.

It looked as if her plan was working. Whether she liked it or not.

CHAPTER TWELVE

"I don't want to be in the way," Elise had said to him the night before.

In the flurry of activity around getting Camille situated and then consulting with the hospital's chief of oncology, Dr. Harding, Edward had forgotten all about their houseguest. He focused on Elise then, and thinking only of the long, lonely vigil ahead, replied, "If you don't mind, I could use the company." Only afterward did he realize that, with those words, he'd crossed the Rubicon between merely making nice and opening the door to future possibilities with Elise.

They sat in the visitors' lounge most of the night, talking. Elise's calming presence kept him from wearing a hole in the floor with his pacing, and by the time the sun came up, he had become better acquainted with her than with people he'd known for years. Elise was a good person, but her niceness wasn't the sugary-sweet kind; she had an inner strength and wasn't afraid to stretch the boundaries of her small-town upbringing. She was what one would want in a wife: lively and intelligent, sensitive to the needs of others, good with kids. Also, undeniably easy on the eye.

When Camille's fever broke, he and Elise headed back to the house. They arrived to find it quiet, everyone else still asleep. They were both hungry so Elise, without being asked, fixed them some scrambled eggs and toast. Afterward, they retired to their respective rooms.

When Edward woke several hours later, it was with gritty eyelids and what felt like a mouthful of cotton balls. He showered and shaved, then headed downstairs to the kitchen. The kids had already blown through, as evidenced by the juice glasses and cereal bowls in the sink; only Holly sat at the table, in her robe and slippers. She was sipping coffee, reading the morning paper.

"Decaf," she said, lifting her mug. "Someday this kid's going to know how much I sacrificed on his behalf and he sure as hell better appreciate it." Her smile fell away and she regarded him with worried eyes. "Is she any better? Has the fever gone down?" she asked. They'd kept in contact throughout most of the night, but it'd been hours since he'd last given her an update.

He nodded in assent. "The antibiotics seem to be doing the trick." Holly didn't need to be told that, with an immune system as compromised as Camille's, even a common cold was potentially deadly. Like him, she was a veteran of this war. "She's still weak, but she's on the mend."

"Did the doctor say when she could come home?"

Edward helped himself to some coffee from the pot. "They want to run more tests, but Dr. Harding says she should be ready to come home by tomorrow at the latest, if she remains stable."

Holly expelled a slow breath. "Thank God. I was so worried." She looked worried still, the kind of deep, systemic worry that didn't wear off. They both knew this was only a temporary reprieve.

Edward fetched a carton of milk from the fridge and poured some into his coffee. Normally, he took it black, but the numerous cups of coffee he'd consumed the night before in an effort to stay awake had left him with a touch of heartburn, so he was going easy on his stomach today. He was lowering himself into a chair when the children charged in. They were wearing their swimsuits, and Zach was carrying a beach ball. "How's Mom? Is she going to be okay?" Kyra asked.

"Your mom's going to be just fine," he assured them, before cautioning his daughter in a mock stern voice, "Which is more than I can say for any young men I catch ogling you in that bikini." Kyra rolled her eyes, but he could tell she was secretly pleased. In her new two-piece, which wasn't quite a bikini but skimpier than he would have liked, he hardly recognized his daughter. Where had his flat-chested, pigtailed little girl gone? Who was this shapely young woman with her coltish legs and budding breasts? Soon there would be boys showing up at their door. There would be fights over curfews and car keys. *How will I get through all that without Camille?*

"When's she coming home?" Zach wanted to know. He'd sprouted several inches this past year, on his way to becoming a gangly adolescent, but right now looked like he had his first day of kindergarten as he stood clutching his beach ball as if it were the only thing between him and certain disaster.

"Soon," Edward told him, keeping it vague.

"Can we go see her, or do they have rules about kids like at the other hospital?"

"Right now, she needs her rest, so it's probably best if she doesn't have any visitors. But I'm sure she'll want to hear from you. Why don't we give her a call before Aunt Holly takes you to the beach?"

"You're not coming with us?" Kyra eyed him expectantly.

After his all-night vigil, he wanted nothing more than to climb back into bed, but his children needed him right now, he realized, more than he needed another few hours' rest. "I wasn't planning on it," he said, "but come to think of it, it might be just what the doctor ordered."

Kyra giggled. "*You're* the doctor, Daddy."

"So I've heard," he replied with a sage nod.

"Can Elise come, too?" his son asked eagerly.

Edward's gaze was drawn upward by the sound of footsteps overhead. Their houseguest was up and about, probably awakened by the noise downstairs. "Sure, if she wants to. You'll have to ask."

Zach went racing upstairs to enlist Elise, and Kyra tagged along. When Edward and Holly were alone again, she cast him a meaningful look over the rim of her mug as she sipped her decaf.

"The kids seem to like her," she observed.

He shrugged. "What's not to like?"

"You like her, too, don't you?"

"Sure, why wouldn't I? She's a nice person." He directed his gaze out the window, watching a squirrel forage for nuts in the backyard while doing his best to ignore the implication in Holly's line of questioning. No such luck—seeing he wasn't going to bite, she stated it outright.

"A nice person whom my sister thinks would make a good wife."

He brought his gaze back to Holly. The robe she was wearing, one of Camille's—blue terry trimmed in darker blue satin piping— was a painful reminder that soon it wouldn't just be someone else wearing his wife's clothes. "I think the less said about *that* the better," he replied tersely.

"Hey, don't bite my head off. I'm on your side. I was no more in favor of the idea than you were when Cam first proposed it. I still think it's crazy, but now that I've met Elise . . ." Holly held his gaze, and he could see in her eyes that she was searching for something that made sense in the midst of all the madness, same as he. "Well, it's hard not to like her. That's all I'm saying."

Edward grunted and took a sip of his coffee.

"Maybe it wouldn't hurt to have her around. We need all the friends we can get at a time like this, right?"

He shot her a dark look. "With friends, I don't have to think about possibly booking a church down the line."

Holly sighed. "I know. I can't quite picture that, either."

Edward pushed his chair back and stood up. Holly looked up at him questioningly, and he smiled to let her know he wasn't angry at her for bringing up a sore subject. Besides, she was right about one thing: He wouldn't be able to get through this without the help of his friends. And the night before, when he'd needed one, Elise had been there for him. "Speaking of our guest," he said in a neutral voice, "I should go see how she's doing. Knowing my son, he'll sweet-talk her into coming with us when she'd rather stay here and catch up on her sleep."

"Well, if you're taking the kids to the beach," Holly said, "I'll head over to the hospital."

"Nothing doing. You're coming with us," he ordered.

Holly shook her head. "Someone should be with her, and you were there all night."

"True, but that was when she was too sick to have a say in the matter. Now that's she's better she's back to calling the shots," he informed his sister-in-law. "And she was very insistent that our weekend not be spoiled because of her. She says she'll be sleeping most of the day, anyway."

"All right, if you say so," Holly relented. "I'll go see her after we get back from the beach, in that case." She gave a rueful shake of her head. "God, she can be so stubborn sometimes."

Tell me about it, Edward thought as he headed upstairs to check on Elise.

AN HOUR LATER they were all piled in the Volvo headed for Cooper's Beach. It was still early in the day so the beach was fairly deserted when they arrived, and they were able to stake out a prime spot. Edward spread the beach blanket over the sand, and Kyra positioned her towel a short distance away, just far enough to be able to pretend she wasn't with her family if any cute boys should happen along. While the others headed down to the water, Edward stretched out and closed his eyes. Before he knew it, he was asleep. When he roused a short while later, Elise and Zach were tossing a Frisbee back and forth farther down the beach and Holly was wading in the surf.

He thought back to summer days when the kids were small, Kyra and Zach chubby little figures in orange life vests digging for sand crabs or collecting seashells in paper cups, before cancer had come crashing in, like a rogue wave smashing a sand castle, to lay ruin to their carefree existence.

Before he'd come to feel unwanted by his own wife.

He knew it wasn't because she'd stopped loving him. Still, it hurt each time she turned away from him in bed, too tired or sick to make love. He couldn't recall the last time he'd felt the light touch of her hand on his thigh or heard her voice murmur seductively in his ear. He missed that. Yearned for it. Even so, he might have found a way to deal with his frustration if not for this crazy scheme of hers. What wife who truly loved her husband would willingly relinquish him to another woman, whatever the circumstances? And in his case, there was more than one candidate, if you counted Kat Fisher. Though ironically, it was that very thing—Kat's having been sprung on him without warning—that had led to his friendship with Angie. A friendship he'd kept hidden from Camille, for reasons he didn't quite understand.

His gaze drifted back to Elise. She was another surprise. Upon meeting her, he'd been determined to be polite and nothing more, but she'd quickly won him over on the bus ride to Southampton. As Holly had observed, it was impossible not to like Elise. The secret he hadn't told his sister-in-law was that he'd begun to think maybe his wife was right. He hadn't thought so in the abstract, but Elise in person was another matter. Now that he'd gotten to know her, he could see how having her around in the months ahead would be to his and his children's benefit. She'd proven herself an ally and the kids already seemed to adore her. She was also a breath of fresh air.

"Mind if I join you?"

At the sound of her voice, Edward looked up to see Elise standing over him, her face flushed with exertion. He gestured toward the vacant spot next to him on the blanket and she collapsed onto it, reaching for her water bottle. "I hope my son didn't wear you out too much," he said. "A little," she admitted, taking a gulp of her water. "But considering I didn't get any sleep last night, it's a wonder I was able to keep up at all." Despite her words, she didn't look as if she'd spent the night camped out in a hospital visitors' lounge keeping a worried husband company—she was her usual sunny, ebullient self. Her gaze traveled to Zach, now splashing in the surf with his aunt Holly. "He's a good kid. They both are. You and Camille must be very proud."

He nodded, his throat tightening.

She went on, "A lot of the parents I deal with don't know the difference between what a child wants and what he or she needs. They seem to think giving them whatever they ask for is a substitute for time and attention." She smiled at him. "Which is a long-winded way of saying I think you're doing a wonderful job raising your kids."

"Most of the credit goes to my wife," he demurred. Camille was the one who enforced rules and saw the kids off to school most days, who made sure teeth got brushed and homework got done.

"Don't sell yourself short," she told him. "They say it takes a village, but it really just takes two. I have several kids in my class whose dads are absentee, and they're the ones who are the most disruptive and who have problems getting along with the other kids." Edward, reminded that his own children would soon be at a similar disadvantage, felt his chest constrict. The shift in mood must have shown on his face because Elise was quick to add, "Kids are resilient, though. And one loving parent can make up for a lot."

Edward envisioned himself, years from now, lying on this beach with Elise, the sun shining as it was now and his world once more spinning smoothly on its axis. Elise, his wife and the stepmother to his children. He'd never stop grieving for Camille, of course, but at least, he'd have the comfort of knowing he was honoring her wishes rather than dishonoring her memory.

On impulse, he took Elise's hand and squeezed it. "Thank you," he said.

"For what?" She turned to face him, her lips curled in a questioning smile.

"For not running out on me last night."

She blushed. "No need to thank me. Really, it's what anyone would have done."

"Not true," he disagreed. "Most people would've taken off at the first hint of what they were in for."

She held his gaze, and he was struck by the extraordinary translucence of her eyes. "That's not how I was raised," she said simply.

"In that case, remind me to thank your parents if I ever meet them."

The color in her cheeks deepened. "Well, since they live in Wisconsin, I don't think there's much chance of that, but I'll be sure to give them the message." She spoke lightly, but it was obvious his casual remark had deeper meaning for her. He made a mental note to watch his step from now on. "Oh, and about last night? I didn't stick around just to be a Good Samaritan. I . . . I had a nice time. I mean, as much as possible given the circumstances," she was careful to add.

"Me, too," he said, meaning it.

Elise's gaze dropped to his shoulders. "Um, I hate to be the one to break it to you, but that's a pretty nasty sunburn you have. You ought to put some sunscreen on before it gets any worse."

Only then did he become aware of the prickly heat on his back and shoulders. He grimaced and reached belatedly for the tube of sunscreen he'd brought. "Usually, my wife reminds me."

"Allow me." Elise plucked the tube from his hand.

He stretched out on his stomach. It had been so long since he'd felt a woman's touch, he gave himself over to the sensation of Elise's hands smoothing lotion over his back as he lay with his eyes closed and his head cradled in his arms, sinking into it as he would a comforting embrace.

ELISE COULD FEEL the tension that had Edward's muscles in knots, even in his relaxed state, as she applied sunscreen to his shoulders and back, and her heart went out to him. At the same time, she took pleasure in the borrowed intimacy of the act. The last time she'd had her hands on a bare-chested man stretched out beside her was when she was married. Mentally, she drew comparisons. Edward was swarthy whereas Dennis was fair, with a leaner build than her ex-husband and a mat of dark hair on his chest that tapered to a narrow trail where it disappeared below the elastic waistband of his swim trunks, in marked contrast to the dusting of golden hairs on Dennis's. And the differences between the two men didn't end there. Dennis had loved her in his own fashion, she supposed, but like the old cars he liked to rebuild in his spare time, he wasn't able to go the distance, whereas Edward's love for his wife was built to last. She knew because she'd witnessed it in action. It had also been evident in the way he'd spoken of Camille the night before as they'd sat up late talking.

"You know what the toughest part is?" he'd said as he sat hunched over with his elbows propped on his knees, cradling a cup of coffee that had gone cold. "I'm a doctor, and there isn't a damn thing I can do. I can't make it better. And I can't stop it from getting worse."

"You're a good advocate, though," she reminded him. She had never seen anyone mobilize the forces faster in getting someone admitted to a hospital. "I don't know anyone else who could have gotten that doctor on the phone as quick as you did . . . not to mention get him to come in when he was in the middle of watching a baseball game." Edward shrugged, a crooked smile forming. "It didn't hurt that the Mets were down twelve runs."

"You're also a good husband," she added.

He gave a short, harsh laugh, as if he might beg to differ with her on that count, but she chalked it up to the sense of helplessness he must feel. "What good will it do in the end, when she's dead and buried?" She flinched at the stark finality of his words. Exhaustion had caught up with him, she could see, stripping away his defenses and any optimism he might have felt.

"I know this is hard for you," she said gently.

He shook his head, saying in a tight-lipped voice, "You don't know the half of it. Have you ever had to watch someone you love slip away bit by bit?" His anger wasn't directed at her, she sensed, nor was the question—he was only voicing his frustration. But she responded nonetheless.

"No, but I know what it's like to lose someone you love. When I found out my husband was cheating on me, it felt like a death. What made it even worse was that I didn't see it coming." Though, looking back, she could see the signs had all been there; she'd simply chosen to ignore them.

Edward tilted his head up to look at her, squinting a little. "Knowing what lies ahead doesn't make it any easier, believe me," he said. With his bloodshot eyes and beard stubble, he reminded her of the men who came to the soup kitchen at her church, where she volunteered, some more presentable than others but all with the same look of despair. "It's just a longer good-bye."

Elise felt an urge to comfort him the only way she knew how— the same way she would if it'd been one of her students who was hurting, with a hug—but she held back. This experience had brought them closer than would otherwise have been possible in so short a time, but the fact was they hadn't known each other long enough for her to take the liberty of putting her arms around him.

Now, as she felt the knotted muscles in his back start to give under the pressure of her fingertips, she felt something loosen inside her as well—the part of her that hadn't dared risk getting her heart broken again. For the first time since her divorce, she allowed herself to think about getting married again one day and having children. Whoever she married would have to be special. Someone smart and kind and, most of all, trustworthy. *Someone like Edward.* She couldn't bring herself to imagine it might actually be him—the possibility was too remote at this point . . . and too charged. But the thought remained nonetheless, teasing at the edges of her consciousness.

She thumbed the cap closed on the tube of sunscreen. This weekend wasn't turning out the way she'd expected, and not just because of the scare with Camille. Elise had intended only to satisfy her moral obligation in honoring Camille's request. Her imagination hadn't stretched any farther than the possibility of her becoming a friend to Edward and Camille and their children, nothing more. Instead she found herself drawn to Edward in ways she wasn't prepared for or entirely comfortable with. She had no idea where it would lead; she only knew there was no turning back. She'd known, in her heart, the instant she'd spotted him as she was stepping out of the cab yesterday at the East Fortieth Street jitney stop. She'd recognized him from the photo Camille had shown her, except he wasn't smiling like in the photo. Taking in the sight of the tall, well-dressed man with the solemn dark eyes and dignified bearing, she'd thought of the lines from the poem "Richard Cory." *He was a gentleman from sole to crown. / Clean-favored, and imperially slim.* A poem with a tragic ending, she recalled belatedly.

"You'll find someone to love again," her friend Glenn had said to her once in the thick of her post-divorce misery. He'd come over that evening to console her, as he had the previous evening and the one before that, bearing a Netflix DVD in one hand and box of microwave popcorn in the other. She felt more miserable than usual on that occasion, having wept her way through *Saving Private Ryan*, selfishly thinking only of Dennis and not the real tragedy of D-Day when so many lives had been lost. Glenn didn't seem to mind, though; he was used to it by then.

"If I do, how will I know I'm not making a mistake?" she moaned, disconsolate. She'd made a mistake in choosing Dennis and had as little faith in her instincts as she did in her ex-husband.

"You'll know," Glenn replied calmly, passing her the bowl of popcorn.

"How?"

"You just will."

Now, thinking of Glenn, she felt a twinge of guilt. She'd been looking forward to spending the day with him and his parents tomorrow; instead all she could think about was how sorry she'd be to say good-bye to this family. Despite last night's ordeal, and in some ways because of it, she was having a good time. Also, she could see where she might be useful. Growing up in Grantsburg, she'd been taught to pitch in when a friend or neighbor or fellow congregant at her church needed help, whether it was tending to someone who was gravely ill or babysitting someone else's sick child so they wouldn't miss a day of work. As a doctor's daughter she had also witnessed firsthand what terminal illness could do to a family. Last night was just a sample of what was to come, and there would be times it would be more than Edward and Holly could cope with on their own. They would need outside help, if only someone to pick up the slack with child care and chores.

Still, she couldn't keep from questioning her motives. She looked down at Edward, dozing beside her. *Would I be doing it purely out of the goodness of my heart?* It was one thing to help another woman in need, another to develop feelings for that woman's husband in doing so.

HOURS LATER, AFTER Zach's sand castle had fallen victim to the rising tide and Kyra had grown tired of waiting for some cute boy to notice her (the chances of which would have been dramatically increased if she hadn't sat self-consciously hunched over with her knees to her chest the entire time), no one raised an objection when Edward suggested they grab a bite to eat and then head home.

They went to Shippy's Pumpernickels, on Windmill Lane, where Zach ordered the same thing he always did—the butterfly shrimp—and Kyra and Holly split a pastrami sandwich. Edward put away an entire order of Shippy's dauntingly apportioned Weiner schnitzel while Elise nibbled daintily on her shrimp salad. The only solemn moment was when Zach said he wished his mom could be there. To which Edward responded with a lump in his throat, "Me, too, sport."

He phoned Camille as soon as they got home.

"Did you guys have fun at the beach?" She sounded tired but upbeat.

"Not as much fun as we would have if you'd been with us. But we worked up an appetite, at least. You should have seen all the food our son packed in at Shippy's." He paused before asking gently, "How are you feeling?"

"Better than yesterday, that's for sure," she reported. "Dr. Harding says I can go home tomorrow, on one condition: I had to promise to have Regina look me over as soon as I get back to the city."

"Do you need me to make an appointment?"

"Already taken care of. I'm seeing her first thing Monday morning."

"Great. I'd like to have a word with her, too." He hadn't given up yet on pursuing some form of treatment beyond just palliative. To that end, he'd consulted with Camille's doctor on prior occasions as well as other hematologist-oncologists whom he'd worked with in the past. He also continued to scour the Internet for word of new protocols or cancer drugs in development. He was determined to leave no stone unturned. Camille may have given up, but he hadn't.

"You don't have to come with me," she told him.

"I know, but I'd like to."

"Really, Edward, I'm perfectly capable of getting there on my own. There's no need for you to rearrange your entire schedule when I can just call for a car. You have your own patients to tend to."

"You're more important," he said, his voice firm.

"All right, if you insist." Camille sighed as if too tired to argue. After a moment, she ventured, "How's Elise?"

"Fine. She seems to be having a good time," he answered cautiously.

"I feel bad about ruining her weekend."

"You didn't ruin it. It just didn't turn out the way you planned."

"Well, I'm sure you'll find a way to make it up to her," she said.

Edward bristled at the implication. What, was he supposed take Elise to a candlelit restaurant? Wine and dine her while his wife lay sick in the hospital? *Christ. What kind of man does she take me for?* Lately, he'd begun to suspect, to his ever-growing dismay, his wife of twenty years didn't know him at all.

LATER IN THE afternoon, Holly took the kids to visit Camille. It was after dark by the time they returned. In the meantime, Elise had prepared supper: salmon poached in white wine, a loaf of bread, and a green salad. After they'd eaten, Edward lit a fire in the hearth, and they played Scrabble. It wasn't long, though, before all the excitement of the night before, coupled with a day at the beach, began to take its toll and the children started to droop. "Come on, guys, time to hit the sack," Holly ordered. For once, they didn't protest.

"You must be tired, too," Edward said to Elise after Holly had shepherded the kids upstairs to bed. The room was quiet—too quiet. The only sounds were those of embers crackling in the fireplace and the creak of footsteps overhead.

"You'd think so, but strangely, I'm not." She sat curled in the armchair by the fireplace, looking no older than Kyra, in her cutoffs and faded Camp Cheyenne T-shirt. She'd been a camp counselor the summer before her senior year of high school—one of the many things he'd learned about her while they'd sat up late talking last night. (She was also a huge Bon Jovi fan and had a weakness for candy corn.) He pictured her now seated before a campfire, sur-rounded by a gaggle of children, leading them in a chorus of "Kum-baya" or telling kid-friendly jokes like the ones that had had Zach in stitches at lunch.

"Me, either," he said. "Actually, I was thinking of taking a walk."

Edward didn't particularly feel like company right now but didn't want to risk hurting her feelings, especially after she'd been so kind—not only in staying with him at the hospital last night but in keeping his nine-year-old entertained today at the beach while he caught some shut-eye—so he asked, "Care to to join me?" Elise nod-ded, looking pleased to have been asked.

They donned their jackets—the weather had turned nippy—and headed out, walking in the direction of the beach, past the other houses that lined the street, saltbox cottages and quaint, shingled Cape Cods like the one he owned, some peeking from behind overgrown trees and hedges. The air was cool but clear, the moon and stars shining brightly overhead, seeming almost close enough to touch.

As they strolled along the sidewalk, Edward thought back to summer nights when he and Camille used to go for walks on the beach after the kids had been put to sleep, when Holly was there to keep an eye on them. One warm night, when the beach was deserted, Camille had impulsively stripped off her clothes and gone racing down to the tide line to plunge into the surf, swimming out beyond the waves. He followed a minute later, gasping when he hit the ice-cold water.

"It's freezing! Why didn't you warn me?" he yelled.

"Because you're you," she called back playfully.

He swam over to her. "What's that supposed to mean?"

"It means you'd still be standing on the beach with your clothes on if I'd warned you." She wound her arms around his neck, press-ing her slippery body against his and giving him a salty kiss. "Don't worry, I'll keep you warm." She grinned. "In fact, I see a dune with our names on it."

They swam back to shore, where they used their discarded clothing to towel themselves off as best they could, before tumbling naked into the leeward side of the dune, where they would be hidden from the view of any passersby. She straddled him, her wet hair dripping onto his torso and her pale skin glowing in the moonlight, and it took all his restraint to keep from coming as soon as he entered her. She felt both cool and hot to the touch. She tasted of the ocean.

They made love that night on a bed of sand, under a blanket of stars.

"That was fun, today at the beach. The whole day, in fact. I've really enjoyed getting to know your family," Elise remarked, interrupting his thoughts. "It's a shame Camille had to miss out," she hastened to add.

Edward, roused from his reverie, turned his attention to her. "She was more concerned about you, actually. She feels bad about not being able to fulfill her hostess duties. I told her you were a good sport about it, and that you even cooked us supper—which, may I add, was delicious, and also above and beyond. In fact, we'll be sorry to see you go." Her friend was picking her up tomorrow morning after breakfast. He realized, somewhat to his chagrin, that he really would miss having Elise around. In the short time she'd been with them, she'd integrated herself into his family nicely but not obtrusively. He wondered if she saw herself becoming a part of their lives. He had mixed feelings about it himself. Part of him continued to balk at the notion, while another part of him thought, more rationally, *No one is out to replace Camille. But if having Elise in our lives would make things easier for all concerned, why not, if she's game?*

Still, he was relieved when Elise only said lightly in response, "Hopefully, we can do this again sometime."

"I'd like that," he said as they crossed to the other side of the street on their way to the beach access path. He was careful to strike a casual tone. "Though I'll have to bone up on my knock-knock jokes for next time, if I'm to keep up with you. Your repertoire is pretty impressive."

She laughed. "I owe it to Glenn. Every lame joke I know, I learned from him."

Glenn was the friend whose folks lived in Amagansett, Edward recalled, the one whom Zach had been referring to dismissively as "that guy." As in, *I don't know why she'd rather be with that guy than with us.* Zach was put out, and maybe a little jealous, that "that guy" would be spiriting Elise away tomorrow. "Have you two known each other long?" Edward asked.

"Gosh, yes—years and years. Glenn's my dearest friend. I don't know what I'd have done without him when I was going through my divorce." She spoke with such affection, Edward wondered if they were perhaps more than just friends. Not that it was any of his business. "It left him with a permanent dent in his couch cushions from all the times I was over at his place, not to mention a total dislike of my ex-husband. He thinks Dennis should be strung up by his—" She broke off, giving a laugh that held no humor. "Well, you get the picture."

"From what you've told me, that sounds about right. He did cheat on you."

"True," she said, sighing.

They reached the end of the path, where they paused to take off their shoes. "So, was it a one-time thing or was he a serial cheater, your ex-husband?" Edward asked as they stepped onto the sand, the deserted beach silvery in the moonlight, the ocean glistening in the distance as waves rolled into shore.

She was quiet a moment before answering, "As far as I know it was only the one time—an office romance. They're married now, with a baby on the way, last I heard. So I guess it worked out for the best—for him anyway." Her tone was matter-of-fact, but he heard the underlying bitterness in her voice. "Not that I'm sitting around feeling sorry for myself. Not anymore. Once I got over that, I realized I'd rather be alone than stay with a man who didn't love me enough to be faithful."

"You never thought about giving him a second chance?"

"Maybe, for about two seconds. But I realized even if I could forgive him, I could never trust him again. I could barely stand being in our apartment after he left. Partly because I missed him—or, rather, I missed what I thought I'd had—but it was also because every time I sat on the sofa or climbed into bed, I wondered if he'd done it there with *her*. When we divided up our assets, I let him have every stick of furniture—I didn't want any of it."

"No regrets?"

"No," she said softly. "I only wish he'd been the man I thought he was when I married him. It was good in the beginning—better than good, I really thought we had it all." She sighed again. "Regardless of what Glenn might think, Dennis isn't a bad person. He was just a bad husband."

"'Better to have loved and lost than never to have loved at all,'" Edward quoted.

"When Tennyson wrote that, I doubt he was going through a divorce," she said with a rueful chuckle.

"Do you think you'll ever get married again?" He glanced at her out of the corner of his eye, gratified to see that her expression remained serene. Whatever agony she'd gone through in her divorce, she seemed to have put it behind her for the most part.

"Maybe. Someday," she said. "But I'm in no hurry. And even if I were to fall in love again and this hypothetical man were to ask me to marry him, I don't know that I could trust myself to make the right decision."

Edward reflected on this as they strolled along the tide line, the packed wet sand cold against the soles of his feet. He felt a heaviness inside him at the thought of what the future might hold for him and his children. "I always thought Camille and I would grow old together," he said, adding with a mirthless laugh. "Now it looks as if I'll be the only one of us with gray hair."

He thought back to when he and Camille were first married, how happy they'd been despite how little they'd had in the way of money or material things. One night, they'd decided to pool their resources so they could go to the movies, only to discover they were a dollar short of the price of admission for two. They scoured their studio apartment for loose change, making a scavenger hunt of it and crowing in triumph with each coin unearthed from the back of a drawer or under the radiator or between the sofa cushions. He found two quarters in the pocket of his winter overcoat and she a cache of pennies in a jar in the kitchen cupboard. Before long, they had enough money. But by then, they'd worked up such an appetite, they decided to go out for pizza instead. He could see her in his mind's eye now as she'd looked that night, sitting across from him at V & T, a tuft of hair sticking up in one spot and her purple and white NYU T-shirt smudged from having crawled under the bed in search of buried treasure. She said with a grin as she helped herself to another slice, "Now, isn't this better than watching Bruce Willis kill bad guys?"

He roused from his thoughts to find himself standing at the water's edge, gazing sightlessly out to sea. When he looked over at Elise, she was regarding him with compassion. She reached up to brush her fingertips over the silvering hair at his temple, a touch so light it might have been the wind blowing. "I think you'll look very distinguished with gray hair," she said.

"Even old age has its compensations, I guess." He aimed for a laugh that fell short of the mark. They were both quiet after that, each wrapped in his or her own thoughts, mindless of the surf washing in to baptize their bare feet. After a minute or two had passed, he said, "We should head back."

By the time they arrived back at the house, it was half-past ten and all was quiet. He switched off the lights downstairs and poked at the fire in the hearth to make sure it was out; then he and Elise went upstairs. At the top of the staircase, he paused and turned to her before they headed for their respective rooms. A band of moonlight from the clerestory window on the landing slanted across her face, accentuating the curve of a cheekbone and underlining the angle of her jaw.

"Good night." He spoke softly so as not to wake the others.

"Sleep tight." Elise leaned in and kissed him on the cheek.

THE FOLLOWING MORNING, after Elise had gone off with her friend Glenn, who'd arrived to pick her up after breakfast, Edward was on his way to the hospital when his cell phone trilled. Angie's voice greeted him. "How'd it go?" she asked as if picking up a conversation from five minutes ago.

"Don't ask." He groaned.

"That bad, huh? What, does she chew with her mouth open? Open beer cans with her teeth?"

It was a moment before he realized she had been referring to Elise. "No, she was the perfect houseguest, as it turns out. It's my wife—she took a turn for the worse. She's in the hospital."

Angie instantly switched gears. "Oh, my God. I'm so sorry. Is . . . is it bad?"

"Not as bad as it might have been, but she gave us quite a scare," he reported. "Good thing we got her to the hospital when we did. In fact, I'm on my way there now to pick her up."

"So she's okay?"

"She's fine." *For now.*

"What a relief. Still, sounds like quite an ordeal," she said, and he was warmed by her sympathy, knowing it wasn't just for Camille. The trouble with being a "rock," as Camille was fond of calling him, was that rocks weren't supposed to crumble.

He let out the sigh that, it seemed, had been pent up for the past two days. "It wasn't exactly the weekend we had planned."

"No shit. How did your, um, houseguest deal with all the family drama?" she asked cautiously. During their last phone conversation, he'd told her about Camille's having invited Elise for the weekend and had shared his apprehensions about the mystery woman's upcoming visit.

"Surprisingly well." Though maybe not so surprising, given how good-natured Elise was. "She was a good sport about it all."

There was a brief pause at the other end. "What's she like?"

"Elise? Let's see. Late thirties. Brown hair, green eyes, medium height. She's from the Midwest—Wisconsin, I think she said. Oh, and she's a schoolteacher—she teaches fourth grade."

"I didn't ask for her résumé," Angie said dryly. "What's she like as a person?" She didn't need to ask, *Is she someone you could see yourself with?* He could hear the question in her voice.

"She seems nice, but I don't know her well enough to form an opinion." He purposely downplayed it.

"Bullshit." In the background, he heard what sounded like the droning of an electric mixer. "I never met a guy who didn't know within two seconds flat whether or not a woman was his type."

"Well, I wasn't looking to make a lasting connection, but I suppose most men would say she was attractive." He kept his voice light. The whirring noise grew louder. "What are you making?"

"A cake." She raised her voice to be heard above the droning.

"What kind?"

"Vanilla, with chocolate frosting."

"Mmm. My favorite. What's the occasion?"

"My nephew's birthday—he just turned nine. That would be Susanne's eldest, Danny. My sister's throwing him a party and we're all invited."

At the note of weariness in her voice, he asked, "Is there a problem?"

"Kind of, yeah." The whirring noise stopped. "Considering that in my family it's somebody's birthday practically every other week.

All that forced togetherness wears on you after a while. Not to mention, I'm the one making all those birthday cakes."

"Do you have to go to every party ?"

"It's either that or face the wrath of Loretta D'Amato."

"I'm sure if you explained to her . . ."

"Not a chance," she said. "We're talking about a woman who once stormed the principal's office at Immaculate Conception and threatened to take it to the Vatican if Father Mulroney didn't apologize for having forced my sister Julia to kneel on the chapel floor for all of first period, as punishment for wearing her skirt too short."

He chuckled. "She sounds like a pistol."

"One you don't want get on the wrong end of," she said. "And my sisters aren't much better, except for Francine. They're constantly telling me what to do, even though I keep reminding them the term limit on my being the baby sister they can boss around ran out a long time ago."

"When I was growing up, I used to envy the kids in my neighborhood who had brothers and sisters, which was pretty much everyone except me."

"You should have been counting your blessings instead. Big families are like amoebas—they tend to clump together. They're also noisy and fractious and generally a pain in the ass, especially when they're all in the same room together. Mine is . . . Boisterous is the polite word for it. No bloodshed—yet—but it's come to blows on more than one occasion." Despite her words, he heard the affection in her voice and knew she wouldn't be baking all those cakes, or bowing to her mom's wishes, if it was purely out of a sense of obligation. "Oh, by the way, speaking of get-togethers, I'm meeting up with some of the old gang from Emilio's on Wednesday night, to shoot some pool. If you don't have anything planned, why don't you join us? Bring Camille, if she's feeling up to it."

"I haven't played pool since college," he said, to buy time before giving her an answer. There was nothing he'd enjoy more than a relaxed evening hanging out with Angie and her friends, but he hesitated to accept the invitation. Camille didn't know he'd become friendly with Angie. Worse, it had gone beyond his simply choosing not to inform her of the fact. The other night, he'd told his wife he had a seminar when he was actually at Angie's cooking class. He'd been shocked by how easily the lie had sprung to his lips. Also, it made no sense. Why did he even feel the need to lie? He had nothing to hide. It wasn't as if he was having an affair or was planning to.

He wondered if the reason was because he needed something that didn't have Camille's handprints all over it; something that wasn't complicated or weighted with responsibility and, most importantly, that didn't come with a set of expectations. *As long as it's innocent, what's the harm?* he told himself.

"Were you any good?" Angie wanted to know.

"I was no hustler, but I won my share of beer bets."

"In that case, the beer's on you if you lose."

"You're on." He pushed aside his misgivings. Didn't he deserve an occasional night out? Why did he always have to be the sober, responsible one—life's designated driver? "As long as you're not scared that I'll show you up in front of your friends."

"In your dreams, pal," she growled.

CHAPTER THIRTEEN

"There's a new cancer drug . . ." Regina poured tea into the cups on the low glass table in front of her. They were in her office, on the furniture by the windows, where they always sat, post-exam, to discuss treatment options or go over test results. Usually, the news wasn't good, but this time Camille and Edward perked up as the hematologist-oncologist went on, "Early results have been promising—in mice, it shrank eighty-five percent of the tumors—though we won't know how effective it is with humans until after the trial phase."

He asked, "Is that the hormone-based drug?" Regina, wearing a crisp white blouse and tailored gray slacks, nodded in response and handed him a steaming cup. "I didn't know it was in trials."

"It's not." The trial was months away yet, she told them. "But I've spoken to Dr. Rose about it, and given the urgency in Camille's case, he's agreed to make her a test subject." Dr. Ira Rose, an old friend of Regina's, was head of the research team at MD Anderson that was developing the drug. "That is, if you're willing." She directed her clear-eyed gaze at Camille as she passed her a cup, which clattered in its saucer as Camille took it from her with trembling hand.

"And you think I'd make a good candidate?" she asked.

Regina sat in the wing chair opposite them, where the sunlight slanting through the windows revealed the tiny lines in her face. When she spoke, it was in a measured voice. "Yes and no. As you know, patients with stage-four cancer are less likely to have a . . . positive outcome. That said, since you wouldn't be foregoing other treatment options, you'd have nothing to lose."

"I . . . I don't know." Camille stammered. Out of the corner of her eye, she could see her husband staring at her in stunned disbelief, no doubt wondering why she wasn't jumping at this opportunity. But if she wasn't, it was only because she was fearful of getting her hopes up. Because they could so easily get crushed. She had worked so hard at acceptance, and now she was being asked to give that up, to be plunged back into a sea of uncertainty. "What are the risks?"

"There's no way of knowing at this point. You'd be the canary in the coal mine, so to speak." Regina paused, as if to let this sink in, before going on, "There could be side effects, possibly debilitating ones. Or even fatal." She always told the truth, even when it was brutal; it was one of the traits Camille admired in her doctor, though right now she could have used some sugarcoating.

"In other words, I could die sooner rather than later?" Camille began to shiver and wrapped her hands around her steaming cup to warm them, though it did nothing to relieve the chill she felt.

"Yes. But there's also the possibility you could improve."

"What are the chances of that?"

"Impossible to say at this point." Regina leaned back in her chair, sipping her tea. "But there have been many cases in which experimental drugs have saved lives, even with patients in the final stages of a terminal illness. I've seen it with some of my own patients. So, yes, there's always hope."

Hope. There it was again, dangled before Camille like a prize in the dime-toss booth at a carnival. *Step right up. You could be our lucky winner!* Or, more likely, she'd lose. Not just the battle, but any control she had over her fate. Even her body would cease to be her own; it would once again become the property of doctors and nurses and lab technicians, theirs to poke and prod and subject to endless tests. She recalled when she'd been hospitalized the last time, in an isolation unit for weeks on end, more dead than alive. She'd gladly have finished the job had she had the strength or means.

On the other hand, this drug could work. Even if it didn't cure her, it could buy her time—years maybe. Years in which to watch her children grow and to mend what was broken in her marriage. How could she say no to that? "I suppose it's worth a try," she said, giving a tentative smile.

Edward took her hand, squeezing it. Regina looked pleased. "I'll let Dr. Rose know," she said.

"How soon can she start?" Edward asked eagerly.

"Hopefully, by the end of the week. The first shipment is on its way as we speak," she informed them.

Camille tilted her head at her doctor. "You knew my answer would be yes?"

Regina smiled at her. "Let's just say I hoped it would be."

Camille knew it was the only answer she could have given; even so, minutes later when Edward turned to grin at her as they were being ushered out the door, beaming as if they'd just won the Mega-Millions jackpot, she wanted to caution him, *Don't count the prize money just yet.*

She took his arm as they strolled along the sidewalk. Normally, they would have headed straight to their respective workplaces, but with this news to absorb, they were taking their time. They were on East Sixty-First Street, approaching York Avenue, when suddenly it all caught up to her. Her step faltered, causing her to clutch more tightly to her husband's arm. Longingly, she eyed the wooden bench up ahead, in front of the Abigail Adams house. "Do you mind if we sit down?" At the worried look he shot her, she assured him, "I'm fine. I just need to catch my breath."

"It's a lot to take in, I know. But this is good news!" he said after they'd settled onto the bench. His face was animated, and there was a light in his eyes where before there had been only the dull gleam of whatever dark thoughts lay within; it had been a long time since she'd seen him this excited. "There's been a lot of buzz online and in the journals about this new drug. They're saying it could be the next big breakthrough in cancer research. If it is, it could also be the answer to our—"

"Let's not get ahead of ourselves," she cut him off. "We mustn't get our hopes up too much."

"But at least there *is* hope."

"Yes, but it's still a long shot. And there could be side effects. I could end up in even worse shape."

The light in his eyes dimmed, giving way to a frown. "You can't think that way."

Camille regarded her husband of twenty years, still as handsome as on their wedding day, more so in some ways, even with gray hairs and his face showing evidence of the strain they'd both been under. Dear Edward, who had been sorely tested and would be tested further. She wanted to believe, as he did, that this could work. But hadn't her mother clung to the same hope?

There was something else weighing on her mind, too. Elise had phoned yesterday, inviting them to supper, to repay them for their hospitality this past weekend, she'd said. (Though, really, if anyone was indebted, it was them—Elise had been a godsend during a tough time.) They'd set a tentative date, and Camille had promised to get back to her as soon as she'd checked with Edward. But she had mixed feelings. She'd hoped her family would grow to love Elise in time, but had been unprepared for the quickness and wholeheartedness with which they'd embraced her. The kids were apparently crazy about her, and though Edward hadn't voiced his opinion outside a few neutral comments, his silence on the subject spoke louder than any words. Clearly, he was taken with her (and why not? She'd been hand-selected, with exquisite care, by the expert) and had decided the less said about it the better. Camille would long remember the picture Edward and Elise had made standing at her bedside in the hospital. She was jealous, she realized. Despite her best efforts to contain it, the green-eyed monster was on the loose.

"By the way, Elise called and invited us to supper," she informed him a few minutes later when they were standing on the corner of York Avenue and First, waiting for a cab to come along. "I told her I'd have to check with you." She wanted to give him an out, should he wish to decline. Part of her, the selfish part, wished he would. Hadn't her doctor provided the perfect out: a possible cure? At the same time, Camille knew it was wrong to wish for that. Chances were this new drug wouldn't work. She couldn't lose sight of what was best for her family. In her absence, they would need the constant, loving support only someone as kind and giving as Elise could offer.

She studied Edward as he stood at her side, his gaze trained on the traffic whizzing past, keeping an eye out for a cab that had its light on. What was he thinking? He appeared to have warmed to Elise, but she never knew with him anymore—his mind was a locked vault. Perhaps he was only pretending to like Elise, though she doubted he was that good an actor. Also, there was the way he'd looked at Elise, that day at the hospital—like they were already married, a couple visiting a sick friend.

Her heart sank at his reply, even though she knew it was for the best.

"Sure, sounds good," he said distractedly. "Just let me know the date, and I'll put in on my calendar."

CAMILLE ARRIVED AT her office later that morning to find a stack of pink message slips on her desk. The top one had Stephen Resler's name on it and was marked "urgent." She phoned him at once. She hadn't heard from him in over a week, which normally wouldn't be cause for concern except that Stephen was one of those clients who was in the habit of checking in with her daily (she'd once told him jokingly that his Bluetooth device would have to be surgically removed when he retired). She'd meant to call earlier to see how things were progressing—or not—with Carole Hardy. Though she had nothing to worry about on that score, as it turned out.

"We're engaged!" he announced. "I popped the question last night, and she said yes."

Camille didn't know what to say. Normally, she'd have cheered at such news, but she couldn't help wondering if he was jumping the gun. He was still on the rebound, which tended to cloud one's judgment. It might have been wiser to have waited another month or two, at least. Finally, she rallied and said, "That's wonderful! Have you two set a date?"

"Not yet. We still have a few kinks to iron out."

His guarded tone prompted her to ask, "Such as?"

"I told her I wanted a prenup. She was fine with that, but here's the thing . . ." He paused, and she braced herself. "She offered to have one of the other partners at her firm draw it up, free of charge."

"And that's a problem?"

The question was met with another, longer pause, and she sensed a shift as the old, once-burned Stephen Resler took the place of the new, happily engaged one. Finally, he burst out, "How do I know she's not in cahoots with this other lawyer? I don't want to get screwed in another divorce!"

"I see." Camille took a moment to process this. "And have you told her how you feel?"

"Are you kidding? She'd think I didn't trust her!"

"It sounds as if you don't."

"It's not *her*—she's great. It's just . . ." Stephen exhaled audibly. "My ex-wife really did a number on me, so I have some trust issues."

"With reason. But if you allow yourself to get bogged down dwelling on the possible pitfalls, you'll never be able to move on," she advised. "Sometimes you have to take a leap of faith." She thought of her own leap of faith in agreeing to try this new drug. And before that, with Elise.

"I hear you," he said. "And I'm willing to take that leap. I wouldn't have put a ring on her finger if I wasn't—which, by the way, cost me a bundle. But if, God forbid, this doesn't work out, I can't afford to be taken to the cleaners a second time. I gotta make sure I'm protected."

"Then you need to tell her you'd be more comfortable using your own attorney."

"Won't she be insulted?"

"Stephen, this is the woman you're engaged to," she reminded him. "If you can't be honest with her now, what will it be like once you're married? If this is a deal breaker, better to know now."

He sighed. "So you're saying I gotta bite the bullet?"

"Yes."

After she'd hung up, she declared, "Lord help us. It'll be a miracle if that man ever makes it to the altar. If he does, I'll dance at his wedding even if I have to be carried onto the dance floor."

Dara looked up from her computer. "Speaking of which, don't forget you have a wedding on Sunday."

Camille frowned, struggling to remember which of her clients was getting married, before it finally came to her. "Right. Georgia and Mike. Thanks for reminding me." It had slipped her mind in all the confusion of the previous weekend. Now she thought back to when she'd first met Georgia Dershaw, at the same fundraiser, coincidentally, at which she'd been introduced to Elise, who was a close friend of Georgia's. At the time, the attractive blond advertising exec had been single and looking. (Georgia had jokingly remarked that if she were to meet a man who had all the right qualities, she'd think she was hallucinating and that it was time for the men in the white coats.) Four months later, she was engaged to Mike Kennedy, the handsome, dynamic software engineer she'd met at the meet-and-greet to which Camille had subsequently invited her. "I should get them a gift. Do you know offhand where they're registered?"

"Already taken care of it," Dara informed her. "A lovely set of crystal goblets, if she should mention it. I also arranged for a car to pick you up—eleven o'clock sharp." The ceremony and reception were to take place at the bride's parents' estate in Greenwich, an hour's drive from the city. "Oh, and you need to pick up Edward's suit at the cleaner's. The claim ticket's on your desk."

Camille regarded her former assistant turned partner in wonderment. No one would ever know it to look at her, especially in the over-the-top outfit she had on—a frilly, semitransparent fuchsia top, paired with an above-the-knee coral skirt and tangerine platform heels, that brought to mind a tequila sunrise, attire more suitable for a hostess in an upscale cocktail lounge than a professional matchmaker—but Dara was the soul of efficiency. "You put me to shame, you know that?"

Dara shrugged modestly. "Just doing my job."

"More like both our jobs."

"Don't worry about me. Just look after yourself. Or I'll be stuck going to all those functions in your place while you enjoy your eternal rest," Dara quipped, and then quickly ducked her head, though not quickly enough for Camille to miss the gleam of tears in her eyes. That was another thing about Dara—if she was a tough cookie, it was the kind with the soft center. "By the way, I spoke with Georgia, when I called to find out how many of those goblets she'd need. Sounded like she had a handle on things—none of the usual bride jitters. Did you know she hired Angie to cater the reception?"

"No, I didn't. But I'm glad that worked out." It had been Camille who'd suggested it. It was only fitting, since Angie was the official Harte to Heart caterer, and it had been at one of their meet-and-greets that Georgia and Mike had become smitten with each other.

Camille remembered something else: Elise was one of the bridesmaids. Another thing that had slipped her mind in the haze of the past weekend. She wondered if Elise had mentioned it to Edward. If so, he hadn't said anything to Camille about it. Either it had slipped his mind, too, or she'd been right in suspecting he was keeping his true feelings for Elise under wraps. At the thought, the green-eyed monster stirred to life once more.

*   *   *

ON THURSDAY OF that week, Edward was putting the finishing touches on a speech he was to give at Johns Hopkins the following Monday, the last chore before heading home, when Angie phoned. He broke into a grin at the sound of her voice. "Well, if it ain't Minnesota Fats," he teased.

Angie gave a wicked laugh at the reminder of how she'd beaten him at pool. But as embarrassing as his performance had been, he couldn't recall when he'd last had so much fun. Hanging out with Angie and her pals, Miguel and Julio, shooting pool and knocking back beers, he'd felt like he was back in college. When he told her as much, she said, "I'm glad you enjoyed getting your butt kicked, but I didn't call to gloat."

Ignoring the open document on his laptop, he leaned back into his chair, suddenly in no hurry to get home. "Oh? What's up?"

"Your umbrella. You left it behind last night. Lucky for you, I'm good at rescuing strays."

He chuckled. "I didn't even notice it was missing. But, hey, thanks."

"*De nada.* Least I could do after wiping the floor with you."

He gave a mock groan. "I thought you weren't going to gloat."

"Well, maybe a little. Serves you right for bragging about what a hot-shot you were in college."

"I never said I was a hot-shot, just that I'd won my share of beer bets. Keep in mind, it's been a while since then."

"Ha! Likely excuse. Why don't you just admit it? You got beat by a girl, fair and square."

"Okay, but I plan to even the score next time." He'd already challenged her to a rematch.

"You're on, buddy. And don't even think about wimping out on me."

"How could I, with you holding my umbrella hostage?"

"Speaking of which, I hope you have a spare one," she said. "Otherwise you'll be walking home in the rain, if today's forecast is accurate."

"In that case, you leave me no choice—I'll have to come get it," he said, only half in jest. "If you're not doing anything, we could catch a bite to eat afterward." Why not? Camille had taken the kids to Brooklyn to visit Holly, so he had the evening free.

"Believe me," Angie said, "I'd love nothing more, but I'm up to my eyeballs." She sounded genuinely regretful. "I have a bar mitzvah on Saturday and a wedding on Sunday, so I'm totally slammed."

He felt unreasonably disappointed but was careful to conceal it. "It wouldn't be the same wedding Camille and I are going to, by any chance?" It stood to reason, since the bride and groom were clients of Camille's.

"Greenwich?"

"Bingo," he said.

They exchanged a laugh. Then she said, "I could bring it to you on Sunday, if you like. The umbrella," she added when he didn't reply. But if he was hesitating, it was only because of the dilemma it presented. Camille would want to know what Angie was doing with his umbrella, and what would he say? *I've been secretly meeting with her, but don't worry, we're just friends.* It would drive a wedge between him and Camille, just when he'd begun to feel hopeful, for the first time in months, with this new drug that could be a game changer. What he wanted more than anything was for them to get back to being the loving couple they'd once been.

"No, don't bother," he told Angie. "I can get it another time."

There was a pregnant pause at the other end. He hadn't told Angie he was keeping their friendship a secret, though she must have guessed from the way he had demurred whenever she'd suggested Camille join them. Now he mentally kicked himself for possibly sending the wrong message. Though if Angie wondered why he was keeping her under wraps, she didn't comment on it. She only replied, "Sure, but if you get caught in a downpour, I can't be held responsible."

"Believe me," he said, "that's the least of my worries."

CHAPTER FOURTEEN

"Sweet. Check it out."

Angie looked up from spooning pickled salmon onto endive leaves to find Tamika standing in the kitchen doorway, at the Dershaws' Greenwich estate, peering into the hallway beyond. She hurried over in time to see the bride descend the staircase, resplendent in ivory silk and a cloud of tulle. The bride's father, a tall, silver-haired man in a bespoke suit, beamed up at her from below, then leaned in to murmur something in her ear, when she reached him, that made her smile. Then they made their way arm-in-arm to the French doors that opened onto the terrace and that provided a partial view of the two hundred guests seated in rows of folding chairs on the lawn below. Beyond, Angie could see the tent, which would soon be crammed with people needing to be fed, luffing in the mild breeze that was blowing. The strains of Pachelbel's Canon in D drifted from the garden, where a string quartet played.

It was all so perfect. Like a fairy tale.

Angie's dreamy smile gave way to a frown of annoyance. She'd been at countless weddings. Why get dewy-eyed over this one? She knew the reason: one who stood six-feet-four inches tall, with curly dark hair and eyes the deep amber of double-malt Scotch. She'd spotted him earlier when he arrived, with his wife. She'd been in the kitchen slicing a baguette for crostini when she happened to glance out the window just as a black Town Car was pulling into the circular drive. Seconds later, Edward emerged from the back, so handsome and elegant, in his formal suit, it took her breath away. Literally—she forgot to breathe. She watched him turn to help Camille out of the backseat—Camille, wan and lovely in a pale yellow dress made up of layers of chiffon that floated around her like wilted petals—and then the two of them disappeared from view, escorted by one of the attendants down the stone path that led to the grounds in back.

Now she and Tamika slipped down the hallway to peek out the French doors. The procession of bridesmaids had already taken place, and now the bride and her father were making their way at a stately pace down the rose-petal-strewn runner that stretched to the altar, where the groom and minister stood under a bower entwined with baby roses, flanked by the bridesmaids and groomsmen. The guests were all smiling, some dabbing at their eyes, though no smiles were brighter than those the bride and groom wore as they were joined at last.

Angie recalled the meet-and-greet at which Georgia and Mike had met. The entire time, they'd had eyes only for each other. Whenever she spotted them, they were deep in conversation, oblivious to those around them. She recalled joking to Cleo at the time, "Another one bites the dust."

Now the joke, apparently, was on her. She could no longer feel superior to others—her sisters in particular—for avoiding the mistakes they'd made. Not when she yearned for . . . something. Something more than what she had. She couldn't put her finger on what it was, exactly; she only knew that meeting Edward had changed her perspective. She understood now why a smart, independent woman like Georgia Dershaw would pitch herself headlong onto the shoals of married life. Georgia was in love—the kind of love that renders you incapable of sound judgment or caution.

Tamika nudged her and pointed out a familiar face, seated in back: a tall exclamation point of a man amid a sea of commas. Edward. Angie's heart started to race, and she felt the slow burn in her belly—two parts desire and one part frustration—that she'd felt watching from afar when he and Camille had arrived. But it was useless to indulge in wishful thinking, she told herself. Even if he'd had designs on her, which he clearly didn't (he treated her the same way her brother-in-law, Big Nick, did—like the kid sister he never had) there was no getting around the fact that he was married. To a woman she liked and admired.

One thing puzzled her, though. The other day, when she'd called to let him know she had his umbrella, he'd said something that confirmed what she'd suspected for some time: He hadn't told his wife about her. The question was, why? It couldn't be because Camille was the possessive type. She even had his next wife picked out, for God's sake! (Something Angie had difficulty understanding—she'd been brought up by a mother who'd be issuing dire warnings from her deathbed, threatening to come back to haunt her husband should he so much as look at another woman before she was cold in her grave.) So what was it, then? Maybe he was just a man who held his cards close to his vest. Which made her wonder: *What isn't he telling* me? Not that she had a right to know every detail of his personal life—they'd only known each other a short while, though it seemed longer. But still.

She thought of the pretty schoolteacher. What was up with *that?* As far Angie knew, he was only going along with it to humor Camille, but when Angie had asked about Elise he'd acted weird, like he'd barely noticed her the entire time she'd stayed with them, which made no sense at all unless he was hiding something, or perhaps lying to himself. Angie's mind swam with questions, her emotions in a similar tumult. *Get a grip,* she ordered herself. *You're not being paid to stand here mooning.* With that, she turned and headed back to the kitchen.

EDWARD, AS HE watched the bride and groom exchange vows, found himself thinking back on his own wedding day. His and

Camille's had been a far more modest affair, with just close friends and relatives in attendance. They'd been cash-strapped, still paying off his student loans, and Camille too obstinate to accept more than a modest contribution from her father, so the ceremony and reception had taken place at a garden center in Westchester owned by the parents of Camille's college roommate Melissa. Camille wore her mother's wedding gown, altered to fit her slimmer figure, and he the one good suit he owned, purchased for his college graduation. He was so nervous, he'd fumbled and nearly dropped the ring attempting to slip it on her finger. In contrast, Camille was as relaxed as if she'd been preparing for that day since the moment they'd met. It was a trait he admired in her: that she always seemed to know how any given story would turn out. It was why she was so successful in her career. But did she know what she was doing this time, in deciding his fate? Did she have any idea what she'd wrought?

Edward's gaze strayed to Elise, standing with the other brides-maids, all dressed in identical lilac-colored gowns. He took in her pink cheeks and sparkling eyes, her light-brown hair that fell in loose, shiny waves around her shoulders, in contrast to the elaborate coifs of the other women. She'd make an even lovelier bride—almost as lovely as Camille on their wedding day. At the thought, he felt a lump form in his throat and the scene before him dissolved in the wash of tears that momentarily blurred his vision. He blinked hard and reached for his wife's hand.

I MUST BE losing it, Angie thought. Maybe her mom's theory, that prolonged spinsterhood (coupled with sexual deprivation in her case) led to early dementia, wasn't so wacky after all. She couldn't keep her mind on her tasks. She inadvertently scraped the parsley tops into the trash instead of the stems and shredded several sheets of the phyllo dough she was using to wrap the cubes of beef for her mini–beef Wellingtons. At one point, as she was chopping chives, the knife slipped, nearly taking off the tip of her index finger. "Shit!" she swore, and then caught herself before she could utter a string of even more colorful curse words.

Tamika looked up at her. "You okay, Miss D?" She'd been a last-minute replacement for one of the waitstaff, Brianna, who'd called in sick. She was the most reliable of Angie's students, and Angie knew she could use the money—she was saving for college. So far, she'd proven useful, doing whatever was needed without complaint, even the grunt work like taking out the trash, and with only a few minor screwups. She wasn't quite ready for front of the house, but in her "uniform"—the plain white shirt and black slacks Angie had told her to wear—with her hair pulled back in a neat chignon and her only jewelry the diamond stud in her nose, she looked the part.

"I'm fine," Angie replied in a forcibly upbeat tone.

"Mmm-hmm. Just like when me and Daarel is fightin' and I ain't gettin' none. Girl, I saw the way you was lookin' at the doc." Tamika lapsed into ghetto speak, as if Angie was just another girl in the hood—which she supposed was a compliment, though right now she was too annoyed to see it as such.

These kids, thought Angie. They thought of nothing but sex. But it had been the same when she was that age, she reminded herself. Hairstyles and fashions were the only things that changed. She hadn't been as promiscuous as some of the girls in her class at Immaculate Conception (where there had been nothing immaculate about the conceptions that had taken place), but there had been boys, boys with whom she'd fallen in and out of love—or like—with the ease of a swimmer changing strokes. It wasn't until she was living on her own that the pickings grew thin. And now she was reduced to having a sixteen-year-old comment on her sex life—or lack thereof.

She cast Tamika a stern look. "The only thing you need to focus on is doing your job. That is, if you plan on keeping this one after today."

Tamika's face lit up. "For real?"

"Yes, though it'd only be part-time, on weekends. I wouldn't want it to interfere with your studies."

Tamika beamed at her and said in her National Merit Scholarship voice, "I won't disappoint you, Miss D."

Soon the appetizers were ready to go out. In addition to the ginger-pickled salmon on endive leaves and mini–beef Wellingtons, there were pot stickers stuffed with sautéed Napa cabbage and bits of pancetta, crostini topped with deviled crab and asparagus pesto, and grilled swordfish on skewers with Asian dipping sauce. While Stylianos passed around flutes of champagne to the guests now crowded into the tent, Pat and Cleo circulated with trays. Meanwhile, Angie remained behind the scenes, where she could supervise Tamika and where she wouldn't risk running into Edward and Camille, which could prove awkward.

It wasn't until the guests had sat down to eat that she put in an appearance—she was short-staffed, so it was all hands on deck—but even then, she was careful to avoid the table at which Edward and Camille sat, which she'd assigned to Cleo. When she finally caught his eye at one point, she only smiled, not stopping to chat. A smile that communicated *Your secret is safe with me.* Though it seemed strange to be keeping their relationship a secret, when it was perfectly innocent. When she glanced over at him again, he was chatting with the woman on his right—one of the bridesmaids, a pretty brunette who appeared to be hanging on his every word.

Angie felt a stab of jealousy, thinking, *Of course.* He probably had legions of women secretly lusting after him. Many of whom would glom on to him when he was a widower like fat ladies flocking to the dessert table at a buffet. Women no doubt far more suitable in every way than she was.

It took every ounce of effort to stay focused as she bustled about. She and her crew got out the next two courses and had just finished plating the dessert—*panna cotta* with pomegranate syrup, and lemon shortbread stamped with the newlyweds' initials—when the band struck up. Angie was passing by Edward and Camille's table when she saw him lean in and murmur in his wife's ear, as if asking her to dance. Camille smiled and shook her head, and though he appeared to take it in stride, Angie didn't miss the look of disappointment that flashed across his face. He turned back to his seatmate, the pretty brunette with whom he'd been chatting earlier.

She didn't see Camille again until they ran into each other a few minutes later as she was stepping out the back door, carrying a loaded tray. Camille was on her way in to use the restroom. "Want me to hold your plate until you get back?" Angie offered after they'd exchanged greetings.

"Thanks, but I'm going to have to skip dessert," Camille told her. "I don't think I could squeeze in another bite. Everything was delicious, by the way. You really outdid yourself."

Angie felt her cheeks warm. Did Camille suspect anything? But what was there to suspect, after all? She'd done nothing wrong. "Thanks," she murmured. "You look nice, by the way." Camille was a bit paler than usual and much too thin, but she looked more ethereal than deathly.

"Do I?" Camille smiled, her gaze turning inward. "Well, maybe there's something to be said for tilting at windmills."

Angie didn't know what to make of the cryptic remark.

She took advantage of the lull, after the desserts had gone out, to steal away for a quick break. Earlier, she'd spied a secluded patio off the breakfast nook. Sheltered by latticework covered in climbing vines, it looked out on a small garden with a pond at the center. She was relieved, when she pushed open the glass door onto the patio, to see that no one else had discovered it. There was only the cat curled up, asleep, one of the rattan chairs and the koi swimming in the pond.

She stretched out on the chaise. It was sheer bliss to be off her aching feet, the sun on her face. The only sounds were the droning of bees and, farther off in the distance, that of toasts being made to the newlyweds inside the tent, accompanied by enthusiastic applause and whistles. Then the band struck up again—a familiar tune that soon had her humming along. She closed her eyes and allowed her mind to drift, picturing herself gliding over the dance floor in Edward's arms.

"THIS TIME, I'M not taking no for answer," Edward told his wife as he pulled her to her feet and onto the dance floor.

Camille had begged off before, but now she smiled and moved into the circle of his arms. As they waltzed to the music, he thought of all the times through the years they'd danced together like this. It felt so familiar . . . and at the same time like something he'd forgotten he knew how to do, like the games he played with his children—Wiffle ball and badminton—that he hadn't played since he himself was a child. Would they ever find their way back to where they'd started? Two people, young and in love, who'd wouldn't have let anything or anyone come between them.

"It's been a while since we've done this," she murmured, as if picking up on his thoughts.

"Too long," he said, pulling her closer.

"What were you thinking of just now?"

"Our wedding day." He smiled into her hair.

"It was nothing like this one, that's for sure. Talk about low budget. If it weren't for my sister, we'd have been dancing to that old boom box of yours instead of the free band she scraped up."

"Well, it was memorable, at least."

"In more ways than one. Remember when my friend Annabel got stung by that bee? I was getting ready to walk down the aisle, and she was yelling for a doctor." Camille chuckled at the memory, though it hadn't been so amusing at the time, Edward recalled. Annabel was allergic, it turned out, and if his friend and fellow intern Phil Terzian hadn't had his black bag in the trunk of his car, she might have died. "I still think the outdoors is more romantic than a church, but you *do* have the insects to consider. All in all, though, I'd have to say it was the perfect wedding."

"Way better than a banquet hall at the Ritz," he agreed.

"Yes, though this is nice. The only thing that really matters is if you're happy." Her gaze strayed to the newlyweds, who glided past just then, their eyes locked on each other's as they moved over the dance floor in perfect unison. His throat tightened, and tears rose once more. He bit back the words he didn't dare voice. *Remember when we used to look at each other like that?*

When the dance ended and another one began, she said, "I think I'd better sit this one out."

"Are you feeling all right?" he asked as they headed back to their table.

"I'm just a bit tired, is all," she said. "Why don't you ask Elise to dance?"

Edward felt a flash of annoyance. If Elise wasn't within earshot, he would have made up some excuse. But he didn't want to be rude, so he turned to Elise and smiled. "May I have this dance?"

She nodded, and together they moved onto the dance floor. As he took her in his arms, he was struck by how robust she seemed, slender though she was, with her firm flesh and rosy cheeks—the picture of health. Out of the corner of his eye, he could see Camille watching them, wearing a bright, fixed smile. It made him clumsy all of a sudden. "Sorry I'm such a klutz. I'm a little out of practice," he apologized after he'd stepped on Elise's toes.

"You're doing just fine," she told him, trying not to wince.

He drew back to eye her bemusedly. "Are you always this polite?"

She laughed. "I can't help it. I'm from the Midwest."

"You put me to shame," he said after another spin around the dance floor, during which he was as clumsy as she was light on her feet, though he did manage not to step on her toes again.

"My parents made me take lessons," she told him. "I was thirteen, and they must've thought it was the only way I'd ever get a boy to dance with me." He drew back to cock an eyebrow at her, finding it hard to believe the lovely Elise had ever had trouble getting boys to dance with her, and she confided, "In seventh grade, I was a head taller than the tallest boy in my class, which doesn't do much for a girl's popularity. Every school dance, I'd come home crying."

"You should've seen me when I was that age," he said. "I was over six feet by the time I turned thirteen. The other kids nicknamed me Stork. You and I would have made a good couple."

He saw her cheeks color, and immediately regretted his ill-considered words.

When the dance ended, he escorted her back to her seat. One of the servers, the light-skinned black girl he recognized from the meet-and-greet, was clearing the table, and he thought of Angie. He'd spotted her earlier but hadn't had a chance to say hello. Now might be a good time. He excused himself, ignoring the questioning look Camille darted him, and headed for the house.

"THERE YOU ARE. I've been looking all over for you."

Angie gave a guilty start, embarrassed to have been caught napping on the job, and then thought, *I know that voice.* She turned, registering Edward's presence as he stepped onto the patio. No, not a dream—here in the flesh. She broke into a grin. "I'm taking a cigarette break," she told him.

"I didn't know you were a smoker," he said.

"I'm not, but I figure I'm entitled to the same perks. Ever notice how no one ever questions it when someone slips out back for a quick smoke? If you totaled up all those five-minute breaks, it'd come to a week's vacation. Me? I'm lucky if I get five seconds to myself." He smiled as he lowered himself into the rattan chair opposite her, which creaked agreeably with his weight. "In my line of work, you've got to be on your toes every minute. Because it's always something—an oven on the fritz or a delivery that got waylaid, or someone got careless with a knife and needs stitches. Today one of my staffers called in sick at the last minute, so I was left shorthanded. Remember Tamika, from my cooking class? I hired her to fill in. But she's new, so there's a learning curve." Angie was aware she was babbling, using words to construct a not-so-solid wall between her and Edward, but she couldn't seem to stop. "What about you? What are you doing hanging out with the hired help when you ought to be dancing with your wife?"

His smile faded. "She wasn't feeling up to it—she's still a little under the weather."

Angie wasn't quite sure how to respond. What do you say to a man whose wife is dying? *Cheer up! She'll be back on her feet soon!* "I ran into her earlier," she said. "She looked good for someone who just got out of the hospital. In fact, I was surprised when you told me you were coming. I didn't think she'd be up to it. But that's Camille for you—she's a trooper."

"I don't think she knows how to slow down." He smiled thinly.

"She said something about tilting at windmills. Do you know what she meant by that?"

He thought for a moment, then said, "No, but I have a pretty good guess." He explained that Camille's doctor had just started her on an experimental drug. "It's totally untested, so we don't know what to expect."

"Sounds hopeful," Angie replied guardedly, not sure if a show of enthusiasm was called for. All she knew about experimental drugs was what she'd picked up watching doctor shows on TV. In real life, it was probably different. Not everyone got cured in the space of an hour's viewing time.

"I think so, but Camille sees it as . . . well, apparently, just another windmill to tilt at." His expression clouded over.

"But if it works, that's all that matters, right?"

"Sure. I just wish she had a little more faith."

"Either way, it won't change the outcome." Angie reached to pet the cat, a marmalade tom, which had relinquished its chair to Edward and settled onto the chaise. "I was raised Catholic, and when I was a kid I used to pray for stuff. My mom told me it didn't work that way, that prayers weren't like a Christmas wish list, but it wasn't until I was older that I realized she was right—it's all pretty random. Not that I stopped believing in God; I just don't see Him as a Santa in the sky. Either you'll get what you want or you won't. All you can do is hope for the best."

"This isn't like the battery-operated car I wanted when I was ten," he said dryly.

"No," she acknowledged with a somber nod. "By the way, did you ever get that car?"

"Yeah," he said, a corner of his mouth lifting in an ironic smile. "Minus the batteries."

They were quiet for a minute, gazing out at the pond where koi swirled and darted like handfuls of tossed confetti. "So, does this mean the deal's off?" Angie ventured at last.

"What deal?" He brought his gaze back to her.

"You know. With the schoolteacher."

"Oh, that." Edward sighed. She waited for him to elaborate, and when he didn't she employed a trick that had always served her well, as the youngest of five sisters who were immune to being outshouted: She stared at him with one eyebrow arched, until he finally divulged, "She's having us over for dinner next weekend." As if that answered the question, which she supposed it did.

"I see," she said. "So even though her services may no longer be required, you're keeping her around just in case?"

"It's not like that," he said, frowning.

"And just what *is* it like?"

"Elise is . . . a family friend."

"Oh, so she's a 'family friend' after just one weekend? Fast work on her part." A nasty edge crept into her voice.

"You make it sound calculated. But if you met her, you'd see she isn't like that. She's a nice person."

Angie felt a stab of jealousy. "A nice person who just so happens to have designs on a married man." *Isn't that the pot calling the kettle black?* whispered a voice in her head. She herself didn't have designs on Edward, at least, not the kind that involved a ring on her finger and silver and china patterns registered at Bloomingdale's, but the fantasies she'd been having about him (her favorite was the one in which they reenacted the scene in *The Postman Always Rings Twice* where Lana Turner is ravaged on the kitchen table like an all-you-can-eat buffet) hardly qualified her for sainthood, either.

His frown deepened. "You've got the wrong idea," he insisted.

"Why don't you explain it to me, then?"

His shoulders sagged. "All I know is, Camille wants this, and I'm not going to deny her. If it gives her comfort to go on believing her family won't be left high and dry when—if—she's gone, then I don't see the harm. She doesn't have to know I have no intention of ever marrying Elise."

Angie grew very still. So still, there was only the beating of her heart, which seemed to fill her entire body. "You don't?" she squeaked.

"No," he said. "I like her a lot, but we'll never be more than friends."

Angie felt a heady rush of relief. Though it didn't change anything as far as she was concerned. She thought: *Is that how he sees me, too—as someone who could never be more than a friend?* "When did you know?" she asked.

"I think I knew all along, but it wasn't until today that it hit me. When I was dancing with her. There I was, a beautiful woman in my arms, one I happen to be fond of, and I felt . . . nothing."

Angie eyed him in confusion. "You mean she's *here*?"

He nodded. "She and the bride are old friends—she's one of the bridesmaids."

No doubt the same one Angie had seen him chatting with earlier. *Oh, what a tangled web we weave* . . . "And have you told Elise she shouldn't get her hopes up?" she asked, her jealousy of a moment ago turning to sympathy. She and the schoolteacher were in the same boat.

"Not in so many words. But I don't have to—she feels the same way I do. We both got roped into this."

"Well, it didn't look like she was in a hurry to be untied."

He eyed her uncomprehendingly. God, men could be so clueless! He said, shaking his head, "I don't know what you thought you saw, but it's not like that, I'm telling you. She went through a rough divorce, and she's not looking to get into another relationship."

Angie wondered again how someone as smart as Edward could be so stupid. She recalled the adoring look on the brunette's face when the two had been chatting. "Maybe not," she said. "But love has a way of sneaking up on you." She ought to know; wasn't that what had happened to her?

In a fit of frustration and self-loathing, she leaped to her feet and stalked to the edge of the patio, where she stood with arms crossed over her chest, scowling in the direction of the pond. She should have ended this . . . whatever you wanted to call it—friendship? An exercise in frustration?—weeks ago, as soon she realized her rogue heart wasn't taking orders from her head. But she hadn't, and now she was paying the price. She heard the scrape of his chair, and a moment later felt his touch on her arm.

"Angie. What is it? What's wrong?"

She let out a breath, and to her horror, a tiny sob escaped along with it. Oh, God. Why didn't she just put an announcement in the *Times*? Then she could make it public. "Nothing," she said.

"You're angry." He put his hand under her chin and tipped her head up to meet his gaze.

"Okay, *yes*, but not at you. I'm mad at myself!" she burst out. "Because I care about you, damn it. I never expected to, I thought we could just be friends." She gave a harsh laugh at the perplexed look he wore. "Yeah, I know—so tenth grade."

"I didn't know you felt that way," he said.

"Then that makes two of us. God, I feel so stupid!" She balled her hands into fists.

"You're not stupid." He put his arms around her, pulling her to him to console her.

She was just tall enough for her head to fit snugly against his breastbone, where she could hear the strong, measured beat of his heart. He smelled of a mixture of wine and cut grass and the more subtle scent that was his alone. She tipped her head back, and they both stared at each other for a second as if to say *What now?* He didn't seem to have any more of a clue than she did. Then, as if drawn by some centrifugal force, their lips met, and she had the most peculiar thought: *This must be what it's like to get shot.* Except it didn't hurt. There was the shock of impact, followed by a sudden lightness of being as her muscles went slack and her knees started to buckle. A warm, tingly deliciousness coursed through her. She parted her lips and felt him respond in kind, with an intensity that took her—him, too, she suspected—by surprise. He crushed her to him, and she felt a shudder go through him. A low groan escaped his throat. She wanted to say to him, *Slow down, there's no rush,* but she knew this might be all they'd ever have.

When they drew apart, he rocked back on his heels and blew out a breath. "Jesus. I didn't see that coming." He gave a shaky laugh. "What did your bartender put in those drinks anyway?"

Angie felt as dazed as he looked. "That was some kiss."

"In my defense, it wasn't premeditated."

"You make it sound like murder."

"Maybe just manslaughter." He smiled, a smile that fell away as soon as it formed. "Angie . . . look, I don't know what to tell you. I'm not even sure what just happened."

She sighed. "It's complicated, I know." She paused before adding in a more resolute voice, "There's just something you should know, so there's no misunderstanding: I'm not the friends-with-benefits type. I may not look it, but I'm an old-fashioned girl at heart." She might not believe in marriage, but she want to be loved by whoever she was with, if only for the duration.

"I don't think of you that way," he said.

"Which leaves us . . . where exactly?" Angie felt as if she were in a car careening down an unfamiliar road at night.

"Honestly? I don't know."

"Should we stop seeing each other?"

"That would be the sensible thing, yes. But you know what?" He placed his hands on her shoulders, looking deep into her eyes. "I like you, Angie. I like being around you. You make me feel like . . . like I'm alive instead of barely functioning. I don't know that I can give that up. I know that sounds selfish, but that's how I feel."

She eased the air out of her lungs. "I see," she said, though she didn't see anything at all, except the man standing before her, wearing a look that was equal parts confusion and tenderness.

"But I can't make any promises. If you had any sense, you'd walk away right now, before it's too late."

Angie knew he was right—she should walk away, get on with her life, and leave Edward to muddle through his—but it was already too late. Her fate was sealed the second his lips touched hers.

The band started up again inside the tent, the music drifting toward them. Distantly, she could hear the lead singer (a veritable Bono compared to most wedding singers) crooning a familiar tune—"Stardust"—a standard at wedding receptions and one she'd heard a million times, humping trays while others danced. Now, though, it was if she were hearing it for the first time.

"Well, what do you know?" she said. "They're playing our song."

Edward smiled at her. "I didn't know we had a song."

"We do now." She held out her arms, and they began to dance.

CHAPTER FIFTEEN

The first week in August, Camille arrived home from work on Wednesday to the unexpected, and totally unprecedented, sight of her father seated on the living room sofa with Zach. They were playing an Xbox game—"Arctic Thunder" from the looks of it—both so absorbed they didn't notice when she entered the room.

"Dad! What are you doing here?" she cried. She hadn't even known he was in town.

He looked up at her, breaking into a grin. "Well, at the moment my grandson here is proving it's apparently not too late to teach an old dog new tricks." He relinquished the controller, then stood and crossed the room to where she stood, giving her a kiss on the cheek. "Hi, honey. Sorry to drop in unannounced, but you weren't answering my calls, so I decided to surprise you."

There was no hint of reproach in his voice, but she felt a stab of guilt nonetheless. She'd been meaning to get back to him for weeks, but there had always been some reason to put it off: It was too late or too early in the day, she was tired or not feeling well, or it was at an hour when he was likely to be on the golf course. But mainly, it was because she didn't think it mattered to him one way or the other. He'd made the effort; now he could cross that item off his list. He didn't really care about her; he was only going through the motions.

Or so she'd thought. Apparently, he cared enough to pay her a visit.

"Don't worry, I booked a room at a hotel," he said, at the panic that must have shown on her face. Zach peeled his eyes from the TV screen to ask, "Can Grandpa Larry stay for supper?" He wore a hopeful look. Never mind that Grandpa Larry was a virtual stranger to her children. Visits were rare, and the only regular contact, outside the annual family dinner at the Waldorf-Astoria or when Camille put the kids on the phone to say hello, were the cards their grandfather sent for their birthdays, always with a twenty-dollar bill tucked inside, and the presents at Christmas.

She hesitated, and Larry was quick to interject, "If you have other plans ..."

"No. Of course we'd love to have you, Dad," she said, her manners kicking in belatedly. She put on a smile. "It won't be fancy, but I'm sure I can rustle up something. Can I get you a drink?"

"I wouldn't say no to a Scotch and soda," he said, looking as if he'd been granted an executive pardon. Was she really so hardhearted he had to be grateful to be asked to stay for supper when he'd come all this way? She felt another stab, then resented him for making her feel guilty.

She went into the kitchen. Did she even have any whiskey? She couldn't recall the last time a guest in her home had requested hard liquor. Most people these days drank wine. She rooted around, finally unearthing a dusty bottle of Johnnie Walker from the pantry cupboard. She was pouring some into a glass when Kyra came flying in, wearing her Lululemon bike shorts and a purple tank top, her hair in a messy ponytail and her feet bare, revealing neon-blue toenail polish.

"Mom, look what Grandpa Larry gave me!" her daughter cried excitedly, waving something at her—a check, she saw, made out to "Kyra Constantin" in the amount of one hundred dollars. "He gave one to Zach, too. He said we could buy whatever we liked. Isn't that awesome?"

"Awesome," Camille echoed with considerably less enthusiasm. "You shouldn't spoil them," she chided her father after Kyra had dashed off. She poured soda into the glass, then handed it to him. "What else am I going to spend it on?" he said with a shrug. *You can't buy love.* "It's fine just this once, as long as you don't make a habit of it," she told him. "Remember, Edward and I still have to live with them after you turn them into monsters."

While Larry sipped his drink, she began assembling ingredients for a stir-fry. She was surprised when he said, "Can I give you a hand with that?" She couldn't recall him ever lifting a finger in the kitchen.

"Since when do you know how to cook?" she said, giving him a wry smile.

"Since I had to learn to feed myself." He stood up, removing his seersucker blazer and draping it over the back of the counter stool on which he'd been sitting, then walked around to where she stood. "You can only eat out so many nights a week, and I never wanted to be one of those old people who subsist on frozen dinners."

She arched an eyebrow. "You mean you don't have a bevy of women waiting on you?"

"That gets old."

"What, the women or them waiting on you?"

"Both. Not that I'm getting any younger myself." He chuckled as he rolled up his shirtsleeves, then his good humor gave way to a melancholy look, as if at the reminder that his eldest daughter might not have the luxury of growing old. He asked, "What's the latest word from the doctor?"

"Nothing much to report." She kept it light, not wanting to get into a heavy discussion. She regretted her outburst that night at the Waldorf. Look where it had led. "Except she has me on this new drug." He perked up at that, and she was quick to explain the drug was experimental and thus completely unproven. Also, she reminded him, experimental drugs that actually lived up to their hype were rare—the equivalent of a hole in one in golf, to use a metaphor he could relate to. "So far it doesn't seem to be having any effect, but the good news is, I'm not any worse."

At regular intervals, she dutifully made the trip across town to New York–Presbyterian Hospital, where she rode the elevator to the third floor of the Payson Pavilion and then made her way down the corridor to the infusion suite (a route so familiar by now she could've found her way there blindfolded). There, she lay in a recliner for two hours tethered to an IV, trying to think positive thoughts while toxic, and possibly lethal, substances circulated through her bloodstream. She was receiving the new drug along with the chemo, so her routine had remained unchanged—four days on, four days off. The only difference was the reintroduction of the "thing with feathers" from the Emily Dickinson poem: hope. Hope that, in her case, flew on wings grown clumsy with disuse.

"You'll let me know if there's any change?" Larry said.

"Of course." She handed him a bag of carrots and the vegetable peeler, which he contemplated as if it were some complex piece of machinery. "Does Holly know you're in town?" she asked as she dumped the other vegetables she'd scrounged from the fridge into the colander to be rinsed.

He looked up at her and nodded, breaking into a smile at the mention of his youngest daughter. "As a matter of fact, I'm meeting her for lunch tomorrow. I was hoping you could join us."

Camille felt miffed at being an afterthought, then thought, *Why should I care?* She had no wish to be her father's favorite. "Tomorrow? Sure, I think I could swing that. I'm supposed to have lunch with one of my clients, but I'll see if I can reschedule." She didn't think Kat would mind.

"She's bringing her friend Curtis. She wants us to meet him."

"Well, it's about time." Camille was anxious to meet the new man in Holly's life. He'd put in for a transfer after learning Holly was pregnant and was now back in his old job at his firm's Wall

Street offices. Though, for whatever reason, Holly hadn't been in a hurry to introduce him to her family. Camille didn't know if it was because she hadn't yet figured out what role he was going to play in her life and that of their child, or if she thought her big sister might disapprove.

"I just hope he's nothing like her former boyfriends," Larry said, voicing Camille's concern.

She sighed. "Amen to that." For once, she and her dad could agree on something. Holly's taste in men had always been questionable at best. Her previous boyfriends included an unemployed high school dropout who'd sold weed to support himself; a lead singer in a garage band that never made it out of the garage; a bouncer at a nightclub, with a shaved head and massive arms covered in tattoos, who answered, for reasons unknown to her, to the name Squid; and, most recently and famously, legitimate rocker Ronan Quist, whose weakness for drugs, alcohol, and groupies (Holly once caught him having sex with two girls at the same time, both underage) was well-documented by the tabloids. There had been no one since Ronan, except the occasional fling. Camille could only hope her sister was ready for a grown-up relationship now that she was about to become a mother. She was encouraged by the fact that Curtis was a) gainfully employed, and b) obviously wished to play a part in his child's life.

"He sounds normal from Holly's description, and his job doesn't involve burning guitars onstage," she listed the positives as she sliced mushrooms. "Also, he's prepared to take responsibility for Holly and the baby. That says something. Though I don't know if Holly got the memo."

"Maybe she's finally ready to settle down," Larry said hopefully.

"I wouldn't rule it out." As a matchmaker, Camille had seen it time and again. People who broke their pattern of entering into bad relationships (usually because of some seminal event, such as a death in the family or, in Holly's case, an unexpected pregnancy) and found true love at last. "While it's true that a leopard doesn't change its spots, it can always find new hunting grounds."

"Speaking of which . . ." Larry looked up at her, a carrot in one hand and the peeler in the other, a curly strip of peel dangling from its tip. From the nervous look he wore, it was obvious something was weighing on his mind, but typical of him, he was going to make her dig for it.

Swallowing her impatience, she asked evenly, "What is it, Dad?"

"Oh, nothing. It's just . . ." He cleared his throat and began again. "I want you to know I've thought a lot about what you said the last time, and I've decided . . . well, the thing of it is . . ." He trailed off, color rising in his cheeks beneath his golfer's tan. He put the peeler down and reached for his drink, taking a fortifying gulp, the sound of the ice rattling in the glass loud in the stillness. When she just stood there, silently waiting for him to go on, he cried, "Damn it, Cammie, you don't make it easy! I always feel like I'm saying the wrong thing with you."

"As opposed to ignoring me, you mean?" she replied coolly.

He dropped his gaze, staring fixedly at the polished granite countertop, where his hazy reflection stood out like a spot she'd missed when wiping up. "I guess I deserved that," he said, his voice soft with regret. "You're right—I wasn't the greatest dad, and there's no excuse for that. But after your mom died . . . well, you were so angry with me. If I stayed away, it was because I couldn't bear the way you looked at me. Like I was the bad guy. You still look at me that way."

A flurry of angry responses stormed through her head, only to melt, one by one, like snowflakes, before they reached her lips. "I do?" She hadn't realized she was so transparent. She realized something else then: Moments like this one with her dad were numbered along with her days. If she wanted to make peace with him, she would have to start somewhere. "Okay, so maybe I wasn't the greatest daughter, either," she conceded. "But I was just a child, and Mom was gone. Even if I was acting like a brat, I still needed my dad. You pretty much checked out on us."

Larry hung his head. "I suppose it's too late to ask for forgiveness."

"Why now? Is it because I'm dying?"

He winced at the reminder. "No. I should have done it years ago. You're right—I did check out. It's no excuse, but when I lost your mom, I lost my bearings. I didn't know who I was anymore, without her, much less how to be a proper dad. I let you girls down. I let *myself* down."

A memory surfaced, of sitting on her father's lap when she was three or four. He'd been smoking his pipe, she recalled, the pleasant fruity smell of the tobacco mingling with the scent of his aftershave as she nestled against him with her head resting on his chest, the wool of his blue golf sweater scratchy against her cheek—the safest of havens. *He loved me back then,* she thought. Maybe Holly was right. Maybe he'd loved her all along but just didn't know how to show it.

She wanted to forgive him. But it wasn't going to happen overnight. "Well, you're here now, so why don't you make yourself useful," she said briskly, indicating the half-peeled carrot in his hand. "Step it up, Dad, or we'll be here all night." His face relaxed, and he resumed his task.

Edward showed up as they were all sitting down to eat. "Well, isn't this a nice surprise!" he exclaimed at seeing his father-in-law. His delight was genuine, she knew—he and Larry had always gotten along well. Too well, for Camille's taste. "To what do we owe the pleasure?"

"Oh, you know, it's been a while. I figured I was overdue for a visit." Larry rose to give Edward a handshake coupled with a manly clap on the back. "Good to see you, son. You're looking well."

"So do you. You in town for long?" Edward pulled up a chair.

"Just until Friday. In fact . . ." He cast a tentative glance at

Camille. "I was thinking maybe the kids could fly back with me if they don't have other plans. I'd love to have them, and there's no shortage of activities—we've got the pool, tennis, shuffleboard, croquet, you name it." He turned to Kyra and Zach, asking in a hearty voice, "What do you say, kids? Would you like that?"

Zach brightened. "Cool! Can we?" he asked eagerly, his gaze darting from Camille to Edward.

Kyra looked horrified. "Zach doesn't need me to go with him, right?" Her voice rose on a shrill, panicky note. Then she caught herself and said, "I'd love to, Grandpa, but I . . . I have this, um, thing with my friends." An invented excuse, no doubt—most of her friends were either still away at camp or vacationing with their parents. Not that Camille blamed her daughter. Forced exile in a retirement community, if only for a few days, with a grandparent who was practically a stranger, fell into the category of cruel and unusual punishment for a teenager. Besides, Kyra had just gotten back from camp, in Maine, where she'd spent the better part of June and all of July.

"I'm sure Grandpa understands," Camille put in before he could comment. She was mindful of the fact that he was honoring her request, but she wasn't ready to place her children in his care just yet. She turned to Zach. "Aren't you supposed to go kayaking with your day camp next week?"

"Yeah, but this might be the only chance I get to visit Grandpa Larry!" he pleaded.

From the mouths of babes. Camille glanced at her father and saw the inference wasn't lost on him. He looked chagrined that it had taken him this long to extend the invitation. The question was, did it come from a genuine desire to get to know his grandchildren? Only time would tell. And time was running out. "It's all right by me if your dad says it's okay," she told her son.

"I don't see why not," Edward said.

Larry looked pleased. Zach was beside himself.

"Yay! I'm going to Florida!" He jumped up, nearly knocking over his water glass in his haste to run over and hug his mother. "Thanks, Mom! You're the best!"

"What am I, chopped liver?" Edward groused good-naturedly.

Belatedly, Zach darted over to give his dad a hug, and as he did, Edward's eyes met Camille's over the top of their son's scruffy brown head in a wordless exchange. Her being the go-to parent had never really been an issue until now, but all of a sudden it seemed like a very big deal.

Later that night, after they'd seen Larry out and sent the children off to bed, Camille said, "By the way, I spoke with Elise today." She was in the walk-in closet in their bedroom, changing into her nightgown. From her vantage point, she could see her husband partially reflected in the full-length mirror on the back of the open closet door—he was seated on the bed, unbuttoning his shirt—but he couldn't see her, as she stood still and alert as a deer at the edge of a clearing.

"What's new with her?" he inquired pleasantly.

"She has two extra tickets to an off-Broadway play a friend of hers is starring in. She wanted to know if we'd like to come as her guests."

"What night?"

"Friday of next week. I told her I'd have check with you. But I was thinking . . ." She paused before proceeding with caution. "She happened to mention she was free this weekend, and I was wondering what you'd think about inviting her to the country." She held her breath. Ever since that first visit, she'd been listening for it: the note of hesitation . . . the pregnant pause . . . the meaningful silence . . . that would signal an underlying hesitation where Elise was concerned. But so far, there had been nothing to suggest he didn't thoroughly enjoy Elise's company. The two times Elise had had them over for supper, he'd seemed to have a good time; nor did he balk whenever she, Camille, suggested a get-together, even when it was just him and Elise—like the night he'd taken her to the opera, when Camille wasn't feeling up to it herself.

"Sure, why not?" he said now, and she felt a peculiar heaviness settle over her. It was what she wanted, what she'd been working toward, but still it left her feeling sad and lonely.

"It'd be just the three of us," she reminded him. Zach would be in Florida with her father, and Kyra had been given permission to spend the weekend with her best friend, Alexia, at Alexia's parents' country house in Rhinebeck. She pulled her nightgown over her head and stepped from the closet. Edward still sat on the bed. His shirt was off, and now he was bent over untying his shoelaces. She watched the play of muscles in his broad shoulders and back and felt some of the old thrill from when they were first married, when she'd regularly think, *I can't believe I have this beautiful man all to myself.* Was that still true? Did she still have him all to herself?

He pulled his shoes off and straightened. "Is that a problem?" he asked mildly.

"I wouldn't want her to feel like a third wheel."

"Why would she feel that way?"

"I don't know. I was just wondering if it might feel a little . . . forced."

"You think she might get the wrong idea, is that it?" He frowned, an edge creeping into his voice.

"No. But you might." The words were out before the thought was fully formed.

He eyed her with reproach. "You think I'm lusting after Elise?"

Would it be so surprising? she thought. God knew his needs weren't being met at home. They hadn't made love in . . . how long? She'd lost track. Not that she didn't still find him desirable, but desire was a thing of the past—another thing her cancer had laid claim to. At night, when got they got under the covers and settled on their respective sides of the bed, they seemed separated by more than an expanse of mattress—it felt more like a gulf. Yet the thought of her husband sleeping with another woman was torture. Emotions churned in her: regret at having to do the unthinkable in setting those wheels in motion; sorrow at what she'd be leaving behind when she died; but most of all, a deep and abiding love for the husband she'd set adrift and who was now slipping away. She sank down beside him on the bed. "I'm sorry I can't give you what you need," she said in a choked voice.

He shook his head slowly, and she saw the gleam of tears in his own eyes. Then he pulled her into his arms. For the longest time, he just held her, stroking her hair, not saying anything. When he drew back at last, she wordlessly peeled off her nightgown. Edward regarded her quizzically as if to say, *Are you sure?* She nodded, closing her eyes, giving herself over to his touch. She'd missed this, she realized. The feel of his hands on her body, the sense of closeness.

She lay down on the bed. She was naked except for what Holly jokingly called her "big-girl" panties, but right now she didn't feel like a big girl; she felt as vulnerable as a child. He kissed her, first on her mouth and then on her neck, before tenderly pressing his lips to the hollow at the base of her throat. His breath was warm and smelled faintly of cloves from the spiced pears she'd served for dessert. She thought of all the times they'd made love like this in the past, taking their time, savoring each moment, because didn't they have all the time in the world?

With featherlight strokes, he caressed her breasts and between her legs. She felt herself stir to life where she'd been dormant. He unbuckled his belt and slipped off his trousers, and she ran the palm of her hand over his muscled belly and below, feeling his erection through his boxers.

Tears filled her eyes when he entered her and began to move inside her. She felt blessed to have a husband who still desired her, though she was no longer desirable, with her ribs showing and the port that had been surgically inserted just below her clavicle protruding like some strange and incongruous appendage. How could she ever have doubted his love? Afterward, they didn't get under the covers right away; they lay nestled together on the bedspread, their limbs entwined.

"That was nice," she whispered.

"Mmmm," he murmured contentedly.

Camille roused herself, finally, to pull her nightgown back on. Then they climbed under the covers, and before long she was fast asleep, dreaming of when they were in their first apartment, on 115th Street, with its toilet that wouldn't flush properly, its paint that was forever flaking from the ceiling. In her dream, it didn't seem so long ago; it was as though they were still that carefree young couple, so certain in their belief that love would conquer all and the best was yet to come.

THERE WAS ONLY one word to describe Curtis McBride: normal. Wonderfully, refreshingly, even shockingly normal after the string of losers Holly had dragged home through the years. He was the perfect combination of clean-cut banker and hipster, well-mannered but with a quirky style—evident in the porpoise-patterned tie he had on—and a gleam in his eye that let you know he could rock it out when the occasion called for it. He had an open, boyish face framed in longish brown hair, dimpled cheeks, and blue eyes that seemed permanently crinkled from the smile that was as much a part of him as his nose or ears. Over lunch at Peels, he entertained them with his tales of life abroad.

"I used to think the Brits were like us, only with an accent," he said. "But every day, you're reminded you're in a foreign country. Like, when they talk football, they mean soccer. Braces are to hold pants up, not straighten teeth. If you're 'wet,' it's because you're a stick in the mud, not because you just got out of the shower. And . . ." He paused before delivering the pièce de résistance, his eyes twinkling with mischief, "if another guy at work asks if you happen to have a spare rubber, you do not, I repeat *do not*, offer him the condom from your wallet."

Everyone roared with laughter, Holly loudest of all. "You *didn't*," she sputtered when she'd caught her breath.

He grinned. "True story."

"If you'd used that thing with me, we wouldn't be in this boat," she teased him.

Larry coughed into his fist, wearing an embarrassed look.

"Ah, but then we'd have been just two ships passing in the night," Curtis said. "I wouldn't have gotten to know you . . . or Junior here." He placed a hand on Holly's now sizable baby bump.

His comment might have seemed odd to anyone who wasn't apprised of the situation, but it made Camille smile. Though seeing them together, seated alongside each other at the window table Curtis had charmed the hostess into giving them, it was hard to imagine a more unlikely pair: Holly in her shredded jeans and vintage smock-dress that doubled as a maternity blouse, a stack of silver bangles on each wrist . . . and Curtis in his custom-made suit and trendy tie. Camille knew it was possible for two people with so little in common to make a go of it—she'd seen it happen with clients—but it was unclear, despite their obvious affection for each other, whether either Holly or Curtis was so inclined. Holly was evasive whenever Camille tried to pin her down.

And yet there they were, parents-to-be.

"So, do you plan on staying in New York?" Camille asked him after their entrées came, *Niçoise* salad for her—her default choice these days because it was usually the least filling thing on the menu.

"For the time being, yeah." If Curtis felt pressured by the not-so-subtle attempt to take his measure, it didn't show—he seemed relaxed and untroubled. "Down the line, who knows? My bank has offices in cities all over the world. This time next year, I could be living in Tokyo or Dubai."

"Curtis is their golden boy." Holly spoke with pride. "When he asked to be transferred back to the States, they promoted him when anyone else probably would've been fired."

Larry, dapper in a cream linen blazer and palm-frond-patterned shirt, lifted his head from the pork chop he was sawing at to issue an approving smile. "Still, it doesn't take away from the gesture," he remarked, turning to Curtis. "That was very noble of you, son. You did the right thing."

"Actually," Curtis confessed, "when Holly told me she was pregnant, I was looking to make a move; that was just what decided it for me." He wore a vaguely sheepish look—that of someone who didn't want to be portrayed in a bad light but who wasn't going to take full credit where it wasn't due. "I hated living in London. The cold and damp alone are enough to drive a sober man to drink."

Camille wondered what to make of it. He was honest—she gave him points for that. But was that all Holly and the baby were to him, an excuse to change locales? She glanced over at her sister to see if she'd taken offense at Curtis's candor, but Holly's face was smooth and unperturbed.

"I spent a fair bit of time in London myself, when I was flying for Pan Am." Larry stepped in to ease the awkward moment. He grew expansive as he went on, "As a matter of fact, it was on a flight from Heathrow to JFK that I met the Duchess of Windsor. We're talking 1974 or 1975, roughly thereabouts—I remember, because it was all over the news about Watergate at the time."

Camille and Holly had heard the story so many times they knew it by heart, but it was the first time for Curtis, who perked up, wearing a look of interest. This was Larry at his best, when he reminisced about his adventures as an airline pilot back in the days when air travel was glamorous—when passengers dressed up, and being a stewardess, as her mother had been at one time (she'd met Larry on what she later called, jokingly, her "maiden voyage"), was considered an exciting career—before it became the equivalent of being crammed into a flying sardine can. "We'd hit some turbu-lence coming in for the landing," he went on, "and after we'd taxied to the gate this very elegant older woman, thin as a rail, wearing a black dress—it had a jeweled brooch pinned to it; I remember because it was so unusual, shaped like a panther—came up to me as first class was disembarking. She said, 'Well done, Captain.' I thought she looked familiar but didn't know who she was. It was my copilot, Dick O'Brien, who clued me in. 'There goes the woman who brought down the British throne,' Dick said. 'And to think we had to fight the Revolutionary War to do it.'" Larry chuckled at the memory, and the others at the table joined in.

Holly got their father to tell the story of where he'd grown up—in one of the mansions in Newport, of all places; not one of the grand, beautifully-refurbished ones that offered guided tours but the crumbly, old, small-by-Newport-standards kind belonging to formerly wealthy folk who could no longer afford the upkeep—while he was on a roll. Afterward, Camille asked, "What about you, Curtis? Where did you grow up?" *Somewhere in the Midwest* was all she had been able to glean from the bits and pieces of information Holly had seen fit to impart.

"A little town you've never heard of—Miami, Oklahoma," he replied, breaking into a grin as he added, "I know—when you think Miami, you think palm trees and ocean views, but all we had was cows and cornfields." Whereas someone else in his position might have put on airs, he seemed proud of his humble beginnings. He'd been raised on a cattle ranch where his dad was the foreman, he said, and had gone to Stanford on scholarship. He was recruited by HSBC right out of college and had been with the bank ever since. "The first time my folks came to visit me in New York, they didn't know what to make of it. They were glad to see me, but just as glad to go at the end of their stay."

What would they make of an illegitimate grandchild? Camille wondered.

"I'm getting Curtis his very own Snugli," joked Holly, when talk turned to the blessed event. "Can't you just see it—Mr. Wall Street here, with his BlackBerry and a baby strapped to his chest?" Curtis laughed, but his laughter seemed a bit forced.

"Won't the logistics be tricky, with you living in the city and Holly in Brooklyn?" Camille asked him, ignoring the warning look Holly shot her. He hadn't said anything about giving up his Tribeca loft or having Holly and the baby move in with him. "We haven't figured out all the details yet." Holly jumped in before he could respond. "We're, um, sort of playing it by ear." As if everything would magically sort itself out once the baby came. *Dear God. They really have no idea.* But that was Holly for you. Her existence had been marked by lifestyle choices that ranged from the mildly reckless to the downright scary—like the time her ex-boyfriend Ronan was driving drunk, with her along for the ride, and they collided with a tree (luckily, no one was seriously hurt). Though Holly was lucky in one sense: She hadn't suffered any lasting damage from the repercussions of those choices. But it was one thing to go out on a limb, another to do so with a baby. Camille could only hope she'd have some company out on that limb.

"I hate to break it to you, guys, but babies have their own agenda. Remember how I was with Kyra?" she reminded her sister. To Larry and Curtis, she said, "I'd read every child care book I could get my hands on, so I thought I knew what to expect, but those first few weeks after Kyra was born, I felt totally out of my depth. I could barely cope, much less get her on any kind of schedule."

"Life seldom works out the way we plan," Larry observed, his gaze turning inward as if he were reflecting on opportunities missed. Then he roused from his reverie, and switched to a safer topic. "Now, who wants dessert? Lunch is on me, so order up. I, for one, have my eye on the pear tart."

"I'll have the same," Holly and Curtis said in unison, then laughed.

"Me, too," chimed Camille, though she knew she wouldn't be able to finish hers—she'd only managed to eat half her *Niçoise* salad. Whenever she and Edward ate out, he usually ended up eating most of her dessert. She pictured him and Elise sharing a piece of pie or cake in some candlelit restaurant and felt her stomach twist. It was worse somehow than the thought of them kissing.

After they'd eaten and Larry had paid the bill, Curtis said his good-byes before heading back to work. Camille hugged him, saying warmly, "I hope we'll be seeing a lot more of you." Perhaps a strange thing to say to the father of her unborn niece or nephew, but the situation itself was strange.

"I hope so, too," he said, his blue eyes crinkling.

Minutes later, the sisters were strolling along Bleecker Street, with its storefronts featuring everything from housewares to sex toys, on their way to a children's clothing shop Holly wanted to check out. Their dad had left to go back to his hotel—he had some calls to make, he'd said—so it was just the two of them. Camille sensed her sister waiting for her to render an opinion on Curtis, but she had decided to keep it to herself until asked, if only to confirm her suspicion that Holly wasn't as la-di-da about all this as she pretended to be.

It was one of those rare summer days that New Yorkers live for, hot but not unbearably so, perfect for dining in sidewalk cafés, sitting out on stoops . . . or strutting one's stuff. They passed a homeless man in rags sporting a pair of glittery red sneakers, then a woman in hot pants and fishnet tights who teetered along on five-inch platform heels, never mind she looked old enough to collect Social Security. A bike messenger, in a bright pink helmet and Kelly green Spandex shorts, whizzed by on his ten-speed, nearly colliding with a teenage girl in tight jeans and a midi top. Camille felt a great affection for the city she'd lived in all her life and loved as she would an eccentric relative, one that was both delightful and abrasive. It wouldn't miss her when she was gone—she was but a grain of sand in its sea of humanity—but she'd been indelibly shaped by it.

"So?" Holly asked, finally. She turned to Camille with an expectant look.

"He's a good guy," Camille said. "And quite the charmer. Not the type you usually go for, which, believe me, is a plus," she added wryly. "I could see you two together. The question is, do *you* see yourself with him?"

"That's not what I asked. I only asked if you liked him," Holly replied irritably.

"Well, you *are* carrying the man's child."

"I got knocked up, okay. You don't need to be in a long-term relationship for that. In fact, I probably wouldn't have seen him again if it hadn't been for the baby."

"Yes, but with babies you can't just wing it. You have to have some sort of plan."

Holly shrugged indifferently. "You know what they say—we're all raised by amateurs. None of us knows what we're doing. You said so yourself. You didn't have a clue when you had Kyra."

"The difference is, I wasn't in it alone—I had a husband."

"Just because you have a husband," Holly said, "it doesn't mean *I* have to. We can't all have the perfect marriage like you."

Camille frowned, thinking, *Perfect marriage? Far from it.* Maybe it had been at one time, but that no longer held true.

They came to a stop in front of a tastefully appointed storefront, with a yellow-and-green striped awning and flowers in planters out front. Child-size mannequins in the front window displayed European-made children's clothing that probably cost as much as a trip to Europe. They went inside and made their way to the infant wear section in back, where Holly held up a tiny, pink smock appliquéd with ducks. "What do you think? Should I ask if it comes in a more gender-neutral color?"

Camille bent to peer at the price tag. "Only if you plan on taking out a bank loan," she said. Holly glanced at the price tag, too, and quickly returned the item to its rack. "You'll definitely need a second income if you plan on buying anything in this store," Camille told her.

Holly just shook her head.

Looking around at the tiny outfits and onesies, it seemed impossible to Camille that her children had ever been small enough to wear clothes that size. Just as impossible as her belief, back then, that nothing could ever come between her and her husband. How naïve she'd been! The marriage she'd once thought a fortress was really more like the mansion her father had grown up in: once grand and since fallen into repair. The question was, could they fix it before it crumbled down altogether? When it was her time to go, she wanted the good memories to outweigh the bad; it would be easier for Edward if he had no regrets.

Camille felt so sad then, she wanted to curl up amid the downy piles of terry and soft cotton knits and be a baby again herself, not a care in the world and with her whole life still ahead of her.

CHAPTER SIXTEEN

"By the way, Ruth enjoyed her lunch with Camille," Hugh remarked as he and Edward were toweling off in the locker room after their showers, following a vigorous game of racquetball at Hugh's athletic club. Their wives had met for lunch the previous week.

"Camille enjoyed it, too." Edward kept his voice light, but at the mention of his wife, he felt the muscles loosened by his workout start to tighten again.

Hugh, naked as a Sasquatch and just as hairy, reached for his boxers. "Ruth thought she looked well, considering. Other than being much too thin, of course. Though if anyone can remedy that, it's my Ruthie. You know her, she never met a knish or a kugel that didn't have someone's name on it. Usually mine." He chuckled and patted his ample belly.

"All donations gratefully received. We never say no to Ruth's cooking."

"You could use some fattening up, too, my friend," Hugh observed, shooting him a pointed glance. Edward had lost weight in the past weeks, not enough to be noticeable, in terms of girth, but enough to accentuate the haggard look he wore. "Just remember, you won't be much good to your wife if you don't take care of yourself."

Edward gave a dry laugh. "I'm not much good to her either way, it seems."

Hugh paused to eye him gravely. "You're doing what you can. The rest is in God's hands."

But not in the control of Camille's oncology team, it appeared. It had been eight weeks since they'd started her on the new drug, and so far she'd shown no sign of improvement. She was no worse, but Edward took little comfort in that, knowing it was likely due to the chemo, which was aimed at slowing the progression of the disease.

"No disrespect, but I don't have much faith in God right now," he said. "Or in the miracles of modern medicine."

"Give it time. It's too soon to say."

"Time? I'm afraid we're running a little low on that," Edward replied with a bitter laugh, and then at the concerned look Hugh gave him, he thought, *Jesus, I sound like the Grim Reaper.* He went on, in a forcibly upbeat voice, "But you're right—it's too soon to say. Hopefully, we'll see some results in the next few weeks. We should know more with the next batch of tests."

"In the meantime, your wife isn't the only one in need of looking after," Hugh said. "You're not eating, you're not sleeping, and frankly it shows—you look like hell. You should see someone."

Edward paused as he was pulling his clothes from his locker. "You mean a shrink?"

Hugh ignored the disdain in his voice. "It wouldn't hurt. You have a lot on your plate right now, and since you won't talk to me . . ." He trailed off. "I could give you some names, if you like." Edward shrugged in response, keeping his back turned. A moment later, a meaty hand fell on his shoulder. He turned to find Hugh eyeing him with concern. "There's no shame in it, you know."

Edward felt the coiled spring in his gut tighten another half turn. Shame? What would Hugh, who as far as he knew had never looked at a woman other than his wife in the forty-five years they'd been married, know about shame? "Jesus. Don't you guys ever give it a rest?" he said as he snatched his shirt from the locker and shoved an arm into the corresponding sleeve.

Hugh eyed him with mild reproach. "You always were a tough nut to crack," he said. "Didn't anyone ever tell you life's not a contest to see who can go the longest without crying uncle?"

Edward exhaled forcibly. "Look, I appreciate your concern, but I just don't see the point. It won't change anything." He fumbled with the buttons on his shirt, his fingers suddenly thick and clumsy.

"It's not always about finding a solution," Hugh said. "Sometimes it helps just to talk."

"Yeah, I know, but with you guys, it never ends there."

"There's a reason we get paid to listen."

"I know. So tough nuts like me can go home with a few extra cracks."

"All right, since you're so determined to make me work for it, I'll make an educated guess as to why you're behaving as if you'd sooner get bit by a snake than get professional help," Hugh pressed on regardless. "It wouldn't have anything to do with the lovely Elise, would it?"

Several weeks prior, Edward had run into Hugh and Ruth at the opera. They had season tickets to the Metropolitan, as did Edward and Camille, except that night Edward hadn't been with his wife—Camille hadn't felt up to going and didn't want her ticket to go to waste, so she'd insisted he take Elise in her place. When he'd bumped into Hugh and Ruth during intermission, he could see them struggling not to raise an eyebrow when he'd introduced them to Elise, even after he'd explained the circumstances. He could also see the wheels turning in the older man's mind.

Edward replied gruffly, "There's nothing going on between Elise and me, if that's what you're implying. If you don't believe me, ask Camille. The whole thing was her idea, remember."

"I'm well aware of that," Hugh said. "But now you have a stake in it as well, it would appear."

Edward, frowning, wrestled with the top button on his shirt. He wished now he hadn't told Hugh about Camille's plan. Naturally

Hugh would make assumptions, having met "the lovely Elise." Never mind Edward's feelings toward her were entirely platonic, and she was no more infatuated with him than he was with her. Elise had made it quite clear, that first weekend, she wasn't looking for more than friendship.

"I'm not cheating on my wife," he stated in no uncertain terms.

"You don't have to, to be in love with another woman. Or for her to be in love with you."

Edward's scowl deepened. "It's not like that. I told you, she's a friend, nothing more."

"Well, *you* might feel that way, but she clearly has other ideas."

"And you deduced this after talking to her for all of ten minutes?" Edward scoffed.

"Actually, it was Ruth," Hugh told him. "Trust another woman to know—they can always spot it. She said Elise looked at you like you'd hung the moon. Naturally, she didn't take it seriously. She knows the devastating effect you dark, brooding types have on women. But it got me thinking. I couldn't help wondering if this plan of Camille's might have worked a little too well."

THE FINAL BELL had rung ten minutes ago, but Elise was still cleaning up the mess her students had left when Glenn poked his head into the classroom. "What's cooking, good looking?"

"Nothing except the usual mayhem," she said, prying a lump of modeling clay from one of the desks. "Some of the kids got into a clay throwing match while we were doing our class project."

"You could always threaten to put those to use, to keep the little monsters in line." He gestured toward the aforementioned class project—childish renditions of ancient Egyptian funeral jars, in the form of lumpy clay pots—arrayed on the row of cabinets below the windows.

"Very funny."

Glenn wandered over to pick up one of the pots. "Do they know what these were used for back in the day?"

"Not specifically," she told him. "I didn't want to give them nightmares."

He nodded in approval. "Not exactly *Toy Story 3*, learning about a bunch of dead pharaohs having their vital organs plucked out and stored in jars, for their second life in the netherworld."

"Except the heart," she reminded him. "That, they got to keep."

"Why was that? I forget."

"So it could be weighed when they got to the other side, to see if they'd led a virtuous life."

"And if it should come up short on the scale?"

"I don't know. I suppose you'd get thrown back."

"I see. So if you were a class-A jerk, you got to live longer?"

"Something like that."

"Figures," he said with a sigh. "In that case, I'd better enjoy life while I can, because I'm sure to die young." He returned the clay pot to its shelf and ambled over to her desk, leaning against it with his legs outstretched. She felt his eyes on her as she moved about, gathering up scraps of construction paper and stray bits of clay. "Hey, you doing anything after this? I was thinking we could check out that Monet exhibit at the Frick."

"I can't. I'm meeting someone," she told him. Her cheeks warmed, and she felt a flutter of anticipation.

"You have a date?" he divined.

"None of your beeswax."

"Ah, the plot thickens." Glenn waggled his eyebrows at her.

"It's Edward Constantin, if you must know."

"Oh. I see." Glenn's playful look gave way to a serious one.

She'd told him the whole story, on the way to his parents' house after that first weekend in Southampton, but even after she had laid out all her reasons for doing so, he still thought it was a bad idea for her to get involved. "This isn't a used car you're test-driving," he'd cautioned. "People have feelings, and feelings can get messy. Or ugly."

"It's not what you think," she told him now, "so you can stop giving me that look. I'm a friend of the family, nothing more."

She felt herself blush, even so. When Edward had phoned earlier in the day to ask if she would meet him for coffee after work, she'd felt a secret thrill at knowing it would be just the two of them. He'd said there was something he needed to talk to her about. What could it be? she wondered. Whatever it was, it clearly wasn't something he wanted his wife to know about.

"If you say so," Glenn said flatly.

"Why are you being this way?" she cried in annoyance. "You act as if you suspect I'm having affair!" *Oh, God. Did I just say that?* Now he would think the lady doth protest too much.

Glenn straightened and crossed the room to where she stood, putting his hands on her shoulders and looking her in the eye. "Just be careful. I see the way you light up when you talk about him. I don't want you to get in over your head." In his khakis and rumpled shirt, a stray lock of brown hair falling over his forehead, he didn't look any older or wiser than his eighth-grade students, though she knew he spoke the truth. The problem was she was already in over her head.

"I appreciate your concern," she told him, "But I promise I'm not in any danger of drowning." She could see how it might look suspicious to Glenn, her meeting alone with Edward, but it wasn't like that. Even if Edward had feelings for her, he'd never act on those feelings, not while his wife was still alive.

Did he have feelings for her? Was that what he wanted to talk to her about? He'd given no indication of it so far, but then he was a man, like her father, who didn't wear his heart on his sleeve. The mere thought made her own heart race. Though it meant they would have to be more vigilant than ever. The idea of sneaking around behind Camille's back was abhorrent to Elise. Camille was so trusting, inviting her to take part in family activities and encouraging her to go on outings with Edward and the children, and once with just Edward, the evening he took her to the opera (an evening she would long remember). How could she ever betray that trust? Never, not for a minute, did she lose sight of the fact that her gain would be another woman's loss. A woman whom she'd grown fond of.

"It's not what you think," she insisted.

Glenn held her gaze. "Okay, but remember, that's how these things start," he said. "You tell yourself nothing's going to happen; then before you know it, you're checking into a motel—the kind where they don't ask too many questions. Isn't that what happened with your ex-husband?"

His words stung. "There's no comparison!" she cried hotly.

"Even what's-his-name isn't the heartless creature you make him out to be. Hey, I'm not defending your ex," Glenn said, holding his hands up as if to deflect the scathing look she directed at him. "But in all fairness, it's not like he woke up one morning and said to himself, *Today I'm going to cheat on my wife,* then went out and found someone to cheat with. It doesn't usually happen that way."

"And what makes you such an expert? You're not exactly the Dr. Phil of romance," she tossed back at him. When he ducked his head, she knew he was keeping something from her and had a pretty good guess what it might be. "Don't tell me. You've met someone." He lifted his head, and when she saw his red cheeks, she grinned. "Aha, so I'm right!"

"That's for me to know and you to find out."

"You sound like one of my fourth graders," she said.

"Most of whom, I assure you, see more action than yours truly," he said.

"Come on, give it up. Who is she? Did you meet her online?"

"No."

"Oh, so it was one of those random meetings?"

"If I tell you, will you promise not to laugh?"

"Cross my heart, hope to die," she vowed, drawing an invisible X over her chest.

He closed his eyes and said in a rush, as if to get it over with, "We met in the cheese section at Whole Foods." A giggle escaped her, and mindful of her promise, she clamped a hand over her mouth. He mock glared at her. "Yeah, I know—cheesy. But it's not like our eyes met over the Gorgonzola, and we knew instantly we were meant for each other. Nothing will come of it, I'm sure."

"Why do you say that?"

"Because we chatted for all of five minutes, and it wasn't like I was trying to pick her up or anything. She was having trouble deciding what to get for this dinner party she was having, so I told her which cheeses would go best with which wines." Glenn might not fit the profile, but he was a true epicurean; everything Elise knew about gourmet food and wine she'd learned from him. Their salaries didn't allow for much in the way of fine dining, but he often cooked for her at his place on weekends—linguine *alle vongele*, beef bourguignon, curried shrimp over Basmati rice. "The fact that she didn't say no when I offered to give her my number, in case she needed any advice later on, doesn't mean anything, except maybe that she was too polite to reject me on the spot."

"Don't underestimate yourself. You've just had a run of bad luck, is all. Any woman would be lucky to snag you."

Unfortunately, Glenn didn't seem to share her high opinion of him. "Like I said, it was no big deal. I don't know why I'm even telling you. I just thought . . . well, she seemed nice." He groaned, as if suddenly realizing something. "Oh, God. She probably thought I was gay."

"Why would she think that?"

"Hello. A neatly dressed man who's suspiciously knowledgeable about entertaining?"

"Okay, but even if she thought that, it only means she's more likely to call."

"Why is that, oh, sage one?"

"Women adore gay men. Plus, if she thought you were gay, she wouldn't be worried that you were coming on to her. And by the time she realizes you *are* coming on to her, she'll be smitten."

He shook his head, as if at the impenetrable workings of the female mind. "It's a moot point, because she won't call."

"How long has it been?"

"A couple of days."

"Give it time. She's probably still recovering from the dinner party—all that wine and cheese you had her buy." Impulsively, she leaned in to plant a kiss on Glenn's cheek. He smelled pleasantly of chalk dust and the aftershave he wore. "Whatever happens, I'm proud of you."

"For what?"

"For not giving up."

His mouth slanted in a rueful smile. "You know us dependable types—we take a licking and keep on ticking."

Minutes later, she was strolling along Christopher Street on her way to meet Edward. The sun was shining, and she was pleasantly aware of the hem of her dress fluttering against her knees. She was glad she'd worn this dress, the blue flowered one that tied in back; it was among her most flattering. At the thought, she felt the excitement she'd managed to keep tamped down all day flare. She might have been on her way to meet a lover. She frowned at the thought, and her step momentarily faltered. But she'd done nothing wrong, nor would she, she reminded herself. If she'd lost her heart to a married man, there was no harm in it as long as she didn't lose her head.

She hadn't expected to fall in love, and certainly not so hard and so fast. But the more she got to know Edward, the more convinced she became that Camille had been right in choosing her as his future wife. Her dad always said of his relationship with her mom that they were like "peas and carrots," and that was how she felt about Edward. They shared the same values and interests—they both loved music (though she was more into classical and he into jazz), and nostalgia in the form of classic films, vintage posters, and club car diners—and she adored his children. She recalled with a smile the hot July day they took Kyra and Zach for a walk along the High Line, then to lunch afterward, at The Diner. Edward ordered a round of milk shakes to go with their burgers.

"Dad, do you know how many calories there are in a milk shake? About nine billion," Kyra said. "Seriously, do you think Mom would approve of you feeding us this stuff?"

"I don't know, sweetie. Why don't we get another woman's opinion?" He looked to Elise, asking with a twinkle in his eye, "What do you think, Elise? Would my wife disapprove?"

Elise chose her words carefully. "What I think is that you and your wife raised a sensible daughter who's smart enough to know one milk shake isn't going to kill her." She turned her smiling gaze on Kyra. "Even if it has nine billion calories," she added, trying not to think about her own waistline.

"Good save," he whispered in her ear.

Elise knew she could never replace Camille in his affections. He loved his wife; anyone with eyes in their head could see that, but there were different kinds of love. Even if Edward saw her, Elise, only as someone he could potentially love down the line, she was willing to take that chance.

Her thoughts drifted to Glenn. She puzzled once more over the fact that there had never been so much as a glimmer of spark between them. Well, except that one time, after Dennis moved out. Glenn had come over for his nightly "tour of duty," as she'd called it, but there was no consoling her that night. She'd just found out her estranged husband was shacked up with his girlfriend, after he'd told her (the lying bastard) he was staying with a friend. The news had sent her into a tailspin of self-pity and renewed outrage.

"It's not that I care that he's still sleeping with her!" she railed.

"We're not together anymore, so he can do what he likes. It's just that . . . he . . . he . . . well, it's the blatantness of it!"

"I don't think that's a real word," said Glenn, attempting to lighten the mood.

She began to weep in earnest, and he put an arm around her. Finally, when she wouldn't—couldn't—stop, he guided her into the bedroom and eased her onto the bed. Still, the tears continued to flow, like blood from an open wound. Someone else might have been at a loss as to what to do, but not Glenn. He took off her shoes and then his, and stretched out beside her on the bed. He held her until his shirt—a gray polo, she recalled—was damp in one spot from her tears.

"Have you ever heard of anyone calling 911 because they couldn't stop crying?" she asked in a choked voice. She was only half joking.

"I don't know," he said. "But if you think it'd help, I'd be happy to make the call." His breath smelled pleasantly buttery from the popcorn they'd been nibbling on while watching the Netflix DVD he'd brought over that night, a hokey 1950s movie starring Troy Donahue and Sandra Dee that he'd ordered only because he thought it would cheer her up. Glenn was the only man she knew, other than her dad, who'd willingly sit through *A Summer Place*.

"You would, wouldn't you?" she said, her runny nose inches from his.

"I have no shame. You should know that by now."

She managed a feeble smile. "Look at you, you're as bad as I am. Worse even. I can't help myself, but you're *choosing* to hang out with a woman who clearly needs psychological help."

He held his handkerchief to her nose and ordered her to blow. "Maybe we both belong in the nuthouse," he said after she'd obeyed. "Can't you just see us in his-and-her straitjackets?"

Elise laughed at the image, a loose weepy laugh that rattled in her throat like phlegm. *I must look awful,* she thought. But it was just Glenn, she reminded herself, and he didn't care what she looked like. He loved her for who she was on the inside, the way only a best friend can.

At some point, she drifted off to sleep. Hours later, she woke in the night to find her head resting on Glenn's arm, his other arm draped over her. He was snoring lightly. She wondered how long he'd stayed awake after she'd fallen asleep. Long enough for his arm to grow numb, no doubt.

He must have felt her stirring because his eyes opened. He smiled, as if he was in the habit of waking up next to her. For the longest time, neither of them spoke. They just lay there, smiling at each other like a couple of kids in a blanket fort hiding out from their parents. In that moment, she realized something she'd known all along but that hadn't really sunk in until then: She wasn't alone. And she never would be, not as long as she had Glenn.

That was when he kissed her. Not a romantic kiss, but it wasn't exactly *un*romantic, either. She felt the light pressure of his lips against hers, as gentle as an exhaled breath, and closed her eyes, imagining it was Dennis. Dennis's mouth on hers, his fingers brushing her cheek.

When she opened her eyes and saw it wasn't Dennis, the spell was broken. Glenn must have sensed it because he drew back at once, wearing the irreverent smile of the Glenn she knew. Perhaps he hadn't meant it the way she imagined, she thought. Perhaps it was only an affectionate kiss. She knew this to be true when he didn't act at all embarrassed. Instead, he teased, "Do you still want me to call the men in the white coats, or do you think it can wait until tomorrow?"

Elise, lost in thought, blew by the outdoor café where she was to meet Edward. She didn't realize it until she was almost to the end of the block and noticed the addresses were getting higher. She was doubling back when she spotted him at one of the tables under the blue-and-white awning in front of the café. She halted in midstride, taking in the sight of him. How noble he looked! A patch of sunlight had crept past the awning to gild his profile, with its aristocratic nose and defined jawline: that of a Roman emperor on a gold coin. His dark curls gleamed as if he'd just showered. She pictured him stepping from the shower, naked, and felt a warmth steal over her that was part desire and part shame. At that exact moment, he caught sight of her and waved. When Elise waved back, her arm seemed to float up of its own accord.

"I haven't kept you waiting, I hope," she said when she reached him.

"Not at all. I just got here a few minutes ago." He gestured toward the iced coffees on the table. "I hope you don't mind, I ordered for you. Double decaf espresso with skim milk, right?" She nodded and smiled as she sat down, touched that he'd remembered. "You look nice, by the way," he said.

"Why, thank you. So do you. Some men are born to wear a jacket and tie, and you, sir, are one of them." She was careful to strike the right tone, playful without being flirtatious. "You're like my dad—he always wears a coat and tie to work. He says being a country doctor is no excuse for lowering your standards. My mom's the same way—she wouldn't dream of showing up at church in a pantsuit."

"You've told me so much about your parents, I feel as if I know them."

"You'd love them," she said, adding silently, *and they'd love you.* "They're great people. It's a little embarrassing to admit this, but I think I had pretty much the perfect childhood."

"Why embarrassing?"

"Well, when I was little, I used to think all parents were like mine. But when I got older and started spending time at my friends' houses, I realized not everyone had it as good as I did. My mom and dad never fought, for one thing—they only disagreed from time to time—and although they were strict with me and my brothers, they never spanked us. They didn't get drunk, like my best friend Courtney's mom who was always causing scenes. They weren't always off doing their own thing, either—we did things as a family. We played card games after supper, like you and Camille do with your kids, and every summer we went camping up at the lake." Elise felt a tug of homesickness at the memory. "Nowadays, when I listen to my friends talk about their childhoods, I'm afraid if I tell them what mine was like, I'll sound like a Pollyanna. Either that, or someone who's hopelessly deluded."

"I can see you in one of those big old farmhouses with a tire swing out back."

"White clapboard with blue trim, and yes, there was a tire swing—it's still there, in fact. There's also a barn and chickens and an old pony named Popcorn that my brothers and I used to ride. He doesn't do much anymore besides munch on grass, but Mom and Dad keep him for sentimental reasons."

"Zach would think he'd died and gone to heaven."

"Except the nearest golf course is miles away."

Edward gave a knowing chuckle. Zach had returned from his trip to Fort Lauderdale lugging a set of pint-size golf clubs, a gift from Grandpa Larry. He'd spent the rest of the summer, whenever he could cajole one of this parents or Elise into taking him, at the driving range at Chelsea Piers. "If he ever decides to give up golf for farming, we're in real trouble," he joked.

They chatted about other things while they sipped their coffees. She asked after the children and Camille, who was soon to undergo another round of tests, she learned. He seemed interested in hearing about the field trip Elise had taken her fourth graders on, to the Museum of the Moving Image. Finally, when enough time had elapsed for it not to seem as if she were dying of curiosity, she asked, keeping her voice light, "So, what was it you wanted to see me about?"

Edward shifted in his chair, looking uncomfortable all of a sudden. She felt a trickle of unease in her belly. A trickle that became a flash flood with his next words. "Elise, I know we've talked about this, but I thought I should make myself clear, in case you've changed your mind or . . . or gotten the wrong impression: There's no future with me. I like you, and enjoy your company, but . . ." He trailed off at the stricken expression she must have worn, realizing, as he must have, that his suspicion was correct: She *had* gotten ideas, despite what she'd told him initially. His face creased with concern. "If . . . if I've inadvertently led you on in any way, I'm sorry."

"Oh." She couldn't think of anything to say. She kept her smile locked in place as her heart sank.

He placed his hand over hers. "Not that I don't value your friendship," he went on, in the same kind voice. "It's been wonderful getting to know you, and the kids adore you. But it would be selfish to string you along if you're looking to get married again someday. You deserve better."

Elise was suddenly having trouble getting enough air into her lungs. She concentrated on slowly inhaling and exhaling, until she could breathe normally again. Finally, she said in what she hoped was a reasonable tone, that of a sane person who wasn't in danger of becoming hysterical, "I'm glad you think of me as a friend. I think of you that way, too. But we don't know what the future holds—we haven't gone down that road yet. I know it's not something you want to think about right now, nor do I, but someday we might feel differently." As if she weren't in love with him already. "Don't you think we owe it to ourselves to, at least, be open to the possibility?"

He shook his head. She saw the regret on his face—regret at having to hurt her, not because he had misgivings. "I don't see myself ever loving you the way I'd have to in order to make that leap."

"Because you love your wife?"

He hesitated before answering, "Yes."

She took him at his word, but that beat of hesitation made her wonder. What if it wasn't just that he loved his wife? Suppose *she* was lacking in some way. Maybe he could never love her for the same reason Dennis couldn't stay faithful. Whatever it was, she needed to know. "Is that the only reason?" she asked. He froze, and at the guilty, almost panicked expression that came over his face, she realized he'd misunderstood. She, on the other hand, understood perfectly. She knew that look all too well: It was the same expression Dennis had worn when she'd confronted him about the affair. "Oh, my God. There's someone else, isn't there?" she whispered.

He didn't answer. He didn't have to. The look on his face said it all. "I see. So I wasn't the only one," she went on, her voice hardening. "Camille had someone else lined up in case I didn't pan out. Maybe I wasn't even her first choice."

"No, no, it's not like that," he assured her. "Camille . . . she doesn't know."

This was an even bigger shock. Elise didn't ask if he was cheating on his wife. She wasn't sure she wanted to know, though she hoped he wasn't—she hated to think of him being anything like Dennis. Besides, it was enough to know he was in love with someone else. Though, judging by how tormented he seemed, it was bringing him more grief than joy. "Well," she said, after the shock had worn off, "I can't say I saw it coming, but I appreciate your honesty."

"If it means anything, I'm sorry," he said.

"I know. Me, too."

"You'll find someone, and when you do, he'll be worth the wait." He brushed his fingertips over her cheek, an affectionate gesture that was like antiseptic poured over an open wound.

"We'll see. I'm not holding my breath," she said.

"Trust me, he's out there."

Elise started to choke up. She'd thought she *had* found him— that special someone with whom she could curl up in bed at night, go on trips, exchange sections of the *Times* while they lounged in their pajamas on Sundays drinking their morning coffee. Someone who'd father the children she hoped to have someday. She drew in a shaky breath. "So," she said, "I guess this is it then. Will you tell the children good-bye for me?"

"It doesn't have to be good-bye," he said. "We can still be friends, can't we?"

Elise was on the verge of answering, *Yes, of course*—because wasn't that what nice girls said to make the other person feel better?—but she couldn't; it would be wrong. She couldn't be friends with him without wanting more. "No, I don't think so," she told him. Struck by the absurdity of the situation, she smiled. "Silly, isn't it? I haven't done this since elementary school."

"What?"

"Break up with someone I've never even kissed."

ANGIE GRITTED HER teeth, wishing she were home right now with her feet up instead of scurrying around inside a cold, drafty tent trying to keep the cans of Sterno under the hotel trays from going out, while rain sluiced down outside. The event she was catering (a.k.a. the Wedding from Hell) was Murphy's Law in effect: Everything that could go wrong had. It started with the ceremony, on a cliff overlooking the ocean in Montauk. Storm clouds began to mass as the vows were being read, and she and her staff had barely gotten the 150 guests corralled into the tent before the heavens unleashed. And the downpour showed no sign of letting up anytime soon. It was coming down so hard, they'd had to place champagne buckets throughout the tent to catch the drips. The strong winds had also brought a sharp drop in temperature. Those guests who weren't too inebriated to notice how cold it was stood huddled in groups, as if for warmth.

Naturally, this did not sit well with the bride. Her Big Day had been ruined, in her view, and because she also happened to be a world-class bitch who'd had no business getting married in the first place (her hapless bridegroom would soon wish he'd gone up in 747 with the shoe bomber instead), she was wound tighter than a tourniquet. The bride had been bitching nonstop—the food was cold, the drinks weren't flowing fast enough, the crust on the salmon Wellington was soggy. When she wasn't throwing a fit about some little thing, she was issuing dire threats under her breath, smiling all the while for the benefit of her guests. Not only would she *not* be recommending Angie's services to any of her friends, she hissed after declaring the gazpacho shooters "a disaster," she would use her blog to spread word of Angie's "gross ineptitude."

The groom, for his part, had responded to the extreme conditions, and his bride's even more extreme displeasure, by getting trashed. Angie was bent over one of the hotel trays, battery-operated lighter in hand, attempting to reignite a can of Sterno, when she glanced up and saw him weaving his way toward her. It quickly became clear it wasn't a second helping he was after.

"Hey, sweet thing. Wanna dance?" he slurred, slipping an arm around her waist.

Sober, he was attractive enough in an affable frat-boy way—a good foil for his dark-haired, Ginsu-knife-faced, Pilates-toned bride. Drunk and red-faced, and sweating despite the chill air, he looked about as appealing as the steamed dumplings Angie was attempting to keep warm.

She eased from his grasp. "Sounds tempting, but I think I'll pass."

"Oh, come on. Don' be like that. Wha's wrong with a lil' fun?"

"Well, for one thing, I'm working, as you can see," she pointed out.

He leaned in, his moist lips brushing her ear. "Yeah, I know," he whispered. "It'd really piss her off, wouldn't it? You 'n' me, ha-cha-cha." He gave her a wink that was more comical than seductive before casting a mutinous glance at his bride, whose attention was fortunately directed elsewhere.

"Look, because you're drunk and I don't get paid enough to put up with this kind of shit, I'm going to pretend we never had this conversation," Angie said in as nice a voice as she could muster. "I know something that'd piss her off even more," he went on, ignoring her. He cast another look at his bride before bringing his bloodshot gaze back to Angie. "How 'bout you and me have a drink in the limo? Nice and dry in there. Whaddya say? Toast the bride and groom?"

If he weren't being so obnoxious, Angie might have felt sorry for him, knowing he faced a life sentence, or at least the next year or two until he wised up, with Bridezilla. But she'd used up her last ounce of goodwill somewhere between the flat tire she'd gotten on the way there and the bride's carping at her a minute ago because the champagne wasn't chilled to her satisfaction. Angie was sick of it all: sick of the rain, and getting blamed for not having proper kitchen facilities or even a power source. Now, on top of it all, she had the drunken groom hitting on her.

To add insult to injury, he pulled her close and ground his pelvis into her. It was the last straw. Angie dropped the lighter and, slick as butter on a griddle, her hand shot down to grab his balls. She squeezed hard enough to make him wince. "Keep it up, and you'll spend your wedding night cuddled up to an ice pack instead of your bride," she growled. *Though you probably wouldn't know the difference.*

His eyes flared in surprise and pain; then he jerked free and staggered back, nearly knocking over a tray of glasses when he bumped into the table behind him. He glared at Angie, sober enough now, after having his balls tenderized, to realize he'd picked the wrong person to mess with. "Bitch!" he spat.

"You took the words right out of my mouth," Angie muttered, but she was looking at the bride, who was staring at them now, her face more thunderous than the sky outside, when she said it.

Hours later, on the ride back to the city in the company van, all she could think about was the hot shower and stiff drink that awaited her at home. It was well past dark by the time Stylianos dropped her off in front of her building. She let herself in with her key, pausing only long enough, once she was inside, to slip off her mud-caked Crocs before heading down the hallway to her ground-floor apartment.

She wasn't just drained; she was dispirited. Today's nuptials were further proof that "happily ever after" existed only in fairy tales. And look at her own track record: One loser boyfriend after another, until finally she'd found the One, who turned out to be the One Who Got Away. They'd had their moment—that one, magical kiss—then *poof!* It went up in smoke. She and Edward had gotten together a couple of times since then, once for the rematch (he won that time) and then a few days later for the lunch she'd promised to treat him to if she lost (she'd taken him to her favorite taco truck), but the way he acted, it was as if the magic moment at Georgia and Mike's wedding had never taken place. Had she only dreamed it? No. She knew she hadn't because she'd caught him once or twice eyeing her with—what, regret? Longing? Maybe this was all he could handle right now.

Whatever, it was pointless to speculate, because she'd made the decision to end it—whatever *it* was. She couldn't go on this way, wishing for what could never be. The fact was, he was married. To a woman he loved; a woman who was dying. It didn't get more complicated than that. She planned to email him that very night, in fact; it would be easier than telling him in person. Still, as she headed for the shower to wash away the day's grime, it was with a heavy heart.

Minutes later, as she was toweling off, she heard a knock at the front door. *What the . . . ?* Frowning, she threw on her robe and dashed to answer it. Most likely it was her neighbor, Justin, from down the hall, who was always showing up at her door in need of something—a coffee filter, milk for his cereal, and once a condom (he'd been going at it with his girlfriend when he'd realized he was fresh out). But when she peered through the peephole she saw it wasn't Justin.

Her heart leaped, and she flung open the door. "Edward! What are you doing here?"

"I tried calling, but I kept getting your voicemail," he said as he stepped inside, soaked from the rain still pouring down outside. Angie realized she hadn't checked her messages since leaving Montauk.

"How did you know I'd be home?" she asked.

"I didn't, but I took a chance. I figured even if you'd hit traffic, you'd have made it back from Montauk by now." At the blank look she must have worn—she was still struggling to sort out the emotions tumbling around inside her—he added, "I would have buzzed you on the intercom, but one of your neighbors happened by just as I was about to. He said he lived down the hall from you."

Fucking Justin, she thought. "I wouldn't have heard it, anyway. I was in the shower," she said stupidly.

"Yes, I can see that."

She felt suddenly self-conscious in her robe, an old cotton kimono worn to a whisper. "Is everything okay?" she asked. In the 'burbs, it wasn't unusual for people to drop by unannounced, but in the city no one ever did, unless it was an emergency or a drunken ex-boyfriend showing up at your door in the middle of the night. Edward didn't appear frantic; nor had he been drinking, as far as she could tell. Still, it could be bad news, the kind he'd felt compelled to deliver in person. Maybe he'd come to the same decision she had, that this dance they'd been doing had to end. Her heart plummeted at the thought, even knowing it was the only sensible course of action.

"Everything's fine," he said, but she could tell he was nervous. He reached into his coat pocket and pulled out an envelope, handing it to her. "I just wanted to drop this off."

"What is it?" she asked.

He grinned. "Open it and see."

"Let's get you out of that coat first. Look at you, you're soaked."

She tucked the envelope into the pocket of her kimono, too overwhelmed by his presence to be curious about its contents, and helped him off with his overcoat. "What is it with you and umbrellas, are they against your religion or something?"

He grinned, his double-malt eyes crinkling at the corners. As they stood facing each other in the cramped confines of the vestibule, she could see he was having trouble keeping his gaze from straying. It made her nervous but also gave her a perverse satisfaction, knowing he wasn't immune to her charms after all. "I forgot," he said simply, not taking his eyes off her. If she hadn't brought it to his attention, he probably wouldn't have noticed he was wet.

"Well, come in and sit down. Can I get you something to drink?"

"You're sure I'm not catching you at a bad time?"

"After the day I just had? It would take a weapon of mass destruction to top that. Long story," she said at the quizzical look he gave her. "First, I need a drink."

She ushered him into the area that served as living room, dining room, and kitchen, in the cozy if cramped seven-hundred-square-foot space she called home. Situated on the ground floor of a five-story building, its one selling feature was the patio in back, just big enough to hold some potted plants, her Weber grill, and a wrought-iron café table and chairs: her own pocket-size paradise.

"Nice," he said, glancing around him. "I like what you've done with the place."

"I call it Early Cul-de-Sac," she said, explaining that most of the furniture was hand-me-downs. "My mom figures if she can't lure me back to the 'burbs, she'll bring the 'burbs to me. Have a seat." She gestured toward the rolled-arm sofa upholstered in chocolate plush that had come out of the den of her childhood home and had witnessed more than one teenage make-out session.

She fetched a bottle of red wine from the kitchen. It wasn't until they were both seated and the wine poured that she remembered the envelope, tucked in the pocket of her kimono. She pulled it out, and when she opened it and saw what was in it, gave a whoop of sheer delight. It was a pair of tickets for the Bon Jovi concert at Madison Square Garden the weekend after next. "Holy buckets!" she cried. "Who'd you have to knock off to get these?"

"No one," he replied with a chuckle. "My sister-in-law is friendly with their road manager. When you told me the concert was sold out, I asked Holly if she could pull some strings."

"Well, I'm forever in her debt. But since there are *two* tickets, I assume you're coming with me."

"I wish," he said with regret. "Unfortunately, I have a conference in Denver that weekend, which I promise you will be every bit as dull as it sounds. But I'm sure you'll have no trouble finding someone to go with you."

She felt a stab of disappointment, but quickly rallied. "I'll ask my sister Frannie. She's an even bigger fan than I am, if that's possible. We had all their albums." They'd even had the obligatory poster on the wall of the bedroom they'd shared, right next to the Jesus plaque from when Frannie was confirmed. "Thanks, it was really sweet of you to think of me. I'm curious, though . . ." She reached for her wineglass, taking a sip. "Why come all this way when you could've just sent me the tickets?"

"Would you believe it if I told you I was in the neighborhood?" he said.

"It's not exactly your neck of the woods."

"True, but it's only a twenty-minute cab ride."

"You uptown guys are all the same—you'd never deign to live here, but you enjoy slumming."

He chuckled. "Something like that."

He held her gaze a beat too long, which reminded her, she was still in her kimono. She thought about excusing herself to throw on some clothes, but no sooner had the thought entered her head than it melted away. She was having too much fun. As they sat on the plush sofa sipping wine, she told him about the wedding in

Montauk, describing in gruesome detail the torments she'd been subjected to at the hands of Bridezilla and Dr. Octopus, the groom. Amazingly, she found she could laugh about it now whereas before she'd wanted to scream in frustration.

"Wow. Remind me never to get on your bad side," Edward commented, wincing at her recounting of how she'd blocked the groom's drunken pass. "Though I can't say I blame the guy. From your description of his bride, I'm sure you were a lot more appealing."

"Actually, I think it had more to do with the fact that he was wasted."

Edward gave her a long look as he lifted his wineglass to his lips. "What was my excuse then?"

A jolt went through her at the memory, the low-voltage version of what she'd felt when they'd kissed at Georgia and Mike's wedding. "Oh, that," she said lightly, as if she'd forgotten all about it. "Weddings will do that to you. It kind of goes with the territory. Don't beat yourself up about it." Clearly, that's what he wanted to hear. Wasn't that why he hadn't made a move, or so much as referred to the incident since then?

He reached up to brush back a tendril of hair that clung to her cheek, tucking it behind her ear. She grew still, as if the moment might burst like a bubble if she moved a muscle or so much as breathed. "I've been telling myself the same thing," he said, "that it was the occasion, or that I'd had one too many glasses of champagne." He held her gaze. "But if that's all it was, why can't I stop thinking about it?"

"I don't know. Why?" she said in a queer, cracked voice.

He leaned in to kiss her, gently—as if asking a question rather than answering one—cupping her face in his hands as his mouth closed over hers. She was zapped by another, stronger jolt of electricity, which shot straight down through the pit of her stomach to her groin. The very air around them seemed charged.

She parted her lips, catching the tip of his tongue between her teeth. He groaned and pulled her close, holding her tightly as the kiss deepened. She sensed he'd wanted this for a very long time, since before he was even fully aware of what he felt. The heat coming off him was that of an engine that's sat idling too long. There would be no stopping this time.

He pushed the kimono from her shoulders, lightly tracing the curve of her collarbone with his thumbs. "You're so beautiful," he murmured.

She laughed self-consciously. "Freckles and all?"

He nodded and bent to kiss them, one by one, his mouth gradually moving lower. By the time he got to her breasts, she was on fire. She felt a corresponding tug in the deepest part of her when he took a nipple in his mouth and began to suck gently. She let out a long, shuddery breath that was more a moan. She could have come at the slightest touch. When the sensations mounted to the point of exquisite torture, she parted her thighs and guided his hand to her sweet spot.

"Now you," she whispered after he'd made her come that way. She undid his belt buckle and helped him off with his clothes, then took him in her mouth as he arched his back and plunged his fingers into the damp tangles of her hair. She could feel him quivering on the verge of climax; then he abruptly pulled back. "No, I want to be inside you," he said in a hoarse whisper.

What had started slow quickly built, their fevered coupling reaching such a pitch, they ended up on the floor at one point, wedged between the sofa and coffee table. With a growl, he gave the table a hard shove, toppling the empty wine bottle and sending a magazine skidding onto the rug. She tore herself away just long enough to make a dash for the bedroom, to get a condom, and then he was on top of her, pushing into her. They rocked together, Angie crying out in mindless pleasure, until he drove into her in a final thrust that blocked everything else from her mind.

When it was over, she lay limp beneath him, as powerless to move as if she'd been struck a blow. Her throat tightened and the backs of her eyes prickled. She'd heard tell of women dissolving into tears in the aftermath, but never having experienced it herself, she'd seen it as a sign of weakness or possibly a subconscious form of manipulation. Now, she understood: Some feelings were simply too big to contain. When she could bestir herself, she eased out from under him, rolling onto her side. "*That* was amazing." She gingerly ran her fingers over the rug burn on her elbow.

She kissed him before he could respond, letting the pressure of her mouth, the play of her tongue against his, ask the question she didn't dare voice: Was this a one-time thing . . . or the start of something?

Edward kissed her back, not like a man who ought to have been reaching for his clothes, judging by her past experience with men, but as if to let her know he was hers, if only for tonight.

CHAPTER SEVENTEEN

The man at the other end of the phone spoke with a slight but noticeable Indian accent. He was calling on behalf of his boss, he said, and wanted to know if she was free the following Sunday to cater a picnic. "How many people?" Angie asked him as she waved hello to her contractor, Yasser Ali, who'd just walked in with his tape measure. Work on the new space in the Bowery was slated to begin soon; she had all the permits and a crew lined up. Any extra cash would come in handy right now. Though it gave her pause when the man answered, "Two." A picnic for two hundred people on such short notice was a tall order. She'd have to pull out all the stops and pray it didn't rain. Still, she thought it was doable. While her contractor went to work measuring door frames, Angie's mind turned to which dishes would work best for an outdoor event.

"Not two hundred, *two*," the man corrected when she spoke of renting Porta Sans.

Angie was intrigued. This guy's boss was willing to pay triple what a picnic lunch from Dean & Deluca or Zabar's would cost? Probably some rich old dude looking to impress his much younger girlfriend, she concluded. Well, she wouldn't disappoint. The following Sunday, when Angie arrived at the Seventy-Ninth Street Boat Basin at the appointed hour, she was toting her outsize Harrods of London hamper (an eBay purchase and one of her most prized possessions) packed with goodies: smoked-trout pâté, a sourdough baguette from the Sullivan Street Bakery and selection of cheeses from Murray's, corn chowder, grilled-chicken-and-avocado sandwiches with chipotle aioli, and a plum tart for dessert. For beverages, there was bottled water and Limonata. And champagne, of course.

The mystery client was waiting by the marina gate. She recognized him even from a distance and cried out in surprised delight. "You sneaky bastard," she said when she caught up to him.

Edward grinned at her. "Sorry, but it was the only way I could be sure you wouldn't be booked for another event." He bent to kiss her on the mouth, then reached to take the hamper from her. "Here, let me help with that. Good God, it's almost as big as you are. What on earth is in it?"

"Enough to last us through next Christmas." She followed him to where the boat was moored, a vintage double-decker Chris-Craft, its wooden decking and trim gleaming in the sunlight. She broke into a grin. "Well, if you intend to shanghai me, at least we're going in style."

Edward, more casually dressed than she'd ever seen him, in khakis and a navy polo shirt that showed off his muscled chest, paused to admire the boat before they climbed aboard. "Isn't she a beauty? She belongs to a friend of mine. He said I could use her anytime I liked, so I thought . . ."

"You thought right," she said, giving him a proper kiss.

Since they'd become lovers, she'd longed to do this: to kiss freely out in the open, like any couple. She'd broken her formerly ironclad rule—never sleep with a married man—and now she was quickly learning what it was to be a mistress. The hard part was having to sneak around. There was also her Catholic guilt, which kind of surprised her, since she had stopped going to church years ago and couldn't remember the last time she'd gone to Confession. But there it was, nonetheless. She'd regularly think, *I'm committing adultery. I'm an adulteress.*

But not today. Today would be a guilt-free day, she decided on the spot. Edward didn't mention Camille, either, except to say that she'd taken the kids to Southampton for the weekend, in explaining why he wasn't with his family.

Even the weather was made to order: sunny and dry, with the nip of autumn in the air. Soon they were churning their way up the Hudson in the borrowed thirty-two-foot Chris-Craft, under a picture postcard sky. They waved to other boaters, who waved back. It was close to noon by the time they reached the Tappan Zee. Edward slowed the engine to cruising speed after they'd passed under the bridge, so as to better take in the view of the trees that lined the banks, decked in fall finery, their leaves a tapestry of reds and yellows. As they continued on upriver, they passed through several hamlets but saw fewer and fewer boats. At last, he pulled into shore, anchoring in a secluded spot where weeping willows draped over the water to create a sheltered cove. Then there was just the sound of leaves rustling and water lapping against the hull.

Edward disappeared belowdecks and reemerged a few minutes later carrying a folding table and two chairs. They picnicked onboard, in the shade of the willows. It was the first time Angie had catered an event at which she was a guest—the only guest in this case—and she relished every moment as they devoured the feast she'd prepared. She ate until she thought she'd burst, then tossed the crumbs to the seagulls that flocked around the boat. When the leftovers had been packed up, she leaned back in her chair with sigh of contentment, tipping her head to the sun.

"You should hire me to cater more of your events," she said. "Seriously, this is the way to go."

"I would," he replied, "except, as you know, I'm not much of a party animal."

She flashed him a wicked grin. "Actually, I was thinking of something a little more, um, intimate."

They went belowdecks, to the snug cabin which had a built-in bed, where they lay down and kissed until their lips were tender from kissing. They took their time undressing each other. It was like a puzzle in reverse, one that grew closer to completion with each item of clothing removed, until they became, in their nakedness, a perfect, shining whole. He tasted of the champagne they'd drunk and smelled of the outdoors. She wanted to stay tangled in his arms forever.

"Mmm," she murmured. "I could get used to this."

"Me, too," he whispered into her hair as she lay cradled in his arms, the boat rocking gently beneath them.

"We're like the Owl and the Pussycat."

"Which one of us is the Pussycat?" he asked.

"You, of course."

He gave a throaty chuckle. "Only because no one would ever dare call you a pussycat."

"Damn straight," she growled. "Never mess with a lady who's packing knives."

When they finally surfaced, the sun was low in the sky and the breeze had turned cool. "Time to head back," he said with regret. *What are we heading back* to? she wondered as he started the engine. But she didn't ask. Why spoil the moment? When she looked back on this day in the weeks and months to come, she wanted to remember it as perfect—the most perfect day of her life.

CAMILLE WAS HEADED home in a taxicab one chilly afternoon in October, staring out the window lost in thought, when she was pulled from her reverie by her cell phone's muffled ringtone—Alicia Keyes singing "Empire State of Mind." She dug the phone from her purse, frowning when she saw the name on the screen. She was tired and out of sorts, having spent the past two hours at the radiology center being plumbed and probed and scanned. The last person she wanted to hear from was the woman who was rapidly becoming her most exasperating client. But it was business, so she rallied and pressed "Talk." "Kat, hi! You beat me to it. I was just going to call you."

"You didn't get any of my messages?" Kat sounded agitated.

"Sorry, I was tied up all morning," Camille said. "So, how did it go with Jim?"

The current contender for the fair Kat Fisher's hand was a man named Jim Rawlins, forty-one, handsome in a toothy RFK way, and head of his own software firm. The match looked promising on paper: They were both attractive, intelligent, and career-driven. Not only did they come from similar backgrounds, they'd both grown up in Short Hills, New Jersey, where they'd gone to the same high school (though they hadn't known each other then—he'd graduated two years before she had). Nevertheless, given Kat's dismal track record, Camille could only keep her fingers crossed.

She wasn't surprised, only disappointed, when Kat said, "I'd rather not discuss it over the phone." Her voice carried the ring of doom, not wedding bells. "Is there any chance we can meet?"

"Of course. How about tomorrow, first thing?"

"I meant today. It's, um, kind of important."

Camille suppressed a sigh, thinking of the hot bath she'd planned to sink into when she got home. Before Kat, her most exasperating client had been a fashion designer by the name of Annalise Renaldo. Like Kat, Annalise was famously impossible to please. When Annalise turned forty, Camille suggested she throw a birthday party, to which Camille invited every eligible man she could round up, even the thirtysomethings and over-sixty set. That was how Annalise met the man to whom she was now engaged, sixty-two-year-old Belgian sculptor Christophe Loriaux. Maybe that was what Kat needed, to step outside the box. That, or a good talking-to.

Camille broke one of her cardinal rules—*never, ever give a client your home address*—and fifteen minutes later Kat was at her door, looking as flushed as if she'd arrived on foot, her hair in disarray.

"Thanks for seeing me on such short notice," she said, biting her lip and looking down. Camille had never seen her this way. Gone was the glamorous reporter, and in her place an insecure schoolgirl. "Not at all." Camille put a motherly arm around her shoulders as she ushered her inside. Kat seemed distressed. Could the date with Jim really have been *that* bad? "What can I get you to drink? I have some white wine in the fridge," she said as she led the way into the living room. The housekeeper was long gone and the children still at school, so they wouldn't be disturbed.

"Sure, that's fine," Kat said distractedly as she sank onto the sofa.

Camille went into the kitchen, where she made herself a cup of tea, and while it was brewing, poured a glass of wine for Kat. "Now, what's this all about? It sounded pretty grim over the phone," she said when she returned. She handed Kat the glass of wine and settled on the chair opposite her, with her steaming mug. She struck a concerned but not overly dire tone, having learned the best way to keep an agitated client from hyperventilating was to speak in a modulated voice.

Kat took a large gulp of her wine, as if to steady herself. Camille noticed she was trembling. "Well," she began, looking down at the rug. "The date started out okay, but at the end . . . it got ugly."

Camille had a sudden, horrifying image of Kat being date-raped. Had mild-mannered Jim Rawlins become a raging maniac after a few drinks? She shuddered at the thought. Never in all the years she'd been a matchmaker had a female client been sexually assaulted, but that didn't mean it couldn't happen. She heard the tremble in her own voice as she asked, "Did he hurt you?"

Kat's head snapped up and her eyes widened. "Oh, no! Nothing like that. He was the perfect gentleman."

A wave of relief washed over Camille. She blew on her tea and took a careful sip. *Okay, so it wasn't Jim. Good.* It was probably some little thing Kat had blown out of proportion, she guessed, like with Dan Zimmer, the wealthy hedge-fund manager who'd preceded Jim

Rawlins. Dan had committed the unpardonable sin of picking her up in a white stretch Hummer that, she'd sniffed, made her feel like she was going to a prom in Bayonne. But when Camille saw the tears in Kat's eyes, she knew it wasn't a minor thing. Kat was really upset. "What happened?" she asked gently.

Kat heaved a shuddery sigh. "I'm not really sure, to be honest. Like I said, the date went well, and then we went back to his place after dinner. I was fine . . . until he kissed me. That was when I lost it. I broke down and started crying for no reason. Honestly, I don't know what came over me! It wasn't even like I'd had too much to drink. And you know the worst of it? He was really sweet about it. He kept asking if there was anything he could do or if he should call someone." Tears rolled down her cheeks, unchecked. "It was so . . . so humiliating."

"Do you have any idea what might have caused it?" Camille asked.

Kat shook her head, taking another gulp of wine. "No, not really. Except . . . well, like I said, he was the perfect gentleman. He reminded me of—" she broke off, her cheeks coloring. "Someone I once knew," she mumbled. She sucked in a breath and took a haphazard swipe at the tears still running down her cheeks. "That's when I realized how hopeless it was. Whenever I meet a nice guy who I'm attracted to, it all goes to shit somehow. If I can't find anything wrong with him, I'll find a way to sabotage it. Which means there must be something wrong with *me*."

Camille suggested gently, "I think it would help if you saw someone. A professional, I mean," she clarified, at the panicked look Kat shot her. "I'm going to give you the name of a therapist. His name is Dr. McDermott. He's very good, and he's helped some of my other clients."

Kat gave a harsh laugh and said bitterly, "Sure, why not? I've tried everything else. And it's not going to get better on its own." She eyed Camille plaintively. "Is it?"

"Probably not," Camille said. She got up and went into the den, returning a minute later with one of her former colleague's business cards. She handed it to Kat. "Call him. You won't regret it." Kat tucked the card in her Chanel bag, then stood and smoothed her skirt. She was heading for the door when her gaze strayed to the grouping of framed photos on the mantel. There was a black-and-white one of Camille and Edward, at the beach in Southampton, standing with their arms around each other's waists looking out at the ocean, she with her head resting on his shoulder. It had been taken a few years ago, by a photographer friend of hers who'd visited one weekend. *A portrait of happier days*, Camille thought now as she watched Kat pause to study it, a wistful look on her face. "You're so lucky," Kat said. "I just wish I knew your secret."

Lucky? Kat's words stayed with Camille long after she'd gone. The irony was too rich. She was dying and her marriage in shambles. How much more unlucky could you get? If Kat only knew . . .

Edward was working ever longer hours, and when he was home, he was preoccupied much of the time. She used to complain about it, but lately it seemed too much of an effort. And yet he was unfailingly attentive whenever she was in need of ministering: when she'd been up all night throwing up or had a splitting headache or was running a fever. He monitored her temperature and placed cool washcloths on her forehead; he brought her tea and toast in bed and insisted on accompanying her to every doctor's appointment. Sometimes Camille felt like screaming at him, "I want a husband, not a caregiver!" But she never did. She never said a word. How could she? She needed for him to let go of her, not hold on.

And then there had been the peculiar business with Elise. Edward had informed her recently that they wouldn't be seeing any more of Elise. They'd just finished washing up after supper and were settling in to watch a movie on TMC, one of the rare evenings he wasn't working late. The kids were in their rooms. "Really?" Camille said, her hands idle in her lap, loosely holding the TV remote, as she processed this disturbing new development. She was stunned and more than a bit perplexed. Why hadn't *Elise* told her? It seemed out of character. "And what brought this about?"

"She decided it would be for the best," he said.

"The best for whom?"

"For us. She didn't want to make things any worse for me or the kids."

"How could she make things worse?" Kat maybe, but not Elise. Elise couldn't mess it up if she tried.

He shot her a dark look. "Isn't it obvious?"

"Not to me, it isn't."

"What if it didn't work out? Then where would we be?" *With you gone,* he didn't need to add. "The kids don't need any more upheaval in their lives."

But Camille was still perplexed. She'd seen the way Elise looked at Edward: like a woman in love who's trying not to show it. Why would she give up the chance to be part of his future? Unless . . .

"Did you say something to her?" she asked. *Something that could have led her to believe it was a lost cause?*

He gave her another look. "Why do you automatically assume everything is *my* fault?"

"I wasn't accusing you. Why are you getting angry?"

The discussion had ended with his getting up and leaving the room. Typical of Edward. But Camille couldn't shake the suspicion that he was keeping something from her. It had been nagging at her for days, and now all at once the mists cleared. She thought about how close he and Elise had become, and how happy and relaxed he was with her. *He's in love with her.* It must have been Edward's decision to end it. He was torn, and didn't want to risk giving in to temptation. And knowing Elise, she felt the same as he did: She was too principled a person to go anywhere near that slippery slope. *Wasn't that partly why I chose her?*

As Camille picked up Kat's wineglass to place it in the dishwasher, she noticed the clear imprint of Kat's lipstick on the rim of the glass. As she stared at it, it seemed to mock her. *My husband's in love with another woman.* Yet why should that come as a shock? It was she who'd set the ball in motion. She hadn't listened when Edward tried to warn her.

And the worst part, the part so horrible she could scarcely bear to contemplate it, was that she couldn't just let it go. Her husband might have changed his mind, but her circumstances hadn't changed. She was going to die. Sooner rather than later. The new drug wasn't working, and it was only a matter of time before her family would be left to fend for themselves. Panic swelled in her.

I have to talk to Elise.

Not over the phone, though. If she spoke to Elise in person, she'd stand a better chance of persuading her to . . . what? Go against her principles in allowing herself to grow even more attached to a married man for whom she had feelings? Suddenly, it all seemed so impossible. So wrong.

A wave of regret washed over Camille. Edward had warned her she was playing with fire, but she hadn't known the fire would rage out of control, consuming everything she held dear.

SAINT LUKE'S SCHOOL, on Hudson Street in Greenwich Village, was one of a select handful of elite private schools in Manhattan. It was one of the ones Camille and Edward had considered applying to when Kyra was old enough to start school, and she recalled touring the campus and being impressed by the lovely, parklike setting and obvious dedication of its teachers. (Ultimately, they'd chosen the Collegiate School, which had equally strong academics and was closer to home.) But gone were the days when her children's education had been her primary concern. She had more urgent business at the moment, the outcome of which could affect their entire future.

Her taxi pulled up in front of Saint Luke's an hour later. She had timed it to arrive when school was letting out, so as to catch Elise. On the way there, she'd rehearsed what she would say to her. *This isn't what you want, I know—to be in limbo. But if you can be patient a little while longer, it will be so, so worth it later on.* Sure, there was risk involved. But the greater the risk, the greater the reward.

What's my reward? she wondered. Only the comfort of know-ing, when her time came, that her children would be spared the loneliness of an empty house. Though any comfort to be had would be tinged with sadness, she knew; she could feel it now, a heaviness dragging at her, as if she'd been transported to a planet where the gravity was twice that on Earth.

She paid the driver and climbed out, crossing the sidewalk to the wrought-iron gates, flanked by high brick walls, that opened onto the campus, where she paused to steel herself before stepping through them onto the path. The bell had just rung, and students were pouring out of the two-story building at the other end of the tree-lined path, running to meet their parents or nannies. When she reached the entrance, Camille pushed her way in through the door. She passed the administrative offices on her right before heading down the first corridor on her left, which was where she spotted Elise, pretty and fresh-looking in a blue A-line skirt and ruffled pink blouse, standing outside her classroom talking to one of her students, a dark-haired little boy who didn't look too happy. Elise was bent over so she and the boy were eye level. Camille heard her say, "Yes, Manuel, you're still the mural monitor even though Kate and Jonathon are your helpers."

"Yeah, but they have to do what I say!" he declared.

"Being in charge doesn't always mean it's okay to boss people around. Someday when you're a real boss, you can tell other people what to do, but in the meantime, don't forget this is a team effort." She straightened and ruffled his hair. "Now run along; you don't want to keep your mom waiting."

He brightened, flashing her a smile before he scampered off.

"You handled that well," Camille remarked as she approached.

Elise turned around at the sound of her voice. She looked startled for a second, and perhaps the tiniest bit dismayed, but then she broke into a smile. "Camille! What are you doing here?"

"I was hoping to have a word with you. Do you have a moment?" Her heart was pounding hard enough to crack a rib, and she felt sick to her stomach, but she had to see this through.

Elise eyed her apprehensively. She seemed nervous. Camille had a pretty good guess as to why. *You're in love with my husband, and he's in love with you.* But Elise wasn't one to shy from difficult conversations. Camille recalled the story of how Elise had confronted her husband when she'd suspected he was cheating on her, refusing to hide her head in the sand like many wives would. Besides, Elise had nothing to apologize for. "Sure," she said with forced-sounding cheer. "Why don't we step into the faculty lounge?"

A plump, older woman wearing a soft cast on one foot hobbled out the door to the faculty lounge, leaning on her cane, as they were headed in. "'Hi, Flora," Elise greeted her. "How's the foot?"

"Better, now that I have a teacher's aide," the older woman said. "Those kids. They'll be the death of me yet, I swear." She was still shaking her head as she continued down the corridor.

Elise turned to Camille. "That was Mrs. Hobbs. One of her first graders accidentally let the class hamster out of its cage, and she broke her ankle chasing after it. The kids thought it was hilarious until they realized she was really hurt. Now all she talks about is retiring, though I doubt she ever will—she loves teaching." Elise kept up a steady stream of chatter, as if to ease the tension that stretched between her and Camille like an invisible thread pulled taut. They entered the lounge, which was thankfully deserted—the other faculty members must have gone home. "Have a seat." She gestured toward the Formica table by the window, where Camille pulled up a chair while Elise remained standing. "Can I get you some coffee, or maybe a cup of tea?"

"No, thanks. I'm good," Camille said.

Elise sat down, reluctantly it seemed. Camille glanced around the room, taking in the rows of cubbies along one wall, each marked with a different faculty member's name; the notices and sign-up sheets tacked to the bulletin board; the collection of mismatched mugs lining the shelf above the coffee station. It all looked so normal. So safe. A place where the worst that could happen was breaking an ankle chasing after a hamster on the loose. "So," Elise said, "what can I do for you?"

Camille smiled to put her at ease. "I was sorry to hear we wouldn't be seeing you anymore," she began. "I wondered what made you change your mind." She didn't mince words, but her tone was gentle. She didn't want Elise to feel pressured, or as if she was being reproached. "You seemed to enjoy spending time with us, and we certainly enjoy your company. Did something happen to upset you?"

Elise looked startled, and then she blushed and looked down. She seemed rattled for some reason, and Camille sensed it wasn't just that she found it awkward discussing such a sensitive matter. "No. It . . . it wasn't anything in particular," she replied hesitantly. "He . . . we . . . decided it would be best if I bowed out. Things had become . . . complicated. Not that I haven't grown fond of you all, but . . ." Elise trailed off, spreading her hands in a helpless gesture.

Camille sensed she wasn't being entirely forthcoming. Part of her wanted to let it go at that. She'd done her best; she'd been through hell and made sacrifices no wife should ever have to make. But she knew she had to see this through. "Forgive me," she said, "but I can't help feeling I'm missing something here. I realize you don't owe me an explanation, but it would help me if I understood. Please."

Elise was silent for so long, Camille wasn't sure she would say anything at all. Elise's face was troubled as she seemed to wrestle with herself. Finally, she said, "It wasn't my decision. It was Edward's. He told me he could never see me as more than a friend and that if I was looking to get married again someday, he didn't want to hold me back." Her mouth twisted in a rueful smile. "I would have stuck around if it'd been up to me. If it makes you feel any better, you had me pegged correctly. I guess I am cut out to be a wife. I just happened to marry the wrong guy. It wasn't until I got to know your husband that I realized that. He's . . . he's very special."

It wasn't quite what Camille had expected to hear. She'd guessed right but only partly. Elise was in love with Edward, but he wasn't in love with her. The realization was followed by a swift, and entirely selfish, surge of relief. She thought: *Thank God. He still loves me.* But why hadn't he told her the whole truth? Was it because he thought she'd be disappointed that her plan had failed? Whatever the reason, Elise wasn't to blame. *Poor Elise. If I hadn't twisted her arm . . .* She met the other woman's gaze, in which, amazingly, she saw only kind concern. Her throat tightened. "I'm sorry I dragged you into this. I guess I wasn't thinking clearly. I was more concerned about my husband."

"You mustn't worry," Elise said gently. "He'll be all right."

"I'm not so sure, but at least, he won't be alone."

Elise blinked, and let out a small gasp. "You mean you *know*?" she whispered.

"I was talking about the kids," Camille said, frowning. "What did you think I meant?"

"Nothing. I . . . I don't know what I was thinking," Elise stammered. Camille was reminded of the time her daughter had been caught covering for her best friend. Alexia's mother had called asking for Alexia, who, it turned out, was at her boyfriend's instead of spending the night at Kyra's. When the truth came out, the look on Kyra's face was the same one Elise wore now.

"Elise, is there something I should know?" Camille spoke calmly, but on the inside she was coming unraveled. Because she *knew*. She'd known all along, deep down. She thought of the growing distance between her and Edward, his increasingly erratic hours, how closed off he'd become lately.

"You should talk to your husband," Elise said.

CHAPTER EIGHTEEN

Edward arrived home that night to find Camille soaking in the tub. It was after ten p.m. He'd just looked in on the kids, who were asleep in bed. The place was quiet except for the music playing softly on the stereo—something operatic, and tragic from the sounds of it; Puccini, he recognized. He felt a pang as he bent to kiss her moist cheek. "You didn't wait up for me, I hope?"

She shook her head, reaching for the bar of soap in the brass holder. The clawfoot tub was one of the few original fixtures they'd kept when renovating the apartment. Camille loved that she could immerse herself all the way to her chin. It was her favorite place to be after a stressful day at work. "Believe it or not, this is the first moment I've had to myself all day," she said. "I just got the kids off to bed. I let Zach stay up late to finish his project."

Zach's project. Edward groaned inwardly at the reminder. The assignment had been to do a diorama of a Civil War battle, accompanied by an oral report. Zach had chosen to do his on the Battle of the *Monitor* and the *Merrimack*. Camille had helped him with the report, and Edward had gotten him started on the diorama. They'd spent several hours the night before cutting out pieces of cardboard and constructing the wood frame. He'd promised to help with the final assembly, but it had slipped his mind like so much else. *I should've been there,* he thought now.

He had told Camille he was having dinner with an old college buddy from out of town but, in truth, he'd spent the evening with Angie. She'd made him supper at her place, Moroccan lamb stew, which she had left to slow-cook in the oven while they'd created some heat of their own in the bedroom. The memory of which brought a stab of guilt. He knew what he was doing was wrong, but that was the thing about Angie: It *felt* right when he was with her. It was only when they were apart, when he was with Camille, that he felt wretched. Sometimes he wondered if it was possible for a person to literally drown in guilt. Camille had made him promise to keep an open mind about the future, but he had done more than that—he'd opened the floodgates.

"How did the project turn out?" he asked, perching on the rim of the tub.

"Well, I'm biased of course, but I think he did an amazing job," she said. "He was so proud, you'd think it was the actual warships he'd built. He can't wait to show it off at school tomorrow."

She lifted a leg from the sudsy water and gave it a desultory pass with the soap bar. With her hair pinned in loose curls atop her head and her face flushed from the steam, she looked so much like the old Camille, the woman with whom he'd fallen in love, his heart caught in his throat. He recalled when they used to take baths together, soaping each other down with long, leisurely strokes until they became so aroused they had to climb out and finish what they'd started. Often they didn't make it as far as the bedroom. One time after they'd made love on the bathroom rug, she drew a heart with her fingertip on the steam-coated medicine cabinet mirror, with their initials inside it. As if they were young lovers and not a married couple with two children.

"I'm sorry I wasn't there to help," he said.

She shrugged. "How was your dinner?"

"Fine. You know, just catching up on stuff." He could feel the lie stamped on his face, hot and glaring. He dropped his gaze, fiddling with a button on his suit jacket that had come loose.

"What's Ray up to these days?"

"Same old same old. You know how it is with politicians, always looking to get reelected." Ray Walker had been his roommate their sophomore year at Brown. After they'd graduated he'd gone on to law school, and then into politics. He was now mayor of his hometown in West Virginia, or at least, he was the last Edward had heard. They'd remained in touch, though admittedly not close touch. Edward didn't know why he'd used Ray as a cover, and it was a decision he'd soon regret.

"Really? I'm surprised he didn't mention he'd been indicted." Camille's tone was so mild it was a moment before the realization kicked in: She was on to him. "It's amazing what you can find out just by Googling someone." She went on to inform him that Ray had been caught six months ago, in a sting operation, taking bribes from a local mining company in exchange for concessions. "So here's what I'd like to know," she said in the same mild tone. "How did a man who's under house arrest manage to travel all the way to New York City to have dinner with his old college buddy?"

Their eyes met, and there it was; he could see it now. It was like rounding a bend on a dark road at night and seeing the flare of an emergency torch up ahead, knowing there had been an accident. In some ways, that's what it felt like, an accident. Except *he* was the cause. He'd been reckless, and now someone he loved dearly was hurt because of it. He looked down, fixing his gaze on the checkerboard tiles at his feet, black-on-white in a diamond pattern, until they blurred before his eyes. He felt deeply ashamed but also strangely relieved. He was sick of the lies. Not just sick *of* them; they were literally making him ill. Each time he told his wife a lie, he could feel it in the pit of his belly, eating away at him like something corrosive he'd swallowed.

"I'm sorry," he said in a dull voice.

"So where were you tonight, really? With *her*?"

He felt a lurch inside, and his stomach floated up into his rib cage. "Yes," he said.

"Why?" Her voice was a strangled whisper. Just that one word but much was contained therein: whole rivers and valleys, an entire mountain for him to climb. Why indeed? He was as baffled by it as she was. *I love you. I don't want to lose you. I didn't see this coming any more than you did.*

He lifted his gaze, finally, to look at her. She was staring at him accusingly, but her blue eyes, which had always melted him in the past, were having the opposite effect on him now. Anger rose up in place of shame. His voice, when he spoke, was harsh. "*Why?* You don't get to ask that. You don't get to play the injured party. None of this would have happened if you hadn't given up on *us* when you gave up on yourself!" He shot to his feet, leveling a finger at her. "I warned you, you were playing with fire! But you wouldn't listen. Well, you got what you wanted. Only it didn't turn out the way you expected."

"You think I wanted *this?*" She bolted upright, sending soapy water surging over the rim of the tub onto the floor. "You lying and sneaking around behind my back? That was never the plan!"

"The plan? *The plan?*" he hurled back at her. "Christ Almighty, I'm your *husband*, not a 401(k)!"

"I only wanted what was best for you and the kids." A querulous note crept into her voice.

"Really. And what about what *I* wanted? Or did that not figure into your agenda?"

"You make it sound so . . . cold. It wasn't like that, and you know it."

"All I know," he said, "is that your plan backfired. I met some-one."

Camille sat very still, her eyes burning in her pale, lovely face. "Are you in love with her?"

His anger died down as suddenly as it had erupted. His shoulders slumped, and the muscles in his face sagged. "I don't know," he said in a hollow voice. Another lie, perhaps. But what was the joy he felt with Angie compared to the deep bond he shared with his wife of twenty years?

"Let me rephrase it then," she said. "Is it serious?"

He nodded unhappily. "Yes."

Camille's eyes filled with tears. "I see. And do you plan on marrying her?"

He winced. "Jesus. You talk as if you're dead already."

"I will be soon enough."

Her words went through him like a scalpel. To lose Angie would be like cutting off his air supply, but just as unimaginable was the thought of losing Camille. "I don't want you to die," he said.

"I know." Her expression softened. "But it's going to happen whether we want it to or not."

"You don't know that."

"Yes, I do. I don't need test results to tell me the drug isn't working. Look at me, Edward." She rose, dripping, to stand before him naked: a statement of truth in human form. He could see each of her ribs, as clearly delineated as on an X-ray, and the bruising on her arms and legs from the blood thinner she was on—one of the cornucopia of drugs she was taking—the chemo port covered with an adhesive pad. He winced at the sight of her, and yet couldn't take his eyes from her. "You think I liked having Elise around?" she went on. "Sure, I adore her—who wouldn't? But that doesn't mean I didn't want to scream every time she smiled at you or said something that made you smile. I only encouraged it because I believed you and the children would be better off with her than without her. The children, especially." He started to protest, but she thrust her hand out, traffic-cop style, stopping him before he could speak out in his own defense. "No, don't. I've heard it all before. What you don't seem to realize is that kids can't just be put on hold. Where were you tonight when Zach needed help finishing his project? And last week, when you were late picking Kyra up from her play rehearsal? Will they be able to depend on you when it's not just homework or an after-school activity but some crisis that can't wait? When Kyra's heart gets broken or Zach's at an age when drinking and drugs are more tempting than video games?"

"So it's just the kids you're worried about," he said bitterly.

"Oh, for God's sake, Edward! Of course not. If this was just about the kids, I'd be interviewing nannies instead. I want you to be happy. To be"—her voice broke—"to be loved."

"I *was* happy. I *was* loved. Or I thought I was. Until you—" He took a step toward her, forgetting about the puddle on the floor, and felt his right heel skid out from under him. He grabbed hold of the towel rack to keep from losing his footing altogether. But even as he gripped it, he had the sensation of falling. "I never wanted this. She was just . . . there." He spoke the last word in a whisper. He closed his eyes a moment, picturing Angie at the meet-and-greet, with her smile that had been like a door flung open at the end of a dark passageway, letting in sunlight. When he opened his eyes, Camille was hugging herself, shivering. He pulled a towel from the rack and started toward her again, but this time was stopped by the coldness in her voice.

"Who is she? Someone I know, or someone you picked up in a bar?"

He eyed her with reproach. "A bar? Do you really think so little of me?"

"Right now, I don't know what to think."

He gave a harsh laugh. "Well, that makes two of us."

"Tell me her name, at least."

He drew in a breath and slowly released it. "It's Angie."

"Angie?" She frowned in confusion, then, "Angie, the caterer? But how—?" She stopped as comprehension dawned. "The meet-and-greet. Of course." Her baffled expression gave way to a look of panic. "But that's . . . that's . . . She's all wrong! It would never work. She's not the marrying kind, she said so herself. I don't even know if she wants kids. Why *her*, of all people?"

Edward could have extolled Angie's virtues and explained that she did in fact adore children—her nieces and nephews, the kids in her cooking class. He could have told his wife that, though Angie and Elise had little in common, they were alike in one sense: They both had good hearts. But those weren't the words that rose to his lips. "I can breathe when I'm with her," he said.

Tears rolled down Camille's cheeks.

"I'm sorry. I should have told you," he said.

"Yes, you should have."

"I didn't want to hurt you."

She gave a smile that was more a grimace. "I just want to know one thing: Do you still love *me*?"

She began to shiver in earnest as she stood there, naked and dripping and thin . . . so thin. He helped her out of the tub and wrapped the towel around her, wincing at the scars from her various procedures. On her belly, more faintly drawn, were the silvery stretch marks from her pregnancies. He drew her close, murmuring into her damp hair, "Of course I love you. I'll always love you."

He held her, and together they wept. They wept for what was lost and what they had yet to lose. They wept for the milestones in their children's lives that would take place without her and for the grandchildren she'd never know and who would never know her. Most of all, they wept for the young couple they'd been, so full of promise and so passionately in love, who'd naively believed, not only that they had all the time in the world, but that they could survive any storm.

CHAPTER NINETEEN

"Stephen Resler," Dara announced, a hand over the receiver. "He says it's urgent."

Camille eyed the blinking hold button on her phone. Urgent? It had been two weeks since she'd last heard from Stephen. Then, he'd been in a quandary over his fiancée's offer to have another attorney in her firm draw up their prenup. Was he calling this time to let her know they'd set a date for the wedding? She didn't have a good feeling for some reason. Or maybe it was just that it was impossible for her to feel good about anything right now.

She couldn't stop thinking about it. Edward and Angie, Angie and Edward. Her head, her stomach, too, ached from thinking about it. She'd hoped going into the office today would distract her, but as she wrote checks, sorted receipts, and reconciled the previous month's bank statement on QuickBooks, the green-eyed monster continued on its rampage, growling and gnashing its teeth. If she'd felt threatened by Elise, this was a million times worse. She pictured Edward and Angie in bed together. His tongue in her mouth. His naked body moving atop hers. It was all she could do not to scream. As an added torment, there was the possibility—perhaps likelihood—that Angie would one day take her place. This time next year, Angie could be living in her home, occupying her place at the table, sleeping in her bed. Raising her children. Angie, who didn't even *like* kids, as far as she knew. Also, what did it say that she would sleep with another woman's husband? What kind of person did that? Not the kind of person she wanted anywhere near Kyra and Zach.

She picked up the phone and punched the flashing line button. "Stephen. Good to hear from you. How have you been? How's Carole?" It surprised her, how normal she sounded. No one would guess she was a total wreck. Not that Stephen Resler would have noticed either way. It quickly became clear he had his own problems.

"The engagement's off," he informed her.

The news didn't exactly come as a shock—a prenup seldom bode well, especially when one half of the couple was a lawyer—but she made the proper noises. "Really? Stephen, I'm so sorry."

"I did like you said," he went on, in the same grim tone. "I told her I'd be more comfortable using my own lawyer. Carole didn't have a problem with that, so I thought we were cool. Until we got to my lawyer's office, and she started making all these frickin' demands— terms, conditions, you name it. Not like she was afraid she'd get screwed in a divorce, mind you. It wasn't even about that." Camille could hear him breathing heavily at the other end. "It was like she was trying to get the upper hand, you know? And I could tell she was loving every minute of it. So I thought, *Christ, if this is what the next forty years are gonna look like, I'm outta here.*"

"It sounds like you did the right thing." Camille shuddered at his description of Carole Hardy in battle mode. Had she seen that side of her, she never would have taken her on as a client.

"Yeah, I know," he replied unhappily.

"You're not second-guessing the decision?"

"Nah." He sighed. "It's just goddamn depressing, is all. My brothers, the guys I went to school with, the guys I work with, they all have wives and kids. They coach their kids' soccer teams. They take their families on vacations. For them, Six Flags isn't just some creepy bald dude jumping around on TV. Me? I'm forty years old, and what have I got show for myself? I'm like the guy in *Groundhog Day*—every goddamn day I wake up to the same goddamn thing."

Camille briefly commiserated with Stephen before adopting a firmer tone. She gave him the same advice she'd given Kat Fisher, when Kat had come to her in tears (was it only yesterday? It seemed like a hundred years ago). "Listen, Stephen, this may not be what you want to hear right now, but I think it might help if you saw a therapist." The problem wasn't really Carole or any of the other women he'd dated, she told him. It was that he hadn't dealt with his own, unresolved issues surrounding his divorce. "Until you take a good look at that, I don't see how another relationship is going to work."

He blew out a breath. "Jesus. You don't pull any punches, do you?"

"I'm saying this as your friend."

"You must think I'm a real head case."

"Not at all. What I think"—she chose her words carefully—"is that you're a really great guy who will find someone equally great someday but who right now is still licking his wounds."

"I was taught that if you fall off a horse, you should get right back on."

"Women aren't horses."

There was a long pause at the other end; then he said in a resigned voice, "What the hell, why not? It's the one thing I *haven't* tried, so I guess it's worth a shot." She could almost hear the wheels turning in his head, the same wheels with which he ran stock prices and traded vast sums of money, when he asked, "How long you figure it'll take? We talking weeks, months, what?"

"I can't answer that," she said. "These things move at their own pace. Though a lot depends on your willingness." She gave him Dr. McDermott's number, and Stephen promised to call and make an appointment. Though, Stephen being Stephen, he managed to get in the last lick.

"You couldn't set me up with a good-looking female shrink, at least?" he joked.

"I think that would be defeating the purpose, don't you?" she said.

After she'd hung up, she turned to Dara. "That's the second one this week I've had to cut loose. I must be losing my touch." She filled her partner in on yesterday's come-to-Jesus with Kat Fisher.

"Don't worry; they'll be back. They always come back." Dara sounded as if she wasn't sure that was such a good thing.

Dara was in full glam mode today: blood-red lipstick, a fitted calf-length skirt in chocolate suede with a slit up one thigh, her black stiletto Prada boots, and a filmy floral-print blouse with a plunging neckline. Probably she had a hot date lined up for later on. Dara always had at least one guy on the hook at any given time, with several hopefuls waiting in the wings.

If I could distill what she's got and give it to my clients, I'd have a one hundred percent success rate, Camille thought. She recalled a story Dara had told about when she was in high school. Dara had been consoling a friend of hers who was heartbroken over having been rejected by a boy she liked, and the friend blurted, "If I'm so hot, how come *you're* the one who gets all the guys?" Most girls that age would've been deeply offended by such a remark, but Dara had shrugged and said, "Maybe it's because they know I don't need them to feel better about myself."

Camille sighed. "Still. I can't help feeling I failed them somehow."

"There's only so much you can do," Dara reminded her. "You can line up all the parts, but you can't set the wheels in motion. The rest is up to fate, destiny, whatever you want to call it."

Camille's thoughts returned to Edward. When they were first married, she used to think she'd already been through the worst, with her mother dying. Nothing could ever be that bad again, she'd believed. Life as she knew it would continue to hum along, with only minor bumps and obstacles along the way. The children would grow up and get married and have children of their own, and she and Edward would grow old together. But getting cancer had changed all that. It had changed *her*. Her former self couldn't have conceived of a plan that would drive her husband into the arms of another woman. Cancer hadn't just robbed her of a future; it had hijacked her identity. What made it so insidious was that she couldn't pinpoint the exact moment the hijacking had taken place.

Back when she used to counsel couples, a shocking number of wives had confessed, in their one-on-one sessions, to having widow fantasies. One woman had confided, about her husband of twenty-two years and the father of their four children, "Every morning, I wake up next to him and think, *My life would be so much easier without this person.*" Camille had never had such thoughts about Edward. There were times they disagreed or got on each other's nerves, like all couples, but even when the disagreements grew heated, she never regretted marrying him. And yet, while a war was being waged in her body, a stealth attack had taken place from without. An enemy had slipped in on silent ninja feet to capture her, leaving a doppelgänger in her place: not a loving wife but one who'd pushed her husband away when she'd needed him most, and when he'd needed her.

Abruptly, she stood up. Too abruptly. The blood drained from her head, and she grew dizzy. She dropped back into her chair and put her head between her knees. When she finally straightened, the room swam back into focus. She looked up to find Dara standing over her wearing a worried look.

"Camille, are you okay?"

"I'm fine." Camille spoke briskly. "Too much coffee on an empty stomach."

"You look a little pale. Do you need to lie down?"

Camille glanced at her watch, then shook her head. "Later. I'm meeting Holly at her Lamaze class in half an hour, and I have a doctor's appointment after that." When Dara continued to hover, she said, "I'll put my feet up after that. I promise. Okay? Am I excused now?"

Camille fetched her coat from the closet—the weather had turned brisk earlier in the week, slipping from Indian summer into fall seemingly overnight—and put it on. She was heading for the door when Dara remarked, "Just think—next time I see your sister, she'll be a mom. Wow. I still can't believe it. That's like, I don't know, George Clooney getting married or something."

Camille paused and smiled. "I don't think she's quite grasped it, either." For Holly, having a baby was just another fun adventure. A tiny person for her to cuddle and dress up in cute clothes and push around in her nifty new Bugaboo stroller. "She has no idea what she's in for."

"What's with the boyfriend? He still in the picture?"

"As far as I know." She'd only seen Curtis a couple of times since they'd been introduced, and at no point had either he or Holly indicated how serious, or not, their relationship was. They were affectionate toward each other, nothing more, and if Holly had more of a glow about her these days, it could just as easily be due to pregnancy hormones. "He seems excited about the baby." That much she could safely report.

"Do they plan on shacking up together?"

"If they are, I haven't heard anything about it." Curtis and Holly both seemed content with the current arrangement. "Between you and me, I'm not holding my breath," she added as she pushed her way out the door.

HOLLY'S LAMAZE CLASS met on Thursdays, between the hours of one and two p.m., in a Pilates studio on Montague Street in Brooklyn Heights, one flight up from a Vietnamese restaurant. The steamy fragrance of *pho* trailed Camille as she ascended the staircase. She arrived to find Holly seated cross-legged on a mat on the floor, her eyes closed as if in meditation. She was surrounded by a dozen other women, in similar poses and various stages of pregnancy, and their coaches—husbands for the most part, with some moms and sisters and best friends sprinkled in. One woman, a heavyset blonde named Barb, had her lesbian partner.

Camille lowered herself onto the mat Holly had thoughtfully placed alongside hers. "You look like a fat, contented Buddha," she said.

Holly opened her eyes and smiled. "More like a fat, contented cow."

"How's Junior?"

"Busy doing gymnastics at the moment." Holly lifted her gauzy Indian-print tunic to show the walnut-size bump on her belly, just above her navel. Camille placed her hand over it and felt it move. She smiled, remembering when she'd been pregnant and thrilling to the feel of the baby moving inside her, wondering if it was an elbow or a knee that was poking at her.

"Is he always this active?"

Holly grinned. "Only when he's showing off for his aunt."

"Well, if he's anything like you were, you'd better put the number for FEMA on speed dial."

Holly giggled. "I wasn't *that* bad."

"Oh? Remember when you thought it'd be fun to swing from the living room curtain rod?" Camille, who'd been playing in her room at the time, would never forget the loud thump, followed by a piercing wail that had brought her and her mom running. They'd found the curtains in a heap on the floor, Holly tangled up in them screaming and thrashing like a piglet in a sack.

"I was five!" Holly said.

"More like five kinds of trouble. Who got Joey Persky to swallow a mothball by telling him it was a magic pill that would make him invisible?" Joey had lived next door to them growing up.

"I didn't know he'd have to have his stomach pumped!"

"Neither did Joey, apparently."

Holly was giggling uncontrollably now. "Stop, or I'll pee my pants."

Several of the other women glanced their way and smiled. They were used to seeing the two sisters with their heads together, giggling over some private joke. Only with Holly could Camille temporarily forget her woes. Today, she needed that more than ever.

The instructor, a perky blond woman named Natalie who had three children of her own, called the class to attention. "Everyone, I have an announcement! Sarah Tsao had her baby. A boy, nine pounds, two ounces. No complications, I'm happy to report." There was a round of applause, and one of the other women, a petite redhead who looked to be about six months along, muttered, "Nine pounds? Oof. They'd have to knock me out." Her burly firefighter husband looked a little pale.

Camille recalled giving birth to Kyra. Edward had alternately soothed and coaxed her on, holding tightly to her hand as she'd borne down with what little strength she had left after fourteen hours of labor. "You can do this," he'd urged, just as he had years later when she'd been battling cancer. When had he stopped holding her hand? *When you let go of his,* a voice whispered in her head.

Natalie, the instructor, launched into a discussion of last week's homework assignment, which had been to do a food diary recording everything the mothers-to-be consumed over a seven-day period. When talk turned to the nutritional benefits, or lack thereof, of nachos and fries, Holly leaned in to whisper, "Remember when you used tell me if I ate junk food it'd stunt my growth?"

"Okay, so I was wrong about that," Camille conceded. Holly had several inches on her.

"You also said it'd lower my IQ."

"Well, I was right about that."

"Ha! I'm *way* smarter than you."

"So smart you forgot to use birth control."

Holly grinned at her. "Smartest dumb move I ever made."

After the discussion period, they practiced the breathing exercises. Half the expecting moms were opting for natural childbirth, while the others, veterans for the most part, were going for the epidural. Heidi Jenkins, a stay-at-home mom seven months pregnant with her second child, had put it best: "When I go to the dentist for a root canal, I'm not expected to grin and bear it," she reasoned. Holly was of the belief that, if the hippie chicks who'd given birth at Woodstock, in the medical aid station tents, could breeze through it without missing a guitar lick, she should be able to manage just fine. *You have no idea*, thought Camille for the umpteenth time.

After class, as they were putting their mats away, she asked in what she hoped was a casual voice, "Have you and Curtis worked out any sort of arrangement yet for when the baby comes?"

Holly shrugged in response. "Not really, but we'll figure it out."

Camille grew impatient. "Holly." She eyed her sister sternly. "This isn't a time-share we're talking about. You're going to be parents. You have to have *some* sort of plan. You can't just wing it."

"Yeah, I know, but things are kind of up in the air right now."

"How so?"

"Curtis got offered a promotion—his boss wants him to head the DC branch. It's a huge opportunity. He could pretty much write his own ticket from there." They headed for the exit, where they paused to don their coats, Holly's a fringed-and-beaded leather jacket that'd once belonged to the drummer for Pink Floyd. "I told him he should take it."

Camille's heart sank. "Is he going to?"

"He hasn't decided yet, but he's considering it," Holly said as they started down the staircase.

She seemed relaxed about the whole thing—*too* relaxed. Camille wasn't fooled. She knew her sister well. Holly made light of things that would have had anyone else freaking out; it was her way of coping. Camille recalled the time Holly phoned from Singapore, after her then-boyfriend Ronan Quist had left her stranded, following a drunken orgy that she'd walked in on and that had resulted in a huge blowout. Holly had acted as if she were calling from down the block, in need of money for a cab, not plane fare home. Camille waited until they were outside, on their way to the corner Starbucks, to weigh in with her opinion.

"You and the baby should be part of the equation, at least."

"It wouldn't be like before, when he was living on the other side of the Atlantic," Holly reasoned. "DC is only a few hours away by train. He could visit on weekends."

"That's what they all say."

"Who?"

"The divorced dads who relocate. Only somehow it never works out the way they plan."

Holly came to an abrupt halt and turned to face her, the fringe on her jacket swaying with the suddenness of the movement. "Will you stop. Geez. We're not divorced! We're not even married."

"I wouldn't rule it out. You're not getting any younger."

"Where is it written you have to be married by a certain age? Or married at all?" Holly demanded. "This may be hard for you to imagine, sis, but not all us single girls go to sleep at night dreaming of white satin and wedding bells. Some of us are perfectly happy being on our own."

"You won't be on your own. You'll have Junior."

"Yes. Won't that be nice?" Holly's expression turned dreamy, and they continued on their way.

"Trust me, there will be days when it won't seem so nice." Camille had always been the calm, cool voice of reason. Not that Holly ever listened. She took a last stab at it, nonetheless, when they were standing in line at Starbucks. "Remember when Kyra was a baby, and I couldn't get her to stop crying?" Her daughter had been colicky as an infant. "I was so sleep-deprived, I was a zombie." So out of it, she'd once "burped" an economy-size pack of Pampers standing in line at Duane Reade. "There were times, I swear, when I thought about leaving her on some nice lady's doorstep. Either that or jumping off a bridge."

Holly grew quiet. It wasn't until they were seated with their lattes that she ventured cautiously, "You wouldn't, would you? I mean kill yourself for real." Her eyes searched Camille's face.

"I don't know," Camille replied honestly. "I can't say it hasn't crossed my mind, but I'm not sure I could ever go through with it. I guess it would depend."

Holly went pale, and she seized hold of Camille's wrist, saying urgently, "Promise me you won't. At least, not without talking to me first. I mean it, Cam. You have to swear on your life. No, not that . . ." She bit down on her bottom lip as a helpless giggle erupted. "I would even help you if . . . if "—her voice wobbled and her eyes pooled with tears—"if you needed me to."

Camille knew the courage it took for her sister to make such an offer and was deeply touched by it. "Thanks, Dr. Kevorkian," she said, making light of it to keep from puddling up herself. "I always knew you were jealous of me, but I never thought you'd take it to such extremes."

Holly gave a choked laugh. "Shut up. I was never jealous."

"Liar."

"In your dreams."

The sisters lapsed into companionable silence. Camille sipped her latte as she gazed out the window at the pedestrians passing by on the sidewalk. A little kid wearing a helmet coasted along on his Razor bike, his mom trotting after him. Next came an elderly woman walking a gray-muzzled black Lab, and then a young couple holding hands who could barely take their eyes off each other long enough to watch where they were going. Camille, remembering when she and Edward had been that intensely focused on each other, was pierced with sorrow.

"Edward's having an affair." The words slipped out before she was even aware she'd spoken.

"What? Did you just say—*Shit!*" Holly swore. Camille turned to find her sister mopping up a puddle of spilled coffee with her napkin. Holly abandoned her efforts and sat back, staring at her. "No, not possible," she said, shaking her head. "Edward would never cheat on you. Whatever it looks like, I'm sure there's an explanation."

Camille sighed. "He didn't deny it when I confronted him."

Holly's eyes widened and her hand flew up to cover her mouth. "Oh, my God." Then her expression hardened. "Figures. It's always the quiet, churchgoing ones you have to watch out for."

"I'm not talking about Elise."

"Then who—?"

"Her name is Angie. Angie D'Amato. She caters my events—or she used to." Camille had sent her a terse e-mail earlier in the day letting her know her services would no longer be required.

"Is it serious?" Holly's eyes seemed to fill her whole face.

"He's not just in it for the sex." An image rose once more of Edward and Angie in bed together, and she felt her stomach cramp. The smell of the spilled coffee was revolting all of a sudden.

"Oh, Cam." Holly took hold of her hand, squeezing it.

"It's my fault as much as his," Camille went on. "I was the one who pushed Elise on him." Though she'd never imagined, in doing so, she'd be opening a door through which anyone could enter. To be fair, neither had Edward, she suspected. However furious she was at him right now, she knew he hadn't sought this out. *She was there.* Weren't those his exact words? He might have added, *And you weren't.* She'd abandoned him, the way he saw it.

"You were only doing what you thought was best for your family," Holly replied staunchly.

"Maybe I should've thought more about what was best for my marriage." Camille lapsed into thought, gazing sightlessly ahead. When she finally roused and glanced at her watch, she saw that it was three p.m. She rose to her feet. "I better run, or I'll be late for my doctor's appointment."

"Is Edward meeting you there?" Holly asked, eyeing her anxiously.

"No. He wanted to, but I told him not to come." She didn't need to be reminded of the shaky ground her marriage was on while being confronted with the even shakier state of her health.

"I'll come with you, then." Holly rose heavily to her feet.

"No, you stay. I'll be fine. It's just routine," she lied.

In fact, today's appointment was anything but routine: She would be learning the results of the latest round of tests. As Camille bade her sister farewell and hurried off to the subway, she steeled herself for the news that would only confirm what she already knew in her heart.

SHE WAS SURPRISED, when she walked into her doctor's office, to find someone seated in the leather wing chair opposite the desk, talking to Regina. A middle-aged man, bald on top, wearing a herringbone blazer and Liberty of London tie. At first, she mistook him for a patient. But no, the receptionist, Bettina, wouldn't have shown her in if Regina had been with another patient. And now here was Regina rising to her feet, smiling and beckoning to her. The man turned to smile at her, too.

"Camille, this is Dr. Rose," Regina said.

Dr. Rose was head of the team at MD Anderson, in Houston, that was developing the experimental drug she was taking. Her mind raced. What was he doing here? Had he just happened to be in town or had he made a special trip? Either way, it was bad news; she was sure of it. She began to tremble at the thought.

"Ira, please," he said warmly as they shook hands. He had a deep voice and spoke with an upper-class British accent. Other than that, there was nothing remarkable about him; he was short and pudgy, with an unassuming manner. What had impressed her was what she'd learned when she'd Googled him: He'd been educated at Oxford and had gotten his medical degree from Harvard. Since then, he'd subsequently won numerous awards and been nominated for the Nobel Prize for his cutting-edge work in the field of cancer research. "Regina's told me so much about you, I feel as if I know you." Once again, she was surprised by how normal she sounded. But this time, it wasn't the state of her marriage that was on her mind; it was the state of her health. Was this nice man going to give her a death sentence? "I understand you two interned together?"

He turned his twinkly gaze on Regina. "Yes, indeed. We all had to scramble to keep up with Reggie."

Reggie? Camille smiled in spite of her nervousness. She had a hard time picturing her poised, dignified hematologist-oncologist as a striving, and possibly gawky, intern called Reggie.

"And I've been doing my best to keep up with *you* ever since," Regina replied with a chuckle.

"And here we are, united once more in a common cause." Dr. Rose brought his beneficent gaze back to Camille. "I've been following your case with great interest, my dear." He had a warmth and old-world courtliness that soothed her jangled nerves like a glass of dry sherry sipped slow. "Actually, that's why I'm here. I thought we might go over your test results together."

Camille nodded woodenly, her heart pounding. "Yes, of course."

"Should we wait for your husband?" he asked.

"No, he, um, couldn't make it." She mumbled something about an emergency with one of his patients. However angry she was at Edward, she didn't want Regina or Dr. Rose to think ill of him.

"A pity. I was rather hoping to meet him. I read his paper in *JAMA* on the latest diagnostic advancements in his field. Fascinating stuff. Ah, well, another time perhaps." Dr. Rose shook his head with regret before getting down to business. "Well then, shall we have a look?"

Camille went over to the sofa and sat down next to Regina, while Dr. Rose took a seat at the end. On the glass table in front of them was the manila envelope from the radiology lab that contained the results of her latest PET scan. Camille felt dread congeal in her stomach, thick and cold. The last two batches of images had shown no change in her condition. This would be more of the same, or it might show that her cancer was progressing. Either way she was doomed—it was either a slow death or a quicker one.

"Your blood work was the first indication of what we were looking at," Dr. Rose began. Camille might have taken comfort in his calm tone as she listened to him go on about her white cells and red cells, her CBCs and ANCs, except she'd spent enough time around doctors—she was married to one, for God's sake—to know they all talked this way even when the prognosis was bleak.

"What does it mean?" she finally blurted.

"Why don't you have a look and see for yourself?" Dr. Rose gestured toward the radiographic images Regina had withdrawn from the manila envelope. Camille bent to peer at them, and immediately noticed something was different. It took her a moment, though, to realize what it was: She was looking for something that wasn't there. The "hot zones"—areas where the tracer with which she'd been injected showed up in light-colored patches anywhere cancer cells were present—were either noticeably reduced or scarcely visible. She studied the images in mute disbelief, her mind struggling to grasp what was plainly visible to the eye. It was too much to take in all at once.

It was Regina who said, "What it means, Camille, is that your cancer appears to be going into remission."

"It's quite remarkable, actually," Dr. Rose interjected, growing more animated. "Your previous results were, shall we say, less than encouraging. Also, given that your cancer was in an advanced stage, we knew it was a long shot to begin with. We certainly never expected anything like this." He gestured excitedly toward the printouts. "If I were a man of the cloth, I would call it a miracle. But as a scientist, I can only say it has far exceeded our expectations."

Camille was too dumbfounded to respond. She half-listened as Dr. Rose went on, something about having her fly to Houston for more tests. He also seemed eager to introduce her to the other members of his team. "You're our new poster girl," he said. She was opening her mouth to protest, *No, I'm the one who isn't going to make it, remember?* when full awareness finally kicked in.

"Are . . . are you saying I'm not going to die?" she stammered.

Regina beamed at her. "Hopefully, not for some time."

Her numb disbelief gave way to a rapidly expanding euphoria that swelled until it nearly lifted her out of her seat. She felt giddy, drunk almost. Her first thought was, *I have to call Edward.*

Edward . . . oh, God. *Edward.*

She stood up, swaying on her feet as the room slowly revolved around her. Black specks gathered at the periphery of her vision, the figures of Regina and Dr. Rose dissolving like pixilated images on a screen. There was a rushing noise like static in her ears. Then she lost consciousness.

CHAPTER TWENTY

"Okay, guys, listen up!" Angie raised her voice to be heard above the din of eight teenagers all trying to outshout and outdo one another. The Bedford-Stuyvesant Youth Center cafeteria sounded like a prison yard. "Trust me, you're gonna want to hear what's on the menu for tonight."

It was the last evening of her cooking class, and she wanted to end it, as she would a proper meal, with dessert. If these kids retained nothing else from the weeks of learning the skills they'd need to get jobs in the restaurant industry, they'd know what a real cake was. Most knew only the store-bought kind: supermarket fare and cheap bakery cakes that tasted like flavored cotton balls. Also, she figured it would provide a welcome distraction from the drama surrounding Tamika and Daarel's latest breakup, which was simmering like a stockpot on the back burner, the girls siding with Tamika and the boys united in their defense of their man Daarel.

This was their third breakup. It was the same story each time: Tamika was working to better herself, while Daarel's career goal, if you could call it that, was to become a rapper—a restaurant job would only be until he signed his first record deal, he liked to boast. Tamika was fed up with his "foolish" dreaming and he with her nagging. Yet, though they were worlds apart in terms of ambition, their chemistry was such that they could never stay apart for very long.

Angie's attention was diverted by a skirmish that had broken out on the fringes of the group, where Tre'Shawn and Julio were unpacking the bags of supplies she'd brought. She watched big, brawny Tre'Shawn give Julio a rough shove that sent the smaller boy reeling. "Watch yo'self, punk!"

"I ain't no punk!" Julio strutted back over to Tre'Shawn, drawing himself up in an effort to look taller.

Tre'Shawn glared at him. "Then why you ack like one?"

Angie darted over to break it up. "Guys, guys. What's gotten into you?" Julio and Tre'Shawn had always gotten along well in the past. "Will somebody please tell me what's going on?"

Tre'Shawn jabbed a finger in Julio's direction. "He bad-mouthing my boy." Tre'Shawn took his role as Daarel's wingman seriously. The two had been best friends since elementary school.

"I ain't bad-mouthing nobody. All's I'm saying is there's two sides to every story." Julio shot an apprehensive glance over his shoulder at Daarel, a hulking figure to his left. Daarel gave him the stink eye, while Tamika stood with her arms folded over her chest wearing a superior look.

"Right now, there's only one side. And that is, if you two don't get back into line, I'll be royally pissed off," Angie said in her sternest voice. "Whatever goes on outside this room, I expect you to check it at the door along with your attitude. You're here to learn, not beat one another up. And since this is our last night, it'd be nice if we could end it on a positive note. Now, who's up for cake?" She turned to address the other kids, who dropped their defensive postures and brightened. They hooted, and D'Enice did a little dance. Only Chandra looked less than enthused. She cast a dubious eye on the bunch of carrots Julio was pulling from one of the grocery bags.

"What kind of cake?" she asked. Skinny Chandra was not an adventurous eater. The other kids would try anything, and some had even developed a taste for foods that had made them wrinkle their noses at the outset, but Chandra was stubbornly set in her likes and dislikes. She preferred frozen fish sticks to fresh fish properly cooked and boxed mac and cheese to homemade spaghetti *alla carbonara*. She was a devout disciple of Colonel Sanders. Angie considered it a minor triumph that she'd gotten Chandra to eat steak that was medium rare as opposed to well done.

"*What kind? Girl, who cares? It's cake!*" yelled D'Enice.

"Carrot cake to be exact," Angie said. "Which is the closest thing to heaven, in my opinion. Now, there are probably more recipes for carrot cake than there are conspiracy theories on who shot JFK"— she ignored the blank looks at the historical reference, preferring not to be reminded of the glaring deficiencies in the city's public education system—"but this one comes with a pedigree, from none other than the White House. So, if it's good enough for VIPs and visiting dignitaries, it's certainly good enough for you guys." She cast a pointed glance at Chandra. "Okay? Now, if everyone will please put their aprons on, we can get this show on the road."

She showed them the proper way to measure dry ingredients— *spoon the flour into the measuring cup, then level it off with a knife, so you don't put in too much*—and how to cream the butter with the sugar—*add the sugar a heaping tablespoon at a time, until the mixture looks like whipped cream.* Raul and Tamika were given the task of peeling and grating the carrots. Tre'Shawn and Daarel cracked the eggs into a bowl. Julio was in charge of grating the nutmeg, which he did with his usual panache, making believe he was in a mariachi band while singing along in a loud voice, which had everyone cracking up. Even Angie joined in on the merriment.

When the batter was ready, she divided it between three cake pans. After the pans had gone into the oven, she unwrapped the cake layers she'd baked the night before. "Now, for the *really* fun part," she said. Her students looked on, rapt as little children, as she demonstrated the making of the frosting. With the electric mixer, she beat cubes of butter and cream cheese that she'd set out earlier to soften, before sifting a mound of confectioners' sugar into the bowl, over which she drizzled cream, beating all the while. She finished with a splash of vanilla extract for flavor.

She let each of her students take a turn frosting the cake, using an offset spatula, while she supervised. Tamika, Chandra, and Raul each frosted their portion with painstaking care. Julio, Jermaine, D'Enice, and Tre'Shawn's efforts were clumsier—more frosting ended up on their fingers, and subsequently in their mouths, than on the cake. Huge, hulking Daarel, with his hands like catcher's mitts, was the surprise star: He was given the top of the cake to frost and did so expertly, swirling it into little peaks the way she'd shown him, sneaking glances at Tamika all the while.

Angie then handed out plastic spoons and the bowl was passed around so each student could have a lick of the leftover frosting. Tre'Shawn was like a kid at Christmas, so excited he kept snatching the bowl out of the others' hands, amid hollered protests and threats of retribution. When the bowl was scraped clean, they sat down to eat the cake they'd all had a hand in making.

"Damn, that's good!" declared D'Enice after one bite.

The others pronounced it the best cake *ever*. Even Chandra polished off her piece.

Julio asked if he could take home a piece of what was left, so his brothers and sisters could have some, which elicited cries of "No fair!" and "Cheater!" from those who seemed to think it an unfair advantage that he had so many siblings. Angie settled the debate by dividing up the remains and giving each student a piece to take home. Then finally, it was time to call it a night. She climbed onto a chair, a move that brought a wave of mock groans. She grinned. "Don't worry. I'm not known for my oratory skills, so I'll make this brief." She scanned the faces of the boys and girls she'd come to think of as family, as noisy and fractious as her own, lovable and aggravating in equal measure. "Well, this has been fun, hasn't it? Call me crazy, but I'm going to miss your sorry asses. It's a miracle none of you lost a finger or an eye, the way you samurais handle knives.

But you've come a long way, and I'm proud of you." She started to choke up a bit, and paused to clear her throat. "You should be proud of yourselves, too. Believe me, not everyone can fillet a fish or make pasta from scratch. So if any of you should decide to make a career of it . . ."

"Hoo, boy. Not me, man!" interjected Raul. His cousin worked as a short-order cook and the pay sucked, he declared. After he was shouted down, he was forced to concede, "Well, I guess it wouldn't be *too* bad, if it was, like, a real restaurant—you know, with table-cloths and stuff."

"Raul's right—the pay *does* suck," Angie told them. "But you don't do it for the money. You do it because you can't *not* do it. That's what's most important: Whatever you do for a living, you've got to love it. You've got to love it enough to look forward to going to work each day even if your boss is a jerk or your coworkers give you a hard time. Because even though it may not seem like it right now, life is short. Trust me on that. Way too short to waste it on a job that sucks."

After she'd said her piece, she started to climb down. But before both feet were on the floor, she was scooped up by a pair of brawny arms and found herself looking into Daarel's grinning face. He paraded her up and down the length of the cafeteria while she cried out in mock protest and the others hooted and laughed and clapped. When he finally set her down, he did so as gently as if she were made of glass. Then everyone gathered around to say their good-byes.

"We gonna miss you, Miss D," said Julio. He looked as if he wanted to hug her, but ended up giving her a bro handshake instead.

"You know where to find me, guys. Seriously, don't make me come after you." She wagged a finger in mock admonition.

Raul wanted to know if she had a Facebook page. She told him no—when would she have the time?—and he shook his head woefully, saying, "Yo, Miss D. You got to get *down* with it."

D'Enice and Chandra both had tears in their eyes when they hugged her. Tamika was the only one of the girls who didn't puddle up; for her, this was the beginning rather than the end. She would continue to work for Angie, after school and on weekends, until she went away to college next year.

Angie's heart was full as she watched her kids troop out the door, each clutching their wedge of cake, on a paper plate wrapped in Saran Wrap, as proudly as if it were a diploma, which in a way it was. They jostled one another, slapped palms and bumped knuckles, and called out good-natured taunts in parting. Even Tamika and Daarel appeared to have made peace, if only for the moment. They fell into step with each other on their way out, their arms nearly brushing.

Angie thought of Edward. She didn't know what to expect after the email from Camille earlier in the day. The cat was out of the bag, that much was clear. Had Edward confessed, or had Camille found out by accident? Either way, it was awful. *Poor Camille.* Angie felt sick about it. She wondered, too, what it meant for her and Edward. Was this the end? She'd know soon enough. She was meeting him for a drink later that evening. But first, she had dinner with her mom and Francine to get through—they'd made an afternoon of it in the city, and she'd promised to take them to her favorite restaurant in her neighborhood. She could only hope her mom wouldn't catch a whiff of something that didn't smell right.

EVERY OTHER MONTH or so, Francine dragged their mother into Manhattan for a day of sightseeing and culture. They visited monuments and historic sites; they went to the museum exhibits Francine had circled in her copy of that week's *Time Out*, or a Broadway show if they could get good seats via TKTS. Francine was the only one of Angie's sisters who hadn't surrendered body and soul to the 'burbs. And though their mother would've been perfectly content if she never took another trip into Manhattan, she was the only one available to accompany Francine on these jaunts—Julia, Susanne, and Rosemary all worked jobs with less flexibility than Francine's—so she'd become the default sidekick. If Angie wasn't too busy, she usually met them for an early dinner before they headed back to Long Island.

"Cozy," Angie's mother pronounced as they entered the restaurant. "Cozy" was code for cramped. Later on, Angie knew, Loretta would rave to her friends about the "charming" place her daughter, the chef, had taken her to, with its black-and-white floor tiles, punched-tin ceiling and kitschy decor complete with stuffed animal heads on the walls, but in truth she preferred dining out at restaurants like Antoine's, in Oyster Bay, with its ancient, red-jacketed waiters and leather-bound menus as hefty as the stone tablets Moses brought down from the Mount. (Though Angie herself hadn't dined there in years, she was sure if she were to go there now she would see the same steak *au poivre* and crêpes suzette on the menu that she'd thought the height of sophistication when her parents took her there to celebrate her high-school graduation.)

"I'm glad you like it, Ma." Angie was careful to keep her eyes averted from Francine. She'd have only to glance at her sister to get them both started. When they were kids, just the sight of Francine's twitching lips, in response to some remark their mother had made, was enough to send Angie into paroxysms of hilarity. She couldn't count the number of times they'd been banished from the dinner table or sent to their rooms for being "disrespectful." "You should try the lasagna. They make their noodles from scratch just like Nonna used to."

Angie conversed briefly with the hostess, whom she knew slightly, an aspiring performance artist named Naomi whose multi-toned hair and multiple piercings were another thing Loretta would no doubt comment on to Francine on the way home. It wasn't until they were seated at their table that Loretta lit up, at the appearance

THE REPLACEMENT WIFE · 323

of their handsome young waiter. She chatted him up as if they were guests at a party he was hosting. After he'd taken their orders and left, she remarked, "What a nice young man. I wonder if he has a girlfriend."

"Doubtful," Angie replied. Francine gave a snort, while their mother wore a blank look. Angie spelled it out. "Mom, he's gay."

Loretta arched her penciled brows in a skeptical look. "You know this for a fact?"

"No, but—"

"Then how can you be sure?"

"If you see bear tracks, do you need to see the bear to know it was there?" One of her mother's favorite expressions, and one that Angie used now to illustrate her point. "Trust me. I've worked in enough restaurants to know gay from straight."

"Maybe he's a switch-hitter," Francine said.

"Well, we wouldn't want *that*," Loretta said. She was tolerant but only to a point.

We? How had it come to this? Her love life a joint enterprise to be endlessly discussed and dissected. "Ma. Can we please just this once have a nice dinner that isn't about you trying to fix me up with every guy you meet who's the right age and doesn't look like the Unabomber?"

"You should become a lesbian," Francine teased, and this time it was Angie who snorted.

"Go ahead, make fun," their mother said, pretending to be miffed. "But it won't seem so amusing when you're the only one at your class reunion who doesn't have baby pictures to show off."

"Ma, I've never even *been* to any of my reunions," Angie reminded her.

Loretta gave her a look, as if that was another subject on which she might wish to voice an opinion. Angie suppressed a sigh. Her mother had an opinion on everything and the mouth to back it up. She was the Linda Richman character from *Saturday Night Live.*

She even looked the part. Her hair was the same mink-brown bouffant as in her junior prom photo (dyed now), and she dressed like an extra on *Dynasty*, complete with shoulder pads only a fellow 1980s refugee would love, turquoise eye shadow and lipstick the bright red of a hazard sign. Oddly enough, it was one of the things Angie admired about her mother: In an ever-changing world, Loretta D'Amato remained unchanged. Not because she was unaware she was out of step but because she liked herself enough not to care what anyone else thought of the way she looked.

If anyone was changed, it was Francine. In high school, she was voted Most Likely to Succeed. But after graduating magna cum laude from Northwestern and getting her master's in education, she got pregnant. She'd been working toward her PhD at the time, but couldn't see herself becoming a single mom (abortion was out of the question), so she dropped out of the PhD program at Boston University and married her boyfriend Nick. Two years later, when Big Nick was offered the job of assistant coach at Hofstra, they bought a house in Massapequa. Big Nick was now head coach at Hofstra, and Francine taught fifth grade at the local middle school.

Now, after three kids, she'd lost her sparkle but not the twenty extra pounds she'd packed on with her last pregnancy. As a teenager, Francine never left the house looking anything less than MTV-worthy. She wore her hair in the Olivia Newton-John shag that was all the rage back then and was obsessive about her clothes and makeup; she and her friends would spend hours painting one another's fingernails and toenails. Now she lived in mom jeans and T-shirts at home, and couldn't remember the last time she'd had a manicure. She didn't bother with her hair except to have the splitends trimmed every so often, and who had time for makeup?

But if it wasn't the life she'd envisioned when she was younger, she wasn't unhappy. Francine might roll her eyes at what she called her husband's dumb-jock ways or threaten to call Homeland Security when Little Nick and Bobby got into it, or sigh that she'd need a hip replacement from toting around a two-year-old at her "advanced" age, but there was no more devoted wife or mother. And she was still the same Francine in one respect—she was rigorously intellectual. She read voraciously. She subscribed to the *New Yorker* and rarely watched TV unless it was CNN. She kept her car radio tuned to NPR and belonged to a book club that focused on the classics.

While they ate, Francine talked about Little Nick's making the lacrosse team at his school, the new tooth that baby Caitlin was cutting, and the upcoming presidential election. Loretta regaled them with more tales of the Alaskan cruise she and Angie's dad had gone on (from which they'd returned with more photos of icebergs and ice floes than probably existed in the archives of *National Geographic*). Angie brought them up-to-date on the renovations on her new space, which were under way, and talked about the last night of her cooking class and how much she'd miss the kids.

"We made carrot cake," she said.

"Ah, cake—I remember those days." Francine sighed wistfully. "Nowadays you can't bring so much as an M&M to school without the sugar nazis jumping down your throat. The rule at our school is, if you bring something for the whole class on your kid's birthday, it has to be fruit or trail mix, preferably organic." She made a face. "Please. Like a cupcake ever killed anyone."

"If that were true, we'd all be dead by now. Right, Ma?" Angie grinned at Loretta. "There was enough Duncan Hines cake mix in our pantry to wipe out the entire population of Long Island."

"We didn't worry about such things when you girls were growing up," said Loretta as she daintily brought a forkful of lasagna to her lips. "It was enough making sure everyone's teeth were straight."

"And that none of us got pregnant," Francine said.

"Well, at least you got something out if it." Their mother cast a pointed glance at Angie.

"Ma, don't start," Angie warned.

"What, did I say something?" Loretta feigned ignorance.

"No, but I know what you're thinking. And it's no use. You might as well face it. I'm a lost cause. I'm never getting married or having kids." *Not if Camille Harte has anything to say about it.*

Minutes later, after their mother had excused herself to use the restroom, Francine leaned in to ask in a hushed voice, "So? What did he say?" Angie had told her about the email from Camille.

She sighed. "We didn't get into it over the phone. I'm meeting him later on."

"Do you think she gave him an ultimatum?"

Angie bit her lip and looked down. "I don't know. All I know is I don't want to lose him."

Francine patted Angie's hand. Initially, she'd warned against becoming involved with a married man. But once Angie explained the circumstances, Francine saw it wasn't just a garden-variety affair. Also, she'd been through enough changeups in her own life to know you couldn't always play it by the book. "Well, even if you have to stop seeing each other," she said, "it'd only be for the time being. Not to sound coldhearted or anything, but the fact is, the woman is dying."

Angie grimaced. "I don't like to think about that."

Francine nodded soberly. "Yeah, I know." She shook her head. "God, I can't imagine. Though if it were me, I probably wouldn't care if Nick had an affair. I'd be glad he was getting some."

"No, you wouldn't. I know you—you'd cut off his balls and have them bronzed."

"You're right." Francine gave a rueful chuckle. "I would." She cast a look in the direction of the restrooms, as if to make sure Loretta wasn't within earshot, before going on. "But from what you've told me, she wants him to be happy. Sure, she would have preferred it if he'd waited until after she was gone, but in the larger scheme of things, she got what she wanted. And, Ange, you deserve that, too—to be happy. Not to sound like Ma or anything, but you do."

Angie sighed again. "The trouble is what *I* want will be at her expense if I get it. I can't wish for that."

Francine raised an eyebrow. "Since when did you start buying into all that Catholic guilt?"

"Since I started sleeping with a married man," Angie said.

FORTY MINUTES LATER she was walking into Lucky Jack's, on Orchard Street. The bar was packed—she'd forgotten it was rugby night, when all the neighborhood ex-pats gathered to watch whatever game was being broadcast via satellite—but even so, she had no trouble spotting Edward amid the crowd. He was seated at one end of the long, copper-topped bar sipping a beer, dressed in faded jeans and an off-white Irish fisherman's sweater. Her heart leaped, and she lingered a moment by the entrance, taking a mental snapshot for future reference—or perhaps as a memento. She loved looking at him—his beautiful face; the long, lean lines of his body. She loved how self-contained he was in repose, in his own little bubble surrounded by all those people, and that he took no notice of the shapely blonde seated on his left who was busy ignoring him but whose body language screamed *Yoo-hoo! This way! Over here!*

What was he thinking right now? *Is he thinking about me?* He'd never told her he loved her, but she knew he did—he'd demonstrated it in countless ways. It wasn't just about the sex, either. They talked on the phone whenever possible and never ran out of things to say to each other. When they were together, she cooked for him or they went to off-the-beaten-track eateries. He brought her little gifts—teas from the tea shop near where he worked, a bar of lavender soap because he knew she loved the smell of lavender, a stained-glass cardinal to hang in her window (after she'd complained that the birds of NYC only came in two colors: gray and brown). True, the time they spent together was made up of stolen moments and it was never enough. But could he bear to lose her any more than she could bear to lose him?

She threaded her way through the crowd. "Hey, you," she breathed in his ear, sneaking up on him. He turned, breaking into a grin as she slid onto the stool next to his. "Sorry about that," she said, jerking her chin in the direction of the mosh pit at the other end of the bar, where the TV was mounted. "I forgot it was rugby night. Do you want to go someplace quieter?"

"No, it's okay. I can't stay long," he said.

Angie felt a stab of panic. *Not a good sign,* she thought. She watched the blonde slip off her stool and, with a regretful glance over her shoulder, begin winding her way toward the entrance. "Another one bites the dust," she observed, gesturing toward the blonde. "When she saw you were taken, she looked at me like I'd stolen her lunch money. Poor thing. Guess she was hoping to get lucky." Angie knew just how she felt. She, too, was hoping to get lucky, though not in quite the same way.

Edward shrugged. "I didn't even see her."

"That's because you weren't looking."

She ordered a rum and Coke and exchanged pleasantries with the bartender Freddie. She and Edward didn't engage in small talk. He just looked at her as she sipped her drink, and that was when she knew. "So, is this good-bye?" she said. "Is that why you wanted to see me?" She kept her voice light, but her heart was heavy. Not just her heart, her whole body—she felt drugged.

"I'm sorry," he said.

"I see," she said, struggling to maintain her composure. "Well, I can't say it comes as a shock. Generally, when a wife finds out her husband is having an affair, it doesn't bode well for the mistress."

"It's not just that," he said. "Something's come up." His somber face grew more animated. "Remember when I told you about the experimental drug she was taking? The one she didn't think would work? Well, it seems to be working."

Angie was stunned. She could only stammer, "Wow. That's . . . that's . . ."

"Amazing. Yeah, I know." A helpless smile spread across his face. "I admit I wasn't too optimistic at first, either. I *hoped*, of course— you can never lose hope. But I knew it was a long shot."

Angie didn't know what to say. It was a moment before any coherent thought could form. "Well, that's good news," she said at last. "The *best* news. I'm happy for you both." She meant it, truly she did. How could she not see it as a blessing that a life was being spared, that Camille's children wouldn't be left motherless? *Even if it's the end of the line for me.* "Does that sound hopelessly insincere coming from the woman you're sleeping with?"

"Not at all," he said, and she knew he understood.

"Well, I guess this is it, then." She struggled to keep the heart-break from her voice.

His smile fell away. "Angie, I . . ."

"It's the right thing to do. The *only* thing," she went on, know-ing what he was going to say and needing to be the first to say it. "Also, let's face it, you're not the cheating kind. You just took a left when you should've turned right, and I was the accident waiting to happen."

Cheers erupted from the mosh pit as another goal was scored, and the rugby fans began rhythmically thumping on the bar with their fists. Angie could feel each thud in the pit of her stomach. Edward took her hand. "I can't leave her," he said. "Not after every-thing she's been through."

She nodded her head. "Of course not. She's your wife." Nor was it just that he couldn't, in good conscience, abandon Camille. He loved her. They had a history together. She was the mother of his children.

Edward dropped his head into his hands, forking his fingers through his hair. If Angie hadn't been so close to the breaking point herself, she'd have smiled at the picture he made. Like the old joke

So ... a man walks into a bar ... Only this was no joke. This was the man she loved, probably the only man she'd ever love, and she was losing him. Worse, she couldn't think of a reason why he should stay. He didn't belong with her. He belonged with his wife and children.

When he lifted his head, she saw how conflicted he was. "Angie, if you only knew what these past few months have meant to me. How much *you* mean to me." He spread his hands in a helpless gesture, as if at a loss for words. "You were the only thing that kept me from drowning."

"Glad to be of service," she said in a wry voice that came out sounding bitter.

"You know I didn't mean it that way," he said, wearing a pained look.

"Just how *did* you mean it?" she asked. She longed to hear him say the words *I love you,* even knowing it would only cause her more pain. But he only shook his head with regret.

"I can't walk out on her. Not now. I owe her that much."

The selfish part of Angie wanted to cry, *What about what you owe ME?* But she knew the answer: He owed her nothing. She'd entered into this with her eyes wide open, a relationship her mother ... and the shrink she'd need after this ... hell, any random person on the street ... would have warned her to run from as if from a burning building. The irony was, even if he'd chosen her over Camille, it wouldn't have worked. Because then he wouldn't be the man she loved. *That* man would never leave his wife after she'd been brought back from the brink of death.

She finished her drink and pushed aside the empty glass. "In that case, I wish you well. Truly. You deserve it after what you've been through. But right now, I'm going home, where I can get drunk in peace and throw myself the mother of all pity parties. So if you'll excuse me ... ."

She slipped off the stool, but her knees buckled when her feet hit the floor. He jumped up to catch her before she fell. He held her steady, his hands gripping her upper arms, his gaze locked onto hers. The noise at the other end of the bar faded to a hum. In that moment, it was just the two of them: two people who had found each other and who now had to find their way apart.

"At least, let me take you home," he said, as if he thought she'd had too much to drink already.

"No, I'm fine." It was far from true—she wasn't anything close to fine; *fine* wasn't even a word in her dictionary—but saying it was one step toward making it so. "I'll catch a cab."

They were forced into even closer proximity when a heavyset man carrying a stein of beer in each hand muscled his way past them. Angie could feel the heat of Edward's body and smell his scent, which brought to mind the showers they'd taken together and sheets warmed by their lovemaking. He was so close, she could have slipped into his arms as easily as taking the next breath. She closed her eyes a moment, savoring his nearness, before taking a step back. She heard a muttered a curse as she bumped into someone behind her. Then she was pushing her way toward the entrance, her head down, not looking to see who else she might be about to plow into.

Outside, she gulped in air like a drowning person who'd been washed ashore. She glanced over her shoulder, half expecting to see that Edward had followed her, but the only other person in sight, besides the smokers huddled by the entrance, was a homeless man shuffling along the sidewalk pushing a grocery cart piled with his worldly possessions. She didn't know whether to be relieved or disappointed. She was at the corner, about to climb into a cab, when Edward emerged into view. "Angie, wait!" he called, waving to get her attention as he dashed toward her.

She paused, keeping a hand on the open door of the cab so the driver wouldn't think she'd changed her mind. She recalled her friend Marie once remarking, on a night like this after she'd spent twenty minutes trying unsuccessfully to hail a cab, that taxis were almost as hard to come by at this hour in this part of town as a good man. If Angie couldn't have one, she'd take the other.

She touched his arm when he caught up to her. "Go home, Edward. Go home to your wife and kids." She ducked into the backseat and pulled the door shut. She didn't look back as the cab sped away. If she had, she'd have seen a figure standing on the curb, looking as forlorn as she.

CHAPTER TWENTY-ONE

IT WAS TWELVE-THIRTY P.M., the third Tuesday in October, and Edward had just seen the last of his morning patients out the door. His receptionist buzzed him. "Your wife is here," Rosie informed him. He frowned in confusion. Did he have a lunch date with Camille? If so, he couldn't recall making it. It must have slipped his mind. No surprise there—he'd been so preoccupied lately it was a wonder he managed to keep anything straight.

Camille breezed in moments later, bringing with her the scent of the outdoors: fallen leaves and damp sidewalks. She was still too thin, but she'd recently put on a few pounds and there was some color in her cheeks. Most notably, the air of sad resignation she'd worn was gone.

"I called earlier, and Rosie said you had some time before your next appointment, so I thought I'd take you to lunch," she said.

"Ah," he said. "And here I was feeling like the world's worst husband for forgetting we had a date."

"You're not. I wanted to surprise you." She smiled, adjusting the knot on his tie, one of those small wifely gestures that would have gone unnoticed in the past but which brought a lump to his throat now.

"Best offer I've had all day." He grinned, but it felt practiced somehow.

Her smile faded, and a flicker of anxiety crossed her face. "You don't have other plans?"

"Nope," he said. "I'm all yours."

Rosie waved good-bye as they passed by the front desk on the way to the elevators. A plump, older woman with white hair like spun glass, she had a weakness for holiday-themed sweaters like the one she was wearing—black and orange with a jack-o'-lantern motif—and the Reese's Pieces she kept in a locked drawer in her desk at all times. "You kids have fun!" she called.

Camille looked to Edward, her eyes dancing with amusement. "Kids. How long since anyone called us that? God, it's been ages. But you know something, I feel like a kid right now."

Edward squeezed her arm. "You look like one."

"So do you—you look very handsome. Just remember: Handsome is as handsome does."

"What's that supposed to mean?"

She smiled mysteriously. "You'll see."

Edward hailed a cab at the corner of Broadway and Fort Washington Avenue, and fifteen minutes later they were pulling up in front of the Hotel Wales, on Madison Avenue near Ninety-Second Street. "I thought you were taking me to lunch," he said as they stepped through the glass door into the lobby. The Hotel Wales, like most of the city's boutique hotels, didn't have a restaurant on the premises.

"You've never heard of room service?" she replied with an arch look.

"You booked us a room?" he asked in surprise.

She nodded, looking pleased with herself, then leaned in to whisper, "They have day rates."

Edward felt himself start to tense up. There was a time when nothing would have thrilled him more than the prospect of an afternoon delight with his wife, but they hadn't had sex in so long. And so much had happened. An image rose in his mind: Angie naked on the big chocolate sofa in her living room, her eyelids lowered seductively and her mouth curled in a come-hither smile.

Until recently, his fantasies had revolved almost exclusively around his wife. Even after she became ill, when their lovemaking was less frequent, it was Camille he thought of when he mastur-bated or when he lay in bed at night unable to sleep, aching for the touch of her hand on his thigh. It wasn't until he met Angie that he realized how starved he was. Not just for sex, but for the kind of intimacy he'd shared with his wife. And he'd taken what Angie had to give, God help him, yes, he had. Seized it with his teeth and both fists, and still he hadn't been able to get enough.

Now here was Camille, wanting to recapture what was lost.

When they got to their room, he saw that the stage had been set: a bottle of champagne on ice, a plate of sandwiches, and one of strawberries dipped in chocolate. A vase of red roses stood on the dresser. Camille had planned it carefully, down to the last detail. Now it was his turn to step up.

He took her in his arms and kissed her. "This beats a restaurant any day."

"I booked the room under Mr. and Mrs., but the desk clerk gave me a funny look," she said. "I don't imagine too many old, mar-ried couples ask about day rates." Camille put her arms around his waist, and he drew her in so her head rested on his chest. Her familiar scent was balm to his frayed nerves. She was so thin, she felt almost weightless; but at the same time, she anchored him. She was just tall enough so the top of her head was level with his chin, unlike Angie, who was so petite, she had to stand on tiptoe to kiss him. He closed his eyes, willing away the persistent images of Angie. *You got your wish*, a voice whispered in his head. *This is what you wanted.*

They undressed and climbed under the covers. They were ten-tative with each other at first, then Camille gradually began to respond to his touch and the gentle pressure of his lips. He kissed her all over, each kiss a period at the end of a sentence. *I can. I will.*

I must. Camille might know . . . or guess . . . that he still harbored feelings for Angie. But they must never speak of it.

She took him in her mouth. He shut his eyes and struggled to shut his mind against the memory of a different mouth, its featherlight tongue unlike the one teasing him now. It taunted him, and the moments passed in a kind of holographic warp, images and remembered sensations shifting in and out of what he could feel and taste and touch. He shuddered, on the verge of climax.

Then he was inside her, and it was as though nothing had changed: all the familiar moves and rhythms he knew by heart; the way she gripped his buttocks as she was building toward her own climax; the way the arches of her feet pressed into his ankles; the sweet little noises she made—all things that held him in the present and at the same time were but echoes of the past.

Afterward, as they lay curled together, he wondered if she was thinking the same thing he was: that the last time he'd lain like this had been with Angie. If so, she didn't speak of it or allude to it. Nor did she whisper endearments. She was wise enough to know it was best to say nothing. Finally, she stirred and said, "And here you were expecting lunch. You must be famished."

He smiled. "Utterly. If your aim was to have me work up an appetite, you've succeeded."

She sat up, pulling on the complimentary robe that had come with the room. "Why don't you do the honors while I go wash up," she said, nodding toward the bottle of champagne in its bucket.

Their easy banter was familiar ground, but here they treaded cautiously as well. Was this a fresh start or only a trip down memory lane? Was it possible to start over after all they'd been through? *Easy, boy,* he told himself, *one step at a time.* He got up and uncorked the champagne.

But as he toasted the future with his wife, his thoughts were with another.

* * *

CAMILLE ARRIVED HOME to find a message from her father on the answering machine. Typical, she thought. Anyone else would've called her on her cell, but Larry relied on landlines the way he once had on the navigational system by which he'd piloted planes. The year before, Holly had talked him into getting a cell phone, which he'd used exactly one time, as far as Camille knew—to inform Holly of said purchase and congratulate himself on the wisdom of it—before relegating it to his sock drawer. The only time it saw the light of day was when he took it with him on trips.

This time, she didn't delay in calling him back. Her father had his faults, but he *was* trying; she'd give him that. After she'd shared her good news with him, he hadn't retreated into the woodwork as she'd expected him to. He continued to make an effort. And although his efforts were often clumsy or clueless, she appreciated that he was, at least, present and accounted for.

"Hi, Dad. Is this a bad time?" she asked when he picked up after five rings.

"No, not at all. I was just . . . um, taking out the trash."

Immediately, she became suspicious. He sounded out of breath, and since when did taking out the trash constitute a marathon? Did he have some health problem he was keeping from her? She recalled that Grandpa Harte hadn't been much older than her dad when he died of a stroke.

"You okay, Dad?" she asked.

"Me? Never better," he said, a bit too heartily. "More importantly, how are *you*?"

"I'm good," she said, thinking how wonderful it was to be able to say it and have it be true.

"Are you eating? Getting enough rest?"

As if she were pregnant or recovering from the flu. But she smiled and answered dutifully, "Yes, Dad. I'm getting my eight hours and eating my peas and carrots." His awkward attempts at parenting no longer irritated her. She recalled his reaction when she'd called with the news that her cancer was in remission. She would never forget the sound of her father, who'd kept a stoic front even at his wife's funeral, weeping at the other end of the phone. "Is that why you called, to see how I was doing, or was there some other reason?" she asked, not unkindly.

He hesitated, clearing his throat. "Yes, well . . . I, um, have something to tell you. Are you sitting down?" Camille braced herself as she ran through the list in her mind of what she thought of as old people diseases: congestive heart failure, arteriolosclerosis, osteoporosis, prostate cancer. She didn't stop to consider that it might not be his health, that it might in fact be *good* news (depending on one's viewpoint), so when he dropped his bombshell, she was totally unprepared. "Remember when you asked if I'd ever thought about getting married again and I told you it wasn't in the cards?" he said. "Well, it turns out I was wrong: Your old man is taking the plunge."

"Seriously? This isn't a joke?" she said when she'd recovered her wits. Had he been a client of hers, she'd have been congratulating him. Instead, she could only wonder who this impostor was and if the aliens who'd abducted her real father would be releasing him anytime soon.

"If it is, the joke's on me." Larry gave a low chuckle, sounding a bit abashed. "I didn't see it coming. But I guess these things have a way of sneaking up on you."

"That's, um . . . well . . . Congratulations, Dad," she finally managed. "Who's the lucky lady?"

"Her name's Lillian. Lillian Dessler." Larry filled her in on the pertinent details. Lillian was a widow, originally from Boston. She'd lost her husband four years ago, to colon cancer. She had two grown daughters, one of whom was a nurse and the other a stay-at-home mom, and six grandchildren. "She's a great gal—you'll love her. She can't wait to meet you and your sister."

Instead of summoning a gracious response, Camille found herself asking bluntly, "You're sure you're not jumping the gun, Dad? It doesn't sound as if you've known her very long." Lillian had moved to Heritage Acres, into a unit down the hall from his, only six months ago.

"At my age, there's no time to waste. I'm not getting any younger, you know," he reminded her. She heard a noise in the background— it sounded like the shower cranking on—and suddenly she understood why he'd been out of breath earlier. *They were having sex.* Oh, God. She almost choked at the realization. She had older clients and firmly believed in love the second or even third time around, but it was different when it was your father. It also underscored her own loneliness. Today's romantic interlude with Edward had been lovely but not all that she'd hoped it would be. He'd made a sincere effort, but she could tell his heart wasn't in it.

He was thinking of her.

"Have you two set a date?" she asked.

"We were thinking March, when the kids are on spring break. Do you and Edward have plans?"

"Not as of yet." Until recently, making travel plans would have been out of the question. Cancún or Vermont might as well have been a trip to the moon. "What about Holly—would that work for her?"

"I haven't discussed it with her yet. I wanted to talk it over with you first," he said. Camille was surprised and touched. He'd shared his news with her before Holly—that was a first.

"Well," she said. "I doubt she's made any plans. She'll have her hands full with the baby."

"Speaking of which, I didn't want to wait that long to meet my newest grandchild, so you'll be seeing me before then. Lil and I are coming for a visit. It'll give you girls a chance to get to know Lil, too."

"Really? That's, um . . . When are you coming?"

"Three weeks from today, to be exact. I timed it to coincide with Holly's due date." As if babies could be counted on to arrive on time. *Or I didn't have enough to cope with,* Camille thought.

How, in the midst of working to rebuild her health, shore up her crumbling marriage, and prepare for the birth of Holly's baby, was she supposed to deal with a visit from her dad and his bride-to-be? But she could see he was trying, so she rallied. "Great," she said. "I look forward to it."

How can I begrudge him? she thought after she'd hung up. Life was short. Not long ago, she'd been facing certain death; today both feet were planted squarely in the land of the living. Each day was a gift, each moment a blessing. She needed to celebrate that, not scrutinize it for flaws.

"Mom?"

Camille looked up find Kyra standing in the doorway, still in her school uniform. She'd been fooling around with makeup— she had permission to experiment at home—and her eyes were smudged with eye shadow, her cheeks pink with blush; she looked at once years older than her age and like when she was a little girl playing dress-up. Camille no longer felt conflicted about her daughter's growing up. She would be around for it; that was what mattered.

"Yes, sweetie?"

"Was that Grandpa Larry on the phone?"

Camille nodded in response, and arranged her face in an expression suitable to the occasion. "Big news," she said. "He's getting married."

Kyra's mouth fell open. "No way."

"Way."

"But he's, like, *old.*"

Camille smiled at her daughter's assumption that love was strictly the province of the young. Kyra would've been horrified to learn what her parents had been up to earlier. "You're never too old to fall in love. Anyway, I'm sure she's nice. Your grandpa certainly seems to think so."

"He wouldn't marry someone he didn't think was nice," Kyra said. "The question is, will *we* like her?" There was a time it wouldn't have mattered, back when Grandpa Larry was but a remote figure. But now that he was playing a more active role in their lives, Kyra had reason to be concerned.

Camille sighed. "We'll know soon enough. They're coming to visit in a few weeks."

Kyra crossed the room, bringing with her the scent of some light, floral fragrance—whichever one they'd been giving away samples of at Sephora the last time she'd shopped there, no doubt—and sank down on the sofa next to Camille. "Mom, are you okay with this? It won't be weird that she's taking your mom's place?" she asked in her Little Mommy voice. Camille had started calling her that—Little Mommy—during her first bout with cancer, when she'd been hospitalized and it had been Kyra making grocery lists, reminding Edward about school events and game times, and making sure her brother did his homework and that his teeth got brushed. Her heart swelled with love. *My sweet, sweet girl.*

"No one could ever take my mom's place," she said. "But that doesn't mean I don't want Grandpa to be happy."

Her daughter did something surprising then: She hugged her. Kyra was at an age when displays of affection—which for the most part had gone the way of footie pajamas, Flintstone vitamins, and bedtime stories—were seldom initiated and merely to be tolerated when she was on the receiving end, so Camille was more touched than she ordinarily would have been. Kyra, her head nestled against Camille's shoulder, murmured, "No one could ever take your place, either, Mom."

"Good," Camille said, "because I'm not going anywhere."

"I know. It's just . . ." Kyra tilted her head to look up at Camille.

"When your cancer came back and you said we shouldn't worry, I was still worried. I was scared you were going to die."

Camille felt a pang, hating that Kyra and Zach had had to grow up too soon and grapple with realities most young children never have to face. At the same time, she felt hugely relieved, knowing that particular worry wasn't one that was likely, at this point, to become a reality. She would never again take her health for granted—there would always be the threat of her cancer recurring—but the Sword of Damocles no longer dangled over her head. "I know, sweetie," she said. "But that's all behind us now. I'm not going to die. Hopefully, not for a long time." She hugged her daughter, breathing in the fragrance of the scent Kyra wore, and underneath it that of Pantene shampoo and the underarm deodorant Kyra religiously slathered on each morning in the sincere belief that she would otherwise clear out a classroom with her body odor. "For one thing, how could I ever leave you and Zach?"

"Dad, too," Kyra prompted.

"Dad, too."

CHAPTER TWENTY-TWO

Oh, the wealth of days! The abundance! For Camille, each new day was Christmas morning, each hour a present under the tree waiting to be unwrapped. She found deep satisfaction in the simplest of pleasures: sipping her morning coffee as she watched the sun come up, kibitzing with Dara at the start of each workday, or strolling the sidewalks taking in the sights and sounds of the city. Most of all, she reveled in time spent with her children: having them hang out with her in the kitchen while she got supper ready, taking them shopping or to a favorite eatery—Sarabeth's or the Popover Café, the Shake Shack in Madison Square Park—helping them with their homework or playing games with them, which with Zach invariably entailed endless rounds of Wii golf. Even the drives to Southampton, which used to get tiresome when the kids squabbled or whined that they were hungry or had to go to the bathroom for the fiftieth time, no longer made her want to scream in frustration.

Things were more tenuous with Edward, but they were making progress. They went out on dates. He took her to romantic restaurants. They held hands in movie theaters. Once, he'd sent flowers, though it wasn't a special occasion. (The card read, "Thinking of you.") At a recent banquet at which Edward had been an honoree, when the wife of one of his fellow honorees commented that it was nice to see a long-married couple as devoted as Camille and Edward, Camille had smiled and nodded as if their love for each other had never been in question. She'd felt only pride that night, seeing her husband on the podium. *How distinguished he looks!* She had thought. All the more so for the lines on his face and feathering of gray at his temples. And yet . . .

Something was missing. She couldn't put her finger on it but felt its absence as keenly as she would a missing tooth or limb. At times, it was as though the missing thing were within reach; at other times, as though it were forever lost. *Be patient,* she told herself. Fractures need time to heal. Especially those in marriages. Then she'd catch her husband, in an unguarded moment, looking melancholy and know he was thinking of *her.* Each time, it was like a knife in her heart.

We still love each other. She repeated those words regularly like a mantra.

Her father and his fiancée arrived the first week in November on schedule, though the baby still hadn't arrived—Holly was a week past her due date. Larry phoned as soon as they'd checked into their hotel. Camille had invited them for supper that evening, but she was eager to meet Lillian so she told them to come early. They showed up an hour later, Larry looking as dapper as ever and with a new twinkle in his eye, which no doubt had to do with the woman at his side.

She greeted her warmly after she'd kissed her dad on the cheek. "You must be Lillian. Hi, I'm Camille." The first thing that struck her was how tall Lillian was—she stood almost shoulder-to-shoulder with Larry. Nor was she anything like the ladies whom Camille had met the one and only time she'd visited her dad at Heritage Acres—ladies who were perennially blond or brunette (with the odd henna-haired redhead mixed in) and who wore color-coordinated outfits in blended-drink shades, lots of chunky gold jewelry, and way too much makeup. Lillian's hair wasn't dyed, and she was dressed simply and tastefully in a silky tunic top and trousers the opalescent blue-green of mother-of-pearl. She wore no makeup, and her only jewelry was a hammered-silver cuff bracelet and matching choker, which complemented her sleek silver bob.

"My dear, I can't tell you how much I've looked forward to this." Lillian clasped Camille's hand in both of hers. Her blue eyes sparkled. "Your father's told me so much about you, and I can see it wasn't just boasting. You're every bit as lovely as he described."

Camille, unused to praise from her father, even secondhand praise, was quick to deflect it by changing the subject. "Dad tells me you have two daughters of your own."

"Yes—Susie and CeeCee. You'll meet them when you come for the wedding."

"I can't wait," Camille said in a tone she hoped sounded heartfelt.

"Your children are coming, too, I hope?" Camille murmured in assent, and Lillian looked pleased. "Wonderful! CeeCee's eldest, Caitlin, is the same age as your daughter, and Susie's boy is only a year younger than your son, so they should get along just fine. Which will leave us ladies plenty of time for girl stuff." She turned to Larry. "Not to exclude you, darling. But I'm sure you men can find something to occupy yourselves."

The old Larry would have grabbed at any excuse to make himself scarce. The new Larry replied in a mock-injured tone, "If I must. I know when I'm not welcome." He fell into step with Camille as they made their way into the living room. "How's your sister holding up?" he asked.

"Fit to burst, in more ways than one," Camille reported. "The way she carries on, you'd think Mother Nature was doing this just to spite her." Her gaze drifted toward the framed photos on the mantel. One showed Holly, at age sixteen, dressed for the prom: in a vintage ball gown from the 1950s, with a full skirt and satin bodice, and pink Converse high-tops. She explained to Lillian, "My sister doesn't do well in forced captivity. She's . . . well, you'll see when you meet her."

Lillian took her time examining all the photos, remarking on what beautiful children Camille had and what a lovely couple she and Edward made. *Aren't we lucky ladies to have such handsome men!* She took notice, too, of the painting over the fireplace, a still life of a bowl of artichokes, that Camille and Edward had purchased years ago at a gallery in SoHo, their first piece of original art, one that marked the transition from penny-pinching to being able to afford nice things.

"Lillian's an artist." Larry said proudly.

"Now, Larry," Lillian admonished, "I thought we agreed, no commercials." She turned to Camille with a self-effacing smile. "I would hardly call myself an artist. I only paint as a hobby."

"She's being modest," Larry said. "Her paintings are on display at the senior center. She's even sold a few."

Lillian smiled and shook her head. "Two, to be exact, not counting the one your father bought," she told Camille. "But enough about me. I want to hear all about *you*, my dear. I was intrigued when your father told me what you did for a living. I'm hoping you'll share some of your trade secrets. I myself haven't had much luck playing Cupid, though it's not for want of trying."

In the light that streamed in the window, Camille could see Lillian hadn't had any face work. Not that she needed it. She had good bones, and the lines on her face were like tiny cracks on a glazed porcelain vase, making it more interesting than if it had been perfectly smooth. Even the soft folds around her eyes were complimentary than unkind. More than anyone Camille had ever met, she embodied the term "growing old gracefully."

"It's not as easy as it looks," Camille said. "Even when you do it for a living, you can sometimes miss the mark." She thought of her two most recent misfires, Kat Fisher and Stephen Resler, and wondered if either of them had taken her advice about seeing a therapist. A few weeks ago, she'd gotten a brief, chatty email from Kat that made no mention of whether or not she was, and Camille hadn't heard from

Stephen since they'd last spoken. She could only hope they would sort themselves out, one way or another. "But you and Dad are proof that not everyone needs help. Sometimes you just get lucky."

Lillian hooked an arm through Larry's. "Luck had nothing to do with it. Your father is a very persistent man."

Persistent? The man whose own daughter had to be at death's door for him to pay attention? Camille nearly laughed out loud. Instead, she smiled and said, "Well, on that note, I think a toast is in order. Why don't you two make yourselves comfortable while I get the champagne?"

She wasn't just being a good hostess. It was a lot to take in . . . meeting Lillian . . . getting to know this other side of her dad. She needed a moment alone to process it. But when Lillian excused herself to wash up, Larry followed Camille into the kitchen. He was eager to know what she thought of Lillian. He wouldn't ask—it wasn't his style—but she could tell he was nervous.

She put his anxieties to rest. "She's lovely, Dad. You did good."

He looked relieved.

Camille reached for the champagne flutes, on a high shelf in the cupboard above the dishwasher. She noticed as she brought them down that they were filmed in dust—they hadn't seen much use lately. What had there been to celebrate until recently? Camille turned on the tap, filling the sink with hot water and squirting in some soap. She washed while her father dried.

"How are the kids?" Larry asked.

She smiled. "Growing up too fast, as usual."

"Zach ready for the pro circuit yet?"

"Any day now, I'm sure. Wait until you see how much he's improved."

"That's my boy." Larry looked pleased. "About time he started taking lessons, don't you think?"

"I suppose. But we don't live near a golf course, so it's not really feasible."

"There may be a way around that," her father said, working a corner of the dishtowel into the narrow neck of the glass he was drying. She could tell from the expression he wore that he'd already given it some thought. "My friend Don Mayes, you remember him? He runs a golf clinic for kids up at my old club. I spoke to him about Zach. Bob's daughter lives in the city, and she could drive him up there on weekends. Naturally, I'd pay for it. I was thinking, since Christmas isn't too far off . . ."

She gave him a look. "Dad. You have to stop giving them things. I think Zach now has every Wii game on the market. And Kyra doesn't need real pearls at her age. Seriously, you're spoiling them."

"What are grandkids for if not to spoil them?" he said with an airy wave of his hand.

She knew where it was really coming from: He was overcompensating for his past neglect. But she couldn't fault him now that he was trying, even if he was trying *too* hard. "Well, you can discuss it with Zach when he gets home," she relented. Zach was at soccer practice. Camille had arranged for one of the other moms to pick up both boys and bring Zach home.

Larry beamed, and then, as if not wanting to press his luck, he switched to another topic. "Speaking of the holidays, if you haven't made any plans yet, why don't you bring the family down for a visit? Lil and I could look after the kids while you and Edward get some one-on-one time."

"Sounds tempting, but I don't see how I could get away. The holidays are my busiest time," she told him.

"Why, what's special about the holidays?" he asked.

She placed the clean champagne flutes on a tray and went to get the champagne from the fridge. "Well," she said, "if you're single and looking, they can be a reminder of what you're missing. Thanksgiving, you don't want to be the only odd man out at the family dinner. And Christmas makes you think of presents from Santa and stockings lined up on the hearth."

She was horrified to find her own eyes filling with tears. She kept her face averted so her dad wouldn't see, but he must have heard the catch in her voice. She felt his arm settle over her shoulders.

"What is it, Cam? You're not . . . ?" Larry didn't have to finish the sentence; the deep grooves of worry in his face said it all: He thought it was something to do with her health—a setback.

She hastened to put that fear to rest. "I'm fine, Dad. It's just . . . seeing you and Lillian."

He nodded in understanding. "If it makes you feel any better, she isn't looking to take your mom's place."

"No, it's not that. It's . . ." Camille swallowed against the lump in her throat. "You seem so happy."

His face relaxed in a smile. "That's because we are." Then, as if sensing this wasn't just about him and Lillian, he went on, "But it's always like that in the beginning. Once we've logged some miles, we'll be like a pair of old shoes. It wasn't always perfect with your mom and me, you know."

"But you loved each other."

"Sure, but we had our ups and downs, like any couple."

What happens when you fall down and can't get up again?

Lillian rejoined them then. Camille poured the champagne. They all raised their glasses. "To your health!" said Larry, smiling at Camille in a way that made her feel like crying all over again.

"To the happy couple," she toasted.

HOLLY'S WATER BROKE on the D train going over the Manhattan Bridge. The four of them—Holly and Camille, Larry and Lillian—had met for lunch in SoHo, and afterward Holly had insisted on them all going back to her place so she could show Larry and Lillian the nursery. (Camille had already seen it—she'd put herself in charge of stocking it with every conceivable item the baby would need.) Holly had done it up in what she called Early Fillmore:

paisley wallpaper to simulate the light-show effect; original concert posters from that era for bands like the Grateful Dead, Pink Floyd, and Jefferson Airplane; a 1970s lava lamp and custom-made crib mobile fashioned from guitar picks. There was even a plush toy in the shape of a guitar. Holly was determined to pass on her love of rock and roll to Junior or, better yet, have him turn out to be a future Mick Jagger or Pete Townshend.

On the subway, Camille and Holly were having their usual debate about the pros and cons of living in Brooklyn versus Manhattan when Holly gave a sudden gasp and looked down. "Oh, God! Is that *me*?" She stared in horror at the growing puddle at her feet.

"It ain't a busted water main, that's for sure," observed the paunchy, balding man seated across from them, who clearly fancied himself a wit. Wedged in next to him was a heavyset woman wearing an unflattering Elmo-pink velour tracksuit that made her look like a very large raspberry—presumably his wife. She scowled at him.

"Gawd, Billy. Show some respect." She turned to inquire solicitously of Holly, "You okay, hon?"

Holly replied in a weak voice, "I think I'm having a baby."

"No shit, Sherlock," muttered a skinny guy with a scruffy day-old beard.

While the other riders gawked as if at a circus sideshow, Camille did her best to keep her sister from panicking. She used her sweater to blot the wet spot on Holly's jeans. When she looked up, Lillian and Larry were approaching from the other end of the car, working their way through the gaggle of gaping straphangers. Lillian, when she reached Holly, bent to place a hand on her shoulder, saying in a soothing, motherly voice, "Don't worry, dear, we'll get you to the hospital in plenty of time. First babies usually aren't in any hurry." Holly nodded mutely, and Lillian asked, "About how far apart would you say the contractions are?"

"I don't know." Holly looked more confused than panic-stricken. "My back's been bothering me all day, but I thought it was just a pulled muscle. It didn't start to get bad until after lunch."

With each lurch of the subway car, the puddle on the floor spread. A pigtailed little girl lifted her sneakered feet and cried, "Mommy! It's going to *get* me!" An older Asian woman with her head buried in a Chinese-language newspaper glanced down impassively at the rivulet snaking its way toward her, then tossed a section of newspaper over it before going back to her reading. A burly guy in work overalls pirouetted around the pole he was holding, as delicately as a ballerina, to keep his boots from being christened. Camille whispered in Holly's ear, "It's just pickle juice."

When they were young, twelve and ten respectively, they'd once witnessed a similar spectacle. They'd gone to the D'Agostino down the block from their building, to get some things their housekeeper had run out of, and were pushing their cart down the jarred goods aisle when they saw a hugely pregnant lady at the other end jump suddenly and then let out a yelp. Her water had broken. She must have been in a panic, and also embarrassed by the mess she'd made, because she grabbed a jar of pickles and dropped it on the floor, as if to create a diversion. When a clerk came hurrying over with a mop and bucket, she declared loudly, "It's just pickle juice!" To this day, whenever Camille and Holly were in a grocery store together, they couldn't walk down the jarred goods aisle without setting each other to giggling with that oft-repeated line.

This time, Holly only smiled weakly in response.

Larry withdrew a folded handkerchief from his pocket and offered it to Holly. She shook her head, refusing it. "Thanks, Dad, but isn't that like sticking your finger in the dike after it's broken?"

"Shouldn't we call the doctor?" He cast a worried look at Camille.

Camille bit her tongue before she could snap, *What does it look like I'm doing?* She had her cell phone out, on which was programmed the number for Holly's ob-gyn, as well as Curtis's contact info. There was just one problem. "I'm not getting a signal," she cried in frustration.

"Stop the train! Stop the train!" bellowed a homeless man who earlier had been soliciting handouts.

"Dude. We're on a fucking *river*!" yelled a teenage boy in a Hollister hoodie and jeans that bagged to his knees.

The homeless man ignored him, mashing his grimy thumb down on the call button on the intercom. Minutes later, the door at the other end of the car banged open and a transit cop appeared, looking pissed off as if he thought he'd been summoned by a false alarm. The big guy in overalls jabbed a finger in Holly's direction. "She's having a baby! Fuh crissakes, *do something*."

The cop, who sported a goatee and had thinning, close-cropped hair that made Camille think of a newly seeded lawn, had clearly never encountered anything like this outside training. He froze, gaping at Holly as if at a suspicious package that might contain an explosive device. It was several moments before he shifted into gear. "All right, everyone, just calm down!" he boomed, though no one had made a peep; the other riders just stared, as if waiting to see what he would do—all except the older Asian lady reading her newspaper. To Holly, he said, "Ma'am, I'm going to radio ahead and alert the station. I'll have them send an ambulance."

As he was barking into his hand-held, Holly hissed to Camille, "Did you hear that? He called me *ma'am*! What's next, they'll stop carding me in bars? Why didn't you warn me this would happen?"

"You never gave me the chance," Camille reminded her.

"Oh, God." Holly grimaced, clutching her belly. "Now *that* definitely wasn't a pulled muscle."

"I didn't make it to the hospital in time, with my first," volunteered a gum-smacking blonde, a Jenna Jameson look-alike wearing a tight pink T-shirt with the words *Hotter than Your Girlfriend* in big block letters stretched across her boobs. "She popped out in the backseat of my boyfriend's Cutlass, right there on the LIE. Scared the shit out of us. But she's fine—she just turned two."

"That's helpful," muttered Holly.

Lillian squeezed Holly's shoulder reassuringly, while Larry just stood there looking pale and shaken.

Camille found herself thinking of the time Holly, at age twelve, had fallen off her bike in Central Park and split her chin. Camille was fifteen at the time but looked older; no one had questioned her authority when she brought Holly to the ER and handed over her dad's insurance card. Larry had been out of town—where else?—so she was the one who'd held Holly's hand as her chin was stitched up. She'd chattered the whole while to distract Holly. Now, in the same vein, she said, "You think this is bad? I know a woman who gave birth to triplets. She said it felt like Hulk Hogan doing the Heimlich maneuver on her. She swore afterward she'd have her tubes tied before she'd go through that again. But the next time I ran into her, she was pregnant again—with twins. That's when she told me, 'To hell with getting my tubes tied, I'm getting a divorce.'"

Holly mustered a faint laugh, and Miss Hotter-than-Your-Girlfriend smiled as though she were in on the joke. The Asian lady looked up from her newspaper to gaze at them impassively. Mr. and Mrs. Billy flattened against their seats as the homeless man lurched past them, reeking of booze and body odor. Out the window, the iron struts of the bridge flashed by, showing strobelike glimpses of the harbor beyond, gray as the sky above, where storm clouds massed, as the train rattled its way toward the next station. Camille thought they'd never get there.

After what seemed an eternity, the train pulled into the Atlantic Avenue station, where they were met by an NYPD cop: a middle-aged Hispanic woman with a kind face. She escorted them off the platform toward the waiting ambulance, keeping a hand on Holly's arm as if guiding a small child across a busy intersection. "Don't you worry, hon," she said. "This'll all be over before you know it. Piece of cake."

"Bullshit," Holly said through gritted teeth as another contraction took hold.

"It's a conspiracy," Camille said. "Someone figured out a long time ago the only way to perpetuate the human race was to trick women into thinking it's a piece of cake." Holly growled in response.

Lillian stroked Holly's back while she rode out the contraction. "The good news is," she said, "when it's over and you're holding your baby in your arms, this will all be a distant memory."

"Not for me, it won't," Larry said, looking distinctly queasy. "I don't think I'll forget this as long as I live."

"Men." Lillian smiled indulgently and tucked an arm through his as they continued on.

Together they trooped up the two flights of stairs. When they emerged into the daylight, Holly paused once more, on the sidewalk, to ride out another contraction, uttering a string of curses the whole while. Then, finally, to everyone's relief, she was loaded onto the waiting ambulance. Camille, Lillian, and Larry followed in a taxi. A short while later, they were reunited at Kings County. It wasn't the nearest hospital but it was where Holly's ob-gyn had privileges, so Holly had insisted on being taken there.

"Tell Curtis he's a dead man if he doesn't get his ass here pronto!" Holly growled from her semiprone position on the gurney. She'd been trying to reach him, as had Camille, but kept getting his voicemail. When Camille told Holly he was probably in a meeting or on another call, Holly barked, "Fuck that! He missed out on the first half, the least he can do is be here for the closing number."

Camille realized it was no use arguing. Holly was beyond reason in her current state. Instead, she promised to get Curtis to the hospital in time if she had to personally track him down. She was relieved when, minutes after Holly had been whisked into the elevator, she heard the familiar tinkling of her cell phone's ring-tone and saw Curtis's name on the display. *Thank God for small favors.* "Tell her to sit tight, I'm on my way," he panted, sounding out of breath. She heard traffic noises in the background and pictured him racing along a sidewalk somewhere in the Financial District, tie flapping, on his way to catch a cab.

"She's not going anywhere, trust me," Camille told him.

After she'd hung up, she phoned Edward. No answer. She tried the number for his office. "Hi, hon! He's with a patient," Rosie informed her cheerily. "Should I poke my head in, or can it wait?"

"Tell him my sister's in labor. We're at Kings County."

Ten minutes later, Edward phoned back. "How's she doing?"

"So far, so good. The resident on call is having a look at her now. We're waiting for her ob-gyn to get here." Camille was in the corridor outside Holly's room in the meantime. "Her water broke on the subway. You should have seen it. Everyone and his uncle were in on it. You would have thought it was the World Series."

He chuckled. "Sorry I missed it. Do you need me there?"

"No," she told him. "Just feed the kids, and make sure they get to bed on time. This may take a while."

She hung up and went to check on Holly. The resident, a petite Indian woman with an air of authority that didn't match her youthful appearance, shook Camille's hand, introducing herself as Dr. Jayaraman. "Everything appears to be normal," she reported in a crisp, accented voice. "Your sister is six centimeters dilated, and the baby is in a good position. I don't anticipate any problems."

"Where's my doctor? I want my doctor!" Holly sounded like a child demanding a fruit rollup at a grocery store checkout stand.

Dr. Jayaraman assured Holly that Dr. Faber was on her way. "Meanwhile, have no worries," she said. "You are in good hands, I promise you." Holly eyed her dubiously—the resident looked so young, she might have been playing the part of a doctor in a school play—and even Camille had to reassure herself with the thought,

Four years of medical school, two years of internship, and two, maybe three years of residency. Yep, she's old enough to deliver a baby.

"No worries? Is she nuts?" said Holly, after the doctor had gone. "It feels like I got run over by a truck that keeps backing up and running over me again, just to make sure. This can't be normal."

Camille smiled at her. "Welcome to the wonderful world of childbirth."

"No one ever said it would be like this."

"You just didn't read the fine print. Anyway, no turning back now." Camille sat down on the bed, saying in a gentler voice, "Want me to massage your back? Would that help?"

"Ahhhh . . . nnnnhhh." Holly's face contorted as another contraction took hold. She pulled her knees up and wrapped her arms around her belly like a drowning person around a flotation device.

Larry took Lillian's arm and hastily steered her out the door. "If you need us, we'll be down the hall," he called over his shoulder. Clearly, he'd seen enough gritty realism for one day.

The contraction subsided. Holly uncurled from her tuck and fell back, panting. She began to laugh weakly. "Do you believe it? Dad getting hitched? Jesus. I never thought I'd see the day."

"Me, either," said Camille. "But I think she's good for him."

"She'll keep him honest," Holly agreed.

"And who's going to keep *you* honest?"

Holly rolled her eyes. "Oh, God. Not that again."

"What? It's a fair question."

"Fair? Is it fair, your beating up on me when I'm in no position to defend myself?"

"I wasn't beating up on you."

"Fuck you." Holly jabbed a finger at Camille, then flipped her the bird for good measure. Camille gave her an injured look, which Holly ignored. She flopped back against the pillows, grinning up at the ceiling. "God, that felt good. You don't know how long I've wanted to do that."

"What, curse me out?" Camille said. "Am I such a terrible sister?"

"No. It's just that I'm fucking tired of having to be fucking nice to you all the time. Now that you're not dying, I don't have to anymore." She reached for Camille's hand, and they exchanged a meaningful look. Then Holly began to giggle. And before long, both sisters were gasping with laughter, punctuated by grunts and groans from Holly as another contraction took hold. When the giggles and contraction had subsided, Holly wheezed, "Some coach you turned out to be."

"Maybe you should've picked Curtis instead," Camille said.

"Oh, right. When he can't even bother to pick up his phone," she replied in a cranky voice.

"He phoned. He's on his way."

Ten minutes later, Curtis blew in like a bank robber with the cops in hot pursuit, hair mussed and tie askew. He skidded to a stop, then sank down on the bed next to Holly, taking her hand. "Are you . . . is the baby . . . oh, my God, is this really happening?" he gasped between breaths.

"It most certainly is," said Camille.

Holly's face contorted again, this time with relief. She reached for Curtis, burying her face against his chest as he drew her into his arms. "I thought you'd never get here," she breathed.

He stroked her hair. "I came as soon as I got your message."

"We still haven't decided on a name," she muttered plaintively into the folds of his jacket. She lifted her head to inform Camille, "Curtis doesn't like any of the names I picked out."

"We are *not* naming our baby after some dead rock star," he said firmly.

Holly had wanted to go with Jimi (as in Hendrix) if it was a boy, or Janis (as in Joplin) if it was a girl. Camille had assumed she was joking, but you never knew with Holly. Now she watched her sister's expression turn serious. Holly grabbed Curtis by the lapels. "Listen, if anything happens to me, I want you to promise to look after Junior. I don't want him to be an orphan."

The color drained from Curtis's face. "Oh, God, is there . . . is there something wrong?"

"Don't listen to her. She's fine," Camille assured him.

Holly flipped her the bird again, then started to cry as another contraction took hold. Curtis rocked her in his arms. "Baby, it's okay. Shhhh . . . I'm here now . . . I'm not going anywhere."

"Promise?" she whispered.

"Promise."

"You'll never leave me?"

"Never."

Camille chose that moment to slip away, only pausing in the doorway for one last look—the sight of her sister and Curtis curled together, as close as Holly's belly would allow, bringing a tug of envy—before she went in search of Larry and Lillian. She found them in the visitors' lounge down the hall. They were deep in conversation and didn't see her at first. She hung back, reluctant to intrude on what was clearly a private moment. Then Larry took notice of her and jumped to his feet, wearing a look of concern. "Is everything okay? Is Holly . . . ?"

"She's fine. Worn out but hanging in there. Curtis is with her."

"You poor dear. You must be worn out yourself." Lillian got up and went over to Camille, putting an arm around her and guiding her over to the sofa. "Sit down. Let me get you a cup of tea."

"Tea would be nice." Camille *was* tired. She had an urge to drop her head onto Lillian's shoulder, sink into the comfort of a mother's arms. Which reminded her: Kyra and Zach—they'd be home from school by now. She dug her cell phone out from her purse and punched in Kyra's number.

Kyra picked up at once, babbling excitedly before Camille could get a word in edgewise. "Did Aunt Holly have the baby yet? Oh, my God! I can't believe I'm missing the whole thing!"

"The baby won't be here for a while yet," Camille told her.

"Can I come? Please, Mom?" Kyra begged. "I can take the subway."

"I want to come, too!" Zach piped in the background.

"Nothing doing. You two stay put," Camille ordered. "I don't need to be worrying about you and your brother getting lost on the subway—or worse—on top of everything else."

"Fine. Dad can take us, then."

Camille realized she'd been outmaneuvered when she heard Kyra call out, "Dad! Mom says it's okay!"

She sighed and said, "Put your dad on."

An hour later, her husband and children trooped into the waiting room. Kyra bursting with excitement and Edward wearing a vaguely sheepish look at having been played by their fourteen-year-old. Zach seemed more interested in the contents of the vending machine than in whatever was going on down the hall, with his aunt. Camille kissed Edward, gave Zach a handful of quarters—now wasn't the time for a lecture about junk food—and got Kyra to settle down before she returned to Holly. She could hear her sister's screams from as far away as the nurses' station. It sounded as if a murder was taking place.

"Do something!" Curtis cried in a panic when she walked in.

Holly was thrashing about like a madwoman. Camille bent down, placing herself squarely in Holly's field of vision. Holly's eyes were wild. She took hold of Holly's shoulders. "Breathe!" she commanded, blowing out breaths the way they'd practiced in Lamaze. "Hoo . . . hoo . . . *ha* . . . hoo . . . hoo . . . *ha*. Don't wimp out on me now. You can do this. I know you can."

"Hoo . . . hoo . . . *ha* . . . hoo . . . hoo . . . *ha*." Holly picked up on the rhythm, though she sounded more like a drowning woman gasping for breath than one in the throes of labor. When the contraction finally eased—they were coming harder and faster now—she collapsed onto her back with a groan. She was panting. Blotchy red patches stood out on her cheeks and strands of hair were pasted to her sweaty forehead. "Is there such a thing as a timeout?" she asked, her voice a hoarse rasp.

"Afraid not. But you're almost there, kiddo." Camille rewarded her with an ice chip.

Holly glared at her. "I bet that's what they said to the prisoners on the march to Bataan."

"Whining isn't going to help."

"Now you sound like Miss Babcock." Miss Babcock had been their PE teacher when they were students at Riverdale, a tall whip of a woman who used to bellow in a foghorn voice, *Come on, ladies, put some muscle into it!* or deliver pithy comments, whenever someone asked to be excused, such as, *Do you think Babe Didrikson won the LPGA title by whining about her period?*

"At least you don't have your period to bitch about," Camille teased.

Holly made a face. "Very funny."

Her ob-gyn arrived just then, wisps of gray hair trailing from her bun and sensible heels clacking. Dr. Faber snapped on a pair of gloves and said, "Let's have a look." She examined Holly and pronounced, "Eight and a half centimeters. Almost there, toots." She patted Holly's knee.

"What took you so long?" Holly sounded exhausted.

"I had another baby to deliver. Two to be accurate—twins." Dr. Faber held up two fingers. "Consider yourself lucky you're only having one. It could be worse."

"Tell me that when it's over," Holly croaked.

Thirty minutes later, Holly was wheeled into Delivery. The plan had been for her to deliver naturally, in the birthing room, but after consulting with Dr. Jayaraman, who'd noticed a slight irregularity in the baby's heartbeat, Dr. Faber decided to play it safe. Not that Holly cared at that point. She was beyond caring. Her vision of giving birth bathed in soft light and blanketed in her favorite quilt while soothing music played—a mix CD of her favorite rock ballads—had fallen by the wayside as she screamed at the top of her lungs for drugs, an epidural, *anything*.

Camille and Curtis donned surgical scrubs. Holly, even in her mindless state, was adamant about one thing: She wanted them both with her when she gave birth. She clutched Camille's hand, hard enough to break a bone, and rained curses on Curtis when she wasn't begging him not to leave. Curtis came through like a champ; he didn't so much as flinch when she swore at him. In the final hour, he was proving what Camille had sensed all along: He was a keeper.

"Okay, bear down now, Holly," Dr. Faber urged.

Holly did as she was told, with a mighty yell worthy of a Civil War soldier having his injured leg sawed off on the battlefield. Curtis looked a little scared, but he remained calm. "You're doing great, baby! Keep pushing! I can see the head. You're almost there!"

Holly strained and cursed and grunted. After several more pushes, a tiny head with a scrunched face emerged into view; Camille could see it reflected in the overhead mirror. Next came a small body streaked with blood and creamy white vernix. Camille let out a breath she hadn't realized she was holding. She felt a relief so huge it was as if the baby had come out of her and not Holly. "A girl!" crowed Dr. Faber, her brown eyes crinkling above her mask. She turned to Camille and Curtis, the baby cradled in her arms. "Which one of you would like to do the honors?"

Curtis looked to Camille. As head coach, the privilege of cutting the cord was rightfully hers. But she stepped aside, giving Curtis the nod. Moments later, Holly sat propped up holding their newborn daughter in her arms while Curtis stood over them, tears pouring down his cheeks. He and Holly shared a look that told Camille she needn't worry that he would keep his promise not to leave her.

Camille rejoined the rest of her family in the visitors' lounge. "For those of you who were expecting a boy, I regret to inform you," she said, breaking into a grin, "that Junior is a girl."

Larry let out a whoop. Lillian dabbed at her eyes with Larry's still-folded handkerchief.

Edward looked relieved, and Kyra was already texting her friends. Only Zach appeared nonplussed. He'd been hoping for a boy. Camille knew he'd dote on his baby cousin once she was an actual presence in his life, but right now she was just another girl in the family.

"Mother and baby both fine?" Edward rose and walked over to Camille. He looked tired. The last time she'd seen him look this tired was when he'd been studying night and day for his boards—decades ago, another lifetime—his face pallid, his eyelids puffy. She knew he hadn't been sleeping well lately. She'd been awakened in the middle of the night, several times this past week, by the sound of him tapping on his computer keyboard in the study across the hall.

"Right as rain," she reported. "Holly's in seventh heaven, and the baby has all ten fingers and toes. Though I'm not so sure about mine." Camille winced as she flexed her own fingers, which had begun to throb from the mangling they'd endured. "They may take a while to recover."

He only chuckled, where once he'd have taken her hand and tenderly kissed each of its bruised fingers. Her elation gave way to a heavy heart. It was the happiest of occasions—*a baby!*—and yet, she felt bereft all of a sudden, looking at Edward. He was smiling, but his eyes were sad.

When Larry and Lillian took the children to the nursery to see the baby, Camille sank wearily onto the sofa, and Edward sat down beside her. He put his arm around her, and she dropped her head onto his shoulder with a sigh. He'd always been the bulwark in every storm, but now was it enough?

THEY WERE DRIVING home when it began to rain. Fat droplets splattered against the windshield like eggs hurled by Halloween pranksters, quickly becoming a torrent. Camille peered out her window as they inched their way over the Manhattan Bridge in the Volvo, in bumper-to-bumper traffic, to the *swish-thwop-swish-thwop* rhythm of the windshield wipers. The city skyline stretched before them, the tops of the skyscrapers obscured by low-hanging clouds. Thunder rumbled, punctuated by flashes of lightning. Camille observed to no one in particular, "A fitting finale to the day." She turned to address Lillian, in the backseat with Larry and the children. "My sister has a flair for the dramatic. She's not like other people, you may have noticed."

"And thank goodness for it," Lillian replied staunchly.

Kyra said to Lillian, "One time, this totally sleazy cop pulled her over for speeding and then said he wouldn't give her a ticket if she'd give him her phone number, and she told him he could kiss her—" She broke off, darting a look at her mom. "Um, actually I don't know if my parents know that story."

Lillian just smiled. "Well, good for her. The world could use more people like your aunt Holly. People who aren't afraid to speak their mind. In fact, she reminds me of someone else I know." She cast an admiring glance at Larry. "You should have seen your grandfather at our last condo association meeting. He was magnificent—a lion in full roar!"

Larry murmured, "Oh, now, it wasn't quite as dramatic as all that."

"He's being modest," Lillian went on. "It all started with that nasty little man, Lyle Humphries. He and his fellow Fascists think they run the association. The latest was, they tried to vote in a regulation that would ban children under the age of twelve from using the pool. Imagine!"

"That's a stupid rule!" Zach cried. Then in the next breath, "What's a Fascist?"

"Bad people who tell other people what to do," Kyra told him.

"God knows what would have happened if your grandpa hadn't put a stop to it," Lillian said.

Edward grinned. "This I'd like to hear."

"Yes, Dad. Tell us what happened," Camille urged.

"It was nothing, really." Larry ducked his head in modesty.

"Nonsense. He saved the day!" Lillian insisted. "I wish you could have seen it. He organized a coup to oust Lyle before the little Napoleon could get his cronies to push the vote through." She turned again to smile adoringly at Larry. "I think that was when I knew I loved him."

"Wow. I'm impressed," Camille said. "How did you manage that, Dad?"

"I'm friendly with some of the other board members," he said. "Most of them aren't like Lyle. I asked how they would feel having to tell their grandchildren the pool was off-limits. That brought them around to my way of thinking pretty quick. All except Lyle, who doesn't have grandkids. They saw it my way, too, when I suggested it might be time for Lyle to step down."

"Nasty old bugger," muttered Lillian.

"I was thinking of Zach," Larry said. "How much fun we had when he visited." He reached over to ruffle Zach's hair. "Wouldn't want anything to spoil our next visit, would we, son?"

"Which reminds me, Larry and I were hoping the kids could stay on for a few extra days after the wedding," Lillian said. "We'll have my grandchildren, so it wouldn't be just us old folks. Do you think you'd like that, if it's okay with your parents?" She turned to Zach and Kyra.

"Awesome!" Zach cried. As if it had already been decided.

Even Kyra looked as if she'd be okay with it.

"Doesn't sound like much of a honeymoon," Edward commented.

"The honeymoon can wait," Larry said. "When you're retired, there's all kinds of time to take trips. It's time with the family you never get enough of." He cast a meaningful look at Camille.

Camille felt touched. "I don't see why not."

When they got to the city, they dropped Larry and Lillian off at their hotel, on Amsterdam Avenue, and the kids along with them. Larry had promised to bring Kyra and Zach home as soon as they'd been fed. They'd skipped supper and were both starved. Larry had said they could order from room service, which Zach considered the height of luxury.

By the time Edward and Camille pulled into their parking garage, the rain, which had tapered off, was coming down hard again. They left the Volvo with the attendant and made a dash for home, cursing the fact that neither of them had brought an umbrella. They'd made it halfway when the heavens unleashed a torrent of biblical proportions. They ducked into the nearest doorway.

"Next time, remind me to tune in to the weather forecast," Edward muttered as he brushed at the raindrops clinging to his coat.

"Cloudy with a chance of rain, it said. Some chance." She shook out her wet hair. The ledge under which they stood huddled sheltered the lower-level entrance to one of the brownstones that lined their block. A brass plaque beside the wrought-iron gate showed it to be the offices of a Karl Bronstein, MD.

"It doesn't look as though it's going to be letting up anytime soon." Edward peered from under the dripping ledge. The exterior light mounted on the brick wall inside the gate cast an eerie glow over his face, making hollows of his eyes and carving deep lines on either side of his mouth.

"I should have thought to bring an umbrella," she said for the third time.

He turned to her and smiled. "You had a few other things on your mind."

She sighed. "What a day. Don't get me wrong, I love my sister dearly, but the way she carried on, you'd have thought she was the only woman on the planet ever to give birth. Though," she added with a smile, "it *is* quite a story—one to tell her grandchildren someday." The tale of Holly's water breaking on the D train going over the Manhattan Bridge was surely as dramatic as any from those who'd given birth at Woodstock.

"Remember when you were in labor with Kyra?" he said. "The maintenance man who came into your room to change a lightbulb?" Camille smiled at the memory. She'd been in the middle of a contraction at the time, so she hadn't exactly been seeing straight. "You mistook him for a male nurse and asked if he'd kindly hold off on the enema until after you'd seen your doctor." Edward laughed and shook his head. "Poor guy. I never saw anyone take off so fast."

She recalled, too, when Edward had held their daughter in his arms for the first time. The look of tenderness on his face as he'd gazed at the tiny miracle they'd produced. How he'd said to her, Camille, with tears in his eyes, *Do you know how much I love you? Do you have any idea?*

Would he be able to say that to her now? She felt her heart buckle like a weakened girder. "A lot of water under the bridge since then. No pun intended," she added, looking out at the rain.

He chuckled. "At least you haven't lost your sense of humor."

"No, and a good thing, too, because it's gotten me through more than one crisis." She watched a woman passing by on the sidewalk pick her way around a puddle, clutching a wind-mangled umbrella. "Let's see, we've had the biblical plagues and now an epic birth. What's next?"

He didn't respond, and when she brought her gaze back to him, he was staring sightlessly ahead, lost in thought. Something was clearly weighing on his mind, and she had a pretty good idea what it was. She felt a surge of sorrow and regret, pouring through her like the runoff gurgling in the drainpipe that angled down the side of the building. "Oh, Edward. I've really made a mess of things, haven't I?" she said in a choked voice.

He turned to look at her, and she saw the subtle shift as he rearranged his features into a neutral mask. "You did what you thought was best," he said. His voice was kind, and that was what really killed her. He would always be taking care of her, even now that she no longer needed to be taken care of. Even if it was at his own expense.

"And now you're unhappy because of it." There, she'd said it. Part of her wanted to snatch the words back, but she knew if she didn't confront this now, the opportunity would pass, dragging them along with it into some dreadful state of simply making do. She couldn't let that happen. Not after everything they'd been through, after everything they'd once meant to each other. She thought, *I'm tired of pretending everything's going to be okay just because* I'm *going to be okay.*

Instead, it was Edward who sought to sidestep it. "Did I say I was unhappy?" An edge crept into his voice.

"No, but it's obvious. To me, at least."

"We hit a rough patch. It happens. We'll get through it."

"You make it sound like some grim duty."

He lifted an eyebrow. "Do I? Or is that just your interpretation?"

Camille squeezed her eyes shut. Lately, whenever they argued, it was always like this. Nothing ever got resolved; they just became more angry and frustrated. Because they were circling, forever circling, never getting to the heart of the matter. Never touching on the *real* issue.

In a fit of desperation, she grabbed the front of his overcoat, clutching the thick, wet wool hard enough to drive a button into the soft meat of her palm. Blood rushed into her head, a hot surge. "Say you love me then! Say it, so it we can move on. But you have to mean it, or it won't count."

He looked startled by her outburst. She was always so civilized—they both were—so careful not to get too near the chasm that yawned at their feet. "Of course I love you," he said guardedly.

"Why? Because I'm your wife?" She let go and took a step back, her hands dropping to her sides.

"Jesus, Camille. What do you *want* from me?"

"I know you love me enough to stay with me. You've already demonstrated that," she said. Tears prickled behind her eyes. "What I want to know is if you love me the way you love *her*?"

He flinched, and she knew she'd struck a nerve. "I'm not going to answer that," he said coldly.

"Why, because you don't want to hurt me?" As if anything he said to her now could be any more hurtful than what she'd imagined. *You think I haven't noticed how preoccupied you've been lately? Or the sad look on your face when you don't know you're being watched? Even when we make love, you're not fully present—you're somewhere else in your mind.*

"I'm here, aren't I? What more do you want?" he said.

Camille felt her resolve start to crumble, but she knew she had to stay the course. Her life might not depend on it, but her marriage did. "All right, let me put it another way." She sucked in a breath. "Supposing I *had* died. Supposing you were a free man. Would you be with her right now?"

He didn't say anything. He didn't have to. A flash of lightning illuminated the stairwell just then, and in that split-second she saw the answer on his face: in the dark glint of his eyes, and in the set of his jaw. She knew what it had cost him to give up Angie, and the realization was like a shot in the heart. *The truth shall set you free,* she thought. *But free to do* what, *exactly?*

She looked away from him, staring miserably out at the pedestrians slogging their way along the sidewalk, partially obscured by umbrellas, some clutching leashes as they urged on bedraggled dogs. "Yes, I did what I thought was best," she said. "But I was thinking with my head and not my heart. And why was that?" She turned slowly to face him, her gaze locking onto his. "I've asked myself that question a thousand times. And the only answer I can come up with is this: If our love had been as strong as it was in the beginning, would I have done what I did? Would you have agreed to it?

Would either of us have been willing to let go of the other, for any reason whatsoever?"

"I never stopped loving you," he insisted.

"I know," she said. "But it's not the same anymore, is it? It was never the same after I got sick. They warned about this in my survivors' group. About how you can grow to resent the person who's taking care of you. And how that person can grow to resent you. Who wouldn't, having to look after someone who's sick and grumpy all the time, and who looks like hell even on their best day? I thought we'd be different, but it turns out we were just like everyone else."

"I didn't resent you," he said.

"Then you're a better person than I am," she said. *Or maybe just not very honest with yourself.* "I resented you at times, yes. I was grateful to you, but I also resented you. When I was in the hospital, there were days when I thought I'd go mad from the pain and from being cooped up for so long." Even remembering that time was painful. The weeks of being isolated in a sterile unit while she underwent the stem cell transplant: weak as a newborn and with every part of her body aching, her mouth and throat riddled with sores that made it hard to swallow, her eyes burning as if someone had poured sand into them. "I needed someone to blame. And you were there. You were always there. The devoted husband with his wreck of a wife. Does that make sense? Of course not. That's my point: We've been acting on the assumption that any of this makes sense."

He eyed her unhappily. "We can't change what happened, but we can get past it."

She wanted to believe that, but if they could get past it, they would have by now. They would have made inroads, at least. Instead, they were both stuck. "I'm not so sure," she said. "Edward, we crossed a line that should never have been crossed. How do you come back from that?"

"You just do," he said. "Other couples have. Why not us?"

"I don't know. Maybe you're right. Maybe we can." Her head spun; she felt confused. And she wanted so desperately to believe it was possible. "But we can't move forward unless we're honest with ourselves and each other. This isn't just about you having an affair. It's not just about me getting sick, either. After I got better and you started putting in more hours at work, I never said a word, even though it made me angry, because I knew why you were doing it. You wanted to escape. What right did I have to object when you'd sacrificed so much on account of *me*?"

"I wasn't trying to escape."

"Maybe not consciously. But wasn't there a part of you that was tired of me? Tired of being the good guy? I don't blame you. *I* was tired of me, too. I would have escaped if I could have."

"It's not too late. We can fix this." A note of desperation crept into his voice.

"Oh, Edward. I don't know."

Edward felt panic swell in him, clogging his throat, filling his ears with a strange buzzing noise. He took a clumsy step back, as if he could somehow ward it off, and bumped up against the wall behind him, the heels of his oxfords scraping against the brickwork with a sound like a match being struck. Maybe Camille was right; maybe there was a part of him that *had* wanted to get away. It had been a difficult time for them both. But right now all he wanted was to go home.

"What are you saying?" He eyed her apprehensively.

She let out a breath that seemed to release something deep inside her. "I think," she said in a shaky voice, as if she'd just then come to a decision, "we should take a break. Until we can sort this out."

The words landed with a dull thud in the pit of his stomach. "Are you asking me to move out?"

"I think it would be best, don't you? For the time being." Camille fought the urge to backpedal. Or to lessen the blow by saying *Just for a few days.* She prayed for the strength to see this through as she

THE REPLACEMENT WIFE · 371

knew she must. Though, God, the way he was looking at her—as if she'd stuck a knife in him.

At last, he gave a slow nod. She caught the glimmer of tears amid the shadows that partially obscured his face. "What will we tell the kids?"

"I don't know, but we'll think of something."

"We can't lie to them." His expression turned hard.

"No," she said. "We'll tell them the truth."

He gave a dry laugh. "The truth? I'm not sure I know what that is anymore."

"I know one thing: This is the only way we're going to find out."

Edward was silent as he contemplated this, gazing out at the darkened, rain-soaked street. "Look. It's stopped," he said at last. The pavement glistened where puddles had formed. The relentless drumbeat of the rain had given way to the sound of dripping eaves and the swishing of tires from the cars that crawled past. He took her hand, lacing his fingers through hers. "Let's go home."

Home. A picture formed in Camille's mind, of the framed sampler that hung in her kitchen, a wedding gift from her in-laws, its simple homily cross-stitched in threads whose colors had faded over time: *Home is where the heart is.* If that was so, where did her heart belong now?

ELISE HAD HEARD about it by accident. She and Glenn had gone to Kings County to visit a fellow faculty member, Chips Miller, who was in the ICU recovering from heart surgery. His real name was Anson, but years ago the assistant principal, Brenda Phipps, had commented that Mr. Miller reminded her of the character played by Robert Donat in her favorite old movie, *Good-bye, Mr. Chips.* She started calling him Chips, and the nickname stuck. He was not distinguished-looking—he was short and gray and stout—but he had the same exuberant manner, disdain for slackers, and gift for teaching. He was not without a sense of humor, either. He'd roared with laughter along with everyone else at the comic skit written and performed by his eighth-grade students in the school's variety show the previous year, which featured a character called Mr. Chips-and-Dip. He was beloved by staff and student body alike, so everyone was shocked and distressed when the principal, Mrs. Hardaway, announced on Monday of that week, during morning chapel, that Mr. Miller had suffered a heart attack and was in the hospital.

Elise went to visit him the very next day. Glenn, although he wasn't as close to the old man and might not have chosen to go on his own (he and the other faculty members had sent a get well card that they'd all signed, and Glenn had had each of his students write a letter), insisted on accompanying her, so she wouldn't have to go alone.

They arrived at Kings County Hospital to find their colleague resting comfortably and in good spirits. They didn't stay long—visits to the ICU were restricted to fifteen minutes. After a brief chat, Elise said as they were leaving, "Next time I see you, I expect you to be up and about, getting the nurses to write their congressman." Chips Miller was a tireless promoter of doing one's civic duty.

"Count on it," the old man said smartly. "In fact, I'll draft the letter myself. They're underpaid, those nurses, and the deplorable conditions they're forced to work in, why, it's shameful."

"You can write a letter about us poor underpaid, overworked teachers while you're at it," joked Glenn.

Mr. Miller was still chuckling when they left.

"Do you think he'll be okay?" asked Elise as they headed down the corridor.

"Sure. He's a tough old bird." Glenn spoke confidently. "If he had a sign around his neck it would read 'Do Not Bend, Tear, or Staple.'" He grinned. "By government regulation, of course."

They got into the elevator. Three floors down, it stopped and a pair of nurses got on. Both of them young—in their mid-twenties,

Elise guessed—a pretty, freckle-faced redhead pushing an EKG cart and a girl with curly dark hair and an overbite. "Her water broke on the subway," the redhead was saying. "Imagine. Good thing her family was with her or she might've ended up in Brighton Beach; she was in such a panic—she didn't know what continent she was on."

The dark-haired girl laughed. "Thank God for family, right?"

"Oh, and here's the best part," the redhead went on, apparently unaware that Elise was shamelessly eavesdropping. "Turns out Jeanine—you know Jeanine Danziger, works on my floor?—used to date the baby's father. About a million years ago, but still. You should've seen the look on her face when he showed up."

"Was he good looking?" asked the other girl.

"Yeah, but nothing compared to the sister's husband. Oh, my God, you should've seen *him*."

"Whose sister?"

"Subway Mom's."

The two nurses giggled, and the first nurse said, "Talk about hot. I mean, like, *to-die-for*. I swear, the guy was a dead ringer for George Clooney. And get this: He's a doctor. I overheard him talking to Dr. J. Too bad he's not on staff here, or I'd seriously think about switching floors."

"Too bad he's married," the dark-haired nurse said with a sigh.

Doctor . . . pregnant sister-in-law . . . looks like George Clooney. There could be only one person who fit that description, Elise thought. She didn't know whether it was fate or mere coincidence that she and Edward happened to be in the same place on the same day, but it seemed a sign of some kind. She waited for her heart to do its little Saint Vitus's dance, like it always did at any reminder of him. But it maintained its steady, normal beat. She let out a breath. Maybe she was finally getting over him. She felt both relieved and saddened at the thought.

Glenn must have put two and two together, because he was giving her a funny look. Others often underestimated Glenn, because of the way he joked around, but he was more perceptive than most people, or maybe just when it came to her. He didn't question it when she got off on the same floor as the redheaded nurse. Nor did he offer any comment. He merely tagged along. It wasn't until she'd stopped at the nurses' station to ask for Holly's room number and they were headed in that direction that he asked, "You're sure about this?"

"I'm visiting a friend. I don't see what's wrong with that," she said. She was careful to speak in an even, neutral voice.

"A friend who just happens to be related to the guy you're in love with," he stage-whispered.

"The guy I *used* to be in love with," she whispered back. She wished now she hadn't told him about Edward's breaking up with her (if you could call it that). But there had been no one else to confide in, and she'd known Glenn would understand. He never judged her, even when he disapproved. How could he, with his track record? He was the self-proclaimed king of romantic dead-ends. He'd only said: *And I thought I was the only one whose picker was broke. Fine pair we make, huh?*

They'd been walking in Madison Square Park at the time. Glenn had recently adopted a puppy from the SPCA, a dachshund-poodle mix that he called a wiener-doodle and had named Curly, and they were taking Curly to the dog run, the puppy straining on his leash, scattering pigeons and other pedestrians with each lunge. (Glenn had enrolled him in an obedience class, but Curly wasn't making much progress.) "I just wish I'd followed my own advice," she said with a sigh. "I'm always reminding my kids to look before they cross, and what do I do? I walk straight into traffic."

"We all do stupid things in the name of love." Glenn bent to unclip Curly's leash, releasing him into the dog run, yipping with delight, to chase after a blond cocker spaniel. "Look at me. I have the market share. It doesn't mean I was foolish or reckless or whatever." He straightened and grinned. "Well, foolish maybe, but not reckless. Anyway, my point is, it happens and you move on."

She gave a snort. "Look who's talking. Mr. Optimism himself."

"It's different with me," he said, his tone matter of fact. "Whatever I have, it's not what women want. Either that or I'm cursed." The most recent prospect, whom they'd dubbed the Cheese Lady, was, as it turned out, already in a relationship—with another woman. A few days after Glenn's chance encounter with her, he'd spotted her again at Whole Foods, this time shopping with her partner and their little girl. Later, he and Elise had laughed at the irony of his having worried that the Cheese Lady would think *he* was gay. "You, on the other hand, could have any guy you wanted just by snapping your fingers."

"I'm not so sure about that," she said, warming at the compliment nonetheless, "but even if it were true, I don't seem to be very good at holding on to them." She sighed again. "I couldn't even hold on to my own husband."

"Ah, so we're back to that, are we? If what's-his-name only knew, his head would be so swelled it would look like a Macy's Thanksgiving Day Parade balloon. Seriously, Osgood—you're reading way too much into it. He was just a shallow jerk who couldn't keep it in his pants."

"Yes, but don't you see—I *chose* him. Out of all those hypothetical men I could have married, I chose Dennis. Then after swearing off men, I went and fell in love with someone else who was all wrong for me—for different reasons, okay, but still wrong. Maybe it's like you said. Maybe my picker's broke."

"I was only joking when I said that. Or maybe trying to make myself feel better about my own sorry state. Seriously. You struck out a couple times, that's all. And maybe it's all part of the plan."

"What plan would that be?" She squinted at him. It was a chilly day, and he was wearing his green Patagonia windbreaker and winter-weight corduroys. With the sun shining on his face, his eyes seemed bluer than ever. His brown hair was scuffed from the wind and his cheeks stamped with red.

"The cosmic plan," he said. "The one that's keeping you on ice until your prince comes. Who, may I add, could come along at any moment."

"You've been reading too many fairy tales," she scoffed.

"You just wait. You'll see. Though you may have trouble recognizing him at first. Remember, in fairy tales the prince is usually in disguise. A beggar or a frog or . . . you never know," He cast a wry glance at Curly, who'd stopped chasing the cocker spaniel and was now sniffing a Labrador retriever.

She laughed. "I'll keep an eye out, in that case."

They found Holly awake, looking worn out but beatific. Curtis was with her. Elise recognized him from the one time they'd met, several weeks ago, at one of Zach's soccer games. Curtis had cheered louder than any of them, and she remembered thinking at the time, *He'll make a good dad.* Now he was one, and it was clear, from the slaphappy grin he wore, that he couldn't be more pleased about it.

"Elise, hi!" Holly greeted her as she walked in. "Wow. News travels fast."

Elise introduced Glenn, and Curtis stood to shake Glenn's hand. "Welcome to the situation room."

"We were visiting a friend, and we heard some nurses gossiping in the elevator," Elise explained. "About a woman who almost gave birth on the subway. I figured it had to be Holly, from the description."

"It's on YouTube, if you want to see for yourself," Holly reported.

"YouTube, huh?" Glenn looked amused.

"Yep. Some dipshit filmed it with his camera phone." Holly rolled her eyes but didn't sound too perturbed. "Just type in 'subway mom,' and then you, too, can witness my public humiliation."

"Wow. So you're a celebrity," Elise remarked.

Holly grinned crookedly. "I always wanted to be a rock star. I guess this is the closest I'll ever get."

"Fortunately for us," Curtis said, with a wry laugh. He turned to

Elise and Glenn. "You just missed Edward and Camille. They were here not five minutes ago." From his blithe tone, Elise surmised he knew nothing of her involvement, outside normal socializing, with the Harte-Constantins.

"Oh." Elise waited once more for her heart to start doing its little dance, but it continued to beat at its normal, steady pace. "Well, next time you speak with them, tell them I said hello," she replied pleasantly.

"Boy or girl?" asked Glenn.

"Girl." Holly said. "We're naming her Judith after my mom."

"What happened to Janis?" Elise asked.

"Curtis put his foot down." Holly shot him a mock glare.

"Judith is a nice name." Elise turned to Glenn. "Don't you think so?"

"The only Judith I know is my dental hygienist," he said. "But she does a good job cleaning teeth."

Holly rolled her eyes again. "Great. I get clean teeth when I could've had rock royalty."

Curtis bent to kiss Holly on the cheek. "You'll thank me someday. And I know our daughter will thank me."

They chatted a few minutes more, until Elise saw Holly's eyelids start to droop. Then she and Glenn said their good-byes, Glenn joking that Holly needed to rest up for her "press conference." As they were headed out the door, Holly called after them, "If you want to see the baby, the nursery is just down the hall."

"You can't miss her," said the proud papa. "She's the most beautiful baby of them all."

Elise and Glenn found Baby Harte-McBride slumbering peacefully in her Isolette, swaddled in a white blanket and sporting a pink knit cap scarcely bigger than a postage stamp. They stood at the nursery's viewing window, gazing reverently at her. "She *is* pretty cute, I have to admit," Glenn remarked finally. "Usually, they all look alike, but this one kind of stands out."

"She does, doesn't she?" Elise felt herself go all gooey at the center, the way she always did around babies, especially newborns. It made her think of the child she'd hoped to have with Dennis.

"She's clearly destined for greatness."

"Which goes to show, you don't need to be named after a dead rock star," said Elise.

"I don't know. Janis would've been cool, or maybe just Joplin—it has a nice ring to it."

"Sounds more like a boy's name."

"You don't think boys can accomplish great things, too?"

"Sure, when they're not too busy tooting their own horn."

Glenn looped an arm around her shoulders. "You know, Osgood, I've been thinking. Maybe we should give it a go ourselves. Marriage, babies—the whole kit and caboodle. What do you say?"

"Sure, why not?" She played along. "But since neither of us is in a relationship, I don't see that happening anytime soon." If at all. Twenty years from now, she'd be like their school librarian, Miss Appleby, who wore a barrette in her hair, ate the same thing for lunch every day—peanut butter crackers, an apple, two slices of cheese—and kept photos of her three dogs on her desk.

"Yeah, well . . ." He darted her a sidelong glance. "That's sort of what I was getting at. I thought since we're both unattached, maybe we could be unattached together. If that makes sense."

"Glenn Stokowski!" She spun around to face him. "Are you asking me to marry you?"

His cheeks reddened. "Would that be so terrible?"

"You're not *serious*?"

"Serious as a heart attack." He caught himself, wincing as if at the thought of Chips Miller. "Sorry. My bad. No disrespect to the old man." He took her hands in his, looking her in the eye. "Remember that list I made of everything I wanted in a wife? Well, the other day I realized I knew someone who ticked all the boxes. She was right in front of me, in fact, and had been all along." He broke into a lopsided grin. "The same someone who's looking at me right now like she doesn't know whether to believe me or hit me over the head."

"How do I *know* you're serious?" she demanded. Even when Glenn was being serious, he was never completely serious. He usually managed to work in an irreverent remark or note of morbid humor. One time, when she was weeping over Dennis, he told her, "Lucky for him your best friend is a schoolteacher." When she asked why that was lucky, his response was, "I can't afford to hire a hit man."

Now he said, "Want me to prove it? Okay, you asked for it." With that, he took her in his arms and kissed her.

Elise was too dumbfounded to resist. By the time her brain registered the fact that he was kissing her—*Glenn Stokowki was kissing her*—it was too late to put a stop to it. But the most surprising thing of all wasn't the fact that he was kissing her (technically this wasn't the first time); it was the kiss itself. It was so completely and utterly *un*-Glenn-like. She had slept with only two men before Dennis, but she had been kissed by many—in high school, she was a popular cheerleader who had spent her share of time behind as well as in front of the bleachers—so she felt qualified to judge, and this was no ordinary kiss. Unlike his previous kiss, which had been more sweet than romantic, there was no mistaking the meaning of this one. It had power and depth and was remarkably self-assured for a man who claimed not to have had much practice lately.

She was trembling when they finally drew apart. "How long has *this* being going on?"

"Awhile," he confessed, red-faced. "Not just that I've wanted to kiss you. I've been thinking about other stuff, too—you, me, us. Little ones with your nose and my mouth, or my nose and your—" He broke off. "Why are you looking at me like that? You're making me nervous."

"I'm making *you* nervous? How do you think *I* feel?"

"Like a woman about to accept a heartfelt proposal, I hope." The impertinent grin was back.

"Wait a minute. Not so fast. When did you decide I was the One?"

"When you were mooning over that one's uncle." He pointed toward Baby Harte-McBride. "I was never jealous of what's-his-name. Maybe because I always knew he wouldn't go the distance. But I could tell it was different with this guy. Once I started seeing him as competition, I knew." He took hold of her hands, his gaze locking onto hers. "I realize this is probably coming out all wrong, but I love you, Elise. Not just as a friend. I *love* love you. As in . . . well, you get the picture." He gestured again toward the nursery's viewing window.

Tears sprang to Elise's eyes. "You could've prepared me, at least."

"How? Apparently, you're not very good at taking hints."

She gave in to a small smile. "We're not too big on subtlety in the Midwest."

"Ah, yes. Home of Hallmark and Russell Stover, maker of the ever-popular Whitman's Sampler."

"Now you're making fun of me."

"No," he said. His expression turned serious. In his pressed khakis and navy J. Crew sweater, with that swoosh of brown hair dipping over his forehead and his blue, blue eyes searching her face, he looked almost painfully earnest. "I am most definitely not making fun of you. I'm merely using humor as a defense mechanism because I'm actually terrified you'll reject me."

Elise smiled and shook her head. "Somehow I don't see that happening."

A spark of hope flared in his eyes, and he looked as if he wanted to comment on that. But he must have decided he'd said quite enough on the subject for the time being, so he only said, taking her arm, "Let's hit it. I don't know about you, but I'm starving. Should we do takeout? My place? As an added bonus I have the latest selections from Netflix for your viewing pleasure."

"As long as I get first pick."

"Sure. But I didn't order any chick flicks. Just standard fare, I'm afraid."

"I happen to like standard fare." She smiled at him as they strolled arm-in-arm down the corridor on their way to the elevators. "In fact, if you're up for it, we could even make it a double feature."

CHAPTER TWENTY-THREE

"Angie, couldya . . . ?"

"Got it!" Angie swooped in to snatch eighteen-month-old Caitlin out of harm's way. Francine's youngest had been on a collision course with the swing set, where her two older brothers, Bobby and Little Nick, were at the moment attempting to launch themselves into outer space.

The toddler howled in protest. On the lawn nearby, Rosemary's eldest, ten-year-old Jacqueline, was stuffing the family's Chihuahua into an old, pink terry Onesie of Caty's, Twinkie looking supremely put-upon as he submitted to this latest indignity with only a few token wriggles. Julia's adopted Korean daughters, Daisy and Lily, ages four and five, were giggling as they looked on, and Susanne's two boys, nine-year-old Aidan and eight-year-old Patrick (Susanne, whose married name was O'Brien, called them her Irish twins), cracking up like it was the funniest thing they'd ever seen.

Angie set Caty down in the sandbox, where she immediately ceased her howling and grabbed a toy shovel, using it to smack at a Little Mermaid doll lying facedown in the sand. In her quilted jacket, her bottom puffy with a diaper, she looked like a pint-size, curly-haired Michelin Man.

"Good reflexes," said Francine when she caught up with Angie a minute later, after having offloaded the tray of hamburger patties she'd been carrying. She wore her mom jeans and a faded

Northwestern U sweatshirt, her hair in a ponytail, errant wisps curling about her face.

"Don't forget, I've had lots of practice." Francine arched an eyebrow in a questioning look, to which Angie responded, "Just because I don't spend my days chasing after toddlers doesn't mean I'm sitting on my ass. I'll bet you a week's pay I log as many miles as you do on average."

"Speaking of which, this is where we pause for a commercial break and I remind you that you wouldn't have to work as hard if you had two incomes. Angie," Francine deepened her voice in imitation of their mom's. "What's it all for if you come home every night to an empty apartment? No one's telling you to quit your job, but why can't you have both? You want to wake up one day when it's too late and wish you'd listened to your ma?"

Francine's wicked impersonation of their mom—she perfectly captured Loretta's broad Long Island accent (which she, Francine, had sought to eradicate from her own speech) and even broader hand gestures and her way of thrusting out her chest when making a point—was always good for a laugh. This time, though, Angie only chuckled dutifully. Jokes about her single status no longer seemed as funny.

"Thanks," she said. "I'll be sure to keep that in mind. Need any help in the kitchen?" she asked as Francine started back toward the house.

Francine paused and shook her head. "I'm pretty sure Ma's got it covered. When I left her, she was rewashing the plates I'd unloaded from the dishwasher." She gave a long-suffering sigh, turning her gaze heavenward. "If you want make yourself useful, do something about the potato salad, for God's sake."

For every family cookout Loretta insisted on making potato salad from a recipe she'd cut out of a supermarket circular years ago. She was a good cook when she stuck to the basics of Italian-American cuisine. Her spaghetti and meatballs were perfection, as was her lasagna. It was only when she strayed into Betty Crocker territory that the results were mixed. Her potato salad, made with Miracle Whip, was, in a word, dreadful. Her daughters had tried every ploy to get her to stop making it ("Why don't you relax, Ma, and let us do the work?" Or, "Ma, how about we do coleslaw for a change?") or, at least, update the recipe. But she was as intractable about that as she was about her *Dynasty*-era wardrobe or the living room suite from Raymour and Flannigan, with its miles of flocked upholstery, that had been purchased when Bush Senior was in the White House.

"Fine. But don't blame me if it ends up tasting as vile as ever," Angie said.

She lingered on the patio a few minutes more after Francine had gone inside, enjoying the sunshine as she watched her nieces and nephews at play. It was unseasonably warm for late November, with temperatures in the mid-sixties, and though not quite warm enough to eat outdoors, they were going to brave it anyway, since Francine's dining room table couldn't seat the entire clan.

Angie had almost decided not to come. What persuaded her in the end wasn't that she didn't have an excuse not to come—she had the day off for once—or her mom's twisting her arm. It was that she hadn't wanted to spend the afternoon alone. Being alone led to obsessive thoughts. Thoughts of a certain someone she'd just as soon forget.

It had been three weeks since the news about Edward and Camille had trickled her way. She was catering an event that evening, a retirement party for some publishing executive at the Puck Building in SoHo, when she was approached by one of the guests, an attractive blonde she recognized from the Harte to Heart meet-and-greets. Normally, she made it a rule never to socialize with guests, but since she knew the woman, if only vaguely (from what she'd already begun to think of as her previous life), she paused to exchange pleasantries. The blonde commented on Angie's having been absent from the previous month's meet-and-greet. Angie murmured an excuse, something about Camille's wanting "a change," at which the other woman leaned in to confide, "That's not the only change. I heard she and her husband are getting a divorce."

"What?" Angie stared at her, dumbfounded.

At the stunned look she must have worn, the blonde said, "I know. I couldn't believe it, either. I thought she had it all—the perfect marriage, the perfect husband. Makes you wonder, doesn't it?"

Angie did more than wonder. If the blonde could have done a Vulcan mind-meld on her then, the words flashing in her brain would have looked like those in the subject line of the email Francine had subsequently sent, after Angie had informed her of this latest development in the ongoing soap opera: *WHAT THE FUCK?* What shocked Angie more than the news itself was that she hadn't heard it from Edward. Shock that gave way to hurt, and then anger, as the ensuing days passed with still no word from him. Obviously, his feelings for her—if he had any—hadn't factored in his decision. She was of so little consequence he couldn't even bother to inform her that he'd split from his wife.

How could I have been so stupid? She'd thought he cared for her. She'd thought the only thing keeping them apart was the ring on his finger. The night he'd told her it was over, she'd felt for him even as her own heart was breaking. But if he'd loved her even a little, wouldn't he have wanted to be with her now that he was free? Or at least provided an explanation as to why he couldn't be. Really, he was no better than her loser ex-boyfriends. He was worse, actually. At least those guys had never pretended to be something they weren't.

And she wasn't blameless herself. She should have known better than to become entangled with a married man. Instead, she'd gone down that slippery slope like it was a waterslide at an amusement park, convincing herself theirs wasn't just another garden variety affair. Camille was dying and wanted her husband to find happiness again after she was gone. *Why couldn't I be the one to make him happy?* Angie had thought. Wasn't she already making him happy? Now the ugly truth was plain to see: *He was only using me.* How else to explain his indifference (*not so much as a fucking email!*)? He'd used her as a crutch during a difficult period in his life, and now that he no longer needed that crutch, she'd been discarded. Angie felt duped. Crushed. Her heart smashed to bits like a piece of crockery dropped onto a tile floor.

She was yanked from her thoughts when two-year-old Caty sent a shovelful of sand flying her way. Angie brushed off the front of her jacket and looked down at Caty, clutching her red plastic shovel and chortling with glee. Angie grinned at her niece. "Nice shot, you little hooligan." Caty was Francine's "oops" baby, and Francine liked to joke that she'd been playing tricks on them ever since. Her favorite trick, since she'd learned to walk, was toddling around the living room as fast as her little legs could carry her, pulling books and knickknacks off shelves. Though whenever something broke, Francine would just shrug and say it was one less thing to dust.

Angie let herself in through the slider to the den, where she found Julia and Susanne blowing up balloons. They waved hello. Susanne's youngest, Pete, had turned eight earlier in the week and Julia's Daisy had turned five the week before—the reason for today's joint celebration—and after lunch there would be cake and ice cream and games for the kids, including a balloon dart-throw. Angie's dad, Lou, and Julia's and Susanne's husbands, Dan and Tony, were watching the football game, the Giants against the Oakland Raiders, on Big Nick's brand-new 48-inch flat-screen TV. None of the men looked up. Physically, they bore no resemblance to one another—Lou, stout and balding; Dan, big, red-haired, and freckled, with the ruddy face of an Irishman who liked his pint; Tony, slight and dark, with the look of a 1950s crooner—but they all wore identical expressions, those of rabid sports fans hanging on every play. The Giants were down two points. The house could be on fire, and they wouldn't have noticed.

"Pucker up, Ange." Susanne motioned toward the bag of balloons. Her face was flushed and her dark-brown curls looked, as usual, as if she'd blow-dried them without benefit of a brush. She didn't look much different than she had as a teenager coming home from soccer practice, except she was a bit heavier, with strands of gray here and there amid the curls. In contrast, Julia looked impossibly slender and chic wearing size-two bisque-colored jeans, a rust-colored knit shell, and a pumpkin jacket, her buttered-blond tresses messy only because they were styled to look that way. She was still the same weight as in high school (which bugged Rosemary, Susanne, and Francine, all of whom had packed on pounds with their pregnancies, no end). It was easy to see why Julia had gotten signed by a modeling agency at age seventeen, and also why she'd lasted all of three minutes on the open market after her divorce.

"Sorry, guys, you're on your own. I'm wanted in the kitchen," Angie said as she crossed over into the hallway.

Julia winked at her as she passed by. "You saving your kisser for someone, Ange?"

Angie smiled and thought, *Yeah, the man in the moon.* The last guy to lay one on her was the eighty-year-old grandfather of the boy whose bar mitzvah she'd catered the previous weekend. That was the extent of her love life right now. And that was fine by her. She'd seen what love could do.

The tinkling of piano keys drifted down the hallway. Angie popped her head into the living room as she approached the kitchen. Rosemary, in a loose-fitting tunic and drawstring pants, her long reddish-brown hair in a bun skewered with chopsticks, sat on the piano bench next to her seven-year-old, Margaret. Margaret, musically gifted like Rosemary, with the same serious face and composed air, was playing a piece Angie recognized as one her sister used to play when she was that age—a Bach two-part invention. She waited until Margaret was finished, then clapped and called, "Way to go, Megs! You'll be playing Carnegie Hall before you know it."

Entering the kitchen, Angie expected to see her mother going at her usual eighty-mile-per-hour pace, washing dishes or wiping down counters, slapping out hamburger patties or peeling hard-boiled eggs for the deviled eggs. Instead, she found her gazing out the window at the older boys playing Frisbee on the front lawn. Francine's ranch-style house was at the end of a cul-de-sac, so Francine and Big Nick didn't worry about the boys playing unsupervised on the lawn or riding their bikes on the street, where the speed limit of ten miles per hour was enforced by speed bumps. (The only vehicular accident to have occurred on Shadybrook Lane in recent memory was when old Mrs. Blankenship next door knocked over one of Francine's trash cans, on the curb out front, while backing her Pontiac Cutlass out of her driveway.)

"The boys behaving themselves?" Angie asked.

"I'm glad they still know how to entertain themselves." Loretta turned to smile at her. "Kids these days, all they know is computers and video games. Not like it was with you and your sisters."

"Yeah, all we had to corrupt our minds was TV. That and drugs, sex, and rock and roll."

Loretta gave her a chastising look that was halfhearted at best—she might be stuck in the past, but she was not without a sense of humor. "You and that mouth of yours—one day it'll get you in trouble." She'd been to the beauty parlor, and her hair was shellacked into its signature upsweep. She wore the embroidered bolero jacket she'd picked up on the previous year's Mexican Riviera cruise, with a full-sleeve shirt and pleated trousers. She looked like a circus ringmaster.

"Face it, Ma. I'm a lost cause. You should know that by now."

"I know no such thing."

"Even though I'm the black sheep of the family?"

"Who said you were the black sheep?"

"You did. Not in so many words, but you didn't have to—I got the message loud and clear."

"Well, I'm sorry if you felt I was criticizing you. I was only—"

"Jesus Christ, Ma. Don't you know when to quit?" Angie cried in frustration. At the reproachful look her mother gave her, she went on in a lighter tone, "See what I mean? I'm incorrigible. Remember when you used to threaten to give me to the nuns to be straightened out? Maybe you should have." Angie was only half joking. "That's what you get for going easy on me. A daughter with a mouth, who doesn't listen." *And who you would be ashamed of if you knew what she'd been up to lately.*

"You're a good girl." Loretta smiled and patted her cheek.

Angie wished she could believe it. But good girls didn't get involved with married men. A man, in her case, who hadn't really loved her, as it turned out; who couldn't even be bothered to inform her that he'd left his wife. No, she wasn't good. She was rotten. A rotten, horrible person.

She gestured toward the items spread over the counter—jars of condiments, a colander of boiled potatoes, blue cheese crumbles, and bunches of scallions and celery, all the makings for her mother's God-bless-the-Pope potato salad. (Angie and her sisters had dubbed it that due to the liberal amount of Miracle Whip that went into it.) "Need a hand with that?" Her mom gave her the celery to chop, and then dumped the potatoes into a bowl. She was reaching for the jar of Miracle Whip when Angie said, "You know, Ma, it wouldn't take me two minutes to whip up some mayonnaise."

"Yes, but then it wouldn't taste the same," Loretta said, meaning the salad.

Angie almost said something but thought better of it. Better to choke down a few bites of her mom's potato salad than hurt her feelings. Besides, she had bigger problems. She needed to get out of the slump she was in. She had to stop obsessing about Edward. She loved him, and she hated him. She wanted to spit in his eye and to smother him in kisses. She wanted to throw herself into his arms and to be a stone figure, unmoved and unmovable. She wanted . . . she wanted . . . she wanted. She was as stuck, in her own way, as her mom with her potato salad and her turquoise eye shadow and fifty zillion pictures of icebergs. And maybe this was what she deserved—to suffer. She'd stolen another woman's husband (borrowed more like it, but still). She'd sinned. She was a sinner. And the worst of it was, she would do it all over again if given the chance.

She had to find her way back to the person she used to be. Her *own* person. Someone who didn't want for anything or anyone; who lived her life the way she fried eggs: neat and clean, and with nothing sticking to the pan. But *how*? How could she get back there when she'd strayed so far?

Make it right.

It was her mother's voice she heard, if the words were only in her mind. Yes, that was exactly what Loretta would say. The same as when Angie had stolen a pack of gum from Willoughby's Pharmacy when she was seven (old enough to know better but still young enough to do dumbass things without weighing the consequences) and Loretta had marched her back to the store to apologize to Mr. Willoughby and pay for the gum, after finding it in Angie's pocket. Angie would never forget the humiliation. How she'd stood staring down at her feet while she mumbled the words, the blush she wore burning holes in her cheeks, the floor an ocean swimming before her tear-filled eyes, one she wished she could dive into. But afterward, it was as if the weight of the world had been lifted from her shoulders.

Now, standing in her sister's sunny kitchen chopping celery, it came to her: She had to make this right, and the only way she could do that was by making amends. She had to tell Camille she was sorry.

·　·　·

FRIDAY OF THE following week was the evening of the December Harte to Heart meet-and-greet. As Angie stepped through the door to the familiar West Chelsea loft, she was instantly on home turf amid the swirl of partygoers, the buzz of conversations punctuated by bright bursts of laughter, the air filled with the mingled scents of perfume, hot appetizers, and poured wine. At the same time, it felt strange. In the past, she'd always showed up, with her staff, hours before the party started. This was also the first time she'd arrived empty-handed. Normally, she'd have been carrying a stack of plastic tubs or aluminum containers, a bulging canvas bag slung over each shoulder. And yet she had never felt more weighted down than she did now. If this were a pond, she'd have sunl like a rock to the bottom. Camille wasn't expecting her and wouldn't be happy to see her. In fact, Angie was probably the last person Camille would want to see.

But Angie had no other choice. She needed to speak with Camille, and Camille wasn't returning her phone calls or emails. She'd hoped to arrange a private meeting, but that obviously wasn't going to happen. And this had to be done face-to-face. No being half-assed about it; she needed to look Camille in the eye when she told her what she'd come to say. She had to do this right.

As she made her way through the crush in search of Camille, her stomach was in knots and her nerves were like a hot-wired engine being gunned. Was she doing more harm than good in coming here? She was the cavalry carrying the smallpox-infested blankets to the unsuspecting Indians. She'd be infecting Camille with her mere presence. She calmed her nerves by repeating to herself: *I can't make it better, but maybe I can keep it from getting worse.* She owed it to Camille to try, at least.

She spotted familiar faces amid the crowd, but though a few people glanced at her curiously, no one appeared to recognize her; either that, or they couldn't place her. She was out of context. Instead of her chef whites, she was wearing a dress, her all-purpose black one. Even so, she felt conspicuous. She felt like a bank robber wearing a Halloween mask. *Everyone freeze, and no one will get hurt!*

Finally, she spied Camille, standing by the bar chatting with one of the guests, a curvy brunette wearing a print wrap-dress. Something was different about her. But what? Her hair was the same, a deep auburn that fell in soft curls about her porcelain face, and she wasn't made up any differently. Had she put on weight? A few pounds maybe—she didn't look quite so gaunt—but not enough to explain the marked change. Then Angie realized what it was: Camille looked healthy. Like someone in the land of the living.

Camille caught her gaze then, and the animated look she wore instantly fell away. She murmured something to the brunette in the wrap-dress, and began making her way toward Angie. She looked ready to do battle: shoulders squared, eyes glittering, a smile that was locked and loaded. As if Angie were a party crasher whom she planned to eject—politely but firmly. Camille wouldn't make a scene, but she would make damn sure Angie got the message. *You're not welcome here.* Angie fought the urge to bolt for the nearest exit; she had to see this through. So she propelled herself forward, meeting Camille halfway.

"What are you doing here?" Camille kept her voice low, but there was steel in it.

"I need to speak with you. Please. It's important," Angie said.

Camille studied her, as if trying to decide whether it was worth risking a scene, then gave a stiff nod. "All right. But not here. Outside." With her jaw clenched, her lips barely moved as she spoke.

She went to fetch her coat while Angie put on the raincoat folded over her arm, and led the way onto the terrace. In warm-weather months, the terrace, which wrapped around the top floor of the building, with views of Lower Manhattan to the south and the Hudson River to the west, was usually thronged with partygoers. Tonight, however, there wasn't another soul in sight. After the unseasonal warm spell of the past week, temperatures had plummeted; even the smokers were apparently forgoing their nicotine fix in favor of staying inside where it was warm. Angie's raincoat was no match for the cold wind gusting off the river. She'd have liked to sit down, in a sheltered spot, but Camille bypassed the groupings of tables and chairs, walking over to the railing on the side of the terrace that faced the river. Angie followed. It was a clear night, and she could see the dark water glittering below, where a barge cruised slowly by, the lights of New Jersey visible on the opposite shore. She hugged herself, shivering.

"I'm sorry." Angie came right out with it. "What I did was wrong, and you have every reason to hate me." Camille, standing beside her gazing out at the river, gave no indication that she'd heard. She only pulled her sheepskin coat more tightly around her.

Finally, Camille turned to face her. "That's it? You're sorry?" Her hair, whipped by the wind, was the only part of her that wasn't perfectly still. Her face might have been carved of ice. "Well, it's too late for that. The damage is done."

Angie nodded, her teeth chattering with the cold. "For what it's worth, it was never about me. Not really. If you hadn't gotten sick—" At the sharp look Camille gave her, she explained, "He told me. It was tearing him apart. At first, I . . . I was just someone he could talk to. And what he mainly talked about was *you*. How much he loved you, and how he didn't want to lose you."

Camille stared at her, wearing a queer, bitten-off smile. "How touching."

Angie flinched at the sarcasm in her voice. "I'm sorry," she said again.

"Your apology is duly noted. If that's all, you can go now." Camille spoke in a clipped, businesslike voice, though Angie knew it was only because she was struggling to keep from losing control. The heat of emotion had melted her icy facade, revealing the underlying anguish. Angie could see, too, the glow of vitality she'd noticed earlier. Camille might not be too happy at the moment, but she no longer had one foot in the grave. And if that was the case, she had the strength to fight to save her marriage. *It may be too late for me, but it's not too late for you,* Angie thought.

"Don't worry, I didn't come to disrupt your party," Angie told her. "I'm also not here just to ease my conscience. There's something you need to know." She reached to grip the railing, to anchor herself, the ice-cold iron biting into her palm. "I'm sure Edward's told you, but I wanted you to hear it from me: It's over between us."

"What makes you think I doubted that?"

"I heard you were getting a divorce."

Camille gave a harsh laugh. "Is that what you heard?"

"Is it true?" Angie hoped she didn't sound eager.

"Not exactly—we're separated. Not that it's any of your business."

So they weren't getting a divorce. Not yet, at least. Angie felt a flicker of hope, but was quick to remind herself this had nothing whatsoever to do with her. "You're right. It's none of my business," she said. "But if you think he might still have feelings for me, I wouldn't want that to be a factor. You should know it wasn't my decision to end it. I wouldn't have been able to, even though I knew it was the right thing to do. I loved him too much." *I still do.* Angie knew she was only making herself look worse, but she was here to make things right, not portray herself in the most flattering light.

Camille tilted her head, regarding Angie with a curious expression. Her blue eyes shone in the light that spilled across the terrace from the floor-to-ceiling windows. "I thought you didn't believe in love."

I didn't. Until I met your husband. Angie drew in a breath that felt sharp, like inhaling broken glass. "The point is," she said, "it's *you* he loves. He was willing to let me go, but not you."

Camille's mouth curved in smile that held no humor. "And yet look where we ended up."

Angie didn't respond. She hunched her shoulders, shivering.

Camille went back to gazing out at the river—she seemed more sad now than angry. When she finally spoke, her voice was soft, almost as if she were talking to herself. "You know the saying *When one door closes, another one opens*? Well, sometimes the reverse is true: One door opens, and another one closes."

Angie didn't know what to make of it. Was Camille saying there was no hope for her marriage? Or was she only voicing her hurt at having been betrayed? Either way, it was no business of Angie's. She was part of Edward's past, not his future. *Whether he stays or goes, he's moved on as far as I'm concerned.* "If it means anything," she said. "I hope you can work it out." The most damnable part of all this was that she still loved him enough to want him to be happy. If his happiness lay with Camille, so be it.

Camille shrugged in response. The silence stretched out, becoming increasingly awkward, prickling like the chill air needling its way through Angie's raincoat. Angie cleared her throat and said, "Well, I should go. Good luck with everything. I mean that." She reached to touch Camille's sleeve, but some instinct made her stop short, and her fingertips met only with cold air. Camille didn't appear to notice. She remained motionless staring into the distance, lost in thought.

CHAPTER TWENTY-FOUR

"What I'd like to know is how a man with twenty years on me and twice as many pounds still manages to slaughter me on a regular basis," Edward groused good-naturedly as he and Hugh made their way off the squash court. He'd just been soundly beaten, by a six-point margin, the third week in a row.

Hugh flashed him a grin. "Bionic knees." He referred to the double knee replacement he'd had several years ago.

"Seriously, what's your secret?"

"The key is balance, my friend. On and off the court."

"Is that just another way of saying I don't have my mojo on?"

Hugh paused to look at him. "You tell me."

Edward only shrugged in response and kept moving. He didn't want to get into a heavy discussion right now. It seemed all he did these days was talk. With Camille, and once a week with the marriage counselor they'd been seeing the past month and a half. Not that anything had come of it, as far as he could tell. He and Camille were making progress, according to Dr. Santangelo, and while Edward didn't dispute that—his view was entirely subjective, so what did he know?—it seemed all they ever did was go over the same tired ground while grappling with the question at the heart of it: *How could two people who love each other have let this happen?*

He and Hugh showered and got dressed; then they headed out. It was lunchtime, and neither was due back at work for another half-hour. They stopped at Eretz, the neighborhood kosher deli and a favorite of Hugh's, for a bite to eat. Hugh ordered his usual, tongue and corned beef on rye and a celery tonic; Edward, a hamburger and fries, plus seltzer water with a slice of lemon.

"You finished unpacking yet?" asked Hugh as he was tucking into his sandwich.

"You mean all three boxes?" Edward gave a dry laugh. Over the weekend, he'd moved from his furnished sublet on Amsterdam at Eighty-Fourth Street to another one, closer to work. "That would include the Crock-Pot my receptionist gave me, which is still in its original carton." He paused to consider this, taking a sip of his seltzer water. "I think Rosie feels sorry for me."

"Why wouldn't she? Look at you—you're a mess. Can't even beat an old man at squash." Hugh took a bite of his sandwich, chewing with satisfaction. His face was ruddy, and his towel-dried hair stuck out in gray corkscrews all over his head. "So, how do you like the new digs?"

"Can't beat the commute." It was only a ten-minute walk to work. It was also a short walk from the subway station, which was convenient for when his children came to visit. Other than that, it was all the same to Edward. He'd simply slid from one featureless capsule into the next.

"Knowing you, that just means longer hours at work," Hugh guessed correctly.

Edward shrugged. "It's not like I have anyone waiting for me at home."

Hugh sighed in commiseration. "It's not easy, I know."

"No offense, but how the hell would you know?" Edward regarded his long-married friend with a wry gaze.

"Ruth left me once. I never told you that story? It was right after Sarah was born. She was feeling overwhelmed and I guess I wasn't being very supportive, so she went with the kids to stay with her folks in Toledo. She didn't threaten to make it permanent, but I knew it was a wakeup call."

"What did you do?"

"At first, all I did was mope; my pride kept me from begging her to come back. Longest two months of my life," Hugh said, shaking his gray, clock-sprung head. "Finally, I couldn't stand it, so I got in the car and drove straight through to Toledo. Just showed up at my in-laws and announced, 'I'm here for Ruthie and the kids.' Ruth didn't say a word. She just packed up, got the kids, and we drove home. On the way, I did most of the talking. I told her I was an ass, that she'd had every reason to leave me, and that I'd missed her and was lost without her. I said if she ever decided to leave again, she had to promise one thing."

"What was that?"

"To take me with her."

Edward felt a tightening in his gut. Hugh made it sound easy—as easy as swallowing one's pride. *If only it were that simple.* "She knew she had you by the short hairs," he said with a laugh.

Hugh took another bite of his monster sandwich, chewing thoughtfully, then washing it down with celery tonic. "How about you? You and Camille making any progress?" he asked. His tone was casual, but Edward knew that, with Hugh, even the most casual inquiry was a spring-loaded mechanism, one that could catapult him into a discussion he'd just as soon not have.

Edward dragged a french fry through the pool of ketchup on his plate, and popped it into his mouth. "Your friend Dr. Santangelo is probably more qualified to comment on that than I am," he replied cautiously. The therapist he and Camille were seeing had been recommended to them by Hugh. Edward liked and respected Dr. Santangelo. Though he would like her a whole lot more, he decided, if their sessions didn't invariably end with him feeling like he'd been run over by a nine-wheeler. "It seems all we do is go in circles."

"Be patient." Hugh dabbed with his napkin at a smear of mustard that had made its way onto his tie. Hugh attracted food particles and drips the way a magnet did metal filings. "Even when it seems as if you're not making progress, these things have a way of resolving themselves."

"That's what worries me."

"What, a resolution?"

"Yes, if it's the wrong one." Edward stared at the burger on his plate, which had grown cold.

"There's no right or wrong in these situations, only what's right for you," Hugh said. He paused before going on, in a gentle tone, "I know you haven't reached that point yet, and God willing you never will, but you should, at least, prepare yourself for the possibility that this could end with the two of you going your separate ways."

Edward shook his head in denial. He was getting the same, sick feeling he got with Dr. Santangelo—the gripping sensation in his gut; the sense of despair like rising floodwaters. "Twenty years is a long time," he said. "We have a lot invested. We have the kids to think of, too."

Hugh sighed again, his brow creased into meaty furrows. "It's not about what you have invested; it's about what you hope to gain. As for the children . . ." He paused, the furrows in his brow deepening. He was like an uncle to Kyra and Zach, so he, too, wanted what was best for them, Edward knew. Still, he didn't mince words. "If you and Camille decide to make a go of it, it should be for one reason only: because you love each other. Couples who stay together because of the kids aren't fooling anyone, believe me. Kids always know."

Edward pushed his plate aside. He'd lost his appetite. His stomach felt like a piece of aluminum foil balled up and jammed into a crevice of his rib cage. "That's where we keep getting hung up. I love her and I know she loves me, but . . ." He searched for the right words. "It's like when something breaks; you can glue it back together, but it'll never be whole again. That's how it feels with her. Like we can never be whole again. A lot of what we have is good, and maybe that's enough, but if the center doesn't hold . . ." He gave a helpless shrug.

"Yeats was commenting on religion, not marriage," Hugh pointed out.

"Yes, but aren't they the same in some respects? Isn't marriage meant to be sacred?" A corner of Edward's mouth hooked up in an ironic smile. "I know that must sound pretty hypocritical coming from me. But if I was unfaithful, it was only because I felt like Camille had given up on *us*, not just on getting better. That whole business with Elise . . ." He felt himself start to grow angry all over again. "Did you know she wasn't the only one? There was another woman before her. Camille set us up on a date that I didn't even know was a date." He gave a hollow laugh at the surprised look Hugh wore. "She came on to me. Not what Camille intended, I'm sure. And not that I took her up on the offer. But I sometimes wonder if that wasn't when everything changed for me. That night. When I realized my wife had stopped thinking of me as her husband. I was just another . . . project," he added bitterly.

"I'm sure she didn't see it that way." Hugh played devil's advocate.

"No. But that's my point. She was looking to the future; she couldn't see what was in front of her. She didn't see that I loved her, and that I'd have sacrificed anything for her, which I did—even my own integrity."

"Perhaps she didn't feel she had a choice."

"We *always* have a choice, if only in choosing how to play out the endgame." Edward spoke more forcefully than he'd intended, and a diner at the next table, a middle-aged man wearing a yarmulke, glanced his way. He lowered his voice. "Look, I'm not saying we can't get past this. It's just . . . it's not easy."

Hugh nodded in understanding. "And your lady friend? Is she still in the picture?"

Edward felt his heart constrict at the mention of Angie. He'd worked as hard at keeping thoughts of her at bay as he had on keeping his marriage intact. Harder in some ways—because despite his best efforts, those thoughts constantly stole in, like wind through unsealed cracks in a window frame. "I'm not seeing her anymore, if that's what you mean," he replied gruffly.

"But you'd like to." It was a statement, not a question.

Edward shrugged again.

Hugh wiped his mouth with his napkin and sat back, brushing idly at the crumbs scattered over his shirtfront. "Want my advice?"

"Do I have a choice?" Edward muttered.

Hugh's next words were like a punch in the gut. "In order to make this work, you have to be clear on one thing: Is Camille the one you want?"

EDWARD WAS STILL pondering the question when he returned to work. The answer was at once simple and complex, a chambered nautilus that looped and spiraled, leading nowhere except in on itself: *I want it all.* He missed his old life, so much at times it was like a hole in his gut. He missed coming home after work. He missed seeing the kids each and every day. He missed the familiar shape of his wife's body spooned against his in bed at night, and the little rituals that had made up the fabric of their daily lives, a life that felt more like a mass of pulled threads these days.

At the same time he wanted . . . he needed . . .

Angie.

He could see her in his mind's eye, a petite figure in chef whites and green Crocs, her molasses-brown hair pulled back in a ponytail and her cheeks flecked with more than freckles, darting about her stainless-steel prep kitchen, a marvel of efficiency as she alternated between chopping, mixing, tending to pans sizzling on the stove, or pulling pans from the oven. All without breaking a sweat or losing her cool. "Controlled chaos," she called it. She would cringe with embarrassment at so unglamorous an image being the one making him smile now, he knew.

It was agony not being able to see her, touch her, or even hear the sound of her voice over the phone. But he knew if he contacted her, there would be no chance of making things right with Camille. A chain was only as strong as its weakest link, and he didn't dare test the strength of this one, lest the chain snap. He wasn't ready to give up on his marriage. He still loved his wife. And if that love was more complicated, with more moving parts—some in need of fixing—he'd just have to work that much harder at repairing it.

He was glad for the distraction work provided. It was a relief, when he stepped out of the elevator on the seventh floor of the Harkness Pavilion, to find his interns clustered outside his office, awaiting his arrival. It was always slower going when he had interns, but he didn't mind. Their energy and enthusiasm was infectious. It reminded him of when he was an intern, in the Precambrian era of his own youthful enthusiasm.

He chose the most earnest of the bunch—a thin, intense woman named Lauren, who back in his day would have been labeled a "grind" but who, in these more enlightened times, was respected by and even looked up to by her peers—to assist with the first of his afternoon patients, a middle-aged woman who'd presented with a case of spastic hemiplegia. While Lauren carefully threaded the plastic tubing through the patient's nasal passage, under Dev's guidance, in preparation for the endoscopic evaluation, Edward lectured, "The area of the brainstem involved in the control of swallowing is located in the dorsal region, adjacent to the nucleus of the tractus solitarius and in the ventral area in and around the nucleus ambiguus . . ."

The rest of the day went by in a blur, though he remembered to check his watch frequently so as not to lose track of time. He was expecting his children that night for supper—they came twice a week—and wanted to be at home when they arrived, even though Kyra, who as the eldest was in charge, had her own set of keys. At five p.m. on the dot, he rode the elevator to the lobby, where the security guard at the front desk, a beefy ex-cop named Joe Rinaldo, called to him as he passed by on his way out, "Night, Doc. You take care now." Edward contemplated this as he pushed his way out the plate-glass door onto the sidewalk, pulling up the collar of his overcoat at the blast of cold air that met him. *Take care?* Wasn't it a little late for that?

He stopped at the Lucky Dragon on his way home to pick up the order he'd called in. It wasn't the best the neighborhood had to offer in terms of Chinese takeout, but it was only a block from his building and service was speedy. Besides, Zach never wanted anything more adventurous than barbecued spareribs and fried rice, and lately it seemed Kyra was always on a diet. Next time, he would have to stock up on groceries so he could fix them a proper meal. *Right*, said the cynical voice in his head. Didn't he say that each time?

The children showed up within minutes of his arrival. Kyra, slouching through the doorway with her backpack slung over one shoulder, Zach trailing after her wearing a glum look, a green rubber tail poking from a pocket of his North Face parka. "Whatcha got there, buddy?" Edward bent to catch the tip of the rubber tail between his thumb and forefinger.

"It's that stupid lizard of his," Kyra sneered. "I told him not to bring it, but he wouldn't listen."

The toy reptile in question was a souvenir from a trip to Cancún that Edward and Camille had taken years ago; they'd brought it back for then five-year-old Zach, who'd been inconsolable at their leaving. Zach treated the rubber lizard as if it were a live pet; he named it Chico and carried it with him everywhere, even taking it to bed with him each night. He stopped bringing it to school only after some of the other kids teased him about it. In recent years, Chico had lived in the closet in Zach's room, in a box with all the other toys Zach had outgrown but didn't have the heart to give away. The fact that Chico had been brought out of retirement must

mean Zach was feeling insecure. Edward felt a stab of guilt, knowing he was partly to blame.

Zach glared at his sister. "You're not the boss of me!"

Kyra gave their father a look that said, *You see what I have to put
up with?*

Edward hugged his son. "Hey, how about you, me, and Chico get
dinner on the table? Okay, buddy?"

Zach nodded glumly, muttering, "I hate her. She's mean."

"Come on, let's not have that kind of talk. What's with you guys,
anyway? You used to get along," Edward said as he led the way into
the galley kitchen off the living room. The takeout was being kept
warm in the oven; all that was left to do was set the table and make
the salad. Edward made it a point to serve fresh greens at every
meal; it was the least he could do.

While Zach was in the bathroom washing up, Kyra took the
opportunity to inform her father, "He's started wetting the bed
again, too. Mom had to put a rubber sheet on his mattress."

Zach had been a bed wetter as a small child. One day, when he
was six, he'd stopped and they'd all breathed a sigh of relief, thinking he'd outgrown it. Then after Camille was diagnosed with cancer the first time, he started again. It had been on and off ever since.
Edward felt a pang of sympathy for his son. "You used to wet the
bed, too," he reminded his daughter.

"Yeah, when I was *two*."

"Your brother's having a hard time right now. Try to be a little
more understanding." He pulled a head of lettuce, half a cucumber,
a red pepper, and a slightly shriveled tomato from the fridge.

"I *do* try, Dad, but why does he have to act like such a baby?"

Edward turned to face his daughter, placing his hands on her
shoulders. "Honey, I know you're upset, but don't take it out on your
brother. It's not his fault that I can't be with you all the time."

She bit her lip, her cheeks reddening. "Whose fault *is* it then?"

He felt another pang. *Mine*, he thought. *My fault.* If he hadn't moved out, this wouldn't be happening—his daughter wouldn't be acting like a brat or his son wetting the bed. Maybe he shouldn't have agreed so readily when Camille suggested it. He took Kyra's mutinous face in his hands. "Your mom and I are doing the best we can. It's not easy for us, either."

"Whatever." Kyra jerked free, and stomped off to set the table.

Edward decided to let it go. He didn't want these precious hours with his children to be just an endless cycle of them acting out and him scolding them. He was the adult; he needed to set the tone. Fortunately, Kyra and Zach had ceased their squabbling by the time they sat down to eat.

"What's this?" Zach poked suspiciously with his fork at the helping of cashew chicken on his plate.

"Try it. You'll like it," Edward coaxed.

"It has nuts in it." Zach pouted.

"You like nuts."

"Not *in* things."

"What do you think peanut butter's made of, butthead?" Kyra weighed in. She informed Edward, "That's practically all he eats at home—peanut-butter-and-jelly sandwiches. Sometimes he even puts marshmallows in them." She made a face. Then, in the lofty tone of a duchess deploring the crude manners of the peasantry, she said, "He really is the most disgusting child."

"You're just saying that 'cause all you eat is lettuce and stuff," Zach shot back. "It's true, Dad. She thinks she's fat." He sang out, "*Fatty, fatty two-by-four can't fit through the bathroom door!*"

Kyra's face reddened and her eyes welled with tears. She was the same healthy weight she'd always been, which probably wasn't thin enough to compete with the razor-bodied fashion models who set such unrealistic standards for girls these days. "You're not the least bit fat," he assured her.

She gave him a withering look. "That's what parents always say."

"Well, it happens to be true in your case."

"You don't know what it's like," she told him. "It's different than it was when you were my age. The boys at my school are . . ." She bit her lip and looked down.

"They're what?" he prompted.

"They say things," she choked out.

"What things?"

"You know. Stuff about girls."

"Any girls in particular?"

"Peter Karlinsky called Cassie Meyers a fat pig."

"Oh, I see. So, is Cassie Meyers a friend of yours?"

Kyra's head jerked up. "No, but she's the same size as me!"

Edward felt suddenly furious at this Peter Karlinsky, whom he'd never even met. "Boys are stupid," he said. At the indignant look Zach shot him, he reached over to ruffle his son's hair. "Present company excluded." If only he could shield his daughter from the agonies of adolescence! "Don't pay any attention. Boys only talk that way to cover up their own insecurities."

"What does he have to be insecure about? All the girls think he's hot."

"You'd be surprised," he said, recalling his own teenage years.

His daughter gave him a pitying look. "Dad," she said in the kindly tone she would use with someone who was dull-witted. "I know you're trying, but seriously, you *so* don't get it."

Edward decided she was right in one sense. There was a lot he didn't "get" when it came to his children. But he was making progress, if only in fits and bursts. He said a little prayer now. *Lord, is it too much to ask that we get through this one meal without tears?* Last time, it had been Zach crying because he'd burned his tongue on the moo shu pork that had been in the microwave too long.

"Eat," he ordered. If he didn't have all the answers, he could exercise his parental prerogative, at least. "You are *not* fat. You're beautiful, and I'm sure I'm not the only one who thinks so."

Kyra rolled her eyes but took a small a bite of her food.

"I don't think you're fat. I only said it to get back at you," Zach told his sister, giving her a smile of such transcendent sweetness, it brought tears to Edward's eyes. Kyra wasn't unmoved, either, though her way of showing it was to ball up her napkin and toss it at Zach, grinning.

After they'd finished eating and had washed up, Zach took a plate of reheated leftovers down to Henry, the doorman at the front desk that evening. Zach had gotten to know all the doormen in the building, but Henry, a young Jamaican with a smile for everyone and an infectious laugh, was his favorite. Henry always took time at the end of his shift, on the evenings the kids visited, to hang out with Zach in the break room for fifteen or twenty minutes before heading home.

Edward helped Kyra with her homework in the meantime, an assignment for algebra that was due the following day. They were sitting on the sofa in the living room, going over the equations, when she looked up at him and said, "Dad? Did you mean it when you said I was pretty?"

"I most certainly did." He bestowed a kiss to her forehead. "You don't believe me?" At the dubious look she gave him, he adopted a mysterious expression and waved his hands in the air like a fortune teller over a crystal ball. "I see boys . . . dozens of boys . . . all flocking around you. And you're . . . ah, yes, it's getting clearer now . . . *you're smiling.*" He grinned at her. "Now that is something I can't wait to see. You smiling again," he was quick to add. "The boys, not so much."

"Oh, Daddy." She dropped her head onto his shoulder. "I miss you," she said in the soft, little-girl voice he hadn't heard in a while. "I wish you could come home. It's not the same without you."

He swallowed hard. "I know, baby."

"Mom misses you, too."

"She told you that?"

"No, but I can tell."

Edward put a finger under his daughter's chin, tilting her head to meet his gaze. "Listen, honey, I don't want you worrying about your mom and me. We're doing our best to work this out, but whatever happens, one thing will never change. We'll always be there for you and your brother."

Kyra's expression remained clouded. "Yeah, but why does it have to be this way? When Nicole Gerber's parents split up, it was because they fought all the time. You and Mom don't fight."

"Not fighting isn't always a good thing. Sometimes it helps to clear the air."

"So it was just about you and mom not fighting?" Kyra looked confused.

"What I meant to say was, we didn't talk things out the way we should have."

"But now that you know what went wrong, you can fix it, right?" Kyra eyed him hopefully.

"It's not that simple," he said with a sigh.

Kyra dropped her gaze, staring unseeingly at the algebra book that lay open on her lap. "Yeah, but Dad?" She looked up at him with her big, brown eyes, which would one day break hearts and which right now were breaking his. "Just so you know, it totally sucks that Zach and I don't get a vote."

THE DOOR TO the townhouse, on East Sixty-Third Street, that housed the offices of Gabriella Santangelo, PhD, and Lorenzo Santangelo MEd, LMHC, was painted red. A shiny red-lipstick red that practically sang out, as Edward stood with his finger on the intercom buzzer, *Whatever's wrong, we can fix it! Don't despair, you're in good hands!* He was reminded of Dr. Stepanik, their family dentist when he was growing up, who'd practiced out of his South Side row house (the downstairs had been converted into offices, somewhere around the time of the Eisenhower administration, judging by its antiquated equipment) and who'd kept jar of suckers on his instrument cabinet for "good little boys and girls." The false optimism promised by the Santangelos' red door was like the suckers Dr. Stepanik used to hand out: It only ensured future visits.

He was let in by the housekeeper, a dour little mouse of a woman named Sofia who reminded him of women he had known growing up, neighbors and friends of his parents who'd been emotionally scarred by traumas suffered in whichever Soviet-bloc country they'd fled. She silently escorted him down the tiled hallway and up the curving staircase to the parlor floor, where the offices of Gabriella and her husband were situated, Gabriella's on the street side and her husband's overlooking the courtyard in back. The offices were separated by a center parlor, which served as a waiting area; solid oak pocket doors at either end ensured privacy. He knocked on the door to Gabriella's office, and she appeared a moment later to usher him in.

Stepping into the sunny front room, handsomely furnished in antiques, he saw that Camille had arrived ahead of him; she was seated in her usual spot, on the sofa by the fireplace where they always sat together during their sessions. She was more casually dressed than usual, in jeans and a teal sweater that brought out the blue of her eyes, and she looked so much like the girl who smote— there was no other word for it—him at first sight all those years ago, at Barney Greengrass, he broke into a smile. He couldn't help it. Camille smiled back.

He sat down, a polite distance from her but not so far as to seem hostile. "Sorry I'm late," he said, though a subsequent glance at his watch showed he was, in fact, right on time. Camille had gotten there early, which annoyed him for some reason. He felt, irrationally, as if he were being ganged up on.

The sofa faced the Eames chair where Dr. Santangelo normally sat, which at the moment was occupied by her pug, Chauncey. The therapist scooped him up and reclaimed her seat, placing him on her lap, where Chauncey settled with a grunt into his default position: that of canine cushion. Gabriella Santangelo was a slender, olive-skinned woman, in her late thirties or thereabouts, with glossy dark hair that fell in thick layers about her angular face, a prominent nose and large, gray-blue eyes that spoke of a quiet intelligence. She wasn't a beautiful woman, but she dressed beautifully—the way European women did, effortlessly it seemed. Today, she wore slim charcoal trousers and a cowl-neck sweater the creamy pink of a strawberry milk shake, an expensive-looking silk scarf artfully draped around her neck. Born in Italy and educated at Cambridge, she'd gotten her doctorate at Columbia University and done her clinical work under Hugh. She was the most talented of his protégées, he had said, and Edward had no reason to doubt that. The only thing he wondered was if Gabriella Santangelo had any idea what the outcome of these sessions would be. He hoped so, because he hadn't a clue.

"Camille and I were just discussing opera," Gabriella said. "She was telling me about the new production of *Tosca* at the Met. She says it's not to be missed."

"I've heard good things about it," he murmured. He didn't mention to the therapist, who was only making conversation, that he had ceded the remaining tickets of their season subscription to Camille. Though it was obvious Camille hadn't forgotten; she flicked him a glance, and he saw her cheeks redden. Was she sorry she hadn't insisted he take the tickets? Grateful that he'd offered them to her? Wishing they could have gone to see *Tosca* together? There was no way of knowing. His wife had become a mystery to him in many ways. "I'll have to see if I can get tickets for when my parents come to visit."

They were coming the week after next, for four days. Only, for the first time he was putting them up at a hotel. It would be awkward having them stay with Camille and the kids, he knew, and his place was too small. They were confused and upset enough as it was by the talk of separation and "needing time apart." Where they were from, a married couple stuck it out no matter what.

"Are your parents opera fans?" Gabriella asked.

"Not particularly, but it's still a treat for them." His parents' musical taste ran along the lines of show tunes and Lite FM. Edward's love of music, jazz in particular, came from his grandmother. When he was young, the two of them would play Nana Clara's old 78s on the stereo—Duke Ellington, Benny Goodman, Count Basie, Fats Waller—in the afternoons after school when his parents were at work. Edward smiled at the mental picture of his tiny grandmother "cutting the rug," as she called it, to the tune of Goodman's "Sing, Sing, Sing (with a Swing)."

"That will be nice for them, then. They must be looking forward to their visit."

"Yes," he said. "Very much so."

The therapist nodded thoughtfully. "Are you and your parents close?" Her low, faintly accented voice had a musical quality that was strangely mesmerizing. It was a moment before Edward realized they were on the clock; no more idle chitchat.

"I would say so, yes." He gave the expected response. The truth was a bit more complicated. He loved his parents, and he was a dutiful son. But was he close to them? No. As a boy, he'd blamed them for Nana Clara's death. He knew better now, but things were never the same between him and his parents after that. A sacred trust had been broken. As it had with him and Camille.

Gabriella stroked the buff-colored ball that was Chauncey, her eyes on Edward. Again, that conversational tone that wasn't just polite interest, he knew. "What was your childhood like?"

He shrugged, settling back on the sofa. "There's not much to tell. It was fairly ordinary." His dad worked at Miller Brewery for forty years until he retired and his mom had kept house for a family in Story Hill, he told her. "I was an only child," he said, and then hastened to add (because didn't therapists always look for the crack into which to drive their crowbar?), "My grandmother lived with us, though. So I wasn't a latchkey kid.

"She made sure I never sat idle, either," he went on. "If I didn't have homework, she'd put me to work hanging wet clothes out to dry or folding shirts." He explained that she used to take in laundry to help with the expenses, and a picture formed in his mind of Nana Clara, armed with a bottle of spray starch and a steam iron. "She never met a shirt collar she couldn't make stand at attention."

"Fond memories, then."

"Yes." In a softer voice, he added, "She died when I was thirteen."

"That must have been difficult."

"Very." He stopped himself before he could go on. It was still new to him, this business of airing his feelings. He'd been taught to "man up" before that expression was even coined. However, he was learning to open up—it was the one good thing to come out of these sessions. *Feelings aren't like fine wine, needing to age to the proper vintage,* Hugh had once told him. At the time, Edward had thought it just another Hugh-ism, but now he saw the wisdom in it—he felt lighter, more clearheaded after he'd unburdened himself. So he told the story of how his grandmother died. When he was finished, Camille was dabbing at her eyes—the same as when he had first told it to her, on their third date—and even Gabriella Santangelo did not appear unmoved.

"That was a brave thing to do," the therapist said.

He shrugged. "What good did it do in the end? I couldn't save her."

"So, you felt it was your responsibility?" Gabriella fixed him with a probing look.

Edward sighed. "I was thirteen." He looked down at the Oriental carpet on which his feet rested. It was old, threadbare in spots, its intricate pattern so familiar to him by now he could see it with his eyes shut. For the first time, he thought about the person who'd woven it—a person who had lived and breathed; who had been more than just a pair of skilled hands; a person who had had troubles of their own. Gabriella's voice floated like a hummingbird into his consciousness.

"Did you feel that way when Camille was sick, that it was your job to save her?"

Edward brought his head up. He looked at Camille, who eyed him expectantly. He chose his words carefully. "I did what any caring husband would do," he said.

"And that included honoring your wife's dying wish?"

Edward nodded his head slowly. "I thought it would help ease her mind."

"Even though you weren't happy about it?"

"Isn't that what marriage is about, making compromises?" An edge crept into his voice.

"Often, yes. But when it's something you're fundamentally opposed to, it can cause problems."

"All right. I wasn't too happy about it, no." He flexed his fingers to keep them from balling into fists.

"Is it fair to say you were angry, then?" They'd been over all this before, numerous times, but though Edward had learned to open up about other things—his past, his worries about his children, his difficulty understanding his wife—this was a briar patch into which he'd dared not venture too far. *Angry? You bet I'm angry. If you knew the extent of it, you'd be appalled.* It wasn't cancer that had ended life as he'd known it; it was Camille—her damn meddling, her supreme arrogance in thinking she knew him better than he knew himself. Now, though, he felt something shift inside him, clearing away whatever had been blocking him. Camille must have sensed it, because she shot him an anxious look as she sat stiffly upright, tense as a drawn bow. Even Chauncey lifted his head, ears pricked—with his flat, rumpled face and pointy ears, he looked like a canine Yoda.

414 · EILEEN GOUDGE

"Yeah, I was angry. Fuck yes." Edward swung around to face Camille. Normally, he didn't swear, so she looked startled. "You gave up! Not just on getting better, but on *us*."

Camille's eyes welled with tears. "I thought I was doing a good thing. I know now it was misguided," she said in a choked voice. "But at the time—" She broke off, shrinking into the sofa cushions. She looked small and lost. "I only wanted what was best for you and the children."

"The best? Is that what you call this? Christ. Look at us!" He could feel his anger expanding, filling his whole body until there was room for little else. "Or was that your *real* plan all along—to get rid of me?"

Tears spilled down her cheeks. Camille reached for the box of tissues on the piecrust table beside the sofa. Several such boxes were positioned strategically about the office. *They must buy them in bulk,* he thought. He pictured Dr. Santangelo and her husband pushing a shopping cart down the dry goods aisle at Costco, stocking up on enough Kleenex to absorb the miseries of the world.

"It wasn't like that," she protested. "I never stopped loving you."

"No," he said. "You just didn't think very highly of me."

"That's not true."

He shook his head slowly. "It was all part of the plan, wasn't it? You line up someone to help with the children and see to my every need, someone so perfect I'd barely even have to grieve once you were gone. Is that really how you saw me? Did you honestly think I was that shallow?"

"You cheated on me!" She sat up straight, her eyes flashing now with more than tears. "Goddamn you, Edward. Whatever I might have done to you, you got back at me ten times over!"

"I didn't do it to get back at you."

"No, what you did was worse. You fell in love," she choked out.

Edward blinked and sat back, his anger subsiding. What could he say? It was true.

Camille blew her nose into a tissue. Her eyes were swollen and bloodshot. When she was calmer, she went on, "She came to see me the other day. Angie. She wanted me to know it was over between you and her. In case I had any doubts." She fixed him with a questioning look.

Edward's mind reeled at the revelation. Angie had gone to see Camille? He felt something crumble in his chest. He knew what it must have taken for her to do that when she was hurting, too, and it made him love her all the more. "It *is* over," he said, but the words left a bitter taste in his mouth.

"But you're still in love with her."

"I didn't say that."

"You don't have to—I can see it on your face. Remember, it's what I do for a living. And I happen to be very good at my job." She gave a short, dry laugh as she helped herself to another Kleenex.

Edward was torn. He didn't wish to hurt her any further, but to be dishonest would defeat the purpose of these sessions, he knew. He recalled the look on Angie's face when they were standing on the sidewalk saying good-bye for the last time: It was the same look his wife wore now.

Camille echoed his thoughts. "If you love her, why are you here? Why aren't you with *her*? I want this to work, Edward, but you have to make up your mind. Is it going to be her or me?"

CHAPTER TWENTY-FIVE

As a child, Angie had loved holidays. Going on Easter egg hunts. Trick-or-treating on Halloween. Thanksgiving in all its bounty, and the tradition in her family, in lieu of prayer, of having each person at the table say what he or she was thankful for that year—such as Rosemary giving thanks, this past Thanksgiving, for the lump in her breast having turned out to be benign, and Susanne's husband, Dan, for making it through his first year of sobriety. "If it weren't for my AA meetings, I'd be half-crocked by now, so that's something for *you* all to be thankful for," he'd joked.

Christmas had been the most eagerly anticipated of the holidays in the D'Amato household. It began with the trip to Dart's Tree Farm, in Southold, the first weekend in December, to choose the perfect Douglas fir or Scotch pine, which was brought home roped to the top of the family station wagon. Then, there was the elaborate business of trimming the tree. It was Angie's dad's job to hang the lights, which mostly involved a lot of muttering under his breath as he sought to untangle the clumped strands. Angie's mom oversaw the stringing of the popcorn (a large quantity of which invariably ended up on the floor or in the girls' hair before the rest made its way onto the tree). Rosemary, as the eldest, had the honor of positioning the glass angel on the topmost branch; Francine supervised the hanging of the ornaments, and Julia the placement of the tinsel. Angie made gingerbread cookies, which they all decorated and then wrapped in cellophane and hung on the tree. The ensuing weeks brought whispered secrets, the crinkling of wrapping paper behind closed doors, holiday music playing endlessly on the stereo (which everyone bitched about but secretly enjoyed), Christmas cakes and cookies and mysterious packages arriving in the mail. Angie and her sisters took turns opening the cardboard windows on the Advent calendar, and sometimes a squabble would break out when someone "accidentally" took someone else's turn. Christmas Eve, they all went to Midnight Mass at Saint Dominic's. Then finally, Christmas morning, in all its raucous, sugarcoated, stocking-stuffed, gift-paper demolishing, glory, would arrive.

Now that they were grown and Angie's sisters had families of their own, Christmas was a more cumbersome affair. Angie typically spent the morning at Francine's, then made the rounds to her other sisters' houses throughout the day, before the entire family gathered for the annual holiday feast at Lou and Loretta's. Usually, Angie found it enjoyable, if exhausting, but this year her heart wasn't in it. She couldn't stop brooding about Edward. She imagined him reunited with his wife; he and Camille opening presents with their kids on Christmas morning. She wondered if he had any regrets. No, of course not. Why would he? He had everything he could possibly want.

Then, shortly before the first of the year, after making it her New Year's resolution to give up on men altogether, she met someone. It was at a rehearsal dinner hosted by the groom's parents, at their Park Avenue penthouse, that she was catering. One of the guests, a tall man around her age, caught her eye, initially because of his height, but at second glance she saw he was also quite attractive, with a lanky build, close-cropped dark hair, and hazel eyes with thick lashes a girl would envy. She'd clearly caught his attention, too, because over the course of the evening, as she and her staff ferried plates back and forth from the kitchen, she noticed him sneaking glances at her. Finally, as the other guests were leaving and she and her staff packing up the leftovers, he approached her.

"David Blum," he introduced himself, shaking her hand. "I just wanted to say the food was amazing. Best borscht I've had since my *bubbe* used to make it. You wouldn't happen to know her, would you? White hair, brown eyes, about yea high"—he held his hand at mid-chest level—"swears she'd never give out her secret recipe but who's susceptible to bribes in the form of sweets."

Angie laughed. "I know a lot of little old ladies. They always have the best recipes."

They chatted a few more minutes, and then David said as he was leaving, "Why don't you give me your card? I may have a job for you. Not right away, but . . ." His expression clouded over, and at the questioning look she gave him, he explained, "It's my dad—he's dying. You know the saying 'It's your funeral'? Well, with Dad it's not just an expression—he's got his all planned. The only thing left to do is hire the caterer. He's interviewed a few, but none were up to his standards. He wants someone who, quote unquote, won't insult his memory with bad food."

Angie didn't offer her sympathies. From David Blum's matter-of-fact tone, she guessed he'd had his fill of Hallmark-worthy sympathies. She only said, "Your dad sounds like my kind of guy."

David regarded her a moment, then said, "Thank you."

"For what? I haven't done anything yet."

"The last caterer Dad interviewed got so emotional, after he'd explained the circumstances, he ended up having to console *her*."

"Not very professional," Angie agreed. "Though in all fairness, it's the nature of the job. We're witness to the most important moments in people's lives, so it's hard not to get caught up in it to some degree. I confess to having shed a tear or two at weddings." She was thinking of one in particular. But the less she dwelled on *that* the better. "That said, if your dad wants to give me a call, I promise I won't subject him to any emotional outbursts."

David asked if she had any free time the following week to meet with him and his dad.

Angie, in addition to a packed schedule, was overseeing work on the new space, which was in full-on construction mode and had her shuttling back and forth to the Bowery between gigs, but she replied without hesitation, "Sure. How about Tuesday, at two?" She'd find the time, even if it meant getting up an hour earlier that day. How could she say no to a dying man?

Angie and the old man hit it off at once. Mendel Blum, who suffered from congestive heart disease, looked much older than his seventy-eight years, but his mind was still sharp. He was a violinist of some note, she learned: He'd played with the New York Philharmonic, for thirty-odd years, before he became ill. He was also a highly-educated man who'd read extensively and studied the Talmud in his youth. The three of them—Angie, Mendel, and David—chatted while sipping oolong tea and listening to a recording of Beethoven's Fifth performed by the Philharmonic. It wasn't until Angie's next visit that they even got around to discussing menu options.

Afterward, David took Angie to a wine bar around the corner from Mendel's Perry Street townhouse. Over a bottle of Pinot Gris, he told her more about his father's background. Angie learned that Mendel had come to this country as a young boy during World War II, just before the Nazis began rounding up Jews in Europe. When the war was over, he discovered that most of his family had died in the camps. It was a searing experience, and one that made him value his Jewish heritage all the more. His three children, David and his two sisters, had all attended Hebrew school, and their bar and bat mitzvahs had been a big deal, not just an excuse to throw a party.

"I wish I could say I was still observant. But these days, I only go to synagogue on High Holidays," David confided with a rueful shake of his head. "Dad doesn't know, so don't say anything. Oh, and you know those little crab things you served at the rehearsal dinner, the ones I told you I liked? Best not mention those, either."

"Your father keeps kosher?" This was a surprise to Angie. As far as she knew, only Orthodox Jews kept kosher, and no Orthodox Jew would dream of hiring anyone but a kosher caterer.

"No, we're Conservative," he said. "There are just certain things, like pork and shellfish, Dad considers *trayf.*"

"But you don't?"

David gave a wry grimace. She pictured him as the earnest bar mitzvah boy he'd once been, one who'd had every intention of fulfilling his father's expectations. *I'll bet he was a cute kid,* she thought. *Adorable but with moxie, like a child actor in a Neil Simon play.* "My downfall was college," he explained. "I didn't want to be different from the other kids, so I ate what they ate. After that, I was a goner. Now I can't imagine life without lobster rolls and BLTs."

"And you've kept it from your dad all this time?"

"I couldn't find a way to break it to him. Somehow the time was never right, and now . . ." He trailed off with a shrug.

"I imagine he has bigger concerns right now than whether or not his son has developed a taste for BLTs," she said gently. "But if it would put your mind at ease, you should tell him."

"You're right. In the larger scheme of things, it's probably not that big a deal." David smiled at her over the rim of his wineglass as he lifted it to his lips. He sat with his long legs stretched in front of him, his Tod's brushing her well-worn Weejuns under the table. He wore jeans and an off-white crewneck sweater with the sleeves pushed up over his tanned, muscular forearms. She decided it was a better look for him than the suit and tie he'd worn at the rehearsal dinner. "What about you—do you have any deep, dark secrets you're keeping from your parents?"

"No, sadly. I'm an open book." Thoughts of Edward crept in, and she resolutely shut her mind against them. "Though in high school, I did stuff that would've had me grounded for life if they'd known."

His eyes sparkled with amusement. "Ah, so you were one of *those* girls."

"Hardly. You had Hebrew school, I had catechism—we should compare notes sometime. If the thought of confession doesn't cut into your Saturday-night action, the threat of going to hell will. Though it was mostly just stupid teenage stuff—you know, drinking and partying, staying out past curfew. And, yeah, I did my share of fooling around." At David's raised eyebrow, she added with a laugh, "Not what you're thinking; it was pretty tame by today's standards. I was a 'good girl.' I was saving myself for marriage. Fortunately, that thinking didn't last, or right now you'd be talking to one of only ten thirty-nine-year-old virgins residing in the tristate area."

David chuckled, and refilled her glass. "You never thought about getting married?"

Angie shrugged and picked at a partially healed cut on her thumb, which she'd gotten slicing onions for a *soupe au pistou*. "Not really." The thought of Edward stole in once more, and once more she shut it out, this time double-bolting the door. "All I ever really wanted was to cook."

"Well, you've succeeded brilliantly at that." David leaned in to place a hand over hers, a friendly gesture that turned into something more when his hand stayed put, his thumb lightly stroking her knuckles. She felt a rippling sensation in her belly, which might have been pleasure or possibly just a case of nerves. "By the way," he said, "in case you hadn't noticed, my dad is pretty smitten with you. He told me as we were leaving tonight that if I didn't ask you out, he would."

Angie was flattered by David's attentions. But she wondered, *Am I ready for this?* It wasn't that she didn't find him attractive, but she was still picking her way through the rubble of her previous relationship. Did she want to put herself out there with someone else, risk getting hurt again? *Or hurting someone.* Because there was also the risk, with David, that she would end up breaking his heart.

She didn't get the same fluttery feeling with him that she had with Edward—this was a mere tremor compared to a full-scale earthquake. Which could be a good thing, she reasoned. At least she wouldn't be entering another potential disaster zone.

"He doesn't care that I'm not Jewish?" she said.

"Beggars can't be choosers," he said. Like her, David was the only one of his siblings who was still single. His two older sisters had each been married more than a decade.

"Gee, you really know how to make a girl feel special," she deadpanned, at which he broke into a grin. "Seriously, you think your father would have a problem with a BLT if it's okay for his son to go out with a shiksa? Isn't that like worrying about a leaky faucet when your house is under two feet of water?"

He chuckled, then his expression turned serious. "It's not a deal breaker," he said, "any more than being Jewish is an automatic shoo-in. I was once engaged to a woman who was Jewish—an Israeli Jew, who grew up on a kibbutz and spoke Hebrew—and Dad never took to her."

He told her about the former fiancée. Her name was Miriam. She and David had lived together for five years before getting engaged. They were in the midst of planning the wedding when Miriam was offered her dream job. The only problem was, the job was in Chicago and David didn't see himself relocating. So they broke the engagement, and she moved to Chicago without him. He was sad about it for a while, but had since concluded it was the right decision. "If I'd loved her enough, I'd have moved in a heartbeat," he said. "The fact that I wasn't willing said something."

"Has there been anyone since?" Angie kept her voice light.

"No one I was serious about. But when I found out my dad was dying, it was a wakeup call. My parents were married more than fifty years. Even with Mom gone, Dad still has those memories. I want that for myself, to be able to look back one day and know my life amounted to something more than climbing the corporate ladder. I'd like a family of my own. I think I'd make a good dad, though I may need some work as a husband—I've gotten kind of set in my ways," he added with a crooked grin, as if it had just occurred to him he might be coming on too strong.

Nonetheless, he'd made his intentions crystal-clear. And while part of her was flattered that he saw her as a potential wife, it was also cause for concern. Would it be fair to lead him on if she couldn't give it her all in returning his affections? She freed her hand from his, coughing into her fist so the move wouldn't seem deliberate. "Yeah, I can picture you sneaking contraband BLTs into your kids' lunch boxes," she teased, to lighten the mood. David laughed.

Most women would jump at what he was offering, she knew. He was a prime catch, and as her mom was forever reminding her, she wasn't getting any younger. She also liked David. Very much. She could grow to love him in time, couldn't she? So why was she holding back? It wasn't just because she had reservations about marriage in general. Her heart belonged to someone else.

Fuck that, she thought. She wasn't going to let Edward hold her heart hostage. She was taking it back.

The following weekend, David took her to a performance of the Miró Quartet at Carnegie Hall, and to a party at a friend's house the weekend after that. They fell into the habit of having dinner together at least once a week. She would cook for him at her place, or they would go to a restaurant. She also went to see his father every chance she got. Mendel was growing weaker by the day. A slight man even in his prime—in his den there was a framed 8 x 10 of Mendel posing next to Lennie Bernstein, in which he was dwarfed by the much taller man—he appeared swallowed up by the armchair in which he spent the majority of his waking hours. Only his eyes retained their sharpness; they were the jaunty blue of a flag snapping over a bombed-out building.

Mendel told stories of the famous musicians and composers he'd known—Lennie, Isaac Stern, Vladimir Horowitz, Shostakovich, to name a few—and of the Greenwich Village of his day, back when it was a gathering place for young artists and musicians. Angie always brought him something to tempt his flagging appetite, usually Jewish comfort food: potato or noodle kugel; *cholent,* slow-cooked in the oven overnight; *kasha varnishkes*; chicken soup with matzo balls.

"*Bubeleh,* you are to matzo balls what Lennie Bernstein was to music," he declared after tasting the soup.

She smiled. "I didn't know the two were even in the same universe, but thank you."

Mendel leaned in to whisper, "Now, if only you could get that *goyisher* son of mine to like matzo balls instead of the *trayf* he eats." The old man, it seemed, had been on to his wayward son for some time.

January slipped over into February, and then it was March. Almost four months since she'd last heard from Edward—he was officially out of her life. So why wasn't she taking it to the next level with David? Why did she continue to hold a part of herself in reserve? He was perfect for her: attentive without being overbearing; sensitive to her wants and needs. He laughed at her jokes and loved every inch of her in bed. *What's not to like?* as Mendel would say. And yes, she did *like* him. She just wasn't sure if she'd call it love. David, for his part, only refrained from using the "L" word, she suspected, because he'd sensed she wasn't ready to hear it.

He went from dropping hints to asking outright when she was going to introduce him to her family. "My mom would have the church booked before you had both feet in the door. Or synagogue— she doesn't discriminate," she would tell him. "The only thing she cares about is if you're solvent and have lively sperm." But the joke was wearing thin. Each time, she saw the question in his eyes.

Finally, she took him home to meet her parents. Angie's mom, predictably, was overjoyed. At the dinner table, Angie could see from the look on her face, she was already mentally making the seating arrangements for the wedding reception. Her dad was won over by the fact that David, a Princeton man, preferred drinking beer out of a bottle as opposed to a glass and was a diehard Mets fan. He also liked that David was in real estate—commercial real estate, to be exact. Her dad had a mistrust of what he called "paper" professions, such as finance or law, whereas real estate dealt in tangibles. Francine, who found an excuse to drop by while David was there, pronounced him "delicious." Angie, it seemed, was the only one with doubts.

He took her to dinner the following Saturday, at Marea. It didn't seem auspicious when he ordered a bottle of champagne. He'd just closed a deal with a Japanese retailer on a ten-thousand-square-foot space in Midtown, so naturally he wanted to celebrate. It wasn't until talk turned to the newlyweds, Geoff and Brenda, whom he'd had dinner with the night before, that she began to grow nervous. "We all thought Geoff would be the last to tie the knot," he said as they nibbled on the passion-fruit napoleon they were sharing for dessert. "We used to joke that he'd donate a kidney before he'd give up the bachelor life. Now I'm the last man standing. Though hopefully not for long."

With that, he withdrew a jeweler's box from his coat pocket, which he opened to reveal a diamond ring nestled in satin folds. "It was my mom's. Dad wanted me to have it. And I know nothing would make him happier than to see you wearing it." He cleared his throat, asking in a more formal voice, "Angie, will you marry me?"

Angie almost choked on the bite of food she was swallowing. She stared at the ring, dumbfounded. Finally, she managed to stammer, "David, I—I don't know what to say. It's . . . it's so sudden."

"I know," he said. "But I can't stop thinking about my dad. How much this would mean to him. Why not give him this last bit of happiness?" He took her hand, looking deep into her eyes. "Angie, I'm crazy about you. I know it must seem like I'm rushing into this, but you just know when something's right, and I've never been more sure about anything in my life. Dad knows it, too. He said, 'If you don't marry that girl, you're an even bigger *luftmentsh* than I thought.'" David plucked the ring from the box and held it out to her. "Don't you want to, at least, try it on?"

It was the most beautiful ring Angie had ever seen: a cushion-cut diamond flanked by smaller ones in a filigreed white-gold setting. She could see herself walking down the aisle with the ring on her finger, Mendel Blum looking on, beaming, as she and David exchanged vows at the altar, or under the chuppah, or wherever. Mendel's last wish realized. She blinked back tears, and before she knew it, she was holding out her hand. David slid the ring onto her finger. "It looks beautiful on you. Just as I knew it would," he said, bending to press his lips to her hand. She felt a rush of affection and some of the thrill her sisters must have felt when they got engaged.

"It's lovely." She turned her hand this way and that so the diamonds caught the light and sparkled. "And a perfect fit, I might add."

"I borrowed one of your rings to have it sized," he said.

"The silver one I thought I'd lost?" She narrowed her eyes at him. "You sneaky devil. How am I supposed to trust a guy who makes off with my belongings in the middle of the night?"

"Actually, it was broad daylight. You were in the shower." David broke into a grin. "Don't worry, you'll get it back. Unless, of course, it has sentimental value." In other words, a gift from a former boyfriend, said his arch look. "In which case, you'll find it at the bottom of the river."

"Bastard," she said, laughing.

"Should I take that as a yes?" He eyed her expectantly.

She studied him, taking in his hazel eyes with those ridiculously long lashes; his mouth that laughed at her jokes and kissed her tenderly and pleasured her in bed, and which right now flickered with a smile itching to break loose. She had no doubt he would make a good husband, but was she ready to be a wife? She returned the ring to its satin nest, saying, "I'm sorry, David, but I can't give you an answer right now. Don't take this the wrong way, because I care about you. Deeply. And you know I'd do anything for your dad. But I'm going to need a little more time."

His face fell, and she saw how crushed he was. But he quickly pulled himself together and said, "I was hoping for something more definite, but I understand. I know I'm jumping the gun." He flashed her a stalwart grin. "Kind of ironic, huh? The guy who waits till he's forty, then has an itchy trigger finger. It would help, though, if I had something more to go on than a 'maybe.'"

"Will this do for now?" Angie leaned across the table to kiss him—a deep, open-mouthed kiss. When they drew apart, other diners were staring and David was grinning from ear to ear. The thought of Edward flashed through her mind once more. But this time, the pain was tempered by a twisted sense of triumph. *You thought you were the one holding all the cards, but two can play at this game.* It was followed by a surge of guilt. She felt mean and childish. Also, what did it say about her feelings for David? She couldn't call what she felt for him love, not yet, but maybe it was something even better: the soil in which the seeds of a lasting relationship could be sowed. She smiled at him. "Tell your dad I don't think you're a *luftmentsh*, whatever that is."

THE NEXT MORNING, David called early with the sad but not unexpected news that his father had passed away, peacefully in his sleep. His voice was frayed but calm over the phone. Angie, choking back tears of her own, conveyed her heartfelt sympathy and asked if there was anything she could do. David thanked her, but told her no, the arrangements had all been made. The funeral, in accordance with Jewish custom, was set to take place two days hence. He asked only that she accompany him and his sisters, who were flying in from

California, to the synagogue the following evening to say Kaddish. "I know Dad would've wanted you there," he said.

The day of the funeral, Angie was also where she knew Mendel would want her to be: in the thick of final preparations for the reception—or "farewell bash," as the old man had dubbed it—to be held after the service. She slipped away just long enough to cab it over to the synagogue to hear the final prayers read before heading back to Mendel's sister's apartment, on Sutton place. At the synagogue, it had been standing room only, so she knew to expect a crowd. She would have to marshal all her forces. It was important to her, for personal as well as professional reasons, that Mendel Blum get the sendoff he deserved. With that in mind, she had Pat and Cleo inspect the linens, glassware, and cutlery, for any spots, tears, chips, or cracks; she put Stylianos to work checking the wine bottles for any loose corks. Tamika, in addition to her duties as kitchen helper, was given the job of keeping Mrs. Kaufman's teacup poodle, Nibs, who had been underfoot all morning, yapping his head off and nipping at everyone's ankles, from being trampled (possibly on purpose). Tamika solved the problem by tucking the poodle into her apron pocket, where he immediately quieted, content as a baby in a Bjorn.

Before long, people began pouring in: friends and relatives of Mendel's, including several cousins from Israel and a niece and nephew from France; fellow musicians and former students; people with whom he'd become friendly through the charitable organizations he'd been active in; the private-duty nurses who'd tended to him at the end. The apartment, in a prewar building, was spacious enough to stage a hockey tournament, but with so many people, it quickly became jammed. Angie only caught glimpses of David from time to time. He looked solemn and dignified in his dark suit and yarmulke as he acquitted his duties as host, along with his sisters, Ruth and Sophie. (Their elderly aunt was too addled by grief to do more than drift aimlessly about.) He was the earnest bar mitzvah boy all grown up.

Angie had taken at once to David's sisters, when she'd met them the night before last. They were both tall like him, with the same winning smile, though the similarities ended there. Ruth, a women's studies professor at UCSB, was plain and seemed to prefer it that way; she accentuated her plainness the way women like Angie's sister Julia did their beauty. Sophie, a professional photographer, was cuter and fluffier—literally; she had a bush of curly hair that David teasingly called her Jew-fro. Neither had asked what Angie, a stranger, was doing at the synagogue the night she came to say Kaddish with the family. She was with their beloved brother so they had embraced her as one of their own. Which only made Angie feel guiltier about being a . . . what had Mendel called it? A *luftmentsh.* A not-nice person. The kind of person who'd keep a wonderful guy like David on tenterhooks, especially when he was in mourning for his father.

It was an hour or more before David caught up with her. Angie was in the kitchen, sprinkling chopped chives over a platter of Russ & Daughters nova, wafer-thin slices wrapped around a stuffing of horseradish cream cheese (a favorite treat of Mendel's). He pulled her close for a quick kiss. "You," he said, "are amazing. Everything is perfect. I can't thank you enough."

"No thanks necessary, but gratuities gratefully accepted," she said, and then added on a more serious note, "Look, I'd have done this for free. Your dad was special. I just wish I'd had time to get to know him better." She cleared her throat, which had grown tight.

From the dining room and parlor drifted the sounds of lively conversation as those who'd gathered to pay their respects told stories about the old man. Earlier, one of the Israeli cousins, a former member of the Knesset, had spoken movingly about the time Mendel traveled to Jerusalem with the Philharmonic to play for an audience of Holocaust survivors, one of whom was from Mendel's native village in Poland, it turned out. Others spoke of the good deeds Mendel had done in his lifetime, in particular his generosity toward up-and-coming musicians, many of whom he'd mentored. One of those mentees, Reuben Diaz, now an accomplished violinist in his own right, had paid tribute at the funeral by playing a piece he'd composed in Mendel's honor.

"He thought you were pretty special, too." David's eyes searched her face, and she saw the question in them. She needed to give him an answer, soon, but they hadn't had a moment alone together since his father's passing. And an opportunity for them to talk in private wasn't likely to present itself in the days to come. David and his sisters would be sitting shiva, at their father's.

"I think it had more to do with my matzo balls than my winning personality," she said.

David smiled and cupped her face in his hands. He ran his thumb under her eye to catch the tear trembling on her lower lid. His voice was raspy from fielding condolences all day. "You know what my father would have said to that? *'Buba,* you are so much more than your matzo balls.'"

"Yeah, I make a mean kugel, too."

"Listen, what do you say we go out for a drink when this is over? Just the two of us."

More than anything, Angie wanted to go home and put her feet up when this was over, but she couldn't refuse. Not today, of all days. Besides, she knew it wasn't just time alone with her he wanted. So she put on a smile. "Just what the doctor ordered," she said, then groaned inwardly. A Freudian slip? Perhaps. But the last thing she needed right now was to be reminded of Edward.

GRAY SKIES GREETED Edward as his plane taxied onto the runway at JFK later that day. He was exhausted and in a foul mood. He'd flown to Boston earlier in the day, where he'd been a guest lecturer at Harvard Medical School, but the return flight was delayed due to stormy weather. It had meant cooling his heels at Logan Airport for two hours before the plane finally boarded, and it was closing in on four p.m. by the time he disembarked at JFK ninety minutes later.

He was in an even fouler mood by the time he emerged from baggage claim, having run interference with fellow passengers weaving in and out of his path and creating roadblocks with their mounds of luggage. He collapsed gratefully into the backseat of the hired Town Car that was waiting for him at the curb. It almost made up for the fact that he was going home to an empty apartment. He gazed unseeingly out the window as the car eased into traffic and onto the exit ramp.

He was thinking about Angie. All day, memories of her had been playing in his head like the continuous loop on the airport TVs. It had started when he was at the podium giving his lecture. A petite, dark-haired woman (one of the professors?) standing in back had caught his eye, and with the lights dimmed for his PowerPoint presentation, she looked at first glance like Angie. So much so, it had given him a start. He became flustered and lost track of what he was saying and had to pause to shuffle through his notes, his heart pounding so hard he half expected to hear it, amplified by the mike clipped to his lapel, reverberating throughout the packed lecture hall.

It wasn't the first time he'd been thrown by a false sighting. Occasionally, he'd catch a glimpse of a dark, ponytailed head in a crowd, or that of a diminutive figure striding jauntily ahead of him along a sidewalk, and his pulse would start to race. Then the woman would turn her head or he'd catch up with her, and he'd see she wasn't Angie. Sometimes it was memories that ambushed him. He'd be going about his business and out of the blue an image would surface. Angie naked, a freckle-faced odalisque . . . or in the kitchen throwing together an elaborate meal as casually as if it were mac and cheese out of a box . . . or at the farmers' market pondering which head of radicchio to buy as if the fate of the world rested on the decision. In those moments, his heart would seize in his chest and he'd say to himself, *You're a damn fool. You wasted precious time trying to fix something that was broken beyond repair, and now you have nothing.*

There was no question of it now. After months of therapy, he and Camille had finally called it quits. The weekend of her father's wedding was the final blow. Edward arrived at his father-in-law's, on Friday, to find that he and Camille, who'd flown down a day earlier with the children, were expected to share the guestroom. (The children were sleeping in the sunroom.) It seemed she had neglected to inform her dad that they were no longer living together. Her excuse was that she'd wanted to wait until after the wedding so as not to cast a pall, but Edward suspected it was because she hadn't quite come to terms with it. They argued about it, and then spent a miserable night with their backs to each other, huddled on their respective sides of the bed. When he awoke the next morning, it was with a crick in his neck and a pit in his stomach, knowing it was over. Camille knew it, too; he saw it in her eyes.

While everyone else was still asleep, they went outside to discuss it, in a civilized fashion, over their morning coffee. "I don't want it to get nasty," she said. "I can bear anything but that."

"There's no reason for it to get nasty," he said.

"You say that now, but once lawyers get involved . . ."

"It's up to *us*, not the lawyers." They sat on the patio, which was fenced in by stone walls down which spilled rivers of bougainvillea and lantana, a lush display that seemed almost indecent in light of what they were discussing. Edward reached across the gap between their two chairs to take her hand. "We've made it this far without tearing each other apart. Don't you think we can make it the rest of the way?"

She gazed unseeingly into the middle distance. The sun was coming up. In Florida, the sun didn't just rise, it announced itself with fanfare: an array of scarlet and pink and gold that formed a showy backdrop against the palm trees that ringed the golf course on the other side of the walled patio. A mild breeze was blowing, carrying the scent of gardenias. Another beautiful day in sunny Fort Lauderdale. Soon the others would be up and about. Larry would conscript him and Curtis for a game of golf. Camille and Holly, Lillian and her daughters, would embark on preparations for the wedding feast. His kids and Lillian's grandchildren would head for the pool. But at the moment, as he sat watching the sun come up, his only thought was how ironic it was that his marriage was ending, not with a bang, but on a quiet morning with the promise of clear skies.

"Do you remember the first time I brought you home to meet my dad?" Camille turned to face him, wearing a faint smile. "I was so worried you wouldn't like him or that he wouldn't like you." She cast a wry glance in the direction of Lillian's unit, where Larry and Lillian were presumably still asleep. (Larry had ceded the master bedroom in his unit to Holly and Curtis and the baby.) "Instead, the two of you got on like a house on fire, and I ended up feeling a little left out."

Edward smiled at the memory. "We talked golf most of the evening, as I recall. I remember being grateful for the summer I caddied at the Sargents' club." The Sargents were the family his mom had kept house for. When Edward was sixteen, Mr. Sargent had gotten him the job at the club. Good thing, and not just because of the money he'd earned toward college. Years later, meeting Camille's father for the first time, he'd have had precious little to talk about otherwise.

"I used to wonder what you saw in my dad that I didn't. I get it now, but back then . . . ?" She shrugged.

He reflected on their twenty years of marriage. At times, it seemed like only yesterday that he'd first seen her, sitting at the table he later came to think of as "their" table at Barney Greengrass, a blaze of autumn colors. At other times, it felt as if an epoch had passed, with all the seismic shifts, triumphs, and tumults of history books. "It's been quite a ride, hasn't it?" he said.

"Yes, and look where we ended up—the breakdown lane." She gave a low, choked laugh.

They sat in silence, reflecting on this as they sipped their coffee, serenaded by the chattering of birds. Edward heard a distant *thwock* and looked up to see a golf ball go sailing up and up over the trees bordering the eighth green. He was struck once more by the wrongness of this picture. How could his marriage be ending in this peaceful setting on someone else's wedding day?

He brought his gaze back to Camille. "When should we break it to the kids?"

"We'll wait until they get back," she said. "I don't want it to spoil their visit with Dad and Lil."

He nodded. "And Holly?"

"I'm pretty sure she already knows."

Edward hoped his sister-in-law wouldn't feel she had to take sides, because there was no question which side she would be on. The bond with Camille was unshakable, and whereas Holly was deeply fond of him, he knew, he was no longer the go-to guy in her life. She had Curtis now. And the baby, who he could hear whimpering inside; whimpers that would soon be full-bore cries. Camille heard it, too, and rose to her feet with a sigh. "Well, so much for relaxing on the patio and reading the morning paper." She eyed his empty mug. "More coffee?"

Edward was taken aback by her calm demeanor. How could she not be as heartsick as he was? Then something caught her eye, and she turned her head. In the sunlight that angled across her face, he could see tears pooled in her eyes, glittering like broken glass. He understood then: She was hanging on to the familiar language and rhythms in order to keep from falling apart.

Had he known, deep down, all along there would be no putting

Humpty Dumpty back together again? Probably, if he was honest about it. But he'd had to try, for the children's sake and because he and Camille still cared for each other. That hadn't changed. However angry or frustrated he became, his first impulse always was to protect her. Even when he was the source of her pain.

But divorce? Jesus. He'd never imagined it would be this hard. He came home from work each night to an empty apartment. He ate alone when he didn't have his children over or wasn't dining out with friends. He slept in his brand-new, king-size bed that had been luxurious to stretch out on in the showroom but that now felt like an ice floe on which he was stranded each night. To make matters worse, he had to muddle through knowing he'd lost Angie as surely as he had Camille. Countless times he'd picked up the phone, only to have the call go unplaced. What would he say? Would she even want to hear from him after all this time?

He didn't regret having done what he could to save his marriage. He wouldn't have been able to live with himself otherwise. He didn't even see it as a failed attempt—nothing could have saved his marriage, he realized now. What killed him was that it had cost him so dearly. He couldn't just pick up where he'd left off with Angie. *She'd tell me to take a hike, and to be sure my boots were laced tight because it was going to be a* long *one.*

On impulse, he leaned in as the car was approaching the Midtown Tunnel. "Driver? Change of plans." *This is insane, you know that?* said a voice in his head even as he rattled off Angie's address. Who knew if she was even home? But it wouldn't have the same impact if he were to phone her instead. There was no substitute for telling a woman face-to-face how much you've missed her. Even if he was almost sure to be rebuffed.

Twenty minutes later, the car pulled up in front of Angie's building. As Edward go out, his heart was pounding and his throat felt dry despite the bottle of water he'd sucked down on the way there. He instructed the driver to wait, then bounded up the stone steps to the entrance and pressed a button on the intercom. He waited a minute, and when there was no response, jammed the heel of his hand down on the whole row of buttons. Moments later, the buzzer sounded and he was inside. A bearded young man emerged from the first door on his left. "Dude. If you're looking for Angie, she's not here."

Edward recognized him as the guy who'd let him in the first time, and who right now probably was wondering if he was in the habit of dropping by unannounced, or just desperate. Edward had encountered him on several other occasions.

"Do you know where I might be able to find her?" He was careful to strike an even, relaxed tone. He didn't want to sound like some crazed ex-boyfriend.

The bearded man shrugged. "I dunno. She said something about a funeral."

"A funeral?"

"Yeah, some rich old dude. It made today's obits. That's all I know."

Edward thanked him and returned to the car. Fortunately, he'd kept the copy of the *Times* that he'd picked up at the airport. Now he scanned the obituary section. Only three of the deceased warranted a full column. Two were women: a prominent civil rights attorney, and a former state assemblywoman. The third was a man named Mendel Blum, a violinist who'd played with the New York Philharmonic and who'd succumbed, at the age of seventy-eight, to some unspecified illness; he was survived by a son and two daughters. Edward phoned the number for the synagogue and a pleasant-sounding female voice provided him with an address for the reception.

Fifteen minutes later, he was dropped off in front of a building on Sutton Place, one of the beautifully preserved prewars that looked out on the East River. The concierge, an older man with a head of thick, snow-white hair and ruddy cheeks, took one look at Edward in his suit and tie and said, "Twenty-eight C, right? You're a little late. Most folks've already left." He shook his head in sympathy. "Sad about Mr. Blum. Helluva nice guy. Poor Mrs. Kaufman, she's really broken up about it."

Edward hadn't given much thought until now to the bereaved family; he was so intent on finding Angie. It made no sense, this urgency he felt—it wasn't as if she were leaving the country tomorrow for an extended period of time (at least, he hoped not)—but he had the strangest feeling that if he delayed any longer he'd be too late. Still, he couldn't just go blundering in. He didn't want to be disrespectful. Besides, he didn't know if she was even still at the reception, or if she'd agree to meet with him under any circumstances. All he knew was that he had to see her. He fished his cell phone from his pocket and dialed her number.

THEY WERE IN the kitchen, where Angie and Tamika were cleaning up after the reception, while Pat, Cleo and Stylianos loaded up the van. On the other side of the dining room that separated the kitchen from the front room, Angie could hear the sounds of David's sisters seeing out the last of the guests. "I have just one question," David said. For a panicky second, she thought he was referring to *the* question before he asked, "How did you get the latkes to stay so crispy?"

She eased the air from her lungs. "Baking powder," she told him. "I'm glad you liked them."

"I liked everything."

"Apparently, you weren't the only one," she said. "I was worried we'd run out at one point." Good thing she'd made extra of the chicken and pasta salads. She'd learned from past experience that, however counterintuitive, there was something about funerals that made people ravenous.

"It was the perfect amount," David said.

She shrugged. "It's like with the loaves and the fish—somehow there's always enough to go around."

"That reminds me," David said, "My nephew Ethan has a bar mitzvah coming up. The twenty-fourth of next month. Ruth wants to know if you can come. Any chance you can get away then?"

"I don't know," Angie hedged. "I'll have to check my schedule." She felt guilty for not telling him outright: She wouldn't be attending any more Blum family events. There was no future with David. After much thought, she had decided it would be wrong to marry a man she didn't love, even one she would almost surely grow to love in time. Now she had the regrettable task of having to break it to him. Though this was neither the time nor the place—she'd wait until they were alone.

". . . it's not the Ritz, but it has a view of the ocean." Angie tuned in to hear him say. She realized he'd been talking the whole time she'd been lost in thought. "I booked a double, just in case. We could stay at Ruth's, but it would be a bit crowded, with the four of them plus Aunt Esther."

"Your aunt Esther will be there?" she said, making conversation.

"That's the plan. Though, who knows?" He dropped his voice, glancing over his shoulder as if to make sure his aunt wasn't within earshot. "You may have noticed she's a little out of it."

"Understandable under the circumstances."

"It's not just because of Dad," he said. "She's been pretty vague lately. Ruth's been after her to hire a companion, but Aunt Esther won't hear of it. She values her independence too much. Which, by the way, doesn't stop her from calling Ruth half-a-dozen times a day. Poor Ruth. She spends more time on the phone with Aunt Esther than she ever did with either of our parents."

"Your aunt doesn't have children of her own?"

"No. She was widowed at a young age and never remarried. She said she could never find anyone as wonderful as Uncle Harvey. He was her one and only."

A shudder went through Angie. *That could be me in fifty years,* she thought. Still pining over her One and Only. "That kind of certainty comes but once in a lifetime." The words slipped out before she realized what she was saying. Oh, God. Had she really just quoted from *The Bridges of Madison County*? To David, of all people! She must be losing it, herself.

David, clearly misinterpreting, grinned at her: a tall drink of water lounging in the doorway, his yarmulke, blue embroidered with silver threads, askew on his head from his having been hugged by a million people. Damn. Would she ever learn to watch her mouth? "I couldn't agree with you more," he said.

Angie didn't respond.

She went into the butler's pantry to put away the silver she'd washed. The butler's pantry was one of the things she loved best about these old prewars. This one was bigger than her kitchen at home; it had enough storage space to hold place settings for several dozen. Its glass-front cabinets were made of solid walnut and its drawers lined with felt, with slots to separate the various utensils. It had its own sink, with the original brass spigots. She loved how it smelled, too—of Lemon Pledge and the lavender water used in ironing the linens. (Mrs. Kaufman's housekeeper, an older Haitian lady named Eugénie, had been on hand to help out today and she'd shared some of her housecleaning tips.) When the last serving spoon was tucked in its drawer, Angie turned to go. Only to come face-to-face with David. He drew her into his arms.

"I was thinking we could make the announcement when we're in California," he murmured into her hair. Their "engagement" was clearly a foregone conclusion in his mind. And why not? Hadn't she led him to believe her answer would be yes? She had been there for him throughout this ordeal; she'd said Kaddish with him and his sisters; she'd held his hand, earlier, at the synagogue; and to cap it off, she'd just quoted from *The Bridges of Madison County*. What was he supposed to think? "It'll be the perfect time—my whole family will be there."

Angie's heart sank. But she couldn't break it to him here, not with his sisters and aunt in the next room. She had to stall him a little longer. So she only said, "Let's talk about it later, okay?" He smiled as if it were a done deal, which made her feel even guiltier.

Minutes later, her cell phone rang.

EDWARD DRANK IN the sight of her. He felt as if he'd been trapped for weeks in a dark chamber and a door had been flung open, letting in fresh air and sunlight. She wore a dark blue dress and black wool cardigan, low-heeled black pumps, a single strand of pearls around her neck—more conservative attire than he was used to seeing her in. But she was still the same Angie, her hair in a ponytail and freckles showing on her unmade-up face. A face that at the moment was a mask of fury.

"You've got some nerve," she said as she stood facing him, in the frozen food aisle of the D'Agostino at the corner of First and Fifty-Sixth. When she'd met him in the lobby of the building where the reception was being held, they hadn't lingered; she'd gestured, stone-faced, for him to follow her and then had stalked ahead of him down the sidewalk before ducking into the first establishment they came to. It seemed fitting somehow that it was a supermarket: a reflection of their unorthodox relationship. "What the hell did you think were you doing, showing up like that?"

"I needed to see you," he told her.

"Now? I'm on a job! Which you'd have known if you'd bothered to call in advance." If the look she was giving him could cause hypothermia, her voice was an ice pick chipping at his confidence.

"I admit my timing could have been better," he said.

"No shit."

He felt the last of his confidence drain away. He hadn't thought this through, no. Nor had he given her fair warning. She had every right to be upset. "I'm sorry if I caught you at a bad time."

"You couldn't have picked a *worse* time. I'm dealing with a bereaved family here."

"Yes, I know. I'm sorry for their loss."

"And this is how you pay your respects? God only knows what Dav—what the family must think, me running out on them like that." An older, henna-haired lady pushing a grocery cart eyed them curiously. *We must look like a married couple having a spat,* Edward thought. Perhaps about what to have for dinner or over a credit card that had been maxed out. "So, what the hell was so important it couldn't wait?" Angie whispered furiously after the woman had passed them.

"Camille and I are getting a divorce," he blurted, and then winced inwardly. That had come out wrong. He'd meant to begin by telling Angie how much he'd missed her; that he hadn't stopped thinking about her since they'd parted. Instead, stupidly, he'd made it about him and his wife.

Surprise registered briefly on Angie's face. Her eyes widened, and a flush rode up her cheekbones. Then her expression hardened again. "*That's* what you came to tell me?"

"Partly, yes. But . . ." The look on her face stopped him before he could finish the sentence. How could he tell her the rest, what was in his heart, with her looking at him like that?

Angie carried her jacket folded over her arm—her hunter-green North Face parka with the fur-trimmed hood. She put it back on, as if she'd heard enough, and he was gripped with panic. "Wait." He placed his hand over hers as she wrestled with the zipper. She jerked back as if stung.

"Look, I'm sorry things didn't work out for you," she snapped. "But here's a news flash: I've moved on."

"At least, let me explain." Edward started toward her, but she took another step back.

"I get it." She spoke through gritted teeth. "I was Plan B, right? If you couldn't patch it up with Camille, you'd still have me. What, did you think all you had to do was snap your fingers for me to come running?" She was so angry, she was quivering. The old lady pushing the grocery cart paused as she was opening one of the freezer cases, to stare at them. Clearly, they were arguing about something more than a roast versus chops.

"I didn't think of you that way," he said, imploring her with his eyes.

"No, I guess not, because clearly you weren't thinking of me at all. Or you would have called. I don't hear from you in months, *not one frigging word.* I have to find out from some random person at a party that you and your wife are separated. Jesus. Do you know how that made me feel?"

"I knew if I called you, it wouldn't stop at that," he said, but the explanation sounded feeble to his ears.

"I see." Her eyes flashed. "So once again you were only thinking of yourself."

"Camille and I were in counseling at the time." He felt a stab of regret at the mention of his wife, like the phantom pain from an amputated limb, and then it was gone. He would always love Camille, but he was no longer *in* love with her. The woman to whom his heart belonged, and who held his fate in her hands, was standing before him now. "I had to see it through, to be fair."

"What about being fair to me? The least you could've done was drop me a line."

"You're right. I should have. I'm sorry," he said. The cold air had seeped through his overcoat; he felt chilled to the bone. "If you give me another chance, I promise I'll make it up to you."

"It's too late for that. I'm seeing someone." She lifted her chin in defiance.

He'd feared as much—a woman as vibrant as Angie wasn't going to sit around waiting for a man who couldn't make up his mind— but still, it caught him off-guard, knocking the wind out of him. He felt as if he'd been sucker-punched. "Is it serious?" he asked, finally.

"He's asked me to marry him."

Edward blinked, and a black hole opened inside him. "And?"

"I haven't given him an answer yet." Her voice softened the tiniest bit.

Time stood still. He could feel a pulse thudding at the base of his throat. Every detail of his surroundings seemed magnified: the flickering of the overhead fluorescents; the music coming from the sound system—Carly Simon singing "You're So Vain"—the rows of packaged goods inside the freezer case against which Angie stood, with her parka gaping open and her arms hanging at her sides. Finally, in a voice he scarcely recognized as his own, he choked out, "Don't. If you really love this guy, I won't stand in the way. I promise you'll never hear from me again." *Even if it kills me.* "But if you have any feelings for me at all, for God's sake *don't*."

She studied him as if not quite knowing what to make of his words. The flintiness had gone out of her expression, but he heard the challenge in her voice when she asked, "And if I tell him no? What then?"

Edward's gaze locked onto hers. This was his one chance, and he couldn't screw it up. This time, he wouldn't back away from his feelings. He wouldn't come at it sideways or present some watered-down version. "I love you, Angie. I never stop missing you, not for one second." This time, he didn't bother to keep his voice down. "I know I handled it badly, and I'm sorry." Out of the corner of his eye, he saw the henna-haired lady staring openly now. He'd drawn attention from other shoppers as well. He didn't care. So what if he made a fool of himself? There were worse things. "Just give me another chance. That's all I'm asking. I'll do everything in my power to make sure you don't regret it."

Angie was staring, too, and for a heart-stopping moment, when she muttered, "Damn you," he was sure he'd blown it. Then she took a jerky step forward, as if being tugged against her will, and with a choked cry fell into his arms. He hugged her hard, filling his lungs with her scent. "Don't look now," she whispered, "but everyone's looking at us like we're the two-for-one special."

"Then let's give them their money's worth." He tugged the elastic band from her ponytail, forking his fingers through her hair as it tumbled down around her shoulders. Then, her face cupped in his hands, he kissed her. He kissed her as if he'd been born for the sole purpose of doing just that.

They drew apart to the sound of applause. A pair of young women hooted in approval. A balding, middle-aged man lifted a pint of ice cream in a wordless toast. Even the old lady who'd been looking at them askance was smiling.

They held hands as he walked her back to the building. The light had faded from the sky, and shadows were pooled in the recesses of buildings. Spring was just around the corner, playing hide-and-go-seek—snow flurries one day, mild temperatures the next. Today it was cloudy and cold. Not that Edward noticed; they might have been strolling on a tropical beach to which they'd been magically transported.

"So, this Mr. Blum, how did he die?" he asked.

Angie tilted her head to smile at him, her face lit by the glow of the street lamp they were passing under. "You're asking the wrong question," she said. "The question is, how did he live?"

CHAPTER TWENTY-SIX

Six Months Later

"Hold still. Let me see if I can fix it." Camille frowned in concentration as she tugged at the zipper on Kyra's dress. Her fingers felt thick and clumsy, as if she'd spent the past hour shoveling snow on this bright summer day instead of getting the kids ready. *It's not just this zipper that's stuck.*

Relax. Take a deep breath. You can do this, she told herself.

She wrestled with the zipper, and after freeing it from the piece of fabric it was caught on, guided it up the back of the pink satin bodice. "There. Now turn around so I can see." Kyra dutifully swiveled to face her. "Oh, honey." Camille's eyes filled with tears. "I don't know when I've seen such a beautiful bridesmaid. You look"—she was about to say *so grown up,* but caught herself. Kyra didn't like being reminded that she was only fifteen—"absolutely stunning."

"You don't think this dress makes me look fat?" Kyra padded in her stockinged feet to the full-length mirror on her closet door, scowling at her reflection as if squaring off against a rival. She tugged at the skirt that flowed in gossamer layers from the fitted empire bodice, over hips so gloriously narrow it was enough to make a grown woman weep. Camille knew she'd never be that lithe or firm-fleshed again, no matter how many hours she spent at the gym.

"Sweetie, you wouldn't look fat in a flour sack."

"Mom. Be serious." Kyra cast her a reproachful look.

"I *am* being serious. You look gorgeous."

Kyra's frown deepened. "I weighed myself this morning. I've gained two whole pounds!"

"So? You're still growing."

"That's what you always say."

"Only because it's the truth. Ask your dad if you don't believe me." At the mention of her ex-husband, she felt herself start to come undone and quickly reined in her emotions. She didn't want to spoil this day for her children. "Now, do you think you can manage the rest on your own?" The only thing left for her to do was slip into her shoes. "I'd better go see how your brother's doing." For some reason, Zach had balked when she'd gone to pin the boutonniere on his lapel.

She found her son sitting on his bed where she'd left him, wearing a glum expression. He looked handsome in his groomsman suit and, like her daughter, more adult than Camille was entirely comfortable with. His hair glistened from all the gel he'd gooped on, to give it that precise messy look. He'd never paid much attention to his appearance until recently, but since he'd started noticing girls, she'd been buying hair gel and antiperspirant in economy-size jars and spray cans. Next it would be shaving cream and condoms. *Would you please stop growing?* she wanted to command. Though right now, he was acting more like a five-year-old.

"I'm not wearing it," he insisted, glaring at the florist's box on his dresser as if it contained hazardous material and not an inoffensive sprig of white freesia. "It's stupid."

"Why is it stupid?" she asked.

"It just is."

"The other groomsmen will all be wearing theirs."

"That's different—they're older."

"I don't see why that should make a difference," she said, using her let's-not-have-any-more-of-this-nonsense voice. She marched over to the dresser and withdrew the boutonniere from its box. She bent to pin it to his lapel, but was stopped short by the look on his face, which was more miserable than mutinous. Concerned, she asked, "Sweetie, what is it? Are you upset about Dad?"

When he didn't answer, she knew she'd guessed right: Zach couldn't talk about what was really bothering him, so he was making a big deal out of nothing. He pushed out his lower lip, squinting hard as if to keep from crying. "I showed it to Colby," he said. Colby Jenkins was a friend from school who lived in their building; he'd stopped by earlier to visit with Zach. "He said it was *gay.*"

"Well, that's just silly. I don't know why anyone would say such a thing." She refrained from adding that there was nothing wrong with being gay—for a fifth-grade boy, it was the worst insult imaginable, she knew. "Besides, you don't want to be the only one not wearing one. It'll look funny." Perhaps the second biggest fear in fifth grade was of being conspicuous.

The tactic paid off. "Okay," he relented, with a noisy sigh. "But I don't need you to pin it on. I can do it myself."

Twenty minutes later, they were in the Volvo on their way to the Episcopal church in Prospect Heights, where baby Judith had been baptized and where today's nuptials were being held. Camille smiled to herself, thinking of Holly. Her fear that her wild-child sister would never settle down had proved groundless. Holly had found love at last, with a good man who doted on her and their daughter. Even so, Camille knew it was a huge leap of faith for Holly when she accepted Curtis's proposal, and she applauded her sister for taking that leap.

Holly wasn't the only one. This past week alone, three wedding invitations had come in the mail. One was from Elise Osgood, who had found love in the last place she had thought to look: right under her nose. She was marrying her long-time friend and colleague, Glenn. She'd sounded happy when Camille had called to congratulate her. The wedding was in October, in Elise's hometown of Grantsburg, Wisconsin.

It was almost ten-thirty a.m., a few minutes before their scheduled time of arrival, when Camille pulled into the parking spot that had conveniently opened up a block from the church. *You'd show up early for your own funeral,* her sister liked to joke. Camille mentally shook her head, thinking she'd very nearly done just that. She climbed out of the car, and then paused to stretch and take a deep breath. The sun was shining. It was a glorious day—the perfect day for a wedding.

She paused one last time when they reached the steps to the church, checking to make sure Kyra's dress wasn't creased in back, and brushing a piece of lint from her son's suit jacket. "Do you think Aunt Holly's here yet?" Kyra asked, casting an anxious glance at the open doors to the church.

"If she's not, she will be soon." Holly had sent a text message saying she and Curtis were running late—something about a poopy diaper that had necessitated a change of clothing. Luckily, they didn't live too far from the church. "Even the poopiest diaper doesn't take that long to change."

"Eww. Gross." Zach made a face.

"Baby poo isn't as gross as grown-up poo," Kyra informed her brother loftily. She was reveling in her role as Judith's godmother and took pride in having changed her share of diapers.

"It's still yucky," insisted Zach.

"You won't be saying that when it's *your* kid," Kyra told him. Zach gave her a blank look, as if being a father someday was as remote a possibility as being elected president of the United States.

"Trust me, you wouldn't believe the lengths to which parents will go," Camille said. "Poopy diapers is the least of it."

The strains of the organ drifted from the church, and Kyra turned to eye her anxiously. Camille didn't know if it was because her daughter was worried about abandoning her or that she might embarrass her by putting in an unscheduled appearance. Probably a little of both. "Are you coming in with us?" she asked.

"No." Camille kissed her on the forehead. She thought Kyra looked relieved, though she couldn't be sure; the sun was in her eyes, making them water. "I don't belong. This is your dad's day."

EDWARD, SEQUESTERED IN the sacristy with the Right Reverend Caswell, couldn't recall when he had last felt this keyed up, and the elderly reverend wasn't making it any easier. "Did you hear the one about the astronaut and the jockey . . . ?" The old man launched into another of his timeworn jokes—jokes no doubt intended to put nervous grooms at ease but which were having the opposite effect on Edward. He felt as antsy as he had as a kid sitting for school portraits while the photographer told cheesy knock-knock jokes. All he'd been able to think about back then was getting out from under the hot lights and onto the basketball court. His only thought now was of his bride-to-be, who was probably pacing the floor right now, as antsy as he was.

He smiled at the thought. If Angie had ever expressed doubts about marriage, he felt confident that, whatever nerves she was experiencing right now, it wasn't a case of cold feet. The other day, after she'd returned home in a foul mood from yet another fitting at the Wedding Belles bridal salon in Manhasset (owned by her mother's best friend, Nadine Pressman, who'd given them a 20 percent discount), he'd jokingly asked if she had any regrets, to which she'd replied, "The only mistake I made was letting my mom take charge. You'd think it was *her* goddamn wedding." She'd paused to give him that smile of hers that never failed to warm his heart, then said, "*You*, on the other hand, I don't regret in the least. I'd marry you bare-ass naked if I could." With that, she'd led him into the bedroom for a sample of what that might look like.

He blew out a breath, releasing some of the butterflies. The last time he'd stood at the altar, with Camille, he'd been too young and inexperienced to know what was in store. When he'd said his vows, he hadn't given much thought to their practical application. In vowing to love his wife in sickness and in health, he couldn't have imagined an ordeal such as the one they had faced, years later, when she had cancer. He recalled the poster that had hung in his dorm room, his freshman year of college, courtesy of his roommate Todd Engleson; it showed a tarantula clinging to a roll of toilet paper, with the words SHIT HAPPENS printed below. Shit had indeed happened. But he and Camille had had their share of good times as well as bad. Too many people threw the baby out with the bathwater in a divorce, but Edward knew the key to his future with Angie lay in not losing sight of his past. By remembering what he and Camille had done right as well as the mistakes they had made, he stood a better chance of not screwing it up the next time. Love the second time around wasn't simply a triumph of hope over experience; it was the sum of those experiences. When he and Angie exchanged vows, those vows would come not just from their hearts but from the scars they had each acquired along the way.

"Reverend, I hate to cut you short," Edward interrupted the pastor before he could deliver the punch line, "but I think it's time." Through the open door to the sanctuary, he could hear the soaring chords of the organ as it segued into "Ave Maria." After that would come the processional march.

"Quite right, son, quite right," said the reverend. He sounded a bit abashed, the way old people do when they realize they've gone on too long. With his bald head and hunched back, he looked like a tortoise poking its head from its shell. But he gathered himself, smiling and bringing his gnarled hands together in a soundless little clap. "So, are you ready to take the plunge?"

Edward grinned. "Ready as I'll ever be."

He stepped through the doorway into a blaze of jeweled light. He was reminded once more of why he and Angie had chosen this church to get married in. The first time he'd come here was for Judith's baptism, and though the structure itself was modestly proportioned, he'd been struck by its ornate carvings and the beauty of its stained-glass windows. When he'd suggested to Angie it would make a fine venue for their wedding in lieu of her family's parish church, since he was divorced and they were both lapsed Catholics, she'd heartily agreed after she'd seen it.

He spotted his parents in the front row, seated with his aunt Catherine and his uncle Cyrus, his cousins and their wives and children filling the rows behind. His little sparrow of a mother in her canary-yellow dress and straw hat, and his father, grown stout with age, looking uncomfortable in the new suit purchased for the occasion. They both looked slightly baffled, as if not quite sure what to make of all this—the whole notion of divorce was alien to them; they knew it existed but had never expected it to be a factor in their lives. Besides, they adored Camille; she was still their daughter-in-law, as far as they were concerned. They wanted him to be happy, though—that was what mattered most. So they were kind to Angie. He couldn't ask for more.

His gaze drifted to Holly and Curtis, seated a few rows behind his cousins. Initially, Holly hadn't wanted to attend, out of loyalty to her sister; it was Camille who'd persuaded her, insisting that Holly and Edward's friendship didn't have to end just because the marriage had. She'd also made the point that it would feel more normal for Kyra and Zach. Whatever the reason, Edward was glad she'd come. He smiled at the unlikely picture of domesticity she made, seated next to Curtis holding their one-year-old on her lap. Judith stood balanced on her mother's knees, gripping the pew in front of her as she bobbed up and down, gurgling in delight while the adults around her smiled at her antics. She was too young to know the bride took center stage at a wedding.

His best man gave him a nudge, leaning in to murmur, "You holding up okay, my friend?" Edward turned to smile at Hugh, who managed to look rumpled even in his pressed tuxedo.

"Why, do I look nervous?" Edward murmured in reply.

"Like a racehorse at the starting gate." Hugh grinned.

The organist launched into the processional march—Bach's "Jesu, Joy of Man's Desiring." Edward's gaze, along with everyone else's, was drawn to the doors that stood open to the vestibule, through which the bridesmaids were now making their entrance. First, Angie's sister Francine, who was matron of honor, then sisters Susanne, Rosemary, and Julia, in that order, all wearing matching rose-colored gowns. Kyra was last, looking unbearably lovely and just as unbearably self-conscious, teetering in her high heels as she made her way up the aisle. He imagined his daughter, ten or twelve years from now, walking down a different aisle on his arm, and felt his heart swell.

Then *she* walked in on her father's arm, and his breath caught in his throat. He hadn't seen Angie since she was kidnapped by her sister Julia earlier in the day and whisked off to a salon for the hours of primping Julia insisted were required. Nor had he laid eyes until now on the gown that had been the subject of so much grumbling on her part. Yards of white silk organza cascaded from a fitted lace bodice with spaghetti straps, which on any other woman as petite as she might have overwhelmed but which Angie carried off like a queen. Complementing it was the antique lace veil that her grandmother had worn on her wedding day. The "something blue," the sapphire necklace she wore, his gift to her. She had never looked lovelier. But what stood out most was the smile she wore, one bright enough to light up the whole church without benefit of its stained glass.

ANGIE, IF SHE'D had her way, would have opted for a simple ceremony before a justice of the peace. But in the end, she'd bowed to the will of She Who Would Not Be Denied. She owed her mother a church wedding, if for no other reason than that Loretta had kept the faith all these years. Now, as she neared the altar, she spied her mother seated up front next to Nadine. Her hair was sculpted and sprayed into the MGM Productions version of its usual coif, and she wore what could only be described as the mother of all mother-of-the-bride outfits—a brocade suit shot through with shiny threads and a pink blouse with more ruffles than a cancan skirt—though it was no match for her smile, which was wide enough to wrap around her neck and meet itself in the middle.

Angie might have felt drab in comparison, but her gown *was* beautiful, she had to admit. More importantly, she felt beautiful in it. Earlier, when she'd stood in front of the mirror for the final reveal, after her mother and sisters, and the stylist Julia had hired, had finished fussing over her and fiddling with her hair, she had decided it was worth the torture of all those fittings. It was certainly a vast improvement over the gown fashioned out of toilet paper Francine had made for her at her bridal shower, though she'd had more fun being "fitted" for that one. She smiled at the memory. She and her sisters had laughed themselves silly parading around in their toilet paper creations, which had led to more silly games, like seeing who could pile the most cotton balls on her head. Finally, stuffed on sandwiches and petit-fours, and half-drunk on champagne, they'd collapsed on the sofa, snuggled together like a litter of puppies, to watch *Bridesmaids* on DVD.

Angie didn't think that could be topped, until the bachelorette party, at her friend Bartholomew's restaurant in the Flatiron District, where she'd once worked as *garde manger*. Everyone came, even the kids from her cooking class. The highlight of the evening was the rap number composed by Daarel in honor of the occasion, which he performed, quite credibly, with his wingmen, Tre'Shawn and Julio, singing backup. Though it was her karaoke rendition of "Unchained Melody" that brought the house down, albeit not in the way one with aspirations of a singing career would hope.

Now, though, there was only the tall, handsome man waiting for her at the altar. Angie's pulse quickened as she drew nearer. The trip down the aisle was short compared to the much longer journey of getting to this point. A journey that had had its share of tears and setbacks, most recently with Edward's children, who understandably weren't too thrilled about their dad's remarrying (although Angie felt she was making progress, especially with Zach), but that she'd take again in a heartbeat.

Flanking Edward on the right were his groomsmen: his closest friend and best man, Hugh; two of his cousins, Pete and Roman; Darryl Hornquist, his former roommate from med school; and Zach, looking solemn and grown-up. On the left were Angie's sisters: Francine, ten pounds lighter thanks to the Weight Watchers program she was on; Susanne, her curly mane cropped in a breezy new style and the diamond tennis bracelet her husband had given her for their fifteenth anniversary, which they'd just celebrated, sparkling on her wrist; Rosemary, whose offer to play the organ in lieu of acting as bridesmaid Angie had politely but firmly declined; and Julia, sleek and glamorous as a runway model. Angie recalled the prayer Julia had uttered while they were standing outside preparing to make their entrance, one that seemed perfectly suited to the occasion. *Holy Mary, Mother of God, may my baby sister have better luck than I did the first time.*

At the very end stood Kyra, the most gorgeous of them all. Angie thought back to when she'd first met Edward's daughter, who'd pointedly ignored her throughout the meal, at the restaurant to which Edward had taken them. While Zach played with his Gameboy, Kyra directed a bright stream of chatter at her dad, about people Angie didn't know and past events she hadn't taken part in. It had taken her days to recover, and she'd been sure there would be no winning Kyra over, ever. Their relationship was still a work in progress, but Kyra had thawed considerably since then. If the way to Zach's heart was through his stomach (he was a sucker for homemade french fries),

Kyra was interested in how the food was prepared. She often found excuses to be in the kitchen when Angie was fixing dinner; she'd ask questions, or if she was in an especially relaxed mood, offer to help. Angie didn't know if she'd ever be completely forgiven for having replaced Kyra's mom in her dad's affections, but she hoped they would be friends someday. In the meantime, she had her nieces and nephews, and Zach when he was being affectionate, as well as her "posse"—Tamika, D'Enice, Chandra, Daarel, Tre'Shawn, Julio, Jermaine, and Raul—to satisfy her kid fix.

She flashed a grin at her posse, all sitting in the same row and all behaving themselves for a change, as she passed by. They were nearly unrecognizable in their Sunday best, especially Daarel in his suit and tie, meekly holding hands with Tamika, who had taken him back after he promised (in writing) to finish out the school year. Seated in front of them were Pat and Cleo and Stylianos, along with members of the hardcore gonzo crew from Angie's restaurant days, warriors all, wearing their scars the way they did their tattoos, as proud emblems of their profession.

My ragtag family and my real one, she thought. A year ago, who'd have thought they'd all be together under one roof someday? But that was the best thing about all this, that it was so unpredictable. Starting with Edward himself. Whenever Angie used to imagine the man she might marry one day, if she ever got around to marrying, she pictured him as being like the guys she'd dated in the past—someone who cursed a blue streak (as all denizens of restaurant kitchens did) and who was probably covered in tattoos, with pierced ears and not a single tie to his name. Instead, she'd ended up with a man who, in addition to being smart, gorgeous, and sexy, was eminently presentable and had a whole closetful of ties—in short, her mom's dream son-in-law. Though Edward had a wild side, too (which Angie planned on exploring further when they were on their honeymoon in Positano), even if it didn't involve excess facial hair, body piercings, or tattoos.

Looking at him now, she saw a study in contrasts. Someone who was kind and loyal but who could also be stubborn and intractable; who was his own man but also your typical man from Mars; who was always there for her but who had a tendency to hold back when showing his own emotions; who was forgetful at times but who never forgot what was most important. In short, someone who wasn't perfect but who was perfect for her, *because* of rather than in spite of his flaws.

She murmured to her father, who had a death grip on her arm, "It's okay, Dad. You can let go now." He darted her a sheepish look—the man who swore he didn't have a sentimental bone in his body and who'd walk out of the room rather than sit through a chick flick—before releasing her.

At last, she stood before Edward at the altar. He gently, reverently almost, lifted the veil from her face. He stared at her so long, she finally leaned in to whisper, "Don't forget to breathe."

"You look beautiful," he whispered back.

"So do you."

Reverend Caswell cleared his throat, a noise that, amplified by the mike clipped to his vestments, sounded like a train rumbling down the tracks. He spoke about the sanctity of marriage and of the blessedness of the union these two people were entering into. Then it was time for the vows. A hush fell over the church; it was so quiet you could've heard a pin drop as far away as Coney Island. Angie felt everyone's eyes on them, but she had eyes only for Edward. Listening to him repeat the vows in his strong, sure voice, she felt something settle in her.

I'm home, she thought.

EPILOGUE

One Year Later

Camille hadn't known what to expect when Kat Fisher called to invite her to lunch. It had been over a year since she'd last heard from her, not since she'd urged her to seek counseling. She wondered if Kat was ready to start dating again, if that was why she wanted to see her.

In the months since Camille herself had joined the ranks of singles, a lot had happened. Edward had remarried, and now he and Angie were expecting a baby, due in February. When Camille had first found out about the baby, the news had hit her hard, but she'd since come to accept and even embrace it to some degree. How could a new life be a bad thing, especially after what she'd been through? She had looked death in the face, and out of that experience had come the ability to appreciate life to its fullest, even the not-so-good things with silver linings so thin they weren't visible to the naked eye. A baby would be terra firma after the seismic shifts of the past year and a half, a little brother or sister to make Kyra and Zach feel more connected to their father's new wife. Edward had moved on, and the children needed to stop wishing for their parents to get back together.

Camille had moved on, too, though it was a slow process that often felt like a case of two steps forward and one step back.

Sometimes it seemed as though she and Edward had been apart for years, and at other times as though he was merely away on a business trip. At the grocery store, she sometimes found herself absentmindedly reaching for the brand of mustard he preferred or the kosher dills she knew he liked; or when doing the laundry, she'd check for any men's socks that might be clinging to the inside of the hamper. Whenever she came across something of his—a stray cuff link; a book he'd forgotten to take with him; a knit cap belonging to him, in among the ski things; an old prescription vial in the medicine cabinet—she was pierced by a sorrow so keen, it was palpable. It seemed inconceivable that all she had to show for twenty years were these scattered reminders, like shells left on the beach by the outgoing tide. How had it come to this? She prided herself on being able to read other people. How could she have missed the cues with her own husband?

But if she had suffered a loss, she had gained something even more precious in exchange: She had her life back. Two months ago, Camille had been declared cancer-free. Her father and Lillian were among the first with whom she shared the news, after she'd told the children, and they were both overjoyed. Larry had sent her his old pilot wings, with a note that read "the sky's the limit," and Lillian a watercolor she'd painted, done from a photo taken the previous summer when they'd visited Camille and the children in Southampton, of Camille standing on the beach at water's edge, that spoke for itself. When Camille told Holly, her sister burst into tears and then, embarrassed, said jokingly, "Damn. And I was really counting on those pearls." The Barbara Bush pearls, as Holly called them, were ones Camille had threatened to leave to her sister in her will. It seemed fitting, then, six weeks later when Holly walked down the aisle on her wedding day, that she was wearing those pearls—the something borrowed.

Camille counted her blessings. She was healthy, her children were thriving, her loved ones settled and happy, and business was better than ever. Dara had created a niche market among the twen-tysomething set, those still young enough to surf the club scene but old enough to be thinking about settling down. She herself had signed eight new clients since Labor Day (the start of her busy season), one of whom had already become engaged after a whirl-wind romance—a gentle, soft-spoken orthopedic surgeon, with the unlikely name of Lance Fontaine, who'd lost his wife to cancer three years prior. He had found his match in a 9/11 widow named Kate Barlow who had children around the same ages as his. It was love at first sight by both accounts. They were to be married in December. Kate's eldest son, Charles, would act as best man.

Camille arrived at the restaurant, Asiate, on the thirty-fifth floor of the Mandarin Oriental, to find Kat seated at one of the tables by the bank of tall windows that looked out on Central Park. She looked as gorgeous as ever—a queen surveying her domain, poised against the scenic backdrop of trees and miniature horse-drawn carriages below—wearing a gold jacket that brought out the natural bronze of her complexion, and jade drop earrings the smoky-green of her eyes.

When she spied Camille, she broke into a grin and rose to greet her, kissing her on the cheek. She smelled of some citrusy fragrance, and there was a glow to her that hadn't come out of a bottle or jar, and that wasn't the product of her impeccable grooming. Camille took her by the shoulders, holding her at arm's length and declar-ing, "Look at you—If I had to guess, I'd say you were in love."

Kat gave an airy laugh. "Spoken like a matchmaker."

Their waiter appeared, one of those too-handsome-to-be-a-civilian types whom Camille immediately pegged as an actor. Defi-nitely not gay; he was so transfixed by Kat, it was clearly an effort when he tore himself away to fill their drink orders—Campari and soda for Kat, the usual Perrier with lime for Camille. Camille was used to seeing grown men become bumbling adolescents around Kat; what was different this time was that Kat scarcely paid him any notice, whereas in the past she'd always flirted outrageously with men who made eyes at her, to feed her ego.

"So, am I right?" Camille asked.

"About what?" Kat played coy.

"Are you in love?"

"Not so fast. We'll get to that in a minute." Kat smiled mysteriously. "First, I want to know what *you've* been up to. There's a rumor going around that you got divorced." Her smile fell away, and her eyes searched Camille's face.

Camille felt a familiar heaviness settle over her. Unlike with her illness, which she'd managed to keep private, news of her divorce had traveled far and wide. She'd fielded sympathies from everyone from clients to the receptionist at her dentist's office. She was the wronged wife, in their eyes. Her husband had left her for another woman. She'd grown weary of trying to explain it wasn't as it appeared—the divorce had been a mutual decision. Most people didn't want the truth. They wanted the stuff of tabloids; they saw things in black-and-white, not shades of gray.

"I'm afraid it's true." Camille adopted the tone she'd perfected these past months in responding to such inquiries: appropriately solemn but not to the point where the other person would feel the need to hide any sharp objects that might be on hand.

"I'm sorry to hear it." Kat seemed truly saddened by the news. "Honestly? If I'd had to choose one couple who I would have said was rock solid, it was you two. And believe me, I'm not just saying that." Camille wondered if there was something Kat *wasn't* saying—something that might have happened at the ill-fated dinner party, from which Edward had returned in a foul mood and which, looking back, seemed to mark the turning point in their marriage, when he'd broken from her and retreated into himself—but she decided it would be best not to ask. What difference did it make at this late date?

"Nothing is unbreakable, even rocks," she said, careful to keep her voice light. The pain had lessened with time, yes, but it was always there, its edge dulled but still capable of drawing blood. "It seems I'm better at orchestrating other people's lives than I am at conducting my own. Speaking of which . . ." She changed the subject before all this talk of divorce succeeded in thoroughly depressing them both. "I'm dying to know. Did you take my advice?"

Kat sipped her drink, which had arrived in the blink of an eye, their waiter giving new meaning to service-with-a-smile. "About Dr. McDermott? Oh, yeah," she said in the tone of someone who'd done more than make a phone call. "I've been seeing him for the past ten months."

"It must be working, because I've never seen you look happier."

Kat gave a wry laugh. "It's been a real eye-opener, that's for sure. You were right about him, by the way—he's great. He got me to see it wasn't the men who were the problem, it was *me*. I was so screwed up, I didn't know what I wanted. It was tough having to look at that, and that was the easy part. The hardest part was figuring out *why*, and the only way I could get through it was by treating it as I would a news story. Reporters dig until they get all the facts, so that's what I did: I dug and dug until I got to the bottom."

"And what did you find?" Camille asked.

Kat gazed thoughtfully out the window. "A lot of it had to do with my parents' divorce. I didn't see much of my dad after that. Then when he remarried, I saw even less of him." She brought her gaze back to Camille, and Camille could see the ghostly remains of that old pain on her face. "With all those men, I think I was chasing the love I never got from my dad. No one could ever measure up because they couldn't give me what I wanted." She shook her head. "I'm making it sound simple, but it wasn't—it took a while to get there. It's like a jigsaw puzzle. At first, all you have is a jumble of pieces. You don't see the picture until you start putting it together."

"And do you see it now?"

"Mostly. Enough so that I could be in a relationship without picking it apart." Kat blushed. Camille had guessed correctly—she was in love. Before she could ask who the lucky man was, Kat's gaze moved past her to a man who was approaching their table, fortyish, well built and well dressed, with a confident stride.

Stephen Resler.

That was when Camille noticed the table was set for three.

Kat jumped up to kiss Stephen—a kiss that spoke of longer acquaintanceship than their one documented date more than a year ago. Other diners stared, as did Camille. It was hard not to stare. They seemed so happy, two attractive and vibrant people who were obviously, radiantly, blessedly in love. She broke into a grin, though she could scarcely believe what she was seeing.

"Well, well. How long has *this* been going on?" she asked after Stephen had sat down.

Stephen reached for Kat's hand, in the casual way of couples who have been together awhile. "Would you believe it? We ran into each other in the waiting room at the doc's office." He explained that he'd been seeing Dr. McDermott's partner, whom Dr. McDermott had thought would be a better fit for him. One day, when Stephen was waiting, Kat happened to show up at the same time. "We got to talking," he said. "Then I asked her out and she said yes, and to make a long story short, we've been together ever since." He grinned. "I guess you could call it kismet."

"Or maybe just blind luck," Kat said. "Except *we* were the ones who were blind, for not seeing it to begin with."

"Pretty hard to see straight when you've got your head up your ass," observed Stephen with a wry chuckle. "Speaking for myself, that is," he was quick to add at the arch look Kat gave him.

"This is a first for me." Camille smiled as she shook her head in amazement. "I've had couples who didn't click until the second or third dates, but I've never had two people not see each other for a whole year, then have sparks fly. I guess it's true what they say: Timing is everything."

"Either that or it was meant to be." Kat gazed adoringly at Stephen.

"First, I needed to get my head shrunk," he said. "It took a while, but I finally figured out why I couldn't let go of my ex: I'd never walked away from a deal. My ego was all wrapped up in it. Once I realized that, I was able to get a grip and move on. That was when I bumped into Kat."

Kat squeezed his hand. "My lucky day."

Over lunch, Camille heard about their future plans. They were looking at apartments, with an eye toward moving in together. They'd talked about getting married but weren't ready to get engaged, they said, though it was clear the only thing holding them back was the strong desire on both their parts not to screw this up by acting in haste. They wanted to do it right, which meant taking it slow.

Afterward, they all rode down in the elevator together before parting ways, Kat and Stephen to head to the Town Car that idled at the curb, Camille to head back to her office. She walked with a light step, smiling to herself at the thought of how fate had led Kat and Stephen full circle. What would her own fate be? she wondered. Was she destined to find love again . . . or would she live alone once the children were grown and on their own?

Turning the corner onto Columbus Circle, she became caught up in the usual swirl of pedestrians. As she made her way past the Time Warner Center, her gaze was drawn upward and she paused to admire the monument at the center of the roundabout, one she'd passed by a thousand times without paying much attention to it. Perched atop the monument was a statue of Christopher Columbus. Contemplating it, Camille thought she knew how Columbus must have felt setting sail for the Americas. He had to have known there was a far greater likelihood he'd sail to his death than to new territories. It was the same for her on a smaller scale. Each morning, when she woke to find the pillow on Edward's side of the bed as plump and smooth as when she'd turned down the covers the night before, she was reminded that she was on her own, adrift on the open sea of her new existence. She'd weathered her share of storms, and there were storms yet to come. But she was on the path to discovery, which was exciting. Not in search of new territories or even a new relationship at this point, but of the person who was slowly emerging from the wreckage of this last storm, a person with whom she very much wished to become reacquainted.

When she reached the intersection at Eighth Avenue and Fifty-Ninth Street, she stepped onto the crosswalk, walking with a quick, sure stride. A cool, westerly breeze was blowing, a reminder that winter wasn't far off, but the sun was shining, and when she got to the curb on the other side she paused, heedless of the other pedestrians eddying past in a hurry to get wherever they were going, to tip her head back and savor its warmth.

ACKNOWLEDGMENTS

It's been a long road bringing this book home, so first I have to thank my readers, who've patiently awaited its publication. The many emails I received inspired me to finish sooner than I might have otherwise.

Many thanks, also, to the following professionals: Janice Spindell, the *ne plus ultra* of matchmakers, who gave me a peek into the high-stakes world of matchmaking. Her success rate is nothing short of astonishing (given my own track record in fixing up friends on blind dates, which so far has netted zero) and proof, in my mind, that matchmaking is best left to the professionals. I owe a debt of gratitude, too, to the wonderful (as well as tall, dark, and handsome) Dr. Jonathan Aviv, for sharing his medical expertise and allowing me to sit in while he examined patients, and then taking time to answer all my questions.

The Replacement Wife would not have come into being without two special people in my life whose unflagging support kept me going during some dark times: my dear husband, Sandy Kenyon, and my agent and friend, Susan Ginsburg. Their belief in me, and in this book, made all the difference.

It's also been a joy working with and getting to know my editor, Marjorie Braman, and the dream team at Open Road Integrated Media. Finally, none of it would have been possible without Jane Friedman, who had the vision to see the future of publishing and then had the courage to act on it.

All rights reserved under International and Pan-American Copyright Conventions. By payment of the required fees, you have been granted the non-exclusive, non-transferable right to access and read the text of this book. No part of this text may be reproduced, transmitted, downloaded, decompiled, reverse engineered, or stored in or introduced into any information storage and retrieval system, in any form or by any means, whether electronic or mechanical, now known or hereinafter invented, without the express written permission of the publisher.

This is a work of fiction. Names, characters, places, and incidents either are the product of the author's imagination or are used fictitiously. Any resemblance to actual persons, living or dead, businesses, companies, events, or locales is entirely coincidental.

copyright © 2012 by Eileen Goudge

cover design by Mumtaz Mustafa

ISBN: 978-1-4532-5814-9 (paperback)

Published in 2012 by Open Road Integrated Media
180 Varick Street
New York, NY 10014
www.openroadmedia.com

EBOOKS BY EILEEN GOUDGE

FROM OPEN ROAD MEDIA

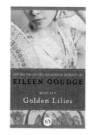

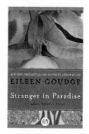

Available wherever ebooks are sold

OPEN ROAD
INTEGRATED MEDIA

FIND OUT MORE AT WWW.OPENROADMEDIA.COM

FOLLOW US: @openroadmedia and Facebook.com/OpenRoadMedia

OPEN ROAD

INTEGRATED MEDIA

Videos, Archival Documents, and New Releases

Sign up for the Open Road Media newsletter and get news delivered straight to your inbox.

FOLLOW US:
@openroadmedia and
Facebook.com/OpenRoadMedia

SIGN UP NOW at
www.openroadmedia.com/newsletters